Lhind
the
Firebird

Set in the Same World:

Lhind the Thief
Lhind the Spy
A Posse of Princesses
Barefoot Pirate
The Wren Series

Lhind
the
Firebird

Sherwood Smith

Book View
Café

LHIND THE SPY
Copyright © 2020 by Sherwood Smith

Published by Book View Café Publishing Cooperative
www.bookviewcafe.com

Editorial team: Katharine Eliska Kimbriel and Sara Stamey
Cover art: Augusta Scarlett
Interior design: Marissa Doyle

ISBN: 978-1-61138-899-2

For K.H.

One

SO FAR, MY STORY has been pretty much all about me.

For most of my life that was all I had — me. I was content enough, even if I often went to sleep hungry, and rarely in the same place for very long. I'd change clothing once a year, always something stolen off a drying line. Some discomfort was a fair trade for freedom.

But then I met Hlanan, and began learning things. Like, theft was bad. But the reward for this exasperating lesson was the gradual discovery of what it meant to have friends.

Then I discovered family.

Two families. Two very, very different families.

Now I had food to eat any time I wanted. I had a home, and a bed to call my own. I could bathe ten times a day if I liked. But I was not content, though I tried mightily to be. Unlike those old, hungry days, I was broken.

Before I go on with that, I'd better start with Hlanan, because this time, the…let's call them adventures, ha ha, didn't just happen to me.

Of course adventure has always happened to others, too, but one of the first lessons in learning how to have friends, and family, was the discovery that what I did affected others. Also, what happened to others mattered to me.

Especially to Hlanan, my first friend. Sweet, scholarly Hlanan, who tries to see the best in everyone, who can rock with silent laughter at unexpected times. Whose kisses — discovered not long before we parted—were as powerful as any of the magical talents I was born with.

Let me begin the day that he—Hlanan Vosaga, youngest of the Empress of Charas al Kherval's four children—left his small bedchamber and went out into the hall, pausing when he saw two sealed scroll-notes and a letter sitting on the tray outside his room.

It was common for palace residents to leave scraps of paper scrolled for one another, but who would send a sealed letter on heavy paper, which had to be carried by hand, instead of through his magical notecase?

He opened the letter first. There, in a very formal, stylized script (probably, Hlanan guessed, from the hand of a scribe), someone requested Hlanan's service. It was signed in a beautifully elaborate signature with four names—so elaborate he couldn't make out any of the names.

What service? Scribe work, of course—had to be. Few knew of the other callings he'd tried and set aside. Brief, bleak humor sparked at the idea that the scribe who wrote this magnificent hand had to employ that skill to request another scribe for whoever wrote that incomprehensible signature. But not everyone from overseas knew any of the various languages found in the Charas al Kherval—at most they might have the basics of the common tongue, Elras.

As Hlanan laid aside the letter, he wondered who Four-Name was, and who would have recommended Hlanan. He wasn't with the scribes now—he had been studying magic with the healers for the past year. But he'd served as a scribe off and on since he was a teen, and he still went around in his scribe robe because it was both comfortable and anonymous. No one paid any attention to scribes unless they needed one.

He set that letter down and glanced at the scrolled notes. The first was an invitation to the wedding of a fellow scribe student from ten years back, and the other's dashing hand was instantly recognizable: Hlanan's half-sister Thianra, writing a single line:

Remember you promised to take breakfast with me. Do not be late!

Hlanan breathed a laugh, knowing that there had to be a message twin to that in his notecase. And if for some reason he didn't turn up, she'd deliver a third message in person, then drag him to the musicians' wing by the back of his collar.

He glanced at his desk where his magical notecase lay. A pulse of duty prompted him to check it, but he turned away again. Who would write to him but his mother?

And what could she want but to express her disappointment, to scold, to list her logical, practical reasons —

Wait.

I think I have to go back a little. If you know the history of the Kherval Empire, skip over this next bit.

Imperial tradition in Charas al Kherval decrees that the ruler's children be raised as commoners until the ruler should choose an heir — if he or she chooses one of their offspring at all. Imperial offspring all *want* the crown, or so history says, but in the Kherval, future rulers are expected to *earn* that crown.

Humans being humans, not everyone who wants it deserves it, and the opposite is true. As a boy, Hlanan hadn't given a future wearing the imperial crown two thoughts. He hated the tedium of court ritual, dressing in elaborate court clothes, and speaking in the equally elaborate formal court mode.

He wanted to see the world for himself, and so at age ten he slipped away from the summer labors he'd been sent to learn — and incidentally evaded the guards who had kept him safe all his short life. He ended up wandering the most dangerous harbor on the continent, staring around as if the world were a stage. That splendid sense of spectacle ended abruptly when Shinjan galley slavers on the hunt for new slaves yanked him off the street and threw him into one of their galleys. The others so grabbed were marked as slaves with magic-laden tattoos and put to work.

He hated remembering those days, for so many reasons: the cold, the careless cruelties of the masters, the eternal hunger, and above all the misery of knowing that slaves' lives were easily discarded and no one cared.

He'd considered throwing himself overboard to drown before he made a covert friendship with a boy a couple years older, Ilyan Rajanas, who turned out to be a prince sold to the slavers by a nasty relative who coveted the princedom Rajanas was heir to. The two made life bearable for each other until Ilyan Rajanas saw a chance at escape from their burning ship during the terrible Battle at Athaniaz Island, between the Shinjans and the equally powerful empire of Sveran Djur.

Ilyan had been training in the martial arts, unlike Hlanan. He led, Hlanan followed. In the chaos of the battle, they made a successful escape, along with a few other galley slaves. One of their first moves after they reached the shores of the Kherval was Rajanas's insistence that they seek a mage powerful enough to remove the magic-laden tattoos marking them as slaves. The magic worked into the ink would trace them for anyone knowing the spells.

Until he was taken, Hlanan had thought little beyond evading lessons he didn't like. At the mage's, he surprised all three of them—himself included—by keeping his tattoo, once the mage cast a permanent block on the tracer so that the Shinjans couldn't track him by magic. He hadn't understood his own motivation at the time, except as a goal to learn enough magic to remove it himself, but he'd come to see the tattoo as a reminder of all those hapless slaves who, somehow, someday, he wanted to rescue.

After that he made his way back home, throwing himself into studies. Once the empress let him loose again, he embarked on a number of apprenticeships, including scribe, but he retained a lifelong interest in magic.

All right, history covered.

Now back to Hlanan after having read those messages.

When he emerged from his private bath, he paused to glance in the narrow mirror to study his reflection, finding nothing interesting in the sight. Skinny ribs, skinny arms (what the guards called 'scribe twigs' not-quite-behind the scribes' backs), slumped shoulders that would probably in a few years start that forward stoop like those of his father the archivist. Brown hair tied back simply, brown eyes. No one usually gave him a second glance.

His father was the least ambitious of the empress's three consorts, but—until recently—it had seemed Hlanan was to be chosen heir.

That was no longer true.

He turned his attention to the tattoo of three intersected diamonds on his shoulder, and laughed internally at himself for his grandiose plans. How he'd impressed the empress with his goal! Except that he hadn't come a step closer to figuring out how to save Shinjan slaves.

That hadn't kept him from making further pompous promises.

How the memory galled him!

A year ago, after my terrible experience in Sveran Djur's capital, Hlanan had even more self-importantly and pretentiously declared that he was going to bring down the Emperor of Sveran Djur.

A fine goal, but really, how is someone supposed to bring down an emperor, evil or not, unless by the equally evil launching of a war? And it would be a nasty one for certain. The Djuran navy was formidable on the seas—only the Shinjans were as strong.

So his determination began to flag. By the time winter iced up the capital, and he hadn't received any answers to certain letters (I'll get to those), he'd decided that he was nothing but a pompous blowhard. The tattoo had become a symbol not of hope, but one of failure. He would never rescue masses of miserable people, or bring down evil emperors—not after a lifetime of never sticking to one course of study. He kept getting sidetracked into other reading, not of the least use: of late, studies of history and linguistics, records of travelers between the continents, customs, governments.

He took the healers' oath to aid all in need, rich or poor, stranger or kin, hoping that would force him to focus on this one calling. And it was a good calling, he knew that. He worked hard at healer magic over the winter, hard enough so that he would fall in bed at night exhausted, which kept him from brooding on his failures. It had felt good to gain enough knowledge to work the first tier of healer spells, but at the same time he was aware of just how much study and practice lay ahead before he could claim real competence.

He turned his back on the mirror, dressed in the first shirt and trousers he laid hands to, and yanked his brown scribe student robe over that. On his way out, he glanced at the letters, and picked up the mysterious one. Though he was now committed to his healer studies, why not serve as a scribe one more time, since this person had gone to all the trouble of asking for him by name?

He left and crossed the wing to the musicians' floor, where Thianra, his half-sister, had her room.

She'd returned three days before from an extensive tour, and was apparently leaving again to hear the legendary Kitharee.

As he walked, he reflected on how the empress, their mother, had during their childhood and early teens favored Thianra as potential heir, but after a year or so of flirting with the idea of being acknowledged the imperial princess, Thianra had decided against it.

"Music is clean. It tells the truth," she'd said to Hlanan when she turned fifteen. "Or most of the time. But even when it prevaricates, it's frivolous instead of cruel. I've been watching court. In spite of all the beautiful clothes, and rituals, and celebrations, the compromise of politics—the smiling lies told to get an effect—makes me feel… compromised. I'd rather be in the gallery playing that beautiful music then down on the floor talking lies over the melodies without hearing them."

And on her sixteenth Name Day, when Hlanan was there, she'd said to their mother, "I understand why you do what you do, and when you must act, but it is not in my nature to follow that path."

Thianra was wiser at sixteen than I am now, Hlanan thought as he reached her room. He tapped, and on her invitation, walked inside—and stopped short.

There, seated in the place of honor at Thianra's little table, was the empress herself.

Thianra and the empress both looked up, two stocky figures, but that was the only resemblance between them. Thianra was darker of skin, like her full-brother Bracan, with hair a richer brown than Hlanan's. The empress was more golden of skin, her hair dark except for the streaks of gray.

"Surprised?" Aranu Crown said ironically.

"Yes. I didn't see any Ravens," Hlanan responded, waving a hand backward—as if the empress's elite guard included invisibility along with their other considerable skills.

"Of course you didn't," the empress retorted. "And have every pair of lips in this benighted palace flapping about how I choose to break the morning fast with a third-level musician? You may be certain, however, that they are around."

Thianra sighed at the brittle tone used by her mother and favorite brother. "Sit down, Hlanan. This breakfast is meant to bring us together again—to talk in comfort the way we used to."

"I," the empress stated, "am perfectly comfortable."

Hlanan took his place on the cushion across from Thianra, at the empress's left. "As am I."

It was not strictly true, but he was determined to act as if he was.

Thianra turned her head from side to side, giving them both a narrow-eyed look. Her expression was habitually pleasant, for she was a cheery, calm soul when left to her music. She liked people, and travel, and she loved her family. "Odd. Here I am back again after touring through four kingdoms playing the winter festivals, to discover that you two have met maybe twice in that time?"

"I," the empress stated trenchantly, "have been occupied with affairs of state."

"And I have been studying," Hlanan stated in exactly the same tone.

"Please help yourselves," Thianra said softly, indicating the fast-cooling muffins, the fresh honey-butter, the shirred eggs with sharp cheese, and the fresh fruit still dappled with dew.

As Hlanan obediently picked up a muffin and broke the crispy crust to release the delicious-smelling steam from the soft center,

Thianra said, "Mother, I know how truly hard you work. And Hlanan, you spent last night telling me—exhaustively—all about scrying and wards, and how backward you have been in both, and how you've been striving to repair that ignorance along with your healer studies. But really, twice?"

The empress sighed as she broke her bread, then scooped dollops of shirred eggs into each half.

Hlanan spread honey-butter on his bread, then bit into it to keep from saying anything.

Thianra said plaintively, "Are you two really that angry with one another?"

"I'm not angry," Hlanan said.

"And I," the empress replied, "am merely waiting for him to recover a proper mental balance."

Thianra laid down her bread. "A proper mental..." she repeated, then turned to their mother, her surprise and disapproval plain. "Is this really still about Hlanan going to Sveran Djur to rescue Lhind?"

Hlanan's eyes narrowed as he regarded his mother.

The empress's eyes narrowed when she saw his expression. "Hlanan," she said, also laying bread on her plate. "I told you I have no objections whatsoever to your romance. Lhind is a dear little thing, though flighty, if you'll forgive a little word play."

Thianra choked on a laugh, and even Hlanan's lips twitched.

"But I *wish* you'd gotten the emotional drama part of romance out of your system when you were a teen. It is simply not reasonable to risk your life haring off straight to the enemy's stronghold after a flirt, when you could as easily have sent one of the many, many skilled people on my extensive payroll I hired specifically to carry out such tasks."

Hlanan also put down his bread. "*I* had to go," he said. "It was I who betrayed her into the enemy's hands in the first place."

"We all know that I did that," the empress stated. "And you know why. I could not let the Djurans discover who *you* were, Hlanan, how important you are to me. Jardis Dhes-Andis would have held you hostage against Charas al Kherval. He sent an *entire army* to seize Lhind, who turns out to be related to him, and he was not going to balk at destroying lives to accomplish that. So I *had* to hand her off to him to keep a bad situation from turning into a slaughter."

"Thereby leaving Lhind to pay the price of my so-called position. Instead of me."

"Be reasonable," the empress pleaded. "That sort of romantic jabber is all very well on the stage, but it is simply not sensible to risk your life for a flirt who will be little but a fond memory by next year."

"Lhind is not a *flirt*," Hlanan stated.

(Yes, it's very odd to write about myself as if I was there, but you'll see why soon.)

Aranu Crown sighed. "Hlanan, grant me my years of experience. You and Lhind are very sweet together, but the two of you are so inexperienced! Of course you are thinking of Forever, and True Love, and all the pretty ribbons of poetry. Life simply isn't like that, and love is the lease predictable and most ephemeral of all the strong emotions. It's a hard lesson that I had to learn early — for the sake of all those I govern."

"If," Hlanan said quietly, "throwing away someone else's life is considered reasonable for a monarch, then perhaps you ought to be speaking to my oldest brother right now. Justeon is very proud of the fact that his romances don't last more than a day at most, and I know he would agree that the helpless don't matter, that the only things of importance are political expedience and military might."

The empress pressed her lips in a line, then said, "Justeon would dearly love to be the next emperor. I am very certain he thinks he will be. But he is excellent where he is, a brave and dashing warrior captain, who will do the needful when necessary. I repeat, *when necessary*, which means as a last resort. I have never succeeded in convincing him that warfare is the failure of negotiation. You know that. I know that. What disturbs me is your using your infatuation as an emotional weapon. What happened to rational discourse?" At that she rose.

Hlanan flushed, rising as well, Thianra slowly and reluctantly followed, her expression dismayed as she looked back and forth between the two.

"Now it is time to return to duty," the empress stated. "We will speak further when we both have had time to reflect."

She walked through the servants' door.

Hlanan caught a glimpse of a black surcoat before the door shut. The Ravens had held the servants' inner corridor empty, so that the empress could come and go unseen.

And that was the privilege of power.

"Well, my peace breakfast was a stunning success," Thianra said, looking down at all the uneaten food. "And to think that I spent half my winter earnings on this."

"Call in a group of your friends. You know they'll scarf it all up," Hlanan said.

Thianra's brief smile was almost as bleak as his. "Yes, we musicians are traditionally hungry, aren't we?" And then, "Hlanan, are you and Lhind really pledged for life?"

"I don't know," he said, running his hands up over his face. He discovered his fingers were shaking. "I've been thinking of finding a mage to remove this tattoo," he admitted, touching his shoulder.

Thianra's expression cleared in relief. "Good! I've never understood why you keep that thing."

"As a promise. Just another promise that I've broken," he said. "That a *rational being* should never have made, I guess." He heard the bitterness in his own voice, and strove for a more even tone. "I don't know what will happen with Lhind — maybe Mother is right and it is over, and I'm the last to find out. But right now, my bond with her feels like a true bond, the only true one in my life. And one I mean to keep. I'm supposed to see that as callow, unreasonable?"

Thianra spread her hands. "It must be so in the political world. One of the many reasons why I told Mother that I could never consider the heirship."

Hlanan sighed. "I'm beginning to think that I will tell her the same. Though she may save me the necessity. Thanks for trying,

Thi. I apologize for leaving, but I'm really not hungry. I may not be emperor material, but at least I can still earn a few coins as a scribe." He patted his pocket, where the letter crackled.

"I'm not going to give up on you," Thianra said as he started toward the door.

"But I already have," he said as he opened it. "And I believe the one thing Mother and I agree on is that she has, too." He went out and shut the door gently behind him.

Out in the main hall, no one was about. Of course he regretted those words. He felt very much like the callow twit his mother thought him.

He leaned against the wall and tried to let his anger wash through him. He knew Thianra meant well—and so did the empress. Somehow that seemed to cut deeper. If he could have seen himself as the victim here…what? He could cling to the pinnacle of self-righteousness? And what would *that* accomplish?

And the worst of it was, he had not heard from Lhind in months.

(Yep, here's me, writing about myself like I'm not here, but I wasn't *there*. So I have to continue right on not being there, until it's my turn.)

He'd sent two letters through the Hrethan ambassador, who had promised to get them to me. Maybe the empress was right, and his bond of love lay only in his imagination.

He pushed away from the wall, hoping to leave the subject behind him, but of course it trailed right with him, stubborn as a stink he'd stepped in. So he walked as fast as he could, and to give himself something useful to think about, pulled Four-Name's letter out again as he traversed the familiar halls.

At the bottom, below the elegant signature with its four names, was an address that Hlanan recognized, a popular inn along the harbor. Well, that made sense if the scribe required translation, and it also explained the foreign-sounding names. Something familiar there?

He grimaced down at the paper, unsure of some of the letters in the elaborate signature. It was so very fine that some of these letters could be read two or three ways. One thing was certain, the writer was unused to the Kherval common language.

Well, the mystery would soon be solved, giving him something else to think about besides his failure.

⟞⟝◆⟞⟝

And *now* it's my turn.

I was at that moment a bird, flying in the high mountains in the far north, where the Hrethan live.

Since my arrival I'd had two goals.

First and most important to me, to get acquainted with the father I'd thought dead until last summer. My father had been born human, a prince of Sveran Djur, but to escape the evil spells laid on him by his own family for daring to escape, he had been transformed by the Hrethan to a bird.

Ordinarily transformation magic is dangerous. Leave someone long enough in a false shape, and they will adapt to that shape. But the Hrethan speak from mind to mind. Mother and the Hrethan had reached him that way, giving him access to the world of the skies as well as that below.

I wanted badly to get to know him, and I knew that he wanted very badly to talk to me, but until I could find a way back to the mental communication that had once been so natural to me, we were confined to relying on my mother translating his thoughts to me. It was slow, cumbersome, and there were some things he wanted to share, important things—but not until I could 'hear' him on the mental plane.

Which I could no longer do. So though we couldn't talk to-gether, we could fly. Those long flights were done in silence, side by side. As we soared over the mountaintops, looking down at glittering blue ice, I found it comforting to glide next to him, the only sound the wind ruffling through our feathers, and soughing over the peaks below.

Bringing me to my second goal, which was to prove to the Hrethan that I was not, in fact, a dangerous criminal who seemed to have caught the attention of the oldest dragon in the world, Rue. A dangerous dragon everyone had thought had been dead for centuries.

But it appeared that—completely by accident—I'd woken him up.

You could say that didn't make me a criminal. But the Hrethan seemed to agree with Aranu Crown, Empress of Charas al Kherval, that it *did* make me dangerous.

More dangerous. It didn't help that when I first discovered I could communicate on the mental plane, it was by accident—and my first protracted conversation was with Jardis Dhes-Andis, Emperor of Sveran Djur, my father's half-brother, though I did not know that at the time. And that some of the powers that I'd inherited, which I'd assumed were so natural and harmless ... weren't.

To the Kherval's Mage Council, and the empress, I was pretty much the perfect example of a walking disaster. But because I was half-Hrethan, the empress couldn't toss me into some convenient mage citadel and lock me up until they decided what to do with me. My mother had gone directly to the empress and made it clear that I should be able to go to the Hrethan mountains to meet my family. The Hrethan are peaceful, but very powerful, and the empress didn't want any trouble with them.

With the Hrethan I could not communicate except by words, which they found clumsy and even untrustworthy. I couldn't defend myself against accusations stemming from my past as a thief. The only thing I could do was confine myself to my family's mountain.

So there I was, flying above the mountains and trying with all my might to be non-threatening, obedient, cooperative, and above all, to be part of a family, after a lifetime of wandering alone, an orphan scavenging on the streets. When I was just with my parents I could be my human self—my mother and I making music together—but the few times I ventured near the other Hrethan, I was always in bird form, because I knew that in my human form I said the wrong things, had no manners, and was generally, well, like the empress once said when she didn't know I was in earshot, unprepossessing at best.

Even I know that the other word for that is 'barbarian.'

I thought longingly about Hlanan often, especially when I flew out into the sunsets, or listened to the rise and fall of Hrethan music. I knew he could travel by magic transfer, but he never came. Of course the empress could keep him busy in the imperial city Erev-li-Erval, and I shouldn't have unreasonable expectations. As little practiced as I was at having family, I was even less practiced at having friends. Especially close friends who one might have kissed.

And most especially close friends one might have kissed who might one day be emperor.

Two

Back to Hlanan.

The letter (somewhat peremptory, Hlanan thought on a second perusal, but then, this was a foreigner) requesting his services designated the time and place for their interview: the largest inn in Erev-li-Erval's harbor.

That gave him plenty of time to make his way down the mountain to the harbor, a pleasant walk that usually cheered him up. Spring was giving way to summer, making the ocean breeze a delicious contrast to the bright, warm sun.

But he wasn't enjoying the spring flowers, the breeze, or the ships floating out there in the harbor below. He was still lost inside his head, trying to declare a mental moratorium on his inability to keep promises he never should have made.

He was certain of one thing. Ineffective people should not be emperors. So he'd go from there. If he failed at his healer magic studies, he could go back to being a scribe. He could work in a stable, or even finish his apprenticeship as a baker. He liked making food. It was a good life, it made people happy. You couldn't always make that claim about emperors...

He raised his eyes, trying to shut his mind away from useless conjecture. He gazed out at the bay, taking in the forest of masts swaying gently on the mild rollers washing in toward the quay.

Big, wide-hulled merchant vessels huddled up closest to the shore, loaded boats plying back and forth. At the two long piers, yachts and ships belonging to important people rode up and down on the rippling tide, some of them very beautiful indeed.

His eye was drawn to a rake-masted schooner, so narrow in the beam it looked like it could give a pirate a race. But this was no pirate—the fine carving along the rail, the dark-wood deck, and the crew dressed in some sort of livery were evidence of wealth and power.

What kind of yacht was that, besides fast? The lines looked … familiar? Not familiar enough to recognize, but then—despite his time in a Shinjan galley as a young boy—he knew little about ships. The slave children stuck up in the cramped stern, driving the tillers, had had no view. What little he'd learned was later, when Ilyan Rajanas bought a yacht, perhaps to rid himself of his own bad memories of their days of slavery on the sea.

Hlanan grimaced and rubbed his shoulder, then turned down the path into the prosperous harbor town, which was busy with local and long distance trade. Wagons, barrels being rolled, bundles of woven goods hoisted on shoulders, flowed toward the warehouses and out of them, and in and around loitering journeymen, pages and prentices dashing here and there on errands, sellers hawking wares, and wealthy folks strolling around looking for entertainment, or places to spend money.

Once Hlanan heard the cry, "Thief!"

His mind flashed to his first encounter with Lhind as seemingly from nowhere the purple-tunicked regular guard appeared, giving chase. Hlanan shook his head, knowing that the thief had little chance of escape; his mother disliked law-breaking at any time, but she considered crime happening in her capital a personal affront. "There is no poverty such as disgusts one in Thesreve," she often said to the smiling courtiers, who of course all agreed.

And it was true, Hlanan had discovered. In Erev-li-Erval—throughout the entire Kherval—the guilds were strictly enjoined to maintain their guild houses for ill, elderly, or otherwise incapacitated members. Then there were the city houses for people who didn't belong to a guild.

Each of Aranu Crown's four children had spent his or her eighth summer in a city house; anyone could stay in one, and be assured of a bed and meals, in trade for labor. But humans, Hlanan had learned, are not so easily corralled into order. That thief, who for whatever reason, did not want to join a guild or a city house, would now be spending a year sweeping, hammering, wanding, or scrubbing—unskilled labors that needed doing—under the stern eye of the city watch. The empress emphasized that this labor was intended to encourage people to learn a skill other than theft.

Hlanan had spent his eighth summer this way, mornings sweeping, and afternoons at the guild school, where he'd discovered that his reading and writing skills were far beyond his age mates'. And so the city house head had sent him to the local scribe school—his mother, at a distance, looking on in approval. At eight, Justeon had been sent to the guard stable, which had eventually led to the army; Bracan had gone aboard a schooner, which had led him to the navy, and Thianra had of course gone to the musicians.

Sometimes Hlanan wondered what might have happened to me if I'd had a city house to live in during my young life.

(Well, so far I hadn't been able to bring myself to admit to him that I'd been in them twice. But both times I'd not made it long; the first because the other children discovered how different I was from other humans. It might have been fine if that house hadn't had a bully as the chief, who thought I made a great target. I ran away. The second house had a nicer chief, but it got to be too hard to hide my differences, because the chief thought everyone should form a big family by eating together, sleeping in a long dormitory, and even bathing in a big pool together. So I ran away again.)

But Hlanan wondered, and that got him to thinking about those unanswered letters, and that made him wonder if the empress was right, and I'd merely considered him a flirt, and moved on to someone beautiful and full of innate talents—someone more like (how he saw) me.

He spotted the turrets of the inn, and, glad for the distraction, turned that way. The carillons at the Guild Hall rang the hour of noon. Hlanan had an hour, so why not get something to eat?

The pulse of hunger made him think of Thianra's breakfast. A grimace of regret promptly killed his appetite again. Thianra had meant well. And he knew his mother. What she'd said was no surprise. He ought to have had better self control—but that was another of his failures. Yes, far better the empress give the heirship to someone more qualified.

He spent the next hour watching silk weavers working in a window to lure customers inside, then a glass blower making swan necks for decorative lanterns, then an entertaining quayside grill skewer-cook, who uttered a stream of patter that made watchers laugh as he chopped vegetables, dipped them in marinade, slipped them onto a skewer with bits of fish, and set them over the grill, splashing spiced wine over them each time he turned them.

Hlanan decided he'd buy one after he got paid for the translation job, and headed at last to the inn, arriving as the carillon bonged musically, noting the first hour after noon, and (had he known it) the top of the tide on the turn.

The echoes of the last chord died among the buildings as he approached the front counter. The woman behind it considered his brown scribe robe, and her expression shuttered.

Hlanan was used to that. He said, holding up the paper, "I am to meet... Am-something. Darabah Vemmm... ari, or eri?" Once again, something about those syllables seemed familiar.

"*Amjaladarusbasvemeri.*"

The voice came from behind, a soft tenor uttering the words so smoothly that they ran together. Familiarity sparked a third time, but he had no time to plumb memory as a tall, thin, young man with short black hair approached. He wore a plain long robe of a soft gray, made high at the neck. Servant? "You are the scribe?" His accent was strong. "I am to say, Amjalad brings himself the message of requirement."

Hlanan returned the man's gaze, completely unable to make sense of that, except it sounded oddly ritualistic. "Where is this... Amjalad?"

"You will me accompany."

The young man in gray walked to the inn doors.

Intrigued, Hlanan followed him back outside, and down toward the quay. The guide never turned as he continued on toward the capital pier, longest and most exclusive in the harbor, usually used by courtiers and aristocrats who were not associated with the navy, who had their own area. Hlanan's sense of intrigue brightened into anticipation when they stepped onto the capital pier, and he was led straight to that beautiful yacht he'd glimpsed from the hillside road.

The livery resolved into cloud-gray tunics over trousers of a dull teal color, with short vests to match, the tunics made high on the neck. The sailors all had short hair, and moved about with assurance, paying no attention whatsoever to Hlanan, who walked behind the silent robed servant along the gangway toward the highly polished stairs that led below to the stern cabin.

At the doors, Hlanan's guide paused and gestured for Hlanan to pass inside. A mild buzz of magic startled him, but he suppressed the urge to test what type of ward it was. Of course so wealthy a ship-owner would arrange for various types of protecttive wards, at the very least water-repelling spells in case of storms. Rich people liked to take art treasures to sea, as if in defiance of weather and water. And Hlanan was still too slow, too unpracticed with such complex spells as testing wards.

Two of the sailors followed Hlanan into the cabin. They stopped inside the double doors, which they pulled soundlessly closed, then they took up stances side by side.

Hlanan approached the lone figure seated on cushions at a low table that ran athwartship, before the open stern windows. The strong light of early afternoon spangled the water outside, throwing writhing reflections of light over the bulkheads and low ceiling, and silhouetting the seated figure, whose lineaments were male.

"Are you... Amjalad?" Hlanan asked.

"You will say Am-Jalad," a precise voice responded in accented Elras. "You are the scribe who brought magic to remove Imperial Princess Elenderi from the governance of her family."

Now Hlanan recognized that accent—it was Djuran.

Hlanan stepped to the side, so that the light didn't dazzle him, and met the cold gaze of a startlingly handsome young man with black hair and bronze skin. "Who *are* you?"

The young man appeared to be only a year or two into manhood, though his height made him at first seem older. He said slowly, with insultingly clear diction, "Did I not state my name in my summons? I am Am-Jalad Darus Bas Veremi. In your language, the Most Noble Darus of Pennon Veremi. I myself brought to your domicile the message summoning you, and now you will in turn summon Her Imperial Highness Elenderi, to be returned to her family, by desire of Emperor Jardis Dhes-Andis."

"No," Hlanan said, and turned toward the door—to find it blocked by the two sailors. Two tall, brawny sailors. Hlanan walked up to them and when they did not part, tried to pass, but one stuck out an arm.

"You are scribe," Darus said, still with that slow, precise diction, as though he considered every word before speaking. "You must do as ordered. I did the Imperial Princess the honor of summoning you myself."

"I came because I thought you hired me," Hlanan said. "I do not take your orders no matter who you are." And he touched the ring on his little finger, which contained a transfer spell. But scarcely had he begun to whisper the word that caused the spell to work when the metal snapped with a green spark—a ward against transfers.

What? And then he remembered where he'd heard the name.

Hlanan whirled around. "You're *that* Darus. You hate Lhind—Elenderi—you wanted her dead. Why are you doing this?"

"What want I matters not. What want you, matters less. Honor and will of the emperor demand her return."

"Jardis Dhes-Andis's will," Hlanan stated, having gone from surprise to shock to anger, "means nothing to me."

I hate writing this part.

Darus flicked a look at the two sailors at the door, who advanced on Hlanan. He tried to struggle, but he was no fighter. One grabbed his arms. The other struck him in the low ribs, then flat-handed his jaw, which caused his knees to buckle. He tried to right himself, but the two dragged him out and down into the hold, where he was dropped into a dark, stuffy space and shut in.

He landed on dank wooden decking, head spinning, jaw and ribs throbbing. As he struggled upright, he became aware of a significant rolling motion: the yacht had put out to sea.

<hr/>

Thianra looked in dismay at all the lovely food she'd ordered and paid for, and decided, why not take Hlanan's suggestion? She went to a friend, a popular tiranthe player, who exclaimed, "A magnificent breakfast waiting to be eaten? Say no more!"

And soon Thianra had a cheerful gathering, which took care of the food, but not her inner turmoil.

She did her best to smile and respond to anyone who spoke to her while she kept glancing at the door, expecting Hlanan back at any moment. But he did not return, and though she counted everyone present as friends, it was a relief when they got up to depart to rehearsals or teaching or private lessons, leaving her alone with the now empty plates and cups and bowls.

Navy Commander Bracan was her full brother. She shared only a mother with Hlanan, but they had always been the closest while growing up. They were also closest in age and in temperament. It bothered her not so much that Hlanan had left annoyed—she ought to have expected that—but that his annoyance had lasted. That was rare. Usually if he went off angry, invariably he came back within an hour, sunny again, and apologetic for his temper. He had never been one to nurse a grudge.

She went to rehearsal, and then to check on her tiranthe, which was being restrung, while mentally reviewing their conversation. Hadn't he said something about earning a living? He usually went about as a scribe, which gave him the freedom of the palace, and the next thing to anonymity.

Thianra launched into her day's activities, but scarcely paid attention to any of them. She was mentally arguing with her mother, and then with Hlanan. Somehow, she had to get those two to see reason, no easy task when she was more used to expressing herself through music than through words.

After a long day of mediocre playing and absent-minded errands, as she constructed careful arguments in her head, the sun finally set, and she was free.

It was easy enough to stop by Hlanan's on her way back to the musicians' wing. A soft knock at his door, then a louder, brought no answer. He must be out—maybe even talking to the empress. Thianra hoped.

When she reached her room at last, she found a note waiting. Written on expensive paper, it contained only a line, in the empress's familiar handwriting, with no signature or address:

Breakfast at first light.

Thianra went to bed, hoping that she'd find everything normal on the morrow. When, just before dawn, she reached her mother's private room overlooking the waterfall, she discovered an unsettling mirror to her own arrangement the day before: a feast awaiting three people.

But Hlanan was not there.

The empress sat squarely on her cushion, arms crossed, brows drawn down into a line over her nose. "Though Hlanan and I have had our disagreements—as have we all—I have never found him cowardly. And he stopped sulking about the time he lost his milk teeth. I thought."

Thianra shook her head, uncertain what to say.

The empress sighed, looking tired, old, and grim. "He ignored a summons I sent yesterday. I sent two of my most discreet Ravens to find him. He is not anywhere in the palace. Did he say anything about leaving, yesterday?"

"Only that he had received a job offer," she replied.

The empress's mouth tightened. "Not through the scribes, he did not. Also, inquiries furnished these tidings: a well-dressed foreigner asked the way to his chamber to leave a message the evening before."

"Might be a friend of his," Thianra said uncertainly.

"I sent my assistant to his room. She found his golden notecase, and two palace messages, one from you and one for a wedding at month's end," the empress said.

Thianra sat down across from her mother. "Perhaps he went to do a favor for a friend who knows him as a scribe."

"That is certainly the most obvious explanation." The empress's brows quirked at a skeptical slant. "Except for the fact that he has always let someone know where he was going."

"That's true."

"So I've ordered the Ravens to send out a party of scouts to make discreet inquiries," the empress said.

"They'll find him," Thianra said with confidence.

There had to be some reasonable explanation, after all. They were all reasonable people.

The empress agreed out loud without either confidence or hope and took her leave, the pressure of the daily ritual inescapable.

She possessed what patience she could as she was robed for the Rising, during which far too many courtiers found ways to beg a private word. She endured the long flattering preambles that they all seemed to think she required — or believed — until at last they came to the point, and she forced herself to listen, and then dispatched them all to her most diplomatic heralds, though she longed to cut them short with an emphatic, "No."

The result would be the same, she reflected with bleak satisfaction as, at last, she withdrew, supposedly to take her brief, private midday meal. But the heralds would repay them with flattery, keeping them busy with vague promises, and then further avenues that would lead around in circles...

As she was doing now, came the unsettling thought as she made her way via private hall to the old archives, her Ravens going ahead not only to scan for possible dangers, but to deflect any wanderers.

The oldest archive smelled musty, like ancient ink and paper. Here, poring over a crackling scroll that had aged to a dull ochre, she found Lian Vosaga, Hlanan's father. The man had scarcely aged, except for the gray in his hair and a more pronounced stoop in his thin shoulders. As she approached, she wondered if he was wearing the same robe he'd worn the last time she'd visited up here, ten years ago. Longer?

At the sound of her footsteps he looked up, blinking, an expression of mild surprise on his face as he said, "Aranu. Shall I rise? Is this a formal call?"

"No," she said, and though their relationship had scarcely lasted five years, she still loved seeing his inky fingers.

But time was short. "Have you seen Hlanan in the past day?"

Lian looked mildly perplexed, as though he had to search his formidable archive of a mind for a Hlanan-shaped scroll. "I haven't seen him for a month or so."

"Flames of Rue!" the empress exclaimed in disappointment— then was immediately distracted. "By the bye, did you know that there is an actual Rue—that that is the name of a dragon apparently dwelling deep under a fire mountain in Sveran Djur?"

"Of course," Lian said mildly. "That is, I thought he was dead, the last dragon. But it appears he is alive after all."

If anyone knew about ancient dragons, it would be an archivist. Lian lifted a hand toward a tall bookcase against the far wall. "There is all manner of dragon lore to be found here, some brought from another continent, and the oldest texts brought through the world gate."

The empress dismissed the bookcase with a jerk of her shoulder. "Never mind ancient lore. All I have time for are today's problems. Which might very well include a powerful dragon living within stone's throw of my worst enemy, Emperor Jardis Dhes-Andis. At least I trust he will not get one of his thrice-cursed mind-controlling fais enchantments around *its* neck!"

"Rue is a male," Lian said equably. "Usually, we are told by the Summer Isles chronicler, queen dragons ruled, however, apparently close to a thousand years ago—"

"Never mind the dragon." She bit back what was about to become a rather heated opinion about dragons, and sighed. "I always thought the expression had to do with the burn of regret. Speaking of, Hlanan seems to have run off somewhere to sulk after he and I had a disagreement, and I cannot find him. I hoped you knew where he might be."

Lian carefully set his reed pen on its holder, and folded his hands. "Aranu, you know Hlanan far better than I," he said in his even, calm, light voice. "It was you who wished to guide his education. But in my time with him, I have never seen him sulk. Are you certain you are not diminishing him in order to palliate your own guilt?"

And that was why she and Lian had only lasted five years, she had to admit. She claimed to cherish plain speaking, but Lian had always been either exasperatingly scholarly and vague, or far too direct—and too right.

They regarded one another. "I've sent the Ravens out," she said.

"Excellent," Lian murmured. "Please let me know when he turns up. I located a record that I believe will amuse him."

Aranu stepped up onto the platform, leaned down and kissed him on the cheek. She was delighted to see him flush like a boy, and chuckled with reminiscence all the way back to the imperial state wing.

Three

WHILE THIANRA AND THE empress spent their day assuming that Hlanan was somewhere close by—and that the Ravens would easily turn him up like a lost coin—he was feeling his way over the dark hold, not so much to find a way out, which he did not expect to encounter, as to sense a weakness in the magical ward that might be worked at so that he could transfer away.

But the mage who had warded the yacht was far more experienced. That much was plain. Still, he continued, as much for something to do as anything else. Hunger and thirst, vague earlier, sharpened over immeasurable time, and now he really regretted stalking away in a snit and leaving Thianra's magnificent breakfast.

Aside from the period of his slavery he had been imprisoned once before, at the hands of Geric Lendan, a sometime childhood friend from court who had turned out to have been suborned by Jardis Dhes-Andis. He had learned that when one is cooped up in the dark, what seems like days can be mere hours. He tried at first to remember all the delicious foods that Thianra had ordered, but that only seemed to worsen the emptiness inside him. So then he tried to dredge up memory of his long-ago Djuran lessons—how to conjugate verbs, the different classes of pronoun depending on whom one addressed—but he didn't have a text to check himself.

The only sense of time passing he could trust besides increased thirst and hunger was the change of the roll of the yacht. Gradually the swells deepened so significantly that he had to wedge himself against a bulkhead and set his feet to the deck to keep from tumbling about. That had to be a summer storm.

At length he found himself sinking into sleep between pitches, until—at last—he was able to lie on his side, arms curled against his chest in the dank, cold darkness, and he slumbered fitfully until a shaft of light struck his eyelids.

Fresh air swept in, bringing the sharp scent of brine. Another pair of brawny liveried men entered, gripped Hlanan by the arms, and brought him out as a third held a lantern, whose light danced crazily in counterpoint to the yacht's pitch and roll.

Thirsty, hungry, grimy, and disoriented, Hlanan did not resist as he was carried up to the captain's cabin again. The clean spacious sweep smelled of sweet spices. It was lit by two very fine glowglobes set on graceful crystal holders shaped like sheaves of barley, set at either end of the long, low table. Hlanan felt even more squalid as he was shoved toward the cool, immaculate Darus, seated again behind his table. That was probably deliberate. He straightened up, anger rushing back.

"You had time to reflect," Darus said carefully, his words sounding rehearsed. "You have nothing to gain in refusal. You will write to Her Imperial Highness—"

"No."

Darus's eyes narrowed, and Hlanan remembered being told about Darus's wolf nature. It seemed very close to the surface as he said, "Your life depends upon it."

Hlanan had to work his mouth to speak, and his voice came out a hoarse whisper: "Do your worst."

Darus half-raised a hand, then frowned. "Why refuse? You are scribe. Scribes obey." When Hlanan did not speak, Darus's eyes narrowed. "You are her pet, then?"

Hlanan didn't answer that. It took all his concentration to stay on his feet. Darus gave him a long, cold, assessing stare. Hlanan stared back. He could see Darus's anger warring with uncertainty.

In his experience, decisions made in anger came quickly. Hlanan considered the expense of the yacht, the long journey, and wondered if he himself was Darus's single clue to Lhind's whereabouts. Killing Hlanan would leave Darus with nothing.

After a tense pause, during which Hlanan swayed on his feet as the ocean washed and slapped against the hull, Darus lifted his head and spoke rapidly in Djuran. All Hlanan made out was the word for 'water' before the silent men took him back to the hold.

A third, bearing that swinging lantern, brought in a ceramic pitcher of water, a single stale bun stuffed with some sort of greens, and left him with them—in the darkness.

Hlanan sank down and felt around for the pitcher. He meant to sip slowly, for he had no idea when, or if, he'd get more, but before he could stop himself he'd swallowed the entire contents.

Now his stomach sloshed. He gnawed at the stale bread, which at least forced him to eat slowly. When he was finished, he felt marginally better, enough to enable him to curl up and sleep.

Once again he woke to the pitch and yaw of a storm, a muffled roar resonating through the timbers. He pressed against a bulkhead, listening to the drips and splashes as water worked its way in. Gradually the noise faded, and he forced himself to get up and move about so that he wouldn't weaken physically.

This time, the servitors brought food and another stale bun stuffed with grilled fish and some kind of dried kelp, and after he'd eaten, he was again brought before Darus, who put the same questions to him.

When Hlanan refused, it was back to the hold, and so it went for another five days—or so he guessed, as it was always dark when he was brought to the stern cabin.

With each visit, though Darus held himself with rigid control, Hlanan could see in that very rigidity how his intransigence angered the Djuran noble. Meanwhile, five days of nothing more than a small jug of water and a stale breakfast roll with leftovers was telling on him physically.

Neither Darus's temper nor Hlanan's wellbeing were helped by a succession of storms. The yacht weathered them beautifully, but Hlanan began to suspect from the number of lookouts on the last night, and the tension he glimpsed so briefly when he was taken from the hold to the cabin, that somewhere along the way they had been driven off course.

At any rate, he was startled out of disturbed dreams by a violent jolt, followed by the frantic footsteps on the deck overhead, very unlike the quieter, orderly footfalls he'd been hearing for uncounted days. Then a lot of high-pitched yelling penetrated down to the hold.

Hlanan's heart thumped against his ribs. An attack? Was it possible it could be Bracan and the imperial navy, somehow to his rescue?

But how would they have even found Hlanan? A fresh surge of regret seized him when he remembered how thoughtlessly — *stupidly* — he'd left the palace without telling anyone anything. He knew better than that, he'd been trained to always let someone know, and so he had, his entire life... until the morning he got into an almighty snit and walked out without talking to anyone.

More snitting wasn't going to save him now. He scrambled up in the stuffy, dank hold, wincing against the crashing of the headache that never quite went away, and pressed as near to the hatch as he could, straining to hear.

A single word in any of the Kherval languages would give him hope. Even pirates could usually be convinced to ransom someone, and Hlanan could count on Ilyan Rajanas to cover him there, without anyone ever revealing who he was.

He did hear words, but muffled and incomprehensible. All the thumping and crashing didn't help. A battle? The thin, acrid smell of smoke heightened his anxiety, until the hatch abruptly crashed open.

Shrouded figures crowded around the opening. Wind-whipped torchlight light jittering wild shadows through the hold. Hlanan winced, turning his eyes away, then started when hard hands gripped his arms.

He said, "Who are you? Are you from the Kherval?"

No answer.

Hope died as he concentrated on getting his feet under him. Ungentle hands yanked him out of the hold, and brought him onto the rocking deck, where more torchlight played over shrouded figures putting out a fire near the foremast. Human-shaped lumps lay sprawled and still on the deck, blood splashes gleaming wetly in the fires.

Hlanan tried to free his arms. The grip tightened mercilessly. No, it couldn't be... the cadences of the low voices aft were heart-sinkingly familiar as he was brought into the cabin, where a man with rusty-gray hair above a domed forehead sat behind Darus's beautiful table (now scarred down the center as if hacked by a sword). The man's jacket was edged in red, with three red chevrons on the arms.

Shinjan.

Darus himself knelt below a bulkhead to the side, his arms bound tightly behind him, two armed Shinjans posted at either side, their faces shrouded by black scarves.

Rust Head addressed Darus in thick Djuran, but Darus knelt with rigid back, gaze straight ahead.

Rust Head turned to Hlanan's escort, who spoke in Shinjan—which Hlanan had never forgotten, "This is the prisoner."

"Did he speak?"

"Some gabble in Elras, the Kherval tongue."

Hlanan knew that if the Shinjans figured out he understood their language, they'd want to know how he'd learned it. He stood there looking at the desk, hoping he appeared uncomprehending.

Rust Head addressed him in Djuran, to which Hlanan shrugged, then said awkwardly in that language, "Prisoner I be. Allow me go, please."

Rust Head made a gesture, and Hlanan's captors shifted, one holding him. Hlanan braced himself for the tattoo search—and death. But to his surprise, no one bothered with his flesh. As one captor held him, the other searched his clothes. His scowl cleared when he saw the little ring on Hlanan's finger, he yanked it off, scraping it over the knuckle, and tossed it onto a pile of rings, earrings, and jeweled clasps, next to a tangle of what looked like silver and gold necklaces.

The little ring had been bespelled with protections and a transfer; Hlanan was too relieved at not being searched for the tattoo to miss it. Yet. Perhaps his being an obvious prisoner somehow obviated the tattoo search. Or perhaps the Shinjans couldn't believe a Djuran prisoner could also be an escaped Shinjan slave.

The booty of necklaces nearly filled a basket at the end of the table. Those had to be the Djurans' *fais*, Hlanan thought—the necklets that enabled them to communicate sub-vocally, and to be traced by magic. The nobles and leaders could also use the magic on their underlings' fais to punish them through nerve-searing magical fire. Breaking the formidable webwork of wards over those fais was not easy. The Shinjan mages must have created some kind of powerful enchantment to break so many so quickly.

Hlanan was muscled out again, and onto the deck, where he was bound, like the rest of the crew, taken aft and forced to the deck.

He sat down, still in a bitter mood over his close escape from the death of escaped slaves, until Darus was brought up, and forced onto the deck a few paces away. Hlanan almost didn't recognize him, he was so battered.

Darus glanced at him with hatred, then turned his one-eyed gaze away, the other eye being swollen shut. He knelt among his crew on the deck, knees together, butt on heels, shoulders straight. His crew respectfully edged away from him as much as possible, leaving Darus in a little moat of isolation.

Hlanan turned away. In the east, under a cloudy sky, ships bobbed on the water, their profile sickeningly familiar. Hlanan did not need the further proof, but there it was: he had fallen into the hands of the Shinjans.

They were kept on deck, through two days (and three storms), given water jugs to pass from hand to hand at dawn and sundown, and once a day fed with pieces of dried fish and kelp cakes.

The water passed in silence. Any time anyone spoke, out came the knotted ropes, burly Shinjans beating the speaker's shoulders with three strokes hard enough to raise bleeding welts. No one spoke after the second such treatment was meted out.

Darus never looked Hlanan's way. On the fourth day, the ship sailed up on the lee side of a huge transport vessel, and the prisoners were forced over a ramp that heaved on the gray sea between the ships.

Hlanan, light-headed from hunger, paused between every step, fighting a nauseating vertigo. It was clear that the Shinjans didn't really care if he fell between the ships into the sea, and for a couple of those wavering steps he was tempted to jump.

Then he was distracted by a splash. Someone behind him had jumped, and when he turned to look, he saw a Shinjan hurl a javelin into the escapee, who floated lifelessly, red clouding the water around him.

The Shinjans sent up a shout of praise.

"Ho-yah!"

"Got him in one!"

". . .stinking Djurans..."

The sailor grinned proudly until a bawl of invective from one of the three-chevron captains got them back to work.

Hlanan walked on. Giving in to suicide was the coward's way. He had no aid but his wits, but at least he had them. He would escape. He'd done it before, he would again.

He reached the deck of the transport and got a shove between the shoulder blades. He fell onto the deck. A huge hand grasped the back of his collar and yanked him, choking, to his feet.

Another shove, and he was manhandled below, where the Djuran crew were funneled down to the hold. Here, their bindings were removed before Hlanan and Darus were thrust into a cubby directly above the hold, small and airless. There, the two of them were left together.

Hlanan could feel Darus's fury—which matched his own. He refused to be the first to speak. What was there to say anyway? "I'm glad they beat you up instead of me?" That would be a fine way to begin what was certain to be a nasty journey.

And it was.

At first, Hlanan expected it to be short. He remembered having heard about the duel between Jardis Dhes-Andis and Darus that Lhind had been forced to witness, and how experienced Darus had been. Hlanan suspected that that deep gouge he'd seen in the beautiful wooden desk was evidence of Darus's fight against the Shinjans, and he wondered as he tried unsuccessfully to find a comfortable position on warped, damp planks of the deck, if Darus was going to attack him. Even when he wasn't starved and light-headed, Hlanan was no fighter.

But Darus kept to his side of the cubby, and neither moved nor spoke.

Hlanan tried to keep himself busy by recollecting his linguistics reading and conjugating Djuran verbs. Far more productive than the maddening internal itch and sting of what-ifs: what if he'd told Thianra where he was going. What if he'd dismissed the question of diplomacy and did a magic transfer to the Hrethan mountains in order to be rejected by me face to face, which would be better than useless wondering.

When he caught himself at it, he forced his mind back to the verbs.

Time ground on, measured by the sound of the Djuran noble's breathing. Hlanan guessed at the passage of time by the food passed in at long intervals, surmising that the morning prisoner feed was continued. By the second time, he could smell the other man who sat so silent in the darkness, the only sound his breathing. Hlanan knew he didn't smell any better — probably worse, as he'd had a few extra days to build up some fine ripeness, thanks to Darus's hospitality on board his yacht.

After a number of dreary days marked off by meals, the sounds above changed, and Hlanan suspected they had reached their destination. He braced himself for whatever was to come next, and presently heard a heavy bolt scrape back outside the cubby.

The door opened, and murky light slanted in, along with a waft of dank air that smelled almost sweet compared to what he'd been breathing.

Pairs of brawny Shinjans hauled the two up to the deck, and then down a ramp to a dock. Against the garish white light under a thin layer of cloud, Hlanan squinted to either side, seeing nothing but Shinjan vessels of various types, mostly the long red-sailed galleys of the navy.

He and Darus were marched behind the scruffy, bedraggled Djuran crew, their livery much the worse for wear. A heavy stone building awaited them at the end of the quay. It bristled with guards.

Hlanan was kept in a hallway as Darus got taken inside a room.

A short time later, Darus came out with his guards. He avoided Hlanan's gaze as he passed, and it was Hlanan's turn to go before another officer behind a desk.

This woman was tall, her face seamed, her pale red hair going white, framing a face dominated by a beak of a nose and a chin that would have set well on one of Justeon's heavy cavalry dragoons. Her short arms below powerful shoulders were marked by three red chevrons.

"You are a prisoner of a very high noble of Sveran Djur," she said in fluent, if accented, Elras. "Who are you? Why did the most noble Darus take you?"

Hlanan shook his head. "Ask him. I know nothing." He plunged his hand into his pocket to present the letter as proof, except of course it had vanished unnoticed some time ago.

Not that it would matter. They'd do what they wanted to do anyway.

"You know something, the both of you," the woman said, laughing softly. "I suspect that proves that you are someone of importance, too, no? In spite of you looking, and smelling, like a dock hand's sorry assistant. Perhaps some of that nobility will wear off after a time at the Barrow. It usually does," she said, and lifted her hand, then said in Shinjan, "Barrow for this one, too."

He and Darus were shoved into a cart with iron bars, where four of the Djurans already waited—all four with healing bruises and cuts. Shinjans of all ages and types went about their morning work, but many paused to stare into the cart at the six, some pointing and laughing, or making raucous comments. Hlanan didn't understand all the slang—he'd been ten when forced onto the galley, so his vocabulary was limited—but he got enough to make him turn his head away.

Darus seemed oblivious. His attention was focused entirely on the remainder of his crew, now being herded in the opposite direction. He followed them with his gaze, turning his head and even pressing his face against the rusty iron bars as he tried to see where they were being taken.

Hlanan had heard of the Barrow. Every slave had. It was the worst prison in the capital, a prison and dungeon combined, and had served as a threat for recalcitrant slaves; if you proved to be too much trouble after a dose of the Barrow, you would be put in the arena as entertainment for the city, who liked the spectacle of people fighting for their lives—and losing.

He wondered if Darus understood where they were being taken, as one of his men muttered something to Darus, to receive a short answer and the slightest shake of his head.

"Shut up, galk," a Shinjan bawled.

Galk. It had been years since Hlanan had heard the term reserved for slaves. It meant beast of burden who speaks, as opposed to *galm*, the beast of burden that doesn't speak, like horses, cows, donkeys, and the other big beasts of burden that walk, because the Shinjans hadn't mastered gryphs the way the Djurans had. Not for lack of trying.

If galks spoke without being spoken to, it meant a beating. That had seemed arbitrarily cruel to ten-year-old Hlanan, but now he could see the cruelly deliberate thought behind it: galks were expected to accept their status as beasts of burden.

This reflection just made him angrier.

He looked away from the confusion that briefly wrinkled Darus's brow, before the noble smoothed his countenance once again, and filthy as he was, assumed his usual hauteur.

Hlanan gazed out. The harbor seemed unchanged from Hlanan's previous visits, caught in brief glimpses when he and

Ilyan had been shifted from one ship to another. He had never been beyond the fortress, where the rest of the Djuran crew were now being marched, to be tattooed by the mages, and then separated out so no man went with a friend or companion when he was chained into galleys.

At least they were adults. For a short time Hlanan was not aware of the creaking cart, the muttering men, the taunts and shrill laughter of the dockside urchins following along; he looked back through time at himself at ten, shivering and bewildered, surrounded by crying children with blood trickling down their arms, as the tattooists were not especially careful of young flesh: the tracer spells were worked into their ink, so the diamonds didn't have to be artistic. Then came the forcible separation, the bigger boys and girls taken in one direction, the smaller and weaker ones in another, and those—like Hlanan—who promised no especial strength or weakness taken to the naval ships.

He and Rajanas had met when forced into the tiny tiller space on the same galley, to serve with two boys almost grown out of the space.

The cart jolted over a hole in the road, bringing him abruptly back to the present, and Darus's frown as he tried to see his disappearing servants.

The cart bumped over the cobbled road up into the city proper, which was as elaborate as Hlanan had remembered.

He remembered learning that Shinjan citizens, who could not bear arms on pain of death, put a great deal of importance in fine exteriors to their homes, elaborate carving and statuary pilasters and other signs that boasted of the family's lineage and success—homes that the slaves in the army and the governmental functionaries were forbidden, along with the creation of families.

But either he had been less observant than he realized, or memory had blurred because proximity revealed cracked and weather-worn carving, ineffectually repaired ironwork, and a general seediness.

Hlanan shifted his attention away from the buildings and observed the people. A cluster of children ran alongside the cart, shouting insults at the galks behind bars, but many of the adults didn't give Hlanan and the Djurans a second glance, any more than they glanced at the animals pulling the cart.

Hlanan noticed two interesting things: first, a group of women talking outside of the awning of a market booth. As the cart approached, they turned as one, then dispersed, each with her basket.

Second, two old men whose long gazes at the Shinjan escort were difficult to interpret, except as... brooding.

But otherwise people went about their business, clearing the street as the escort and cart proceeded down the middle, then filling in behind them again, rather as if they weren't there.

The cart rolled past three-story buildings with elaborately edged roofs, then past smaller, less decorative buildings, then at last past the edges of the city. The sun sank down in the west, lurid light slanting through the gathering shadows when they reached a military outpost at last.

The same food as always was brought to the cart. One man unlocked the iron door, and a brawny woman set a jug and a flat basket of the same food as before inside, then the door was slammed and locked again, after which the Shinjans walked away.

The biggest of the Djurans grabbed everything before anyone else could. Darus spoke for the first time, giving an order in a short voice.

The big man set the basket down, but then regarded his noble with a narrow, reflective stare, which Darus returned steadily.

Hlanan was sure the big guard had begun to understand what it meant that they no longer wore fais. In Sveran Djur, all the Djurans wore the magic-laden necklets, but only the nobles had the ability to administer magical 'correction' — which at its worst felt like being burned alive, though it left no marks. (As well I knew.)

Hlanan held his breath, his heart beating hard against his ribs.

But the big man slowly set the basket back down.

Darus spoke again, and one by one the Djurans took food — leaving the broken bits and crumbs for Hlanan. They passed the jug of water from hand to hand. Hlanan got it last, and was left with scarcely a few sips.

There they were, in the middle of a military camp's courtyard, as a summer thunderstorm blasted through, pelting them with hail, then rain. Hlanan, whose thirst had become unbearable, pressed his face against the bars, his mouth open to catch as much of the rain as he could. He swallowed until he got hiccoughs, then spent the rest of the night shivering in damp clothes, but at least he'd finally had enough to drink.

His sleep was intermittent; he drifted in and out, vaguely aware of soft whispers now and then.

When the sun came up, he found himself pressed awkwardly in a corner, a man's leg jammed boot first against his side. Once one woke, the others did, and as they did, Hlanan saw a new tension in the way they sat—and a new alignment of alliances.

He suspected that the big one was about to go after Darus.

But nothing happened until the basket and jug was brought, this time by a weedy young man with a shock of the red hair that Shinjans prized so much.

The escort drew swords as the cage was unlocked, the basket slung in and the empty one pulled out. A jug was set down, the door locked again.

The Shinjans had scarcely taken two steps away when the big man made his move.

Darus was ready for him—a grunt, a hiss, the meaty thud of a fist in the breastbone, a sickening crack, then the hissing sound of someone strangling. The big man fell back gasping for breath, one hand at his throat, his thumb bent all the way backward on the other hand.

The rest of the Djurans could have piled onto Darus, but either custom or prudence held them back. As the big man cowered back, sobbing, the Shinjans, who had stopped to watch, laughed, and started away again.

"You remember that skinny galk," someone said. "He's got my bet."

Darus paid them no attention as he made a short gesture of command to one of the other men, who divided up the food. This time, Hlanan got a little more than crumbs: not a full share, but better than the night before. The big man got nothing.

After the Shinjans came back for the basket and jug, the cart was hitched up to four horses again, and the journey toward the capital, and the Barrow, began.

FOUR

DEEPLY DISTURBED, THIANRA FORCED herself to continue with her life. She left the capital to visit her instrument maker in the south of Namas Ilan, but as it's said, your shadow sticks to your heels no matter how fast you run, and her worries traveled right along with her.

This family had been making excellent tiranthes for generations; their instruments might not look as fancy as those made by fashionable court instrument makers, but the wood was better seasoned, the strings bringing out a purer sound.

From time to time Thianra took out her one extravagance, a golden notecase for magic-transfer letters, and checked to see if there was any news about Hlanan.

Nothing.

Thianra's instrument was worth the trip, but now that she had it, she couldn't enjoy it. Not with that silence from Hlanan, which had turned from puzzling to alarming. Since the principality of Alezand was not all the far, she went to the local posting inn to find out if there was a post coach, or someone hired to take post, heading for Alezand's border.

"Every third day," she was told. "Leavin' direct on noon bells—you can see 'em hitching the horses right now. And Milsa, who swaps driving with her brother, right there diving into her skilling."

A triumphant hand indicated a woman on the other side of the room, bending over her meal, a driver's coat folded over the next chair.

Thianra said, "Is there room?"

"You'll by rights talk to Milsa about that, but I can tell you, she only has three paid passengers," the woman said, perhaps hoping for an order, as the summer heat seemed to have made the world somnolent, and custom was sparse. No one seemed to want to move except the insects flying in circles near the door.

"I'll take a plate of skilling, then," Thianra said.

And she soon sat before a cold dish of spiced cucumber, tomato, celery and some other greens, with crumbled hard-boiled egg dashed through it, and a savory fish sauce poured on top.

She and Milsa the driver finished at the same time. Milsa, a tall, somber woman about Thianra's own age, thickset and fair-haired, took Thianra's coins and then Thianra settled into the coach, her new tiranthe balanced on top of her travel bundle.

Thianra, as always, offered to play to entertain her fellow passengers, but the stout woman in the opposite corner scowled and said she hated noise. The other passengers, a skinny carpenter and a teenage girl with a basket of combed wool, agreed that it was unconscionably hot, and no one ought to have to travel; the stout woman declared that heat was healthy, and that youth complained about every little thing these days, which had the effect of silencing them all—except when the stout woman chose to benefit them all with her opinions. Needless to say, these were all complaints.

Because of the unseasonable heat, the coach stopped often for the horses. Just before they halted for the night, the stout woman got off. The journey promptly became merry, Thianra playing the while, and the others singing and clapping.

She had learned three variations on a couple of old folk songs before they came at last to Imbradi, Alezand's capital, where ruled Hlanan's old friend Ilyan Rajanas, Prince of Alezand.

Her hopes dashed when she discovered that Rajanas was not there—and neither was Hlanan.

She was given a guest room, where she got through her daily fingering practice until a servant brought word that the prince had returned. Tall, black-haired, and competent, he was also very politically astute, and Thianra hoped that if he didn't know where Hlanan was, he might have an idea.

When she reached the interview chamber, she discovered that he was not alone; his hands snapped and gestured, responded to in a speedy flicker by an equally tall, pale-haired woman wearing a gray uniform.

"Thianra," Rajanas said, his slanted brows rising in mild surprise. "Welcome to Imbradi. Is Hlanan with you?"

There went her last faint hope. "No. I thought he might have come here. Or that you've heard from him?"

"Not since winter," Rajanas said, and with more hand gestures, "May I introduce Ovlan Nath? Soon to be Princess of Alezand."

Thianra cried in delight, "That is wonderful news!"

Ovlan smiled and gestured something as Rajanas said, "In fact, I was going to write to Hlanan again. I wrote to him not five days ago, to let him know — usually he answers within a day or so."

Ovlan glanced from one to the other, gestured to Rajanas, and left.

Rajanas's eyes narrowed. "Where is he?"

"He seems to be missing," Thianra said to Hlanan's oldest and most trusted friend. Rajanas was the only person outside the family who knew who their mother was. "The empress would not like this to go any farther, but…"

Out it all came. Rajanas listened silently, then said, "Has anyone contacted Lhind, to ask if she knows?"

"No," Thianra said.

"You should."

Thianra shook her head. "My mother would object."

Rajanas grunted, but didn't make any more comment than that. He knew that Hlanan was being considered for the imperial heirship, which, if it happened, would change his entire life.

"Listen, I can find a mage to give you a transfer token back to the capital, if you like."

Thianra accepted gratefully.

The next morning, after sharing breakfast with the affianced couple—and learning several words in hand-signing—Thianra braced for the unpleasant wrench of magic transfer.

She came out of it at the imperial palace Destination. She carried her precious new instrument directly to her room, where she found a summons note from her mother, who would of course have been apprised of her appearance.

At the royal suite she was waved right in.

The empress looked old and tired. "Thianra, Hlanan's disappearance, or rather the manner of it, is endemic—part of a larger problem. I have not discussed my inner thoughts with you as you have made it clear that your music is your first priority. I accept that. If you do not want to be involved further, stop me now."

"If it concerns Hlanan, of course I want to hear it, Mother," Thianra said. "What problem?"

"The apparent peace that isn't." The empress walked restlessly back and forth along the massive glass wall that overlooked the waterfall. Dread tightened inside Thianra.

The empress began thumping her fist on a table, a book case, and her desk on each point as she strode around and spoke. "That mage Maita Boniree—on the imperial payroll—squatted there on my border, not a week's ride from this city, while secretly practicing blood magic. Geric Lendan raised without morals or ethics by smiling, flattering parents in my own court—after their having sold that wretched boy to Jardis Dhes-Andis to be turned into a spy. I never knew that. I was told he'd been sent to be tutored to become a better courtier in order to serve. He was! By Djurans! How was that *possibly* supposed to be good for Charas al Kherval?"

"Where are his parents now?"

"Oh, they quarreled with each other and vanished in different directions long ago," the empress said bitterly. *Bam,* her fist hit the desk. "Years before their son got into trouble. Their daughter now rules their land, and thorough investigation has turned up nothing suspicious in her, at least. My Ravens were *very* thorough," she added bleakly.

Thianra thought, here it comes.

"And now, we have Hlanan's disappearance. It seems that he was lured somehow on board a Djuran craft. After the lure was brought *inside. The. Palace.*"

Bang! Bang! Bang! went her imperial fist on each word.

"By not just some spy from Sveran Djur, but by no less than one of their nobles."

"What?"

"All the inn people noticed was that he paid well, he and his servants comported themselves with noble bearing, though they spoke very little of our language. They all wore those damn necklaces, which no one thought to question. In his arrogance, he even used his name, though he wrote it in Djuran, in the registry at the inn down at the harbor. No one thought to question *that*, either!"

Thianra stared, appalled.

"One of my Ravens speaks Djuran, and apparently was the first to notice," the Empress said bitterly. "We seem to have been honored with a visit by Darus Bas Veremi, one of their Am-Jalad, which means something like the old archduke rank. The Am-Jalad Darus who tried to have Lhind killed while she was a prisoner in Sveran Djur."

"This Darus was in *Erev-li-Erval?*" Thianra cried.

"Oh, that isn't the worst of it!" The empress's eyes widened, her gaze angrily sardonic. "The worst of it is, this Am-Jalad Darus Bas Veremi bribed his way into *my palace*, in order to leave some kind of note, or threat, or something, for Hlanan, *at his room*, at the very center of the palace. *Himself.* He didn't send a servant. And no one thought to mention any of this to anyone, until the Ravens scared the spit out of the servants and the lower tier guards by hauling them in to be questioned."

Thianra jerked her thumb at the floor. "Darus was *here?*"

"In and out. Easy as air. Gate and door guards never noticed him. Servants wafted him along, well greased with gold," the Empress said sarcastically. "Of course that's the last gold they'll ever see, at least from me, not that turning them off helps us any. But I sent 'em packing just the same, with a stiff reminder of my magnanimity, as my great-grandfather would have lopped off their ears. And the empress before that, their heads."

Thianra stared, unsure what to say.

"I prided myself on the peace and safety of my own halls, the quiet harmony. Tchah! On every side of me, from high court to assistant cook, people say what they think I want to hear, hiding their true natures as well as their ambitions. Part of me wishes to surround them all with spies, but going down that road leads only to madness. At least I can, and in fact have, ordered a thorough examination of the guard routine. The Ravens," she said with relish, "can be very thorough."

Aranu Crown then rubbed her eyes. "Thianra, I'm getting too old for this kind of trouble. But I must go on as if nothing happened, and wait for Jardis Dhes-Andis to get around to whatever threat he is preparing, because of course that Am-Jalad set sail as soon as he grabbed Hlanan, and slithered straight back to Sveran Djur. And I *hate* the fact that, as your militant brother Justeon would say, Dhes-Andis gets to pick the time, and the ground, of a battle I didn't even know was coming."

"Are you sure? Have you received a threat or message?"

"Not yet."

"From what I remember, he wasn't slow to issue threats."

"He might be waiting for something. Or weather might have slowed that slimy snake Darus, though the Grand Admiral insists that they ought to have reached Sveran Djur by now twice over. The only thing I can think of is that Jardis Dhes-Andis is trying to choke Lhind's whereabouts out of Hlanan."

"Lhind!" Thianra repeated.

"You weren't here last summer," the empress said grimly, "when I had to face a decision that still gives me nightmares. Jardis Dhes-Andis was willing to set fire to entire cities if I didn't surrender Lhind to him. And Geric Lendan stood there ready to slit Hlanan's throat. I think Dhes-Andis is hunting her down by any every underhanded means at his command, and he—being a Djuran—has a quiver full of 'em. But when he gets what he wants, at the very least he will brandish Hlanan and demand a trade. Assuming of course he also squeezes out of Hlanan the truth of his birth."

Thianra's insides roiled when she mentally translated 'choke' and 'squeeze' for torture.

The empress halted before the window. "And I'll do it. In a heartbeat," she whispered huskily. "And Hlanan will not only hate me forever, he'll throw my own words back into my teeth about rational decisions and not letting sentiment rule. Hlanan is my son. The best of all three boys, if only he knew it."

Thianra bit her lip, not wanting to say that this, right here, summed up one of the main reasons why she never wanted to be empress. She gripped her hands together so hard that her fingernails dug into her palms. "He doesn't know it, Mother. If anything, he believes he's a disappointment. That's pretty much the last thing he said to me before he left, that morning."

"And that is my fault." The empress pressed the heels of her hands to her eyes. "He has no ambition, which I find admirable. Infinitely preferable to Justeon's arrogant assumption that he's destined for power. Not that he'd be bad—he's not *evil*—but Hlanan's sense of justice is as acute as his sense of duty. But that's it, he's regarded the prospect of becoming emperor as a duty, preferably for someone else. I wanted him to want it enough to reach for it, to strive, not because he's the least bad choice, but because he's the best. Will make the best emperor. I want him... to have passion."

The empress threw her arms out wide. "You have to have passion, or the sheer work will devour you, if more ambitious people don't."

Thianra had no trouble agreeing with that.

The empress heaved a sigh. "I shouldn't rant at you, especially as you never wanted any of it." She gazed wearily down at the waiting piles of paper on her desk. "Thank you for listening. I must get back to court," she said. "I've kept some of those same smooth-talking, smooth-slithering ambitious snakes waiting—a salutary lesson—but I will lose my position of moral superiority if I prolong it."

She walked to the door and went through, surrounded by her guards, leaving Thianra alone in the room.

She had never wanted power, but that didn't mean she wouldn't try to help her relations when she could. She thought of missing the Kitharee, and anguish gripped her.

Maybe she wouldn't have to go that far. She knew that while the mage guild worked with the empress, everything Aranu Crown did was considered for its consequences, and mages talked as much as anyone else. The empress was angry with the guild for not tending its own problems, like that horrid Maita Boniree, busy killing people while she experimented with forbidden blood magic in an effort to bring a lover back to life.

So the empress couldn't go to the mages to ask for a scry contact without the guild worrying and gossiping about why, but Thianra the musician could, and no one would care.

She went to the heralds and stood in line to be put together with a mage or scribe. As she had expected, no one took an interest in a minor musician; once again she rejoiced at the freedom that imperial custom gave her. Imperial monarchs could keep their families private, until they wished to present them to the world. Each had handled the custom differently; some had raised their children to expect wealth and privilege, paying lip service to custom, while forcing court to defer to imperial blood.

Few of those offspring numbered among the rulers considered good. Some were infamous.

Aranu had made it plain to her four that should any of them let their true birth slip, she would find them a suitable place in court, and protect them, but they would never inherit. She'd expected them to earn their own livings before she chose an heir.

When at last it was Thianra's turn to scry, she found herself sitting with a young man whose bushy brown hair above a pair of

equally bushy eyebrows gave him a permanent look of surprise —
if you didn't notice the bored droop to his mouth.

"How do you do this?" she asked. "I've never scryed before.
Do you need the location of the person, and full name?"

"No," he said, as if he had repeated it endlessly. "It's not like
writing a letter. Put your hands on the base of my scry stone, look
into the stone and let your mind loose. Think about the person you
wish to reach. I'll do the rest: when you see them in the stone, then
go ahead and talk."

"Do you hear what we say?" Thianra asked.

"Of course," he responded, still bored. "But we never talk
about patrons' scryings."

The scry stone was a polished piece of pink quartz, set in a
ceramic holder. Thianra sat opposite the mage and put her
fingertips on the rim of the ceramic holder, and let her mind
conjure up memories of Hlanan.

There were a lot of memories, many of which made her smile.
But after a time, she glanced up at the mage, who frowned, those
bristling brows of his knit together in a line over his nose.

"What's wrong?" Thianra asked.

"I'm not finding your person," the mage said reluctantly.
"They could be blocking us." He shook himself, resettled his bony
body on his chair, and said, "Concentrate on one memory."

Thianra brought up the painful memory of that last breakfast,
but that was no more successful.

He said, "I'm sorry. You could go to one of the masters, but I
don't think you'll get anything better. Your person has us blocked,
or has been warded."

Thianra had to pay anyway, and retreated in defeat to her
room, where she stood in the center with her arms folded tightly
across her front as she stared down at the new tiranthe that she
had saved for, that she'd had made for this trip to hear the
legendary Kitharee, who did not make public performances. You
had to go to them — and few were permitted.

She finally sighed, knowing by her own intense reluctance that the decision had been made. She just had to make the first step, which was always the hardest.

By the next morning, she had everything organized. She told her fellow musicians that she was not going to the Kitharee after all, because she had another project: she was visiting the Hrethan in the north, to seek out the origins of some very old folk melodies.

She sent a note to Ilyan Rajanas, and then left another note, in code, for the empress.

By dawn she was on the road —

She was coming to find *me*.

Five

FOR HLANAN AND THE Djurans still crowded into that barred cart, things worsened when Darus fought back.

Instead of the customary sour-faced woman, who was at least silent, the meanest of the guards one morning brought the food. Arrogant and slipshod, he unlocked the door with one hand and began to sling the pail in—and Darus struck.

He was so fast that everyone, prisoners and guards alike stared in shock. One moment Darus sat there so still, head bent, greasy hair hanging in strings to hide his face, then he had his hands around the throat of the guard as they fell out of the cage.

The shock lasted barely a heartbeat. Before the four Djuran prisoners could crowd out to the attack, the guards reacted, whips swinging, swords ripping out. It took half of them to pin Darus down, mostly by landing on top of him, the other half menacing the prisoners to keep them back.

Darus's target heaved himself free, then stood there whooping for breath, staring down at Darus spread-eagled on the ground as he wiped his bloody nose on his cuff.

"Kill him?" a guard asked—with difficulty, as Darus heaved in his effort to get free.

"And lose the bounty for a Djuran risto?" He snarled, "Break his arms."

They held him down, and the big guard, still wiping his bloody nose, stomped Darus's outstretched one forearm, the other upper arm, grinning at the satisfying cracks.

Then they threw Darus back into the cart and the door slammed so hard it made the cart rock. The lock rattled into place. The driver climbed on in front, and the party began to move.

The Djurans bent over their lord, muttering until the whips cracked between the bars, landing on heads and shoulders with full force. By signs and gestures, the Djurans did their best for Darus—the big man ripped his own clothes to make bandage strips, and the other gently bound Darus's broken arms against him.

The cart's iron bars offered a panoramic view of the Shinjan countryside, in the distance a ridge of mountains jutting unevenly against the horizon, dominated by a great peak. Hlanan, pressed into a corner, peered through the constant pall of dust in the air, raised by the horses' hooves. The state of the road seemed to be either dust or mud, after the occasional storms that rumbled through. The water in the deep ruts shimmered and steamed afterward, evaporating rapidly.

The road was deplorable. It had obviously once been paved, for square stones still lined the edges in a broken pattern, reminding Hlanan unpleasantly of missing teeth. He suspected that stones had been looted by local farmers to repair their houses, judging by the sagging roofs and piebald walls he glimpsed now and then, bolstered by stonework that matched the road paving.

The cart was constantly surrounded by alert guards. The atmosphere remained tense, full of angry looks, curses, and sword tips jabbing through the bars if any of the prisoners so much as looked at the guards. As night fell, the only sound in the cart was Darus's hissing breaths of pain.

Hlanan could look away, but he could not stop his ears.

What now? He knew the spells to bind broken bones. Should he risk giving away his skills by helping an enemy? Supposing he did. These angry Shinjans might well break Darus's arms again, and Hlanan's as well. If the Djurans didn't attack him for his temerity.

He could not transfer away. That ward had been spoken over him on the ship in what seemed standard procedure, but no one had blocked his healer magic. No one paid him the least head. Bowing his chin almost to his chest, he let his hand drift to his shoulder, and he whispered under his breath, a mere illusion, the least of magics, in order to blur the tattoo.

He felt a soft touch like a moth alighting on his shoulder: he knew the spell had worked. So his magic had not been warded, only the transfer spell.

Yet what could he do without his mage book? He had forgotten most of the complicated mage spells he'd been working with in years past. No one memorized those. All he remembered were his basic healers' spells.

He leaned against the bars, tired, hungry, aching, and struggled with the truth: that once again he was an oath-breaker. He could call it prudence, and it was, but he didn't really want to heal Darus, whom he blamed for his current plight.

And so he had to listen to that shivery, hissing breathing, all night long.

———◆◆◆———

When dawn broke at last, the guards hooked up the cart again and they began to move. There was no food or water that morning.

By the time the sun beat down directly overhead, the huge mountain loomed, blocking half the sky. The capital had been built on its slope, towers and rooftops barely visible behind a pall of dust.

As they neared, they rolled into the shade of the mountain, and Hlanan actually felt a sense of relief. By mid-afternoon they lumbered into the courtyard of a fortress bristling with roving sentries. Time to brace himself. He expected the tattooing to come next, as it had when he'd been enslaved as a boy.

He thought about warning the Djurans, then decided against it. From all appearances Darus had passed out. What good would knowing do for them, anyway? It would cause questions that might be dangerous to answer. The Shinjans must not find out that he had escaped them once before, and there was no reason for the Djurans not to tell their captors, if Hlanan shared his knowledge.

Their claim of absolute power and their control of slaves by terror depends upon their threats appearing to be true. If any slave escapes and lives, it gives hope to the others, and hope is a very powerful weapon, the empress had told Hlanan during a lesson on Shinja, after his escape.

Hlanan was almost grateful when the cart's iron door at last swung open and the prisoners were summarily hauled out. Darus swayed with obvious pain, his arms wrapped against his torso with strips torn from his men's shirts. Surreptitiously, Hlanan tested the transfer spell once more—and the warning singe of hot metal caused him to abandon the spell.

Darus's men closed protectively around him. The big man held his lord upright as they were marched inside. Down a side passage Hlanan caught sight of a cluster of abject youths, some with bleeding arms resultant from fresh tattoos, their heads badly shaved, vulnerable scalps nicked and bleeding. *You are no longer a person*, such treatment was meant to convince you. *You are mere galk, property.* Weeping, bewildered, disconsolate, they were herded in another direction.

But he and the Djurans passed by and were forced down the stairs into a tunnel.

It was then that Hlanan thought, *We are not going to be tattooed – death is nigh.*

He had thought he was prepared, but the watery sensation in his knees, his damp palms, the frantic beat of his heart made it plain that he wasn't resigned at all. He forced himself to breathe, to listen, to think.

He did not know if the illusion hiding the tattoo would keep a searcher from discovering it. Illusions were so flimsy. At least the ward blocking the tracer magic on the tattoo had been thorough. He would not be discovered that way.

Their guards halted, grounding their spears. As the Djurans looked on uncomprehending, Hlanan heard the patrol leader address someone on the other side of the stone archway, "The one with the long black hair is a Djuran..." A slang term that Hlanan didn't understand.

That's Darus. The important thing was, it seemed there would be no search for tattoos — but then no one expected to find one on a Djuran noble and his honor guard.

The Shinjan guards pushed from behind, obviously impatient to get this duty over with. Hlanan understood why as he and the others stumbled down a dank stone passage, the stuffy air smelling like sour clothing, rotting food, sweat, the exhalations of too many people, and the stomach-churning tang of worse stenches.

Guards stood weapons-ready as a massive iron gate was unlocked, then swung open to reveal a broad space. As near as he could make out in the thick gloom, walls, ceiling, floor were made of unrelieved stone. No furnishings whatsoever. Murky pre-dawn light filtered in through thin slit windows on one side, high up under the ceiling. People, mostly men, sat, lay, or shuffled like grimy ghosts around this space.

A burly Shinjan with red chevron flashes on his jacket sleeves took a step inside. Five guards, also dressed in black but without the chevron flashes filed in behind him, knotted whips gripped in gauntleted fists. They raised their whips, and the entire gathering quieted instantly.

Hlanan found himself shoved violently inward. He stumbled and fell, one knee smashing onto a broken stone. White lightning seared his sight and he struggled to breathe. He keeled over onto slimy stone as somewhere overheard a harsh Shinjan voice roared, "You know the rule: a hundred lashes apiece for every one of you galk if any of these die. They're marked by Command, same as you."

The iron doors screeched and clanged, the locks clattered, footsteps marched away.

A low, rumbling roar of voices and a rushing, hissing sound of feet on stones brought Hlanan's head up in time for him to be knocked down again, straight onto the already throbbing knee. Blinded, he fell, lungs laboring past the spasm of agony. A foot planted on his back as hard fingers scrabbled at his arms. No, the loose sleeves of his brown scribe robe.

Then the fingers jerked away, and someone behind him grunted in pain. A man landed next to Hlanan, as someone else wrenched at the scribe robe and yanked it free, pulling Hlanan's arms back excruciatingly first.

Someone else started tugging at his linen shirt, grimy as it was, but a roar from the guard outside the iron gate halted the thief: "Mark!"

"Leave him. For now," a man muttered in Shinjan.

Hlanan levered himself to his elbows, his head spinning. Noise to his right brought his attention around. As the stone room jerked and spun, jerked and spun, Hlanan became aware of a huge mass of squirming, kicking, fighting figures. He fought against the dizziness of pain, but could make little out.

The attackers seemed to agree on a truce, or a hiatus, by some signal that Hlanan could not perceive. In ones and twos they picked themselves up and moved away, leaving the Djurans there before the gate.

Darus stood swaying, his feverish face half-lit in the faint, wavering reflected torchlight, arms bound to his sides over his filthy robes. His men had protected him, and now that the attackers had backed off, they sat on the ground in a tight square with Darus as its center.

Hlanan picked himself up, his entire body throbbing around the red-hot pain in his knee. The instinct to get stone at his back overwhelmed him, and he moved crab-wise, as one knee did not seem to want to function, and the left side of his head ached where it had banged against the stone.

He got his back to a bit of wall directly underneath one of the windows, which afforded a trickle of dust-laden air that smelled better than the rest of the space. By now, the illusion over his tattoo had surely faded. It took all his strength to murmur a new spell, flimsy as the magic was.

Then he shut his eyes, and drifted into a nightmarish half-sleep, from which he was woken abruptly from a half-dozing state by a sudden dousing of filthy water in a cascade from the barred window overhead.

It seemed that rain had begun outside. Apparently the ground was flush with the window sills. He recoiled—to the sound of harsh laughter nearby—and moved onto the noisome stones a ways away.

He inadvertently bumped into someone on his blind side, earning a kick that sent him reeling away. Then he sat, gritting his teeth against his chilly, sodden clothes, as he watched several people wearing little or nothing walk up to the windows and stand in the water. When it had sluiced over them, they moved away, to be replaced by others.

That water was still a light brown, but he was desperate with thirst, and so grimy his skin crawled. Why not? He didn't care what happened to him now—he had to drink.

He tried to get up, but his bad knee sent pangs of lightning through him, and he fell back. As he gathered his courage to try again, he watched the others emerging from the gloom outside the shafting light. Those coming to douse themselves were being passed through by a huge, burly man, with two women shoving and yelling, acting as his enforcers.

Scummy water pooled around Hlanan, rilling outward across the stones. He bent down and sucked up the water, which tasted so vile he nearly choked. But thirst was an unrelenting master.

No sooner had he thought that than he noticed the cascade thinning to a trickle. The last people under the windows caught mere drips, then the mass moved farther into the room. Slanting rays of morning sunlight reappeared, the greasily gleaming stones gently steaming where the light struck. The smell of dankness intensified as the sun crawled westward. Hlanan remained where he was, too tense and too overwhelmed by pain to move, and once again fell into a stuporous state, half-asleep.

The light slowly slanted across the floor, turning golden and then ochre, the rays lengthening and then slowly fading. Before darkness closed in, the rumble of iron-reinforced boot heels caused a stilling in the dull roar of voices that Hlanan had not noticed until they fell silent.

The gate clanked, armed guards rolled in a wheelbarrow, and dumped onto the grimy stones a load of... food. "Feed, galk!"

Hlanan tried to get up. His knee, swollen to twice its size, refused to let him stand, but the blinding thirst and his gnawing stomach insisted he move. So he half-crawled to the pile as a small number of others closed in, grabbing with grimy hands at the torn, stale ends of bread, half-eaten apples, grilled fish (mostly spines) and other obvious scrapings, then backed away. Hlanan picked up a bread heel, a plum with one huge bite taken out of it, and a bit of cheese grind, and when he was brutally shoved aside, retreated the same way he'd come, his items clapped under his arm.

Clang! The door shut.

Smash! Lights splintered across Hlanan's vision as someone knocked him flat. His arms flailed—he hit the stones—and when he sat up, his items of food were gone. A narrow, female foot pressed against the back of his head, and nails scored up his back and then over his arms as his shirt was ripped off his body, leaving him there in his trousers. Even his shoes and socks were gone.

At least in the turgid darkness, covered with slime from the filthy stones, no one noticed the illusion over his shoulder tattoo.

He swallowed in his dry throat, trying to work up some spit for a semblance of relief, and watched as darkness closed in. Presently he heard the snores, snorts and snuffles of slumber, and lay back, breathing out slowly. When the aches diminished to a steady dullness, he slipped into cold, shivering sleep.

Six

IT WON'T SURPRISE ANYONE to learn that Hrethans, being dual natured (human and bird) are smaller and lighter than most humans. They prefer living in mountains—the higher the better—and they aren't much for collecting belongings.

Icecrest, the beautiful imperial palace where the Emperor of Sveran Djur lurks—squats—prowls (I'm not even trying to be fair here) is deemed gorgeous by most. Even I, who loathed my stay there almost as much as I loathed its master, had to admit that the place, with all its windows of colored glass, vaulting towers, and graceful carvings, was beautiful. But that's because I did not grow up among the Hrethan.

That palace to a Hrethan would be merely a huge, complicated prison in which it'd be easy to get lost. As for the imperial palace at Erev-li-Erval, its denizens fail to understand why the Hrethan ambassadors decline to stay there, though granted a fine suite with plenty of servants, beautiful furniture, and access to the court, adorned by the Kherval's highest ranks.

The Hrethan don't tell the empress or her people what they really think of those stuffy, confining, confusing boxy buildings.

And so, when Thianra finally gained the mountain heights, after being passed from person to person, then housed in small, minimally furnished way stations, she was astonished to reach what she had been told was the central Hrethan council, the closest they have to a government, to find a couple more small way stations, nothing more than round cottages, with huge open windows, built into the trunks of ancient trees that had died centuries before.

Then she looked up the slope toward the crest of the mountain, where snows never melted in the shadows even at the height of summer, and discovered what looked like large beehives among the trees: she was in the Hrethan version of a city. They had no palaces.

While she was being transferred upward from location to location, she was followed by a bird named Tir.

———◈———

While Thianra jolted unpleasantly from place to place via transfer magic, and recovered between transfers, I sat with my parents in our small house with windows wide enough to let the wind flow through, practicing my music.

My mother was skilled on the harp and the tiranthe, the latter having six steel strings. The harp strings are each tuned to a note, but on the tiranthe, you change chords with your fingers. I love the music of both instruments, and we had begun playing together as my fingering got better.

My father, as I said, was not in human form. He perched on the window sill, a white aidlar with darker feathers edging wings and tail, almost lost against the snowy slope beyond as he listened. He remained near me, his benevolent eye turned my way, though I could not communicate with him, which hurt terribly.

But then *everything* hurt, though my parents strove to create a scene of peace and harmony within my self-chosen exile within the Hrethan world.

My mother conveyed his comments from time to time, as he, too, loved harp music. That was what had first brought them together, their mutual love of music.

The little house, which was basically a roof against storms, sat high on a cliff below soughing firs, the wide windows overlooking undulating quilt-squares of land hazed into a soft blur by distance. I loved that view, so peaceful. Sometimes I flew it in imagination, though that too often triggered memories that hurt, and then the inevitable what-ifs that hurt even more.

Mother kept her blue hair wrapped around her to prevent it from tangling in her fingers. She ran her hands along the harp in glissandos, which was how she warmed up. I'd fwooshed my hair out, and it snapped around me as I determinedly forced myself to concentrate on identifying the chords she played before I mirrored them on the tiranthe.

"You are grieving, my darling," my mother said suddenly.

I turned away guiltily. "No, I'm not," I lied. "It's just that my fingers still aren't nimble enough to shift chords that fast."

"It will come. You have been diligent these past months, and have done very well. It took me years."

My father's head jerked minutely from side to side, his ruby red eyes steady and observant.

"Darling Elenderi, your father says, your gaze strays often westward. Do you wish to return to the lowlands?"

I flexed my hands. My exasperation with my slow progress in mastery of the tiranthe hadn't been a total lie. And the grief my mother sensed over what I'd lost wasn't wholly true. The pain I hid had Hlanan's silence as cause. I had no experience with those feelings—I had no idea how to define them even to myself.

One thing I was sure of, the empress hadn't wanted me around the son she'd chosen as heir. She regarded me as a terrible influence—amoral, undisciplined, uneducated, a disaster.

And it was all true.

But... the heart has its own logic, this much I'd learned. Hlanan knew where the Hrethan lived, he knew magic, he traveled around. If he wanted to see me, he could find me easily. The silence made it increasingly clear that duty to his mother had overcome whatever he felt for me.

And there was nothing that my parents could do.

So I stayed silent, looking back at my Hrethan mother and then at my Djuran father perched on the window sill. I loved them so fiercely, but at the same time I felt helpless, aware that we were united by blood and by music, but by so little else. I was the half-

and-half daughter who'd thought she was an orphan until last summer—who raised herself—who fit in nowhere.

I tried to find words, until I noticed my mother's gaze going distant the way I'd learned meant communication on the mental plane, which the Hrethan do as naturally as everyone else speaks.

"Tir comes," my mother said. "Can you listen for the bird you once called friend?" Her long, thin fingers, with their soft blue down, rose to tap her forehead. Her hair—like mine not actual hair but long feathered strands of a deep blue unlike my silver—rose gently to swirl around her head.

"I can't," I said. And though it made no difference—my mind was locked tight behind a shield of fear—my hands came up instinctively to tug at my neck, which of course was bare. No golden, magical *fais* enclosed my throat, to jolt me with lightning-strikes of pain. I jerked my hands down again, aware of my parents' eyes following the convulsive gesture I was learning to do less often, but still couldn't completely control.

Tir was actually Hlanan's bird friend. I had learned that aidlars as a species were in some way connected to Hrethan, and sometimes chose to serve as messengers, but seldom for humans. Hlanan had befriended the then-young aidlar during his days as a slave aboard a galley. He'd shared his scant meals with Tir, who had been caught up in one of the rare, horrible storms that could sweep birds halfway around the world. Tir had extended companionship to me, too, when I demonstrated my ability to hear the thoughts of creatures—but when I left the capital, Tir had stayed behind, close to Hlanan.

The aidlar sailed in through the window to perch beside my father, a long-bodied, mostly white bird with a seed-picker beak and ruby eyes.

"Lhind come!" Tir squawked. "Friend!"

My father cawed, "Go with! We wait!"

Surprised, I transformed to my bird self, the only thing I'd really mastered all winter—I no longer had to jump off a cliff to force instinct to take over and transform me. I flitted after Tir, high up to the tree city where the Hrethan congregated.

Here, most of the elders lived. I followed the guides down through snow-laden branches until they lit on a window sill in what I recognized as the guest house. It was larger than most, with a fire stick in a ceramic stove that radiated warmth.

Hrethan don't feel cold the way humans without feathers do.

Friend? When I saw the guest house, my heart lightened, and I thought, Hlanan! He's come all this way at last?

But when I transformed and walked into the guest chamber, my gaze lit on—"Thianra?"

"Lhind!" She turned away from holding her hands out to the stove, glanced at me, blushed, then turned back. "Um, did you give up wearing clothes?"

In case you haven't seen us, I ought to mention that Hrethan are covered with down. The true Hrethan are completely covered from their noses up over their eyes, and over the backs of their hands and feet, in shimmering blue of various shades. Only their cheeks and chins are bare, as are their palms and the bottoms of their feet. I, being half Hrethan, have a bare face, hands up the underside of my forearms, and feet, the rest of me covered by down. My hair—which not only covers my back but grows down my spine to my tail, which is also long and feathered—swirled around me like a cloak. I'm never bare-skin naked, but then clothes are a symbol. Humans with bare skin wear clothes, and privacy in that way is considered a fundamental part of civilization.

I'd always hated wearing clothes, which were hot and confining, but I understood the rules. Thianra gazed through the window, as she was always respectful of others' dignity. Even though I'd never had any sense of dignity whatsoever, I found a Hrethan wrap lying over the back of a chair, and pulled it around me, smoothing its folds.

"Civilized now," I said.

She turned. "You look wonderful," she commented.

"And you look tired."

"Oh, no. Cold, a little. And a bit anxious. They have been very kind, but they kept me waiting in all these cold, drafty round houses without glass in the windows, then sent me on by magic transfer. I don't know if their ruler thought I might be a danger?" She spread her still-gloved hands, her breath smoking in the air.

"There isn't a ruler, not in the way you mean. The elders speak for themselves, and everyone else listens, but they all have to agree before action. Everything with the Hrethan takes time. Including what they're going to do about me," I said.

Her eyes rounded. Thianra is stocky like her mother, brown-haired, and quiet, but in her way very expressive. Her eyebrows lifted, and she repeated, "What they are going to do about you? Aren't you one of them?"

"Half. Then there's what I've done. Remember Faryana, the Hrethan mage that Geric Lendan enchanted into a diamond necklace?"

"Oh yes," she said, smiling. "When we first met you."

"Well, I didn't know about Hrethan being able to talk on the mental plane. Then," I said. "Faryana heard everything I was thinking while I wore that necklace. She was finally disenchanted a few months ago, and she felt it her duty to repeat all my thievish thoughts. Along with my conversations with Jardis Dhes-Andis."

Thianra winced. "But you were on your own, trying to survive!"

"I know, I know. And they know my story. But at the same time, they don't know what to do with me. They seem to regard me as if I'm a thunderstorm about to break, though why, I don't know. It's not like I can *do* much of anything."

Thianra said slowly. "I know you do magic, as well as scrying without a scry stone—"

"Not any more," I said, and once again my hand snapped up to claw at my throat for the fais that was not there. "I can't. If I even think about it, I have nightmares, even when I'm not asleep…" I stopped. "Wait. Here I am, whining about what I can't do, and you're *here*. Why? Is there… something wrong with Hlanan? Did he send you with a message to me?"

"Yes, no, and have you read his letters?"

"What letters?"

At that she looked around helplessly, a tangle of her brown hair protruding from the hood of her bulky coat. It hit me then that she was very upset. "Lhind, Hlanan is missing," she said, hands clasping tightly. "I was hoping that his letters might furnish even a bit of a clue—"

"Wait here," I exclaimed, threw off the wrap, and jumped out the window, transforming in a flash.

I flew as fast as I could across the tree city to where I knew the messengers from the Hrethan who served as ambassadors to the human world left communications.

When I passed into the perch, I found the Eldest waiting there. Of course. Even though at present I could hear nothing beyond my steel-tight mental shield, the Hrethan were communicating in the mental realm all the time, and had passed Thianra along, talking ahead all the while.

Politeness among Hrethan is to match whatever form the Elders have chosen. The Eldest was in his Hrethan form, so I transformed. The blue of his feathers had silvered to nearly the color of my own feathers, and his hair and tail had gone bone white. I stared at those old eyes, the deep brown of the trunks of the great trees, and knew he was waiting for my mental voice. But the same instinct for self-preservation that had brought out my bird had shut my inner voice.

My hair whipped up around me as I shook my head. "I can't," I whispered.

His voice was a husky whisper. "You can. But you must learn trust."

"I want to," I said. "I do. But... "

He held up his hand, the talons on the ends of his fingers long and sharp. "You must learn trust." His hand opened toward me, then outward.

Trust. So simple a word, so impossible a concept.

The Eldest brought his hand around in a circle, and I understood the other part of his hint about trust: he knew very well that I had been hiding up on the mountain top with my parents, avoiding the other Hrethan, especially since Faryana's return to her proper form. Or I would have found out about the letters after they came.

Hlanan's letters, two of them, sat in a basket. They were little scrolls, sealed with wax. I wanted to open them right there, but they would be easier to carry in my talons the way they were.

I transformed back, picked them up, and flew to the guest house.

There, I put my wrap back on and carried the letters to Thianra.

"Go ahead," she said. "Read them. I'll wait."

I broke the seal on the first.

> *Dear Lhind: Or perhaps you have made your peace with your given name, now that you are at last reunited with the parents who gave it to you. Let me know. I have practiced saying Elenderi, though I suspect I will never lose my fondness for Lhind.*
>
> *Whenever I miss you — which is every day — I try to imagine you flying about on the mountaintops, as happy as a bird. I wonder if that expression originated with the Hrethan? You will have to tell me.*
>
> *I would say I wish you were here, but I know that would be at the cost of your happiness. And your happiness is what matters most.*
>
> *What are you doing, seeing, learning? At present I have commenced magic studies again, but a new branch, the arts of healing. You will laugh at me for beginning yet another apprenticeship — I have to laugh at myself, as I do every time I try to count up how many occasions I've sat on the back bench with the ten-year-olds. I'm enjoying the new studies, as I enjoy them all.*
>
> *Other matters have been suspended. Sometimes I walk at the waterfall and pretend you are there to talk things over with me. Imagining your dubious gaze as we look over my putative future labors braces me: all the power and glory are nothing if they cannot give she who matters most to me what matters most to her, happiness, and above all freedom.*

That is all to say that the future is uncertain, but today, I am thinking of you. I hope that you, in turn, sometimes look westward from the clouds, and think of me.

"I didn't know," I cried out, Thianra's concerned gaze blurring as tears burned my eyelids. "I didn't know."

She shook her head, her gaze going to the second letter. I ripped it open.

Dear Lhind: I am aware that at least two exchanges have gone back and forth between the Hrethan ambassador and the imperial desk, so I must assume that you have your reasons for not wanting to write back.

Or could it be that Hrethan have a different perception of time? That is the problem with silence, one can fill it with suppositions as well as memories. When we parted, it was with kisses and promises, and I still feel the same, so I've been assuming you do as well. Has that changed? You were always so forthright. I've depended upon that, but people do alter, and move on.

If this is your will, let me fill the rest of this letter not with an account of my days, but with my favorite memories of you. If you have decided it is time to part, I will abide by your wishes, with gratitude for the time we had, and my ...

"I can't read any more," I wailed. "I have to find him! This is terrible! I thought he didn't come because he didn't want to, because it was duty. I thought he understood that I'm only safe high up where Dhes-Andis can't get me, or —" I stopped before I could say *the empress*. Who had surrendered me to Dhes-Andis the previous summer for perfectly understandable political reasons.

Another reason why I loathed politics.

Thianra looked around, then said softly, "The Hrethan didn't tell you about these letters?"

"They probably did. On the mental plane. But I can't lift my... my mind shield. It's hard to explain. It's the nightmares. About last summer. And my mother knows I can't bear to talk about any of it, so I expect she thought mentioning the letters would only hurt me, the way talking about what happened to me in Sveran Djur does."

Thianra held out her hands. "You never told me exactly what happened to you, and Hlanan refused to say anything unless you did."

"Oh, there's little to say." I got up and paced restlessly, my tail and hair swishing violently around me. "Jardis Dhes-Andis put a fais on me—it's like a necklace, but with all these magical spells laid in. Djurans wear them all their lives. The nobles have extra spells, including torture."

"*Torture?*"

"Oh, they *call* it 'correction,' and parents can do it to their children, and they claim it's merely a sting, but it was no sting to me when Dhes-Andis blasted me. It was like being struck by lightning. It's just as effective as nasty implements in dank dungeons, even if it doesn't leave visible scars. Maybe worse, because he can get at you any time, anywhere."

My hands scrabbled at my neck, and Thianra shivered.

I wrenched my hands down. "Ever since I left I've been having nightmares of him scrying for me, and I even get flashes of pain, in memory, like he's got a fais around my neck again. It's like I got away here." I smacked my ribs. "But I'm still his prisoner here." I smacked my head.

"But you're free," Thianra protested. "His evil cannot reach you. So many would defend you, beginning with your own family, I am certain of it!"

"But it's not enough. Because..." I sighed, and forced out the truth. "I'm afraid of *myself*. I came so close to doing what he wanted. You have to realize that my fais had full powers. I could have hurt anyone—except *him*, of course. He wanted me to use it, and I almost did, especially when that horrible Darus—"

"Darus?" She breathed the name.

"What?" I stopped, staring at her in horror. "How do *you* know him?"

"I don't know him. But I'm very much afraid I know a little *of* him," she said. "He seems to be the one who took Hlanan."

"What?" I yelped. "Noooooo!"

She told me what the empress had learned. As she talked, I walked faster and faster, and when she finished, I said, "I've got to do something!" I smacked my fist into my palm. "That horrible Darus! This is all my fault."

"What? No, it isn't," Thianra said, in as exasperated a voice as ever I'd heard from so gentle a person.

"Not in the sense that I caused it intentionally," I said. "One thing for sure, Am-Jalad Darus hated and despised me at least as much as I hated him and his rotten emperor. I'll wager anything that if he kidnapped Hlanan, he's on his way home, where Jardis the Evil Fiend in Man Form will soon be sending a threatening letter saying they'll kill him if the empress doesn't do what he says."

"But they don't know his relationship to the empress," Thianra said. "Unless they were told."

"Not by me! I never said anything about Charas al Kherval," I stated firmly. "Even if I'd wanted to tell Dhes-Andis who Hlanan really was, which I did not, the last thing I wanted was to find myself squeezed between two imperials. All right, then, so if Am-Jalad Darus didn't take Hlanan to threaten the empress, then he has to have done it to demand she hand over me. For some weird Djuran reason, since you'd think he would be howling with gratitude that I was long gone. I better tell Mother I'm leaving."

Thianra blinked at me. "What do you propose to do?"

"Go rescue Hlanan," I said promptly.

"You don't think he can take care of himself?"

"Not against *them*," I said. "He's too gentle, and he forgets to eat half the time, forgets practical things if he finds some old book to track down, or some new spell to learn."

Thianra gave me a crooked smile. "That's very like him, and yet he's gotten along in the world so far."

"But not as a Djuran prisoner," I said grimly. "Besides, he came for me once, and I hope he knows I'd come for him as soon as I could. Maybe I'm not very good at doing relationships yet, but that much I'm sure about!"

She looked perplexed, and so I plowed on before she could draw breath. "But first, I'm going to visit Rajanas, because even though he's almost as much of a poisonous viper as Jardis Dhes-Andis, he does know plenty about self-defense, and if I'm going up against those Djurans, I'm going to need me some lessons."

Thianra said firmly, "Then I am going with you."

Seven

BACK TO HLANAN, LIVING in a world of stinks.

Stenches are one of the few things I'm an expert on. In fact, they were my first and best defense. The reek of very ripe cheese — some stunningly repugnant fish oil, well summered — a visit to a stable floor — all these added to my outer garment armored me nearly as effectively as chain mail and breastplates do for big brawny warriors.

Stinks, in short, can be used as a weapon, and so the Shinjans knew. The sour reek of decay well mixed with the nose-rotting odor of old food the weakened prisoners' bodies got rid of so fast they couldn't do the Waste Spell in time — or they were too weak and delirious to care — mixed with the slime on the stone floor to create a stink with the power of a hundred armies, silent but deadly.

The Barrow's first attack was the environment. Only the hardiest could survive it. Water was runoff that spilled into a trough below the grating channel and drained away somewhere. The spillover through the grating, caused by rain, was what the hardier used to get somewhat clean.

The next morning, Hlanan saw the trough lit by morning light filtering through the grating. He crawled to it and dipped his hands to drink. The water tasted stale, gritty, oily, and his stomach cramped unmercifully from the water he'd drunk off the stones the night before. And again. And again. He whispered the Waste Spell over and over.

He understood then that only the strongest survived. He knew he wasn't strong—he never had been. He'd been fine with that, because he prized wit over brute strength. But here, he was going to need both: strength to survive, and wit to figure out how to survive. Beginning with a way to purify the water and his food.

And then he was going to have to face the truth of his healer's oath, avoided so far in order to hide his skills from the guards.

He did not have that excuse now.

Food was the Shinjans' second weapon, after the environment. The guards arrived in force, dumped a wheelbarrow of scrapings and garbage onto the stones, and then left, not caring if or how it was shared out.

It seemed that the prisoners had become galk indeed. The treatment appeared to be a deliberate policy, intended to get the prisoners to degrade themselves all on their own. The guards didn't have to lift a finger.

Hlanan had difficulty seeing out of one still-healing eye. He took care to be aware of his surroundings as he moved to the water trough, but before he drank, he first whispered the water purification spell over his hands, and then over the water he scooped up. Over and over.

Almost immediately his innards began to settle down. And the next time food was dumped in, he wedged himself among the others and grabbed a handful of squishy something, and that, too, he whispered the purification spell over, revealing old porridge, with bits of fried fish in it.

Eating those few scraps made him feel a tiny bit better. Also, the swelling in his knee began to abate a little.

He recovered enough to watch the guards for any chance of escape. He could not transfer out, but he did know illusion magic. No one could actually make themselves invisible, but illusion could trick the eye away, especially in so dim an atmosphere.

But in order for the eye to be tricked, those eyes had to be looking elsewhere. The guards stood nearly shoulder to shoulder when they opened the iron gates. Even if they wouldn't notice a blur passing within hand's distance, he wasn't certain they would not feel him trying to slip by.

And there were still his vows.

He wrestled with himself every bit as hard as the prisoners did with one another, and with the next morning, when he found himself able to move without becoming dangerously light-headed, he knew he had to act in accordance with those vows.

Though he was not yet even journeyman level at healing magic — that was when they would begin studying the more subtle illnesses of body and mind — he had learned a great deal about wounds, which were anything but subtle.

That morning, he made another swipe at the food, which he could see was crawling with maggots. He snagged a half-eaten but not completely rotten plum, and a hunk of dried cheese, mostly rind. He whispered the purification spell over it. The food shrank as the rot vanished. He ate the little that was left, then repeated the laborious process at the water trough.

He had his wits back, and enough strength to move. It was time to heed his oath.

He gazed past the struggling figures at the food dump. Darus lay still and quiet against the far wall, two of his men on guard and two fighting to get food to share out.

Slowly, expecting — even hoping — to be turned back at any moment, Hlanan ventured toward Darus. A vicious triumph flared deep in the pit of Hlanan's gut at seeing his enemy brought lower than he was, so intense that he was appalled at his reaction. This bleak, triumphant hatred at another's suffering was one very small step from the barbarity going on a few paces away, the grunting, squealing, smacking, writhing scramble for sustenance.

That was mere survival — becoming the galk the Shinjans called them. The life worth living meant keeping to one's promises.

The Djuran lord lay in silence, his breath shuddering. Those broken arms had to be infected, and therefore agonizing, judging by his struggle for breath.

The Djuran guards moved to keep Hlanan away. He cleared his throat. Though he felt somewhat better, his head still ached, and when he tried to remember the Djuran he'd reviewed so diligently in the hold of the yacht, his old Shinjan vocabulary crowded in instead.

So he pointed to his own arm, then to Darus's, and said, "Make good."

He whispered an illusion, of a snapped twig that straightened. One man started, the other warily moved back a pace, but watched with angry intensity as Hlanan bent over Darus, whose light breathing did not change.

No one was around, prisoner or guard. Darus appeared to be unconscious.

I will not be false to my oaths, Hlanan thought, and the hatred he could not suppress drove him to act.

He ran his hand lightly up Darus's nearer arm. Despite it being bound by a filthy strip of shirt, it was easy to find the swollen flesh over the break. It was hot, indicating infection.

Using the lightest of touches, he tested the swelling and whispered the infection-removal spell. The heat began to lessen, and Hlanan knew the swelling would rapidly diminish. Feeling carefully with his fingertips as Darus woke and stiffened in agonized silence, Hlanan found the break, a terrible long fracture leading off it. Binding bone was one of the first spells the healers learned, after mastering the spells to purify infection.

He moved slowly, carefully, fitting the bones back together as he whispered the bone-binding spell over and over. He moved incrementally along the fracture, until his head swam with dizziness. He paused to breathe, and then, though he was fast losing strength, reached for Darus's other arm. This one had a clean break. It was simpler to realign and bind, but it took the last of his strength.

Hlanan rose, bent low, and returned to his usual spot. There, he sank down, weak and drowsy. But as he drifted into slumber, he felt better about himself than he had in weeks.

The next morning, the last guard bawled, "The imperial prince is giving the city an entertainment! You two!" He pointed at a pair of prisoners. "Out, galk. The rest of you stay back, unless you want to feel my whip."

Hlanan watched narrowly. The guards still stood in a cluster — there was no possibility of slipping between them.

The last guard pointed at the brute who had attacked Hlanan. The big man shuffled out. The guards crashed the gate closed and locked it, the other guards shoved the big man into the corridor with their spears, and the group clattered away.

When it was quiet again, the rhythmic thumps and hisses of movement caused Hlanan to peer into the gloom on the other side of the prison chamber. He barely made out figures moving in unison. It was the Djurans, doing some kind of military drill. There in the midst of them worked Darus, in spite of just-healed arms. The bone-binding spell just bound bone until it could heal on its own. The spells did nothing for pain. Therefore the pain had to be significant. But there he was, exercising anyway.

Hlanan settled back with a weary sigh, intending to sleep away the dreary day, when a hard hand smacked his shoulder.

He recoiled, glaring up — at one of four Djuran guards.

"You. Come," the Djuran said — and hauled Hlanan to his feet.

He was not going to struggle. What would be the use? Even at his best health he could never have won a fight against any of the ordinary Djuran sailors, much less Darus's elite guards.

So he perforce must come, his heart hammering his ribs.

In silence the Djuran led Hlanan across the noisome chamber to the corner where the Djurans had taken up residence. There, they waited in a formation, Darus at the front, and the guard halted Hlanan quite firmly behind a pair, and took up station at his right as the fourth stood at his left.

Darus said something in a low murmur, and the guard turned to Hlanan. "Learn. Strong you be."

Hlanan's laugh escaped in a kind of wheeze — and then the Djurans began to move slowly. The guards at either side slapped at Hlanan's arm, his shoulder, his side, his legs, again and again, until he mimicked the movement correctly.

Hlanan had spent enough time with Ilyan Rajanas to recognize what he called a warming drill, the slow preparation of muscles for harder work, integrated with breathing. Ilyan had always been bigger and stronger as well as older, physical skills coming to him naturally in a way that Hlanan could see but never imitate. So he'd ceased trying, in favor of honing his wits and awareness.

This warming drill, he could tell, was going to render him breathless and trembling before he ever got to the strength training.

And so it was.

He was soon stupid with fatigue and dripping with sweat, legs trembling, hands barely lifting. The guard merely continued to slap him through it, hard enough to sting, but not enough to knock him down, until he crowed for breath.

At last the man let him drop down. "Not good. Weak you."

"I could have told you that," Hlanan whispered in his home language.

Darus never turned, just kept working, leading his men, until they were done. Hlanan, highly uncomfortable, pushed himself to his bare feet and made it back across to his usual post, where he gratefully dropped into sleep, as his sweat dried cold on him.

And the next day, after the doors clanged shut, there was the Djuran again. Hlanan glared at him, aching in every muscle. Was this some humiliation? Yes—in a sense. He could see their unhidden scorn for his weakness, but they could have gathered around and thrashed him senseless. He knew no one would have interfered.

But they didn't. So there was another purpose here. Though Darus never looked his way, Hlanan sensed that this was, at least in the Djuran lord's mind, some kind of acknowledgment of the healing.

Hlanan could have told him not to bother, but the Am-Jalad never looked his way.

At any rate, there did not seem to be any way to avoid it, so he forced his unwilling body to follow, and once again, the deceptively slow beginning, their boots clacking and thumping, and his bare feet smacking the dirty, slimy stones, until the racking, gasping point at which he had to sink down and watch the Djurans grunt their way to the end.

And so it went for a stretch of days.

Especially at the beginning, Hlanan wanted to refuse, but he forced himself to his feet. Every day, he eyed the door in hopes of a single inattentive moment, a wider gap between two guards, and finding none, tried to get enough of the scant food, after which the Djuran guard always came for him. He forced himself to fumble clumsily through the repetitive movements made by the Djurans, who ignored him—except if he stopped.

Then, sweaty, shaky, spent, he retreated, sank down, grimacing against the sharp protest of his muscles, and put his head on his knees as he breathed slowly.

Sometimes he was aware of whispered conversation among the Shinjans, but no one approached him.

Eight

FOR THIANRA, THE TEDIOUS reversal of her trip to the mountains: short transfer, recovery, transfer, recovery.

Because I really hate how transfers make you feel you're being turned inside out and then trampled under the hooves of a thundering herd of horses, I flew down as far as I could, to the house on a lower slope that serves as the place where lowland people communicate with the Hrethan above.

When I felt the heavier air tug at my body, I glided the rest of the way to the village, where I transformed to my human self and put on my wrap. There I met Thianra, who'd rested between transfers.

I squinched my eyes and braced my body for a last magic transfer to Imbradi, capital of Prince Ilyan Rajanas's Alezand.

It was interesting to be there again, after all that had happened to me since my last visit. For one thing, I could see many similarities to Djuran fashion in the furnishings and some of the ways space was organized. Rajanas's black hair and light eyes made me wonder for the first time how much of Sveran Djur might be in his background.

Not that I'd ask. He'd only laugh at me, or say something sarcastic, as usual.

Rajanas, I could take or leave, but it was great to see Ovlan again. And though, in losing my ability to communicate in the mental realm I had also lost being able to understand any language as soon as I heard it, I did remember most of the hand-signing language I'd learned, enough to greet her.

However, this I will say for Rajanas. He doesn't fool around with a lot of protocol and ritual if he doesn't have to. As soon as he saw me, he said right off, "Where's Hlanan?"

"That's why we're here. I plan to go find out," I answered, delighted to get things going at once. "But first I think I need to learn some self-defense. In Sveran Djur they fight with these sword things with magic on them."

His slanted brows lifted and he pursed his lips in a silent whistle. But he didn't say anything about Djuran sword-sticks. Using his hands as he spoke, for Ovlan's benefit (or maybe it was just habit by now, especially as she had become fairly adept at lip reading), he said, "From what I recollect, you were not bad in a fight."

"Sure, at deflecting bullies long enough so I could get away. But I don't know anything about actual sword-fighting. Especially those sword-sticks. Even a tap looked like it hurt. They didn't even have to stab each other."

Rajanas crossed his arms, as outside the arched windows of his fine parlor, rain began bucketing down. "First of all, I've never trained in the Djuran arts, though I've heard about them. Second, if you wish to learn the rapier, I take it you're willing to stay here two, three, maybe five years? Train every day?"

"No," I said, my disappointment sharp. "I need to get going if I'm going to rescue Hlanan."

"I sympathize, young thief." His hands swooped and dived in sign language, as Ovlan watched us all with narrowed eyes. "But I could put a rapier in your hands, and all it would do is endanger you. There's little worse than a bit of training."

"You said a heartbeat ago that I'm good," I wailed.

Rajanas turned to Ovlan, the diamond in one ear winking. She signed something—because I my inner shield remained closed I hadn't a clue to what it was. Maybe private shorthand.

Rajanas responded with a slight nod, and turned to me. "You're very adept at acrobatics, and your aim with bottles, pots, and anything to hand is right on target. Ovlan suggests you report at dawn to the Gray Wolves' private court, and drill with them. After that, we'll talk."

Thianra was nodding slowly. "I'll come, too."

Until I was Jardis Dhes-Andis's prisoner, I'd been able to get out of any trouble I'd been in, preferably by wit, but when necessary, I'd used anything to hand to get away from would-be attackers.

Most bullies rely on strength, and on their ability to frighten the weaker. Or they depend on numbers. But when I watched Dhes-Andis duel with Darus that time, I knew that I would never last a heartbeat against either of them.

That night Thianra and I were invited to stay as guests, and to attend the theater down in the main street, where the locals put on a play full of disguises and laughter, mock battles, rollicking songs (joined in on with lusty if tuneless bellowing by the enthusiastic audience) and dancing. If Hlanan's being missing had not weighed on my soul I would have loved it. But though I laughed and clapped, I longed for the night to be over so I could get at that training.

After an equally restless night, dawn had scarcely begun to lift the gloom when I ran down to the kitchens. I ate a hasty breakfast and was the first to the courtyard, keeping well back so I could observe the situation, seeing as how at one time I'd been a target of the Gray Wolves.

They had been the traditional defenders of Thann, a hilly duchy from the other side of the continent. But the duchess before the present one had been ambitious, and used the Gray Wolves as her personal assassination team to get rid of anyone in her way.

That had included, for a time, Hlanan and me.

Later, after the duchess fell, I'd seen first-hand how dispirited the Gray Wolves had become under the command of the erstwhile duke, Prince Geric Lendan. Their pride in always obeying orders had been their own worst enemy, when those orders were evil. Also, not all of them had been averse to outright murder, which had caused internal strife among them.

As I lurked in the shadows, watching them gather in those

cowled gray woolen tunics, I saw that some of the older ones were no longer part of the company. They'd been replaced by younger recruits, who lined up eagerly.

Ovlan took up a position at the front, and signaled the warm-ups. I joined at the back. From the enthusiasm I saw all around me, it seemed that the Gray Wolves had purpose again, and pride.

At first I kept up fine—I've always been very active—but then it came time to take wooden sword in hand and do some of what Thianra whispered to me were basic blocks and lunges.

And here I began to see that my plan was going to splat.

First of all, the wooden sword was unwieldy for someone as short and light as I am. I was slow, and clumsy, and my palm began to sting in a way that I knew was going to mean blisters. And we hadn't even gotten to the fighting yet.

My spirits sank as Ovlan motioned people into pairs. She set Thianra with a girl of about sixteen, and motioned me toward another youngster who was two hands taller than I.

The first exercise was to lunge low, block, feint-then-lunge high, block. I put my entire body into my swings, and could see my partner barely making an effort. And when I blocked her lunge, my hand stung so much I dropped my sword.

My partner rolled her eyes, but waited for me to pick it up again, and we finished the pattern—and I dropped the sword again.

"I give up," I said miserably.

"Hold, thief." That was Rajanas, watching from a window above. He hand-signed to Ovlan—*try... [something]*—and she nodded.

Rajanas said, "Lemic. Bocca. Nils, yes, you, too. And... Enghet. All four of you, attack Lhind—try to capture her. Go, on, thief, show them what you usually do."

I stood there gawking, my hands throbbing, but when Nils—a grinning, golden-haired boy with mischief in his face—and three other determined people in gray advanced, old habit took over.

I leaped over the shortest one, somersaulted in the air, and when they whirled, startled, and Nils charged, with big, brawny

Enghet closing in, I leaped again, putting my back to the stone wall and my feet to the barrel of wooden swords and kicked.

The barrel overturned right in their path, spilling wood right and left. A leap, bounce, and I spotted a drinking bucket next to a stack of towels—dipping the top towel, I snapped it at a Gray Wolf, then flung it with a quick twist to my wrist so that the towel wrapped around her head, clinging the way wet cloth does. As she staggered about blind, clawing at the towel, I shouldered her into Nils, who'd danced past the wood and was trying to come at me from the side.

All four started after me, and I ran, using momentum to leap to a wall and over their heads to where the practice shields were stashed, which I started spinning at them until the sound of Rajanas's laughter broke our attention, followed by Ovlan clapping twice.

We all stopped, whooping for breath.

"Nils! What did you just learn?"

"She cheats!" Nils yelled, fists on hips.

"Are you going to tell street brawlers that they cheated if they get the drop on you during your patrol?"

Nils pursed his lips, then said in a subdued voice, "Then why do we have rules, if no one uses 'em?"

"These rules are to train moves into your muscles as you build strength, so you don't have to think about them. They become habit. Did you see how fast ordinary objects became weapons for Lhind? That," Rajanas said, "is habit." He turned my way. "Thief, what did you just learn?"

My heart had already sunk. "Stick with what I know."

Ovlan clapped again, and gestured the lines to reform.

I looked down at the blisters puffing up red and angry across my palms, and backed out to watch. Thianra finished out the drill. It was clear she'd learned the basics at some time in her life, and though she was far from the best, she was not among the raw beginners, once they got to scrapping.

I watched, brooding. What good would sticking with what I knew do me in Sveran Djur? I remembered that insanely fast, and obviously painful duel between Am-Jalad Darus and Jardis Dhes-Andis—and it hadn't even been a fight to the death. Kicking over buckets and barrels wouldn't deflect either of them for much more than an instant. Even if there were barrels and buckets handily within reach.

When the Gray Wolves finished their matches, they were dismissed to the midday meal, and Thianra and I joined Rajanas upstairs.

"Why the long face, thief?" he asked, as a servant brought me fruit, a baked cheese pie, and crunchy vegetables.

"You don't think I should go rescue Hlanan."

He shook his head. "Never said that. But I do think you should consider what you're up against. Why do you think I didn't sail south for Sveran Djur the day I heard he might be a prisoner there?"

That was unanswerable, and made me feel so miserable I almost didn't eat. I say almost, because I'd gone hungry for too many years to ever completely pass up a meal. But I didn't enjoy it, because I was arguing with myself. The truth was clear to more people than just me: I couldn't possibly be successful in finding and rescuing Hlanan, without an army or two at my back.

To every sensible argument my mind offered, my heart insisted: *I am going to try.*

Thianra stayed silent during the meal, but at the end, offered—as she always did—to play to the company.

Usually I love her music. I love all music. It was music that brought my mother back to me, and they even had a harp here, which I might in another mood have played to accompany Thianra. But I was too dejected for even music.

And so, while they gathered in the music room, I wandered along a balcony, gazing up at the stars, and wondering if Hlanan, as a prisoner, looked at the same ones. Or was he stuck in a dungeon? It had pleased Dhes-Andis to make my prison a pretty one, because I shared his blood. He probably wouldn't do that for Hlanan.

I paced past an open window, then jumped back, my hair and

tail floofing out as Tir sailed in through the window, banked, and then perched on the back of a carved chair.

"Tir!" I exclaimed. "How did you find me?" Then, "Did you find Hlanan?"

"Come! Lhind come!" Tir croaked. "Come! Aw-w-w!"

"Hlanan?" I repeated, though I knew Tir's few human words were clearer than that.

"A-o-o-w-w-w-! A-o-o-w-w-w-!" Tir squawked, flapping in agitation.

In the past I'd been able to understand Tir much better through the mental connection. Animals think in images and scents and sounds, not words, though the bird part of me translated all that into words.

That is, when I was able to do it.

"I'm sorry, I can't hear you." I was more upset than ever. "But I can follow you."

And with that, I leaped out the window into a tree branch, and swung down.

Tir flapped up into the sky to the west, gliding back, then up again, making it clear that I was supposed to fly. That meant toiling and moiling my way up the mountainside until I got high enough. I could have refused, but Tir seemed to be anxious for me to make an effort. Since the aidlar had come all this way seeking me, of course I had to go.

So I bent my head, swung my arms, and started stumping my way straight up the mountainside behind the city. It was thickly forested. Tir flew above me, crying out from time to time. I ran upward until my breath sawed in my throat, until at *last* I sensed the lightening of air that meant I could transform.

I paused, hands on knees, my hair and tail drooping as lifeless as human hair as I tried to catch my breath. Then, muscles trembling, I pushed myself up one more rocky cliff… and the moment I sensed that tingle through my body, I transformed, scarcely aware of my clothes fluttering to the ground.

Tir took off, and I flapped, getting a brief burst of strength in bird form, and followed until I reached a strong air current. Then I rode that up and up, needing only a twitch of tail feathers and primaries on my wingtips to guide me into the wind stream.

As a bird, my thoughts narrowed to the immediate. I gloried in flight—always—and found my strength again. Higher and higher, toward the snowy peaks we flew, Tir and I, until a massive shadow blocked the stars, swooping down.

Then moonlight shimmered over iridescent violet feathers, and I gazed up at a great gryph.

Not just any great gryph, I saw as I flitted closer. I knew this gryph. Firebird was the name the Djurans had given him. His lower neck still bore the remains of scarring left by the heavily decorated controlling fais that had forced the bird to the will of Raifas, one of Dhes-Andis's nobles, and a naval commander. Almost my last act in Sveran Djur had been to break the magic on that fais—and in turn, Firebird had set me free.

"A-o-o-w-w-w-!" Tir cried, a sound echoed by Firebird.

Then I understood: Tir doesn't really say 'r' or 'l' sounds. My name is more like 'Whind' than Lhind, for example, and Tir's name comes out as a screeling sound.

What they were saying was: *Rue*.

The king of the dragons had sent them.

Nine

HLANAN HAD SLOWLY BECOME inured to sleeping on the stones, his skin bare above the waist. Each day he dragged himself through the Djuran drill, his mind so closed off he scarcely noticed the movements becoming incrementally less painful. He purified his water and whatever food he could snatch. Nothing was going to make the latter more appetizing, as it was still scrapings, but at least the rot was taken out by magic.

He slept as much as he could, his only form of escape, as the guards never left space between them when the doors were open.

Then one night noise, clanks, and clatters forced his consciousness upward toward the surface of awareness as the guards pushed the big man in again. The man swayed his way to the back and collapsed onto the ground. The flickering torchlight played over the distortions of bruised and torn flesh, and Hlanan could hear pain in every breath.

So the brute was back again. Hlanan knew that he would make himself go to the man the following day, aware that he regarded this as a duty that everyone around him would scorn in this place of arbitrary cruelty and madness.

But that only made him stubborn.

Next day, as usual Hlanan cleansed his water and his handful of food, which he ate as slowly as he could as if that might fool his stomach into thinking it more. No one attacked him anymore, probably because he'd been marked by the Djurans, who were left to themselves.

When Hlanan finished, sure enough, a Djuran came to summon him. He knew by now that they would not take no for an answer, whatever their motivation—perhaps some odd combination of honor, obligation, and sheer entertainment at his hopelessness.

At least he could better endure the drill now. After it was finished, he forced himself to the next duty, and crossed the slimy ground to the supine man. Even in the dim light from the grating on the far wall, the man's face was almost unrecognizable. He lay on one side, arm cradled against his ribs, the forearm swollen sickeningly in the middle: fractured bones. Equal swelling distending his ear: a shattered jaw.

Hlanan knelt beside him. The man jerked, the dim light filtering through the grating revealing his swollen mouth and bloody teeth. "Uhn." He tried to speak, and to move away. "Uhn."

"Lie still," Hlanan said in Shinjan. "Let me see if I can..."

The man tried again to scramble away, but the effort proved too much, and he subsided into a faint. Good. Hlanan touched his fingers lightly to the swollen, hot flesh of the break.

He eased the swelling by using the infection spell, then carefully felt for the bone fragments below the flesh and massaged them together. After each one clicked into place he bound it with magic, and though he sensed a warning tingle up his arm, and his head panged, he moved to the man's jaw, nudged that into its natural form, and bespelled the bones together.

When he felt his control over the spell wavering, he tied it off, and pressed his hands on his knees, his head swimming as he struggled for breath, then retreated to his usual spot on the greasy stones to recover.

Another long, dreary day passed.

The next morning, instead of the Djuran guard coming to summon Hlanan, he stared up in surprise at Darus, whose clothes looked no cleaner than his, though he'd managed to wash his face, and finger his hair into a semblance of order.

"Comprehend you the Shinjan tongue," Darus stated in Elras.

"Yes."

"What said they? When take they this man,'" Darus demanded.

"I think he's taken out to fight in the arena."

Darus's lips whitened. "Arena? A fight to the death?" His eyes widened. "I welcome that!"

Hlanan said, "I don't know. But a fight, certainly, for the entertainment of the Shinjans."

Darus turned his head and spat. "They can me kill. Entertain them I will not."

"Yes, you will." The gravely voice caused both Hlanan and Darus to turn sharply.

"You who to intrude?" Darus demanded in his accented Elras.

"Call me Sig." The big, grizzled man standing there was the one who had attacked Hlanan for his food—and who now had a discolored jaw and arm, held together by Hlanan's magic. It had to hurt to speak, after only one day of magical reattachment, yet there he was.

Sig's Elras was guttural with a heavy accent, but understandable. "You fight in exhibition. If you no fight, you get whip. Before your own company killed before of you."

"Company?" Hlanan repeated, appalled.

A slight nod. "Us. Captains. You? Entertain city, maybe." He switched to Shinjan. "They pull us out when our companies rotate in. We can fight or be flogged. We are examples to the rest. You are entertainment, maybe before you go to Jaw Box, maybe after." He flicked at look Darus's way. "Tell him."

Hlanan translated into Elras, and Darus recoiled subtly, stilling, his gaze distant. Then he said, "What is Jaw Box?"

"Inter-ro-ga-tion," Sig enunciated, wincing. "You are marks for three reasons. Politics. Information. Ransom. Imperial marks, for arena." He grabbed Hlanan's arm, and spoke low. "It was you, put magic on me."

"Yes."

"Why'd you do it?" Sig demanded in his own language, as Darus stood there, his wary gaze cutting from one speaker to the other.

"Because I took an oath. And will not betray it," Hlanan said.

"Yes." The man grunted a humorless laugh. "You will. We all do. In time. Oaths have no meaning. So what d'you want from me?"

"Nothing," Hlanan said.

Bloodshot eyes narrowed in anger, and Hlanan braced for a beating. He understood that somehow he had insulted this man — no, insulted his authority? No, that wasn't quite right, or maybe only a part. Sig felt he owed Hlanan, was that it? Despite his words, he had enough of a moral sense left to not want to be beholden. So he wanted a trade, to make them quits.

Sig poked Hlanan in breastbone. "You come to me. I tell you who to fix."

Hlanan gazed down at the floor, arms crossed tightly over his chest. This moment—this heartbeat, two, three, was a decision point. Though he had not thought ahead about the consequences of his healing experiments, it seemed that his spells, rudimentary as they were, gave him not a weapon—that would go directly against the healers' vows—but a tool, something to trade.

One choice led toward possible comfort, the other... not. He could not see past that, but he knew this: if he survived, he would forever look back at this moment as judge, jury, executioner.

"No. I aid anyone who needs me. That's the oath healers take."

Sig stiffened. "You are fool."

"I've heard that before. If you want a trade, consider this. I will purify the water trough for everyone. And the food, as soon as the guards depart. It won't look much better, but the rot will vanish. But I'll only do it if there is no more fighting. Everyone gets a share."

And that, Hlanan knew, undercut this man's authority with one hand, but granted him a choice with the other.

He thought he could see Sig considering the question as his expression turned vague, then hardened into conviction. Hlanan sensed in the subtle sounds of shifting cloth, the scrapes of feet moving nearer, and in the harsh breathing, how everyone listened. Sig still had authority: what he decided mattered.

Sig turned his head. "You hear that?"

A gaunt older man stepped up, dim in the gloom. "Fair for all?"

"That's my offer," Hlanan said.

Hlanan could see Sig's gaze going from one to another among the crowd. His enforcers?

Sig said, "Yes." He touched his jaw, then grunted and shuffled away, chuckling low in his chest.

The shadowy figures of the prisoners retreated into the inky darkness, leaving Darus standing alone, having waited all this time.

Darus said in heavy Elras, "What you and him say?"

Hlanan translated, at the end of which Darus made a gesture of command. Hlanan sighed, seeing that he was not going to get out of Djuran warm-ups.

Anyway, he was getting inured to fumbling his way through.

———⊰⊙⊱———

After the drill, he forced his tired muscles back across the room to the trough, and then began another long, wearying session, repeating the spell over and over as he moved along the trough, so that all the water the prisoners drank purified as it sluiced down toward the drain.

When he was done, he sank down where he was, crossed his arms over his knees, and put his forehead on his arms.

He must have slept a little. When he woke up, his shirt lay in a heap next to his feet.

He picked it up and pulled it on. It was filthy and rank with someone else's sweat, but dipping it in the trough—cleaning it— might attract the attention of the guards. He did not want to test his theory that the trough, and the wheelbarrow of dumped food, were all a deliberate tactic to reinforce their galk status.

And everyone else seemed to feel the same, for he saw no one using the trickle in the trough to attempt cleaning their clothing or selves. Instead, they dipped only their hands, most watching the magic flash subtly over them to get rid of the grime, then drinking. Cleaning themselves to be reserved for the sheets of water coming through the grating when it rained.

The next day, they waited in the usual half-circle for the guards to dump the food. There it was, unappetizing as ever. As soon as the guards had gone away, Hlanan was ready—he'd prepared the spell as soon as he woke, so all he had to do was walk around the perimeter of the lumpish mass, whisper, and finish the spell. Silvery green sparkles flashed all over.

The food was still a disgusting mess all tumbled together, but the maggots were gone, the slime, the rot, the dirt.

Sig and the two female enforcers stood like sentinels as everyone filed by to get some. One of the Djurans got Darus's share and took it to him.

Hlanan was left with a bigger share than he'd ever managed to get on his own. No larger than anyone else's, but no smaller.

The next day was a repeat.

The following day began with a deep rumbling beneath the stones, and a tremor that shook the building.

People looked warily at each other. Hlanan's heart thudded, but he breathed away the instinctive panic. Mages for centuries had known how to control ground quakes, diminishing the deep pressures in slow releases that harmed nothing living on the surface. Surely that was also true in Shinja.

The next change was that the guards did not show up with the wheelbarrow of scrapings.

The day otherwise settled into routine. When the food was late, the Djurans still drilled, Hlanan with them. He checked the purification spell on the trough, which was holding. Everyone watched the sunlight shift the bars across the nasty stones of the floor. Grumbling increased, and Hlanan heard someone say, "It's the mage, done for us. Guards found out."

"How?" Sig snapped, still talking slowly, as if his jaw hurt. "I tell you, something was going on when they brought us survivors out of the pit. Not just the mucks and the spears were on alert, but the kips as well."

Hlanan said, "What are kips?"

"Tell him, Trax." Sig rubbed his jaw and winced.

One of the pair of enforcers turned to Hlanan. "They wear the hat, looks like a kiprit fighting lizard. Imperial household guards. They boss the spears, the castle guard. And everybody bosses the mucks. Ours," she added, and made a spitting motion to one side.

Other Shinjans began speaking up to add their opinions of the mucks, in a variety of creative curses. That caused some laughter until Darus lifted his voice – "Quiet."

He said it in Djuran, then he said in Elras, "To not speak."

Sig turned on him, but Darus, flanked by his faithful guardians, ignored everyone, moving toward the grating.

Silence fell, everyone turning to hear the distant sounds of clashes and thuds.

"Ah, probably just a defense drill," Sig began, but uncertainly.

A long, liquid scream, followed by a roar and then the ringing clashes of steel weaponry shut the prisoners up. They moved in a mass to stand below the grating, faces upturned.

The noises moved away, then trumpets blared. Horse hooves thundered across the square, causing shadows to flicker over the grating, and sending gouts of dust to whirl in, bringing the pungent smell of horse.

Once again, from another direction, came the shouts and clangs. "It's coming from the princes' wing," Sig said. "I'm sure of it."

"Another slave revolt?" one of the women muttered.

The prisoners fell silent, then someone muttered 'Zeltzi' and a muffled curse, and someone else made a spitting sound.

"And his mother is fighting back," someone else said.

Wasn't one of the emperor's consorts named Zeltzi? No, wasn't she empress now? And she had a son high in military command, Avejo.

There was another son, by a different consort, what was her name, Lennar? Luenro! She'd come from the Kherval, a king's daughter who'd made a treaty marriage to the Shinjan emperor. Hlanan's mother had remarked wryly that that princess had probably saved Shinja's imperial treasury from insolvency for at least five years—and she had been empress, until some kind of internal politics forced her to a subordinate position, while Zeltzi took her crown.

As quiet fell, Hlanan reconsidered everything he'd seen on the cart ride to the capital: the crumbling streets and ill-maintained buildings, the knots of people scowling. He'd been too thirsty, hungry, and exhausted to recognize what he knew now as signs of poverty. Unrest. Clearly the fortune Luenro had brought with her had been spent.

Quiet fell again, broken now and then by the sound of tramping feet marching in cadence: patrols all through the castle complex. Tension reigned for the remainder of the long, dreary day, until at last night fell. More murmured conversations, too low to hear, their tone anxious and angry, preceded quiet.

When the prisoners woke in the morning, there was the tramp of the guards again, and the day's food dumped—from the smell, it had sat out since the day previous.

The prison guards always had their weapons out before they unlocked the doors, standing in two lines so that a cat or dog would have difficulty getting between them. This particular morning, Hlanan sensed a sharper awareness, as if they expected trouble. No, as if they looked for an excuse to use those tightly gripped weapons. But the prisoners stood away in silence.

"G'wan, galk!" a guard bawled. "Aren't you ready to feed?"

No one spoke or moved. The guard cursed them all roundly, and slammed the door. Then they tramped away.

Hlanan got to work. Magic shimmered over the scrambled mess of food on the floor. The pile diminished perceptibly as the rot was whisked away into the soil below the castle foundations.

Several elbowed forward, and one man snarled at another, but Trax used the wetted end of Hlanan's former scribe robe to whip the man back.

With ill tempers driven by gnawing hunger, everyone got what they could. Hlanan managed to get three fish tails with bits of sesame-oil cooked meat burned on them, some withered greens, and a heel of bread that was so hard it took him a while to gnaw it down.

The rest of the day was measured by the tramp of the patrolling guards. Once, the acrid scent of smoke drifted in, and again, everyone gathered under the grating, looking up in hopes of seeing some clue to outside events.

Then late that night, a bigger contingent of guards approached—from the sound, an entire company, or maybe even more.

The usual prison guards, who the Shinjans called the mucks, were accompanied by tall, fully armored and armed men and women with crested headdresses that came down over nose and cheekbones, partially hiding their faces.

These had to be the kips. The prison guards unlocked the door, and roughly shoved two badly beaten men inside to land on the stone floor. Behind them walked an older woman, dark splatters marring her light-colored silken gown. The flicker of firelight highlighted wrinkled skin and silvery hair as she made her way slowly, hands out. The guards stood away from her, no one touching her, though she felt with thin fingers extended, as though she could not see in the murky dimness.

The rest of the prisoners backed away, a susurrus of whispers ringing outward, too quick for Hlanan to catch.

The woman did not look right or left, but walked straight to the back, until she was no more than a pale wisp, like ghost flame, against the inky blackness.

With deliberate movements she knelt, then lay down. The guards locked up again, and tramped away, their silence much more sinister than the mucks' usual threats and insults.

With the guards went the light, so perforce Hlanan and the rest of the prisoners had to listen to the hissing, broken breathing of the two men.

As soon as it was light, the mucks returned with the wheelbarrow, as before.

They dumped the food out, then one roared, "The prince is giving the city a festival. You might even get to be part of the entertainment!"

No one moved, but Hlanan felt the tension that gripped the prisoners as they side-eyed each other.

The guards departed on this threat, then, aware of being watched, Hlanan went through the spells that became quicker and surer each day. As soon as everyone had their small share of food, one of the Djurans started Hlanan's way.

Hlanan heaved himself to his feet, avoided the Djuran, and crossed to face Darus. "Hurt first," he said in Djuran, pointing to where the three newcomers lay. He tapped his ear, and said, "Very bad."

Darus regarded him in silence, then said something rapidly to his men. Hlanan turned away, hoping they'd get on without him, and so would end the strange experiment.

But no, they ranged up, obviously determined to wait for him.

Hlanan moved to the first of the new prisoners, knelt, and felt gently over the shivering, delirious man, until his fingers encountered the stickiness of slowly seeping blood. Hlanan spread his fingers and whispered the spell to clear the infection away from the lacerations over the man's back. Then came the tougher spell, the one to knit flesh as he pressed together each laceration. This took so many repeats his head began to buzz.

Hlanan finished, checked the man over, found more evidence of torture, and attended that, too. At last he finished and bowed his head, fighting against swarms of darkness across his vision.

He moved to the second man, who lay unconscious.

This time the magic took a lot longer, and Hlanan had to kneel there, head bowed, before he could get up and move.

He forced himself to go to the woman, who had stretched out a little ways away, her body straight, hands at her sides. In the dimness, he saw no obvious wound, though her breathing was slow and harsh with pain.

"Is there anything I can do for you?" Hlanan said in his accented Shinjan.

A scrape, a hissing breath was the first warning that they were not alone. He looked up. A circle of prisoners surrounded them. It was too dim to see any faces.

"Go," the woman breathed. "Go."

Hlanan did.

———❧———

The next morning after drill, Hlanan made certain to take his food first. He got enough for two, braced to be attacked, but though Sig and the others watched him, no one moved against him as he crammed his small handful of stale bread and hardened cheese into his mouth, and made his way to the place where he'd left the old woman. She hadn't moved.

He knelt down. "I have food," he said in Shinjan. "Bread." It was a slightly less stale heel than the one still stuck, dry and stale, in his throat.

The woman was breathing, but she lay still. He touched her hand. "Is there pain anywhere? Can I help you?" He asked first in Shinjan, and then repeated it in Elras, hoping she understood at least one of them.

The woman said in accentless Elras, "Leave me to die."

"Why give them an easier victory?" Hlanan whispered – the argument he used against himself.

Her eyelids were still closed, but the sound of her breathing made it plain that she was awake, and aware. "She has already won."

She? "No," he breathed. "Not while we live. And think. Talk. Plan."

She did not respond.

"Please eat," he said.

A faint sigh escaped her.

Hlanan found one of her hands. He pressed the small bit of bread into it, and the cracked, dried piece of cheese. "I hope you will change your mind."

"It is too late," she whispered. "My son betrayed, and must be dead. I embrace the darkness."

Hlanan moved away reluctantly, and for a time the day measured itself slowly in the barred light shafts moving across the slick, oily gleam of the filthy stones, and the tramp of feet outside.

Then late that night, the tramp of feet approached down the corridor — the guards were back.

The guards creaked the doors open, and expelled what at first seemed like a dozen bloody wrecks into the room. "Prince's marks, so you know what happens if you touch 'em, ha ha ha," the lead guard bawled. "Now, Tastag Company is here. Where are our examples of treachery and cowardice to entertain for Tastag's fine and loyal warriors?"

Mag and Trax, Sig's enforcers, moved toward the guards, who entered to surround them — as if the scrawny, weaponless women were any kind of threat to the armed and armored guards.

The guards' torches flared, and Hlanan turned his head away from the brightness, seeing the rest of the prison cell clearly for the first time. It was as dismal as expected, but even worse, when his gaze fell on the old woman who had briefly raised her head from the filthy ground, there plain to see was what he had missed in the darkness: her sightless gaze, the color of her eyes peculiar, the sclera marbled with gray-blue. She had been blinded by magic.

Ten

BACK TO ME, FLYING southward along the range along the western curve of the Kherval continent.

Of course I was terrified, and wanted to run and hide.

But fear of what might happen if I didn't go was even scarier. I'd seen that dragon named Rue twice, once deep in the Dragon Mountain when Raifas, the Shinjan lord whose land, or pennon, included that mountain, took me to see it. I hadn't told him about the dragon.

The next time I saw Rue, he had burst open the top of the mountain and flew down the island. A single beat of his wings had shattered every window in the imperial palace—and incidentally, the dragon's flight had enabled me to escape, after breaking the power of the fais controlling the gryph Firebird.

I couldn't imagine why a dragon would send gryphs all this way to summon me, but surely it couldn't be just to smite me. Could it?

By the time Firebird led me, still southward, high over the sea, we had been joined by a whirling snowstorm of white birds, at least a hundred aidlars.

Exhilaration thrilled through me as the high air currents carried us in a wide arc over the deep sparkling waters far below. But even drifting on wind currents takes effort. When I spotted some islands dotting the horizon, I was glad I'd been flying so much with my father. Riding the currents still takes work. I might not have been able to endure the long flight without all that practice.

But soon another worry supplanted the sense of increasing fatigue. It looked as if we might land on one of those islands, which gave me a highly unpleasant choice: dropping from a height into the sea, or falling to the ground on land, because already the air was significantly heavier, and I struggled to keep myself aloft.

But Firebird banked, tail feathers spreading, and drifted below me in unmistakable invitation. My heart crowded my throat as I transformed, and plopped with a splat onto his back.

The wind, so friendly when I was a bird, whistled threateningly down my human self. I stretched my arms around his great neck, burying my face in his feathers, below which I could feel the ridges of scarring from that horrible fais Raifas had put on Firebird to control him.

Down we spiraled toward the largest island in the clump, hazed by feathery clouds. A brief, damp period of gray fog as we penetrated the clouds, then the island sharpened into clarity directly below.

The island centered around an enormous pointed mountain, the top of which was entirely hidden by a crown of interwoven *kivedus*, an ivy-like plant I was used to seeing on the high mountains, where it flowered in spring, then dropped nuts in fall. The contours of the mountain's slopes blurred beneath the green of fruit trees. Though I saw no signs of human habitation, I certainly wouldn't go hungry.

We drifted toward the lower mountain slopes. Here, an enormous forest grew, nut trees and firs, tanglewood and a hundred different ferny and flowering shrubs among fruit trees. Wildflowers ruled the meadows, blanketing the lower reaches all the way to the shore. Above these meadows, thousands of different birds soared, chirring, pecking for seeds, preening, nesting.

Birds whirred into the air, squawking and tweeting as Firebird angled down and landed on a grassy hummock. The gryph's great muscles bunched under me, and his wings folded in. I slid off and landed in the soft grass, the rich mud beneath giving. The island smelled of wildflowers and blossoms. I snuffled in the heady scents, feeling better than I had all day — enough to discover that I was ravenous.

Firebird ducked his great head, looking at me from one eye, then the other, ruffled his feathers, and finally made impatient noises that sounded somewhere between scolding and exasperated.

I remembered the mental images from our days as prisoners, he of Raifas, me of the emperor. I touched my head, unsure how much—if anything—gryphs understood, and said, "I can't hear you."

Firebird launched skyward, mighty wings beating the air as he lofted high, and settled on the mountain crown. Against the lurid colors of sunset I made out his profile digging and snapping among the kivedus plants.

So that was what they ate! I remembered stacks of something or other, dried and sorted, in the aviary at Dhes-Andis's royal palace. Here, the gryph could get its preferred diet fresh, and his feathers were the brighter for it.

As for me, I ran up the slope and began picking plums, peaches, tiny purple grape bunches, and on the ground, great melons on their vines. I broke these on stones, and then gathered nuts.

These were going to be difficult to pry open, until a parrot with florid green and crimson and white feathers, with a trailing crest of iridescent blue, hopped on a stone, cracked a nut, and let the halves fall.

When I cautiously reached for one, wary of that beak, the parrot cawed a sound that sounded suspiciously like a laugh, and flapped, but didn't drive me away.

Sweet nuts! Savory nuts, tart, and hot-flavored—what an amazing variety! I ate until I couldn't eat another bite, then sank into the grass as the last of the sun vanished, and Little Moon peeked out at me from the other side of the mountain.

Well, I was here. Firebird had brought me. There was no one to ask for reasons. No clothes to wear, no house to go inside of. I suspected rain would fall before morning, but at least it would be warm.

Early as it was, there was nothing else to do, and flying all day had tired me out. I snapped my hair out to cover me, curled up where I was, and slept.

I was glad I had. Midway through the night a storm moved in. At first the rain was soft and warm, and since I'm covered with down, and my hair and tail are feathers, it didn't bother me unduly. But then the wind began to rise, cold air chasing the warmth away. Blue lightning rendered the world black and white, then a mighty crash of thunder roared.

I scrambled up, groping my way toward one of the thicker trees, in time for a sudden smiting of hailstones. Ordinarily cold doesn't bother me, except when I am soaked to the skin with sleety water. I pressed up against the trunk, shivering, as the branches above me creaked and tossed.

Once again lightning flared, far out over the sea, lighting up a solid white squall. I had to find shelter. I stumbled in the direction of the mountain, fumbling blindly in the thick darkness, until lightning revealed a crevasse up above me.

Here I found a stream-carved little cave. On one side water sheeted down, but on the other I could sit relatively sheltered, as the storm whipped and wailed across the island, rendering my mood dour: a dragon had sent for me for whatever reason, and meanwhile, I was no closer to finding Hlanan than before. Maybe even farther away, now that I was stuck on this island in the middle of the sea.

But storms pass.

The lightning branched farther and farther out to sea. I made out the black silhouettes of gryphs flying overhead, blocking out the occasional stars twinkling between departing clouds.

I curled up and fell into slumber once again, and this time when I woke, it was to find myself surrounded by lizard-heads on long, thin necks, bright eyes turning bird-like to study me.

My gaze traveled down those long, thin necks to small three-fingered claw-hands pulled in tight to broad chests, feathered arm flaps folded in. Below those, two long, skinny legs. Lizardrakes!

I sat up, dried mud glopping off me in clumps, and the

lizardrakes backed up, making little sounds midway between the murml-coo of pigeons and a whistle.

"Ow, I need water," I croaked.

The lizardrakes responded with noises like whistle-quacks as they backed out of the crevasse. I followed, stretching. My body was one giant itch as more mud flaked and clumped off me.

I had scrambled up a fairly steep slope, and began picking my way down, envying the lizardrakes, most of whom stretched out their small wings, which flapped in a blur. The creatures didn't get much lift, but they drifted gently down to the flowery ground at the foot of the mountain, whereas I had to pick my way carefully, often stepping in hidden holes of gloppy mud.

The lizardrakes swarmed to the left, pausing to look back at me. I followed them. When I emerged from under the trees, I spotted gryphs roaming and nesting around a small valley located on the far side of the mountain. Grays, browns, and the big purples dipped heads in water, or sat in the morning sun as aidlars landed on their backs and heads, grooming them with their beaks. Other aidlars glided into the meadows to hunt for seeds, and the gryphs took to the air one by one, flying up to feed on kivedus.

I followed the tiny trickles of muddy water toward the valley, and found a clear-running stream. The sun was up by then, and already warm, so after I dipped my hands to drink, I waded in and sank below the surface of the cool water. When I came up, I was clean again, and soon dry.

I kept wandering, looking for more fruit trees – then stopped when I reached the top of the valley, and looked down into a sheltered area carved by the stream.

On either side of the curving waters little huts stood, their roofs fitted together with fronds. And as I watched, three human shapes appeared from beyond the fronds, and ran into the huts.

At first I thought they were children, they were so small. When I crossed the stream and approached one of the huts, two emerged, both wearing shiny, rippling grass skirts of thin, silky fronds. Their skin was pale, delicately scaled and iridescent, their hair the color and consistency of corn-floss.

Both wore woven flower garlands around their necks, which sent up the fragrances of blossoms. They approached me, their light-colored eyes wide, and chattered in a language I didn't know.

A third emerged from a hut farther on, carrying something in her arms. She met me, held it out, and it turned out to be a grass skirt on a simple tie. I took it, saying, "Thank you!" and tied it on. It felt pleasant, swishing about my ankles. My upper half was covered by my hair.

Small as they were, I could see that they were not children — and sure enough, even smaller ones pelted through the water, laughing and splashing one another.

The hut people led me toward their fruit trees, where I got some breakfast. After a short, unsuccessful attempt to talk to me, they gave up trying to communicate, and smiled, inviting me to gather orchids with them and weave flower garlands, or gather the long grasses, which they wove into mats that formed the walls of their huts.

Some trooped, singing together, out of the valley to a far slope where they weeded gardens. I discovered that they planted what seemed to be sweet potatoes, which they baked to hardness and then stashed against the winter months. The smaller ones harvested the long grasses that grew on the stream banks, then worked them with oils to make the skirts.

I spent two anxious days with the people, learning bits of their language when the rains came through. We sat in the huts as they taught me their weaving.

Then one night I sensed intent.

They went around lighting oil-soaked strands braided tightly together. The oil, something sweet-smelling, reminding me of honey, made the braided fronds burn very slowly. These were suspended inside lanterns made of dried, painted leaves that glowed with light. When enough of them were hung, the village area looked pretty, the nighttime colors softened.

A sound like a rushing of wind through great trees rose out of nowhere. I looked around, then up as the stars vanished from the sky, then the darkness resolved into a mighty flock of gryphs descending to light on the hillside, and the areas outside the village.

As the gryphs hopped in closer, forming a circle around the villagers, the lizardrake people began humming a melody that seemed familiar. At first it seemed sinister, though the melody itself rose and fell in a pleasing way, until I found the connection: it was a simplified version of the Shadow Dance so popular with the Djuran imperial court.

But oh, what a difference!

The people formed into a circle, as the Djurans had. They paid no attention to numbers, unlike the Djurans with their courtly, controlled figures. The island began the familiar dance, but when the melody ended, sparks scintillated around half of the people — and they turned into lizardrakes!

Then the lizardrakes formed another circle, this time joined by a pair of tall, slender people with dark purple skin. No, feathers, grown close over their bodies, much as mine did. Though my covering is mostly down, except for the hair on my head and along my spine to my tail. Theirs was actual feathers, in a deep purple, almost black, complemented by graceful looping folds of some kind of wrap that left their limbs free.

The two joined the dance — the *true* shadow dance — as the people and lizardrakes leaped and twirled joyfully. At the end of each round, humans transformed to lizardrakes, and lizardrakes to human. At the edge of the circle, the pair of gryph people leaped into the air, and for a heartbeat they flashed into their great gryph form, wings outspread overhead, then they blurred with a blue flash and landed again as two-legs, whirling and dancing.

Not everyone transformed. I sensed that many were single-natured humans (whose ancestors might have been lizardrakes, as they resembled the lizardrake humans in every other way), and the single-natured lizardrakes stayed on the edge of the circle, as did the great gryphs. Not just a few, either. When I looked away from the dance, I was astounded to discover a multitude of them, starlight gleaming in their eyes, too many eyes to count. A galaxy of gryphs had gathered, silently watching the dance.

Three times the circles blended and broke, transformed then blended and broke, transforming back again as those in human form hummed. It was a celebration of life—all forms of life.

And at the end, the woman who taught me to weave garlands came to me, her wide pale eyes reflecting the lantern light as she took me by the shoulders.

"For you," she said slowly, enunciating each word. "You see? You hear? For you. Now go, in sky." She raised her hand toward the nearest gryph, its purple feathers highlighted by the golden glow of the lanterns.

The ruffled feathers at the neck—it was Firebird!

The gryph squawked at me, and dipped his head once, twice.

"I can't," I said. I didn't have the vocabulary to explain that I needed to be up higher before I could change—and it saddened me to be unable to communicate, when all my life that had come easily. Naturally.

Then the pair of gryph people approached me, one with shimmering dark blue cloth carried across her forearms.

At first I couldn't tell if they were male or female, as both still wore those wraps of a deep violet with warm brown tones. Both were tall. When they got close, I saw that one's visible limbs were covered in dark violet-blue feathers, the second in feathers of a rich, gold-touched burnt sienna. They both had feathered crests instead of hair, violet on the one and gold-touched brown on the other.

I understood then that these were dual-natured great gryphs in their human form, the violet a male and the brown a female. She held out shimmery cloth to me. It matched the color of their wraps.

As I took it and shook it out, the female said something in a language I'd never heard before. When I did not answer, she looked from side to side, then spoke carefully in accented Elras, "You no longer hear?"

She didn't touch the sides of her head where her ears might be.

She touched her forehead.

I shook my head, amazed at the softness of the cloth. It was a wrap like theirs! The fabric felt softer and lighter than silk, but it was strong. Much stronger than my pretty grass skirt, or my flower garlands. Strong enough to endure wind—in flight.

She nodded encouragement at me, and I flicked it around myself, with one end over a shoulder. I needed my spine hair and tail free, so I wrapped it crosswise, glad to discover that, like Hrethan wraps, there was plenty of fabric. When it draped nicely around me, she gave a little nod of approval.

"Our gift," she said in a language close to the lizardrake tongue. Then she pointed to the great gryph the Djurans had called Firebird. "You fix?"

"Fix?" I repeated. "I don't understand." That phrase I'd said a lot.

"You saw." She indicated the dancers. "You help?" She tapped her head, and indicated the great gryph, with his scarred neck under ruffled feathers. "When he is small, egg from our flock leader." She lifted her hands like wings. "He was taken by bind-one."

"Bind-one?"

"Those who bind." She touched her neck, indicating the magical control necklace the Djurans called fais.

"Yes! Raifas of Ardam Pennon, that much I remember," I said. Raifas had bragged to me about capturing a wild great gryph, and striving to tame and train it. As I looked at those ruffled feathers over the gryph's neck, I mentally changed 'tame and train' to 'torture.' The troubling thing was, while Jardis Dhes-Andis had had no problem with torturing me in order to force me into obedience, I never got the sense that Raifas thought he was torturing the great gryph.

"Kaa is taken very small, forced to stay gryph. Many years. Cannot be human again. You." The female gryph in human form opened both hands to me, palms up. "You hear his pain." She tapped her head. "You hear now?" And her expression changed, as if she were thinking a message at me.

Sick with self-disgust and disappointment, and underneath that the crawling fear that Dhes-Andis was hovering evilly somewhere just outside my perception, waiting to pounce, I shook my head. "I can't hear this way anymore," I said as I tapped my forehead. "Only with these." I tapped my ears.

She turned to the male, and they held a conversation much too rapid to follow: I got maybe five words out of a hundred. But I was fairly certain one of those was 'dragon.'

The female turned back to me. "You free Kaa of pain-binding. Some of us saw. We all know. Come with us." And once again she indicated the great gryph standing nearby, huge round eye switching between us all.

"You mean Firebird?" I asked.

She tipped her head, and the male said, "That is not his name. The bind-folk called him that. He is not a firebird. He is Kaa. You freed Kaa. He brings you to Rue, be healed. Now?"

I turned to regard the neck-scarred gryph. He was once dual-natured? The fact that he couldn't transform to his human self reminded me of my father. My emotions tumbled around inside me, but I tried to squash them down. There must have been a hundred gryphs circling us, all waiting. All watching.

I swallowed in a dry throat. "Kaa, you want me to go with you?"

Kaa danced near, feathers ruffling on his back.

"Remember, I can't fly unless I get up high."

Kaa dipped his head. He clearly understood me. I walked toward him, and placed my hand on his warm shoulder, the feathers soft beneath my hand. He stilled, and so I leaped up, twirling in the air and landing on his back.

The two gryph people transformed into their gryph shapes, and I noted that their wraps vanished. That was interesting — did their people have magic that the lizardrake people didn't?

In another mighty beating of wings, the gryphs took to the air, Kaa in the center, with me on his back.

All the gryphs shot upward into the brilliant, starry sky, as the lizardrake people danced below us, faces upturned.

The wind scoured me, and my garlands showered petals downward, floating on the air currents. My grass skirt also began shedding, strands floating and writhing as they drifted down. But my beautiful wrap protected me from the wind.

We were off again, flying into the night.

The flock of gryphs flew through thick clouds, preventing me from seeing anything much behind Kaa's purple-feathered head stretched out before me. I clung to his back, dampened in the moisture. I suspect if I'd had time to see Sveran Djur's main island appearing below I might have dropped off Kaa in fright, or tried to take wing in order to fly back to the Hrethan heights.

As it was, we suddenly burst through the gray-bellied clouds into clear air, rendered rosy gold in the slanting rays of the sun rising over the sea behind us. Below, I briefly glimpsed the round, upturned faces of Djuran farmers and silk tree tenders. They halted in their morning chores and watched the vast flock of purple gryphs circling the glowing, fuming mouth of the volcano before descending into the caldera.

Then I saw the churning lava below.

The gryphs' wings thundered as they swooped in and lit all around the rough edge of the caldera. Kaa alone drifted into the stunning heat boiling off the glowing lava, and perched on an outcropping of rock where once before I'd stood.

I slid off his back, and he took off at once, struggling against updrafts of hot air until he cleared. I stood alone on the rock, my hair fluffing all around me, my tail switching back and forth as I tried to shade my eyes against the red-hot lava glow.

Then I forgot the heat, and the Djurans, and everything else as a great head lifted out of the smoky vapors, swung about, and a glowing eye taller than me fixed on me.

Eleven

I STARED AT THE dragon who stared back at me.

In a weird way, I forgot the danger. Or maybe the heat—and the danger—became irrelevant because I seemed to have stepped sideways through a veil more felt than seen into a world outside of time.

From a peculiar mental distance glimmered a worry that I would catch fire, but I could not look away from that great eye, the pupil narrowing to a vertical line like a sword. The strange world-beyond-the-world rippled around me as water ripples.

My body vanished from the regular world, and what remained was memory of my body, because all sense—the smell of hot rock, the tiredness gripping my neck, above all that relentless heat—smoothed to nothingness.

In a vast cavern before me—far larger than one would have thought the mountaintop could hold—the mighty dragon sat, ridged tail curled around so that its spear-sharp tip rested neatly by his front claws. Those claws were huge, patterned in scales like a snake, the fore-toe talon as long as my leg from foot to hip. Rue's pose reminded me of a cat, his body somewhere between snake and lizard, except for the mighty folded-back wings, and the long whiskers waving gently in a way that reminded me of my own hair. His scales were a beautiful pattern of deep red shading to peach color on his belly. The ridged spikes down that long curved neck suggested a mane.

Then he spoke, mind to mind: *Thou heedest me not, little firebird.*

I opened my mouth to explain that I no longer had access to the mental realm, but I couldn't speak.

I didn't have to speak.

My instinctive, fearful grip on the protective wall inside my mind had vanished like smoke. The dragon's thought reached across the limitless space of the mental realm, his presence bright as a sun.

Fear not, little firebird. Fear not.

Why am I here?

Thou hast before thee a choice, came the reply, softly spoken and yet so very deep a note the words seemed to resonate through stone and air as well as the fragile bone of my skull.

Choice? If I could have, I would have gulped in my dry throat somewhere on the other side of the veil: in my experience, nobody ever offers you good choices. Especially after dragging you down a continent and halfway across an ocean.

Thou art ignorant, little firebird, once cast into the world to fly as thou wilt. Thou must learn the world of the seen and the unseen.

And with that flowed images: the world as it was centuries before, some rivers different, even some islands. I recognized the shape of Sveran Djur's main island, but there was no proud, towering Icecrest castle commanding the island from the southernmost peak. Instead, woodland covered the island, overseen by the volcano. Wood covered its slopes.

But the most dramatic difference from the present? The sky. Dragons soared against the azure reach, their coloration mostly shades of crimson, glimmering with bronze and gold highlights, smaller dragons shading from sandy to peach to violet, a few of them a soft gray like vapor. I watched them in heart-lifting delight as they drifted and played, diving in and out of clouds, sometimes in train with brilliantly plumaged gryphs. Lower down twinkled white darting shapes: aidlars.

I don't know how long I remained there. It felt like a few heartbeats, but it might have been days, as I watched Rue's memories of life long ago.

In those early days, dragons and other forms of life co-existed peacefully. Dragons dwelled in and on the mountains, where they clawed down deep to eat the veins of ore that fed their fiery natures. The overturned ground they left provided rich new soil for the plants that provided the seeds and fruits for all the dragons' smaller flying kin.

The dual-natured humans living then co-existed with the dragons. In their human form they largely avoided mountains ice-bound during half the year. Those whose other natures included wings soared over the heights in the mild summers, feasting on the fruits of plants that grew only at those heights. Then they flew down again for harvest time, and withdrew into cozy houses for winter, where they made art and music.

Until, through the world-gate, arrived humans bringing their own arts, including steel.

For making more steel they required ore.

My exhilaration spiraled down into sick apprehension as, from the dragon-eye view, I gained a view of history now obscured in human records, or written as the heroic war against the terrible, evil dragons whose entire purpose appeared to be to exterminate humanity.

Rue's memories made it plain that humans and dragons warred over possession of the world's ore. There was plenty of ore. But the humans wanted it all.

Mages and warriors alike did their best to drive off dragon-kind, and attack those who stubbornly remained in their mountains, especially the ranges formed around volcanoes, for in those mountains could be found not only ore, but rare metals and even gemstones. The dragons required the heat of molten rock for their nests, and ore for sustenance.

One by one they vanished — vanquished. Then, as mages and warriors got better at killing dragons, groups and flocks were either killed or driven to leave the world altogether.

Rue, chosen mate of the queen of dragons, and thus their king, fought the longest and hardest, though he was the prime target — a prize that kings and emperors wished to claim if they could only vanquish him. While he was defending a nest far in the icy reaches up north, an alliance of humans went after the last dragons in the south. The northern dragons used a world gate as a last ditch escape, leaving Rue alone. Receiving a cry for aid from his mate, leading that southern archipelago, Rue took off, flying his fastest.

But he was too late.

The last and most painful image to engrave across my inner eye was the dragon queen, a female of rose-gold, falling amid magical flames, her body pierced with thousands of poisoned spears, to crash into the sea and sink to extinction.

After her death Rue withdrew to his fastness here, and sorrow bound him in the twilight world, sorrow not only over the loss of his mate, but over his own kind, as he was the last.

He was slowly starving himself to stone in his grief, when last winter Kaa called to him from Icecrest, leading the dual-natured in their plea for his aid. Though he had nearly shut out the world as he slowly gave himself up to stone, they were close enough for him to hear, and as their king, to respond with his dwindling strength.

That was when Hlanan risked his life to bring me the spell to break my fais.

Now it was my turn for memory: we all stood on the wind-swept terrace high at Icecrest when Rue suddenly blasted forth from this very mountain, stunning the Djurans as well as myself as he flew overhead. With one hard beat of his wings, he'd shattered all the windows in the emperor's mighty citadel. The shock of that moment helped me gain those few heartbeats of time to make a decision: rather than break my own fais, I slapped the spell against Kaa's fais, which enabled him to break free, using his beak to snap the fais from the others left and right. And finally snapping my own, as I fell toward the sea.

Rue had stayed quiet, sharing my memory. *Thou sacrificed thyself for Kaa.*

That was instinct, not courage, I thought, and I felt a tremor of his laughter through heated stone and rippling air. But it died away, and then came Rue's memory of that day: he heard the gryphs, and he heard me, and broke through the veil for the first time in centuries to come to our aid.

But that, he discovered, was a mistake. He was too weakened to do anything but make a circle around the island and return to his fastness again. He had to regain strength, and began to consume the ore that the mountain had silently been extruding down deep, below human reach, over the intervening centuries.

With the slow accretion of strength came increased awareness, and he sensed—across the veil, distant in the world—the tiny lights of a dragon egg clutch slowly incubating.

I was going to ask how long dragon eggs are supposed to gestate, then thought that human time measure didn't seem to mean anything to a dragon. Also, I was seeing all this history in wordless memory, and time between those worlds was probably even more slippery to measure.

The important thing was, it turned out his mate had laid her clutch safely in another volcano, in that mysterious space just outside of time and the physical world, where humans could not find and kill them. But she had been shot with so many poison darts as she led her pursuers away from them that she could not reach Rue mentally to tell him what she had done. It had taken the last of her strength to fly away from that mountain to drop into the sea.

Now those eggs lay in a mountain whose molten rock surged very deep, the top of the mountain long since covered with snows. But the eggs were very nearly ready to emerge into the physical world, shaking their mountain as the eggs finished growing.

So deep are they that to reach them I must tear open the mountain top, which shall destroy all humankind dwelling below.

Shock radiated through me. "Whoever lives on that mountain, wherever it is, didn't kill any dragons," I said. "I think it's horrible, what happened in the past. I hate that! But... isn't there a way to get the eggs out without murdering a lot of people?"

Rue's head swung around, and once again the great eyes slitted as he regarded me. *And so thou art here, little firebird. I deem there is time yet, before the turn of the sun reacheth winter's short days. Thou art dual-natured. Thou canst treat with humans, and my little Kaa extolls thy deeds on behalf of his flock.*

I began my life in peace with thy kind, and thought to end it in their war. Now with the possibility of my kind born again into the world, I would carry on with peace, but thy kind must begin it. Bring forth safely my beloved's eggs, and I will dwell in peace with all the world.

I stared at Rue, totally bewildered. "How can *I* rescue dragon eggs? What mountain? How can I get there? I know I'm dual-natured, well, sort of. I can't seem to get into my bird form unless I am high up."

Thou hast not yet learned to draw from the sun, Rue's voice resonated with amusement.

"I don't even know what that means," I admitted.

Thou art in part a firebird, knowest thou not?

"A what? I thought you were just calling me that because… well, I don't know why. But I don't know what a firebird even *is,* other than the ones in very old tapestries." I thought of the gold and silver-embroidered forms, usually surrounded by artistically sewn flames.

For answer, Rue gave me mental pictures: my father, young, standing on Icecrest Mountain, facing the sun, arms outstretched.

I protested wordlessly: my father was a Dhes-Andis, though a prince. A mere human. Sveran Djur's empire suppressed dual natures with their magical fais, that much I knew.

The dual nature in thy progenitor is suppressed, but by the constraints of magic. He was born with dual nature from both sides, diminished through his father, but the firebird was once strong in his mother's people.

"The Hrethan fear he has been a bird too long. He cannot be human again," I protested.

They know not his line. Give him the sun, take away the false magical wall, and he may recover his nature. More important now, the fire from his mother's line hath come strongly down to you. Call to it! Use the sun's fire to make your firebird form.

"I don't understand."

I thought I was speaking, but it wasn't until I abruptly found myself again in the withering heat above the molten lava that I truly understood I had regained my ability to hear the unspoken again.

Which meant that Jardis Dhes-Andis could scry me—

Permit not thy fears to do the work of thine enemy.

And abruptly I was... *there* again—standing on the rough stone shelf as smoke and swelter boiled up from the churning molten lava below. My hair lifted, my tail fluffed, my beautiful wrap fluttered, singeing—but I warded the heat by an instinct I now became aware of.

Thy firebird nature absorbs the fire-in-air. Draw it in, and thou canst use it.

With the words came an image of a silver-gilt bird breathing fire.

I stood there at war with myself. My first concern was to shutter my mind safely away again, though Rue's words unsettled me. I was not, not, *not* doing Jardis Dhes-Andis's work for him! The Evil Emperor's villainous intent to snare me by scrying mind to mind was no fault of mine.

Even worse was the reminder that half of my blood was Dhes-Andis. I had been pretending it was not true—a pretense made easier because my father was caught in his bird shape.

It is that part of thee that keepeth thee from burning to ash, little firebird.

Now Rue was definitely laughing at me. Dragon-style. I could feel the rumble of laughter through the stone all around me, and I glanced up, spying countless gryph heads far above, peering down over the rough circle of the caldera, Kaa among them—and I sensed that he had been healed during the time I had been getting my personal tour of dragon history.

Hmm. I did not even *like* heat, especially when I was smothered and swaddled in clothing to disguise my nature. I much preferred snowy weather. Was my dislike an instinctive fear?

All that ran through my mind, water over the rocks of my conviction that just as I never passed up a meal, I never pass up a defense. Again without words, Rue demonstrated what I had instinctively managed as a youth, before my horrible encounter with Dhes-Andis: closing an inner eye to ward the mental realm. But I had assumed that there was no step between, that it was either or until my mother tried to teach me otherwise, but I was too afraid to trust her.

Now, sensing Rue's protective shield, I worked on the wall, then an inner eye.

That is good. Look outward, heed outward, but hold thine own thought inward.

I had to use an image to shape the effort. A wall clearly didn't work, so I pictured a dragon eye inside my mind, and reached outward. There were all the gryphs' minds above, brilliant as fireflies dancing in wildly in the air. Kaa's joy gleamed brightly. Why were they flying about so much?

I couldn't let that distract me. I needed to learn what Rue was teaching me.

For a measureless time I worked on that inner eye, and as I did, I began to perceive Rue's other meanings. My nature — my father's nature — Jardis Dhes-Andis had to have known at least something about this inherited access to magic, or he wouldn't have exerted himself to get hold of me, and then make me practice the fire spell, which I had struggled to confine to a "pinhole" made first with my thumb and forefinger, and then a mentally shaped pinhole.

That spell was a limitation. Did Dhes-Andis know that? Maybe he did, but deliberately kept the knowledge from me to maintain a semblance of control over me until such time as I would become his obedient tool.

I made an effort and pushed those memories aside.

Without all the residual fear and anger, I concentrated better. If I drew directly on light and heat, it flowed through me far more effortlessly than when I had to hold the artificial construct of spells in my mind.

Next step: that same power lay behind the instinctive transformation. I had only been able to accomplish the transformation in the heights, where sunlight was sharper, clearer, and I'd needed the shock of falling for my instinct to break past my mental walls.

Now I understood that I could draw sunlight into me from anywhere. I could even draw starlight, which was sunfire at a distance.

I shut my eyes, and imagined the dragon-eye flicking open from deep within my chest—and squawked in shock as the vapors promptly hurled my bird body skyward. I snapped my wings out and fought against the rising drafts until I hovered above the stone, then transformed to my own shape again. My gryph wrap lay on the stone, beginning to smoke. "No!" I grabbed it up.

Thou must take it with thee when thou art bird.

"Is that what the great gryphs do?" I asked—already knowing the answer. They were taught that from the egg, of course. When you grew up in a family, you learned all their ways, as natural as learning to walk.

The old desolation trickled its dampening chill over the joy of discovery. I had never had a family life, to teach me traditions and day to day skills of dual-natured civilization. Oh, I'd been lucky enough to rediscover my family recently, but none of it felt natural. On the mountain tops I'd strained to be what the Hrethan wanted me to be.

I drew in a steadying breath, opened my inner eye, and this time when I transformed to my bird, I mentally pulled my wrap with my body into the bird. Once again, the hot winds rising off the lava vaulted me upward. But I was ready for it, and dove back down, glad to see no wrap on the barren stone.

I transformed to my human self again, wrap intact. That inward pull—that had to be what Rue meant about drawing light and heat.

I gazed determinedly down at the boiling, churning lava in its bright crimson glow, chunks of black rock floating about in it. I emptied my mind of Dhes-Andis's spells, and mentally pinched at that lava.

A spurt of lava blurped up high above me and promptly began to fall. I hastily danced back before it could splat on my head. I was not about to test how far I could endure heated objects.

At least I'd managed *something*.

Always, when I'd discovered something new, I worked and worked at it until it became easy. That went for picking pockets as well as for leaping and turning three somersaults in the air: the one had kept me alive, and the other had made life worth living.

I don't know how long I stayed there in the hideously hot, vaporously fuming caldera mere paces above boiling lava, practicing my inner eye, but at one point I vaguely noticed stars overhead, and dark shapes flitting back and forth across the sky, briefly blotting the light.

I practiced transforming from bird to human, until I could do it in a blink, and take my clothing with me. Somehow—I still don't understand it—having experienced that veil into wherever Rue was made it easier to understand how, while I was in bird form, some of my unnecessary material self, plus clothing, could slip past the veil, and wait there until I needed them again. And understanding made it possible.

Finally I worked on pulling fire up from the lava. The tough part was getting rid of it. At first I tried through concentration, but if I blinked, or my eyes shifted, I lost control. First splotches of lava, and finally pure flame gouted up, but it sprayed all over, and I had to squinch my eyes shut and clench my fists to stop it.

I remembered Rue's image of the firebird breathing fire, but that didn't help me. My short human nose would only breath fire down to toast my front and toes. I still could not transform into a firebird. All I sensed of that ancestral shape was this bit of its power, so I had to find another way to aim.

Since I had hands, why not use them as guide? That made it exponentially easier. Wherever I pointed, the fire shot with satisfactory gouts. And if I clenched my fist, the mental command to close my fingers functioned as command to end the fire.

After that, I happily shot fire all over the cavern, playing until 1) I discovered that I was gnawingly hungry as well as desperately thirsty, and 2) a vaguely distracting sound resolved into the blaring of horns.

Rue stirred. *Thy kind have gathered without.*

My kind? "Hrethan?"

But I knew as I said/thought it that of course Hrethan would avoid Sveran Djur, and its emperor's intent to force everything, and everyone, under control of his fais. It was over the fais that my parents had run away so long ago, resulting in the cruel spell that would kill my father if the Hrethan ever released him from his transformation to a bird, and resulted in my being lost for all these years.

I peered through the smoke at Rue. "Before I go up there and see what's going on, one last question. Where exactly is the mountain where the eggs are that I am to rescue before New Year's?"

Human names for places meant little to Rue. He had been alive for too many centuries, even if he'd had any interest in the rise and fall of human kingdoms and empires after he retired to his mountain to await death. Instead he gave me a glimpse from above, which I tried to translate into one of Hlanan's beautiful maps in the palace archive.

But the dragon's memory did not correspond with the maps I'd glimpsed a few times while at the palace. I did not have time to puzzle over this before the noise outside once again distracted me.

More to test my newfound skills than anything else, I flashed to my bird self and rode the upward draft until I reached the jagged, rocky lip of the caldera, where the winter previous, Rue had ripped upward from the lava below to take flight across the island. I cleared the rocks and gazed down in surprise and indignation at ranks of Djuran warriors, wearing helms and armor, as they aimed their longbows at the sky.

I turned my eye upward toward the gryphs circling overhead. The Djurans were shooting at the gryphs! I drifted over the edge, furious—and then the rising sun caught with glowing crimson light on the overlapping armored plates of the man who had to be the leader.

Did I know that silhouette? His armor was quite handsome, resembling dragon scales, actually. His helm opened across the eyes, permitting him a wider view than those he commanded, and I spotted a pair of black, slanting brows.

I did know him! That was Most Noble Raifas of Ardam Pennon, who had captured Kaa when young, and forced him into a fais.

Raifas did not appear to spot my small, silver-feathered self in the smoke rising from the crater. I took a fast glance around, and spotted a tumbled slope adjacent to the cliff where he stood. The slope lay in a dimple, protected from the bowmen, who were stationed on rises so they could shoot upward.

I lit on a large, flat boulder, transforming to myself, put my hands around my mouth, and yelled, "Stop that!"

Raifas glanced upward, downward, from side to side — then those dramatically slanted brows tilted even more as his eyes widened.

"Princess Elenderi?" he called. "You *are* alive!"

"Stop shooting at the gryphs," I screeched. "They aren't doing anything to you! That's disgusting!"

He stared at me, then with a quick movement pulled his helmet off. Long, dark waving hair tumbled down over his shoulders as he regarded me, curving lips parted. Then he laughed, turned his head, and raised a gauntleted first to someone on the other side of his cliff. He opened his fingers twice, and a trumpet pealed some chords.

The hiss of arrows climbing skyward halted.

"Why has this army of gryphs been gathered about this mountain for the past three weeks?" Raifas called to me.

"Weeks?" I squawked. I really had lost all sense of time while I'd been with Rue in the dragon world.

"Closer to a month," Raifas amended, as hot winds whipped his long hair into tangles. "Which mountain, I might add, is fuming the same as it did when the dragon attacked last winter. We thought another attack was imminent."

"Attacked?" I repeated incredulously. "That was no attack!"

"What else do you call it? They are still repairing the windows at Icecrest."

As he spoke, Raifas leaped down from rock to rock toward me, pausing to wave off his honor guard, who had climbed with a clatter to flank him.

Giddy from the fumes and from hunger, I stared back, slowly realizing that I was surrounded by Djuran warriors. As yet none had closed in. "If Rue wanted to attack, you would have known it," I said recklessly, then saw in the shifted weapons and exchanges of looks that this might not have been the wisest thing to say at that moment.

But it was the truth. And beyond that, I had my own quest.

Two quests. Besides rescuing Rue's eggs, I still faced the problem of that slinker Darus, who had captured Hlanan. But instinct prompted me to be careful. If the Djurans knew how much Hlanan meant to me, it would be them demanding things, not me.

"If you want to talk, then we'll meet elsewhere," I declared, as my head swam. Now that I was back in my body for a length of time, I was so hungry and thirsty I was becoming more light-headed by the moment. I added with a glare at Raifas's force, "Where there aren't a hundred archers within shooting distance."

He paused in his slow climb toward me, gilt armor glittering as he put his hands on his hips. "I would never shoot you," he exclaimed, his tone amused, but a little indignant, too.

"Then you won't mind meeting somewhere else," I retorted. "Minus the arrows."

"A truce," he called back, hands wide. "On my honor." His brows slanted steeply again as he glanced from me to the top of the caldera behind me. "My home here at Ardam," he suggested, pointing westward. "You know where it lies. Tomorrow? It will take us a day to carry out our retreat."

"Tomorrow morning," I agreed.

I leaped backward, my hair and tail fluffing out, then closing around me in a silver cloud as another gout of smoke swirled around me. I had just enough strength to weave what I had once called a shimmer, that is, an illusion, thickening the smoke enough to obscure my transformation to my bird.

Using the smoke as cover, I drifted safely over the heads of the

Djurans, who looked around in bewilderment. A few watched their commander, and others the sky. No one noticed a small silver bird in the dissipating smoke, and so I sped down the mountain, until I found a stream chuckling its way along a verdant slope. There, I transformed back, drank my fill, then helped myself to wild berries, and nearby, a gleaning of nuts. Then finding a secluded grove, I curled up and slept.

Twelve

LATE ONE NIGHT, ONE of Sig's enforcers was thrust back into Hlanan's cell in the Barrow. She lay where she fell. As soon as the guards were gone, a shadow loomed on Hlanan's left, sensed more than seen. It was Sig.

"Mag," he murmured.

"Don't touch me."

"Let's get you out of range. You know they'll dump the fodder right on you when they show up next."

Mag cursed, but pushed herself to her knees.

"I'll help."

Mag snarled another curse, but allowed Sig to pick her up. She was the smaller of the two women who had worked as a team. She was wiry muscle and bone under Hlanan's now filthy scribe robe, which covered her ruined shirt.

"Where's Trax?" Sig asked.

"She won. Kept her for the next, since half Tastag is on duty at the outer perimeter. She's giving the city a show twice a week." Her voice shivered with pain.

"Did you hear who's rotating in next?" Sig asked as he led her away.

She cursed in answer, weakly pushed at his arm with her hand, and Sig let her go. She grasped her shoulder, hunching in pain as she staggered further inside the cell. Hlanan heard her collapse to the ground with a hiss.

Sig said in a low rumble, "We're for it now."

"Who is 'she'?" Hlanan asked.

Sig's head swung his way, and even in the weak, murky light, Hlanan could see his disbelief. Sig only shook his head, muttered, "A mage oughta know better. No names." He shuffled away, leaving Hlanan alone with Mag.

Hlanan did not waste the time explaining that no one could actually bespell names. That is, not that he had ever learned. "Can I do anything to help you?"

"Nothing broke. Just strains. Leave me be," Mag muttered.

Hlanan moved away. He was so exhausted from sustained magical effort, especially while continually hungry, that sleep was the only remedy. He closed his eyes... and fell into so hard a sleep that it came as a shock when the sudden noise of a full company of guards woke him again.

At first he was certain he had not slept at all, but as his awareness widened, he got that sense that one does that the hour was advanced to that time between night and very early morning, when the world seems most dangerous and uncanny.

The ruddy flare of torchlight jerked the iron bars' shadows across the filthy floor, winking back in oily gleams, before the company fanned out purposefully as someone unlocked the gate.

Warriors with drawn steel clattered in—again, not the rough guards they faced every day, but disciplined warriors wearing those intimidating crested helms.

The prisoners scrambled back, out of the light, but not fast enough before the striding guards. Pale faces above grimy rags stilled, eyes wide enough to reflect the torchlight in twin reddish gold gleams as the guards drove the prisoners back and back, leaving one slight figure alone on the floor, the blind old woman.

Then in walked a tall man with a stride that set his cascade of red braids swinging. He wore a beautifully gilt breastplate above a gold-worked belt with baldea straps dangling from hip to thigh, clattering gently at every step. His fine high boots rang on the slick stone ground as he entered the silent ring of his guardsmen.

He ignored the prisoners, many of whom looked away as his eyes glanced around. Prisoners retreated all the way to the far walls in the deep murk that had never seen any light.

Sure this must be one of the two imperial princes.

The prince knelt down next to the old woman, and to Hlanan's surprise, spoke to her in a variant of what sounded like very old-fashioned Djuran verb forms, though the language was Shinjan: "My beloved aunt, I did my best to protect thee. Thou knowest what occurreth when Mother's will is crossed, and mine own temper riseth."

"Oh, Avejo," the woman sighed.

This could only be Imperial Prince Avejo, son of the Empress of Shinja, Zeltzi.

"I will take thee from here this moment," Avejo said. "I should like nothing better, my heart, soul, and will upon it. But first thou art to use thy wisdom and mercy to talk Invey into listening to me. I know I am right — that my will is Shinja's glory."

Invey! This poor woman had to be his mother, the Kherval-born Princess Luenro, famed for the wealth she had brought on her marriage, and her good works afterward.

"Invey liveth?" Luenro spoke, her voice thin and reedy

"Of course, honored aunt," Avejo said soothingly, gently. "Dost thou verily believe I would stand by to permit mine own brother to be slaughtered?

"But thy will... shalt not lead to Shinja's glory," the princess said, her husky whisper gaining the strength of conviction. "War doth not bring glory but briefly, shored up by blood and more blood, built upon broken promises."

"What promises have I broken?"

"I only know that I must confine my trust to what I hear with my own ears, and not what I am told. Too much falsity hath prevailed; I have taken wishes for deeds. What I know is this. My son is not here, therefore he must be dead."

Avejo said, "I've broken no promise. No hand dareth raise against him."

"And yet I am here."

"Thou art safer here than in the imperial chambers at present. But thou canst influence events: I come myself to see that thou livest, and to promise that I shall faithfully carry thy words to Invey. Time is our greatest enemy. I must have thee, and thy son, oath-sworn at my back that I may freely act for Shinja's glory. I know that, I *trust* that, once thy promise is given, thou art true to it, thou and my brother both. Therefore I come to thee, that thou might impart a message to him, counseling him so."

"Why must I speak?" Her voice was hoarse with effort. "Thou shalt put words of thy desire in my mouth, whatever I say."

"Aunt, thou malignest me! I vow on my brother's and my shared blood I will carry no false word."

"Then carry thou this message: hold fast, my son. Hold true."

Hlanan hitched a little closer, in case he missed the princess's voiceless whisper. It was clear that she had not the strength for more.

A slight shimmer along the stylized golden dragon worked into the breastplate, a ticking of the baldea straps, was all the reaction Avejo revealed.

Then he said, "Thou hast always maintained thou knowest little of imperial policy, and this be not the place for discussion of high matters. Thou, beloved and respected aunt, art revered for thy generosity and serenity, far above such strivings. Why wilt thou not extend that generosity to me, and permit me to carry thy wisdom and encouragement to thy son, that we three might unite?"

"Thou knowest my son's vows," she whispered, her consonants sharp and clear with her conviction. "Thou wert adamant in support of his remaining outside of imperial concerns, confined only to his studies. He hath remained true to his vows, and it would be false in me to stir him from them now."

"In peaceful times, I would laud such convictions. But now, in time of need..."

"Now is when he must needs cleave strongest to his vows," she breathed.

Avejo rose to his feet. "I desire thee to understand my grief at thy decision, honored aunt. I say no more here, except to observe that it be strength of will as well as power that shall save this our empire, and that means not flinching at whatever demands it maketh." He then abandoned the formal court form, and said in universal Shinjan, "If you change your mind, you've only to speak. The guards will remove you at once."

He wheeled about, pausing mid-step as something caught his eye: Darus.

Avejo stood there, limned by torchlight, as he studied the Djuran—who, with his four guards, took care over their appearances, unlike everyone else. And though all the prisoners had withdrawn, looking away, only the Djurans and Hlanan kept their places, Darus standing straight and tall, his manner challenging. Hlanan sat in his corner, easily overlooked.

Avejo uttered a soft laugh, no more than an exhaled breath, then exited, the guards closing in behind him in precise reverse order. The gate clanged shut, and boot heels clattered away, not in the usual lazy gait, but in precise rhythm. They took the light with them, until darkness and silence fell once again.

Then the whispers broke out.

"Did you see that? *He* was here!"

"What did he say?"

"That was Dragon Language, empty-skull. If you understood a word of it, then they'll garrote you for presumption."

"Better that than the flogging post in the arena, before our entire company, road-offal."

"Shut yer yaps." That was Sig. "Want 'em back in here?"

A volley of curses was the response, but the voices dropped to whispers, and Hlanan rose to move to Luenro's side.

"I am the healer mage student," he murmured. "What can I do for you?"

Princess Luenro muttered deliriously, "I must survive... I must aid my son."

Hlanan knew she needed food and water, especially the latter. But he had no cup.

He moved to the trough, which dribbled with clean water, thanks to his spell work, but when he tried to dip his hands in, the thin runnel only wetted his fingers. So he muttered the cleaning spell over his shirt, then dipped a sleeve into the water. When it was sodden, he carried it quickly into the darkness where the princess lay. He performed all this aware of watching eyes. No one interfered, though, as he knelt down.

"I am sorry, but you need water, and this is the only way I can get it to you."

She touched the sleeve, and he felt more than saw the slight dip of her chin in acknowledgement. He wrung the sleeve between his hands, and water dripped into her parted lips.

It took four trips before she whispered, "Enough. That is good. I shall sleep, and then try to rise on my own."

Hlanan put his shirt back on, grimacing at the wet sleeve. At least it was no longer grimy — though he knew as soon as he lay down that would change. And just as well. He did not want to risk having the only clean cloth in the entire cell, when next the guards returned.

———⊰●⊱———

Another tremor shook the castle, not as strong as the first, but lasting far longer, so long that Hlanan felt unsteady for a time after it subsided. A little like he felt when he first stepped onto land after a sea voyage.

The next morning, when the guards returned with the wheelbarrow of food, they dumped it and then pulled their weapons with the shivery sound of sliding steel. One group stood shoulder to shoulder across the doorway, as usual. The rest, instead of crowding behind them and making loud comments, entered with knobbed truncheons gripped in their gauntleted hands. They advanced on the Djurans to surround them, weapons raised in expectation.

Darus glanced from side to side, stiff with tension. He might not know the language, but he could see as well as anyone else how very much those guards looked for the slightest excuse to attack the hated Djurans. Apparently deciding that trying to remain in the disgusting cell did not accord with his sense of honor, Darus walked stiffly toward the door, followed by his guards in formation.

The Shinjan guards uttered coarse comments, laughed raucously, and the last of them whacked one of the Djurans as he passed through the door.

They locked the door with a hard clang, and withdrew, leaving silence.

The prisoners waited for Hlanan. When he had done his spell over the food, he took a small helping of greens and half a roast potato for Luenro. He crammed the bread heel that he'd picked for himself into his mouth and took her share to the former empress-consort.

True to her word, she sat up. She took the meager offering on both her palms, as if receiving a gift. With equal dignity she nibbled slowly, and then struggled to her feet.

At that, several people sprang forward. She put out a hand, touching those nearest her, and finding another woman, closed her thin fingers on the woman's thick, scarred wrist. She whispered softly as the big woman guided her to her feet. Luenro followed the former guard to the water trough. This woman, who had stayed in the background until now, murmured in soft tones, as though speaking to an infant, or an invalid.

Hlanan retreated, considering the change in atmosphere: whatever had brought all these people so low, they seemed to exclude the princess from their ire.

Hlanan glanced toward the space previously occupied by Darus and his Djurans, as had become habit, and noticed it was empty. He returned to his own space, with the prospect of a long, dreary day stretching ahead of him. He'd always resented the Djuran exercises—thought them pointless—but as he stood there, he considered how much stronger he felt. He would never be able to do anything with weapons, but if called upon for movement, he could do that. He might even be able to run.

Could he? With nothing else to do, he tried to remember the sequence of exercises. His muscles had become accustomed to the routine, and he worked through with only a pause or two, then he began walking swiftly back and forth along the bars, from the Djurans' old spot to his own, back and forth until he was panting and sweaty, but no longer trembling with exhaustion.

He paused, as did everyone, at the sudden eruption of distant shouts. A susurrus of whispered speculation rustled through his fellow prisoners, then subsided eventually: they could all ask questions of one another, but no one had answers.

Late in the day a rainstorm swept through, gushing water through the grate. This time, Sig moved to the princess, bowing in soldier fashion, fist to his heart. Princess Luenro was offered first chance at soaking herself. The tall warrior woman guided her to the grate, where she stood, blind eyes staring upward, as rain cascaded over her, but she did not stay long.

In silence the others shuffled through. The truce, such as it was, seemed to be holding.

Thirteen

I WOKE UP TO Tir hopping back and forth along a branch over my head, ruby eye cocked toward me. As I stirred, a weight on my wrap brought my attention down to two sprays of grapes and a handful of berries.

"Tir," I said happily. "You found me!"

It took an effort, but I opened the inner eye again, and in flooded Tir's thoughts, in images of course: flying with other aidlars to the island, avoiding the shooters and the fire mountain. The heat was too much for small birds. Even the gryphs had stayed at a prudent distance.

Memory returned, and with it my agreement to meet Raifas.

I grimaced. I'd liked him well enough—for a Djuran noble. But he was also a loyal and dedicated part of Sveran Djur's command structure, and he'd been cheerfully planning to invade the island of Ndai the way someone else might plan a treasure hunt for a party.

I would rather avoid him—I didn't trust him—but I also remembered my promise to Rue. I had promised to save those eggs. I also wanted to prevent a massacre of hapless human populace below the volcano where the eggs lay, wherever it was.

And I had to find Hlanan! Maybe Raifas would know where Darus was, and therefore Hlanan.

It was time to find out.

I had lain down near a little waterfall that filled a pool. When I sat up, the smell of smoke rising from my hair and clothes nearly choked me. I dove straight into the water, wrap and all, and swam about until I felt clean.

The fabric of the great gryph wrap was made of some thin, soft thread, warp in deep violet and weft in ruddy brown, so it shimmered with rich color in the light. It was easily wrung out so that the material was merely damp when I spread it over a rock in the morning sunlight. By the time I'd fluffed the water from hair and tail, the wrap was dry enough to fling around me again.

As I shut my eyes and reached mentally for Tir, I couldn't prevent an inward cringe, but nothing terrible happened. I asked mentally where Tir found the berries, and the aidlar hopped back and forth on a branch, giving me images that promised a short flight.

In the light of a new day, everything I had experienced in Mount Dragon seemed dreamlike, the world beyond the veil unreal. I tried to suppress doubt, exerted that newly-learned inward pull...

And I flitted skyward in my bird self, the wrap gone in the space between worlds.

After scavenging breakfast for us both, Tir led me upward until I spotted the town of Ardam set above a great, curving harbor, the bulk of Mount Dragon rising at the town's eastern end.

A three-towered castle, built on a high cliff, commanded the town and the harbor below. I remembered the tallest tower over the gate, the two at the back corners of the square walls being shorter. I was relieved to see that the town was mostly unharmed, though some walls had cracked from the explosion when Rue first flew out last winter. The lava flow, now hardened, had been confined to valleys between mountain slopes. Spring growth was already blurring a lot of it, the burned area laved by snowmelt and summer rains.

I drifted down and landed in the castle's broad central square, to be greeted by a gray-clad servant who had obviously been hovering about. He led me past the magnificent indoor tree, and upstairs to the elegant room I remembered, with the enormous lancet windows all around. I was glad to see the ones facing the sea open to the summer air, if I had to make a quick exit.

I turned from them to Raifas, who studied me with an amused quirk to his curved lips, deep sardonic dimples at each corner. He was dressed in pale blue, with a long, sleeveless garment of burnt umber silk worn over it, the front folded back to resemble the stole that was part of Djuran fashion. It was embroidered with dragonflies and leaping dolphins in shades of gold and blue.

I remembered that embroidery had hidden meanings, but I couldn't recollect what dragonflies and dolphins indicated, and anyway, he was gesturing for the servant to pour out what smelled like a delicious concoction of citrus and berry juices.

"Already securing your lines of retreat?" he said.

"Wouldn't you?" I retorted.

"Only from enemies."

"Exactly."

"I'm wounded." He pressed a hand to his heart, and gave me a look of mock sorrow. Then his expression smoothed. "I am not your enemy, Elenderi."

"Less lip-flapping and more action will convince me of that," I said, arms crossed, my hair and tail clouding around me, the ends snapping. "So far, the flights of arrows aren't exactly convincing."

"When half Ardam-town ran to hide in their houses, and the other half halted work to watch what appeared to be an armada of great gryphs coming down toward the very mountain that—in recent memory—exploded, raining us with flaming debris, as a dragon emerged to shatter every pane of glass... they might be excused from coming to me to defend them against attack."

"But Rue didn't attack."

"How were we supposed to know that? From our perspective, hundreds of wild great gryphs filled the sky above that mountain. What else were we to think but that they were doing their best to draw that dragon out again? Of course we did our best to drive them off."

"All right," I said. "I guess I can see how frightening that was, considering the fact that none of you have ever tried to communi-cate with the gryphs, just enslave them." And when he let out a sigh, I added, "I hope nobody was hurt. I mean when Rue first came out. The town looks fine from above, but I saw all that lava."

""It was winter, so everyone was either in their houses, or on board ship in the harbor. The damage was all external. Though we did have to send in the mages to heat the houses as pretty much every window shattered."

"I'm sorry for that," I said. Much as I disliked most of the Djuran nobles, who called themselves the Chosen, I had no quarrel with ordinary people. The ones I'd been permitted to meet had been friendly, curious, but not cruel. Unlike many of their nobles.

Raifas looked as if he was going to say something, then his gaze shifted and he lifted a hand toward the low table. "I took the liberty of ordering breakfast," he said. "Remembering that you don't touch meat, but you were fond of our local goat cheese, I asked for cheese tartlets, and…ah. I see you are still fond of them."

I already had one crammed in my mouth as I dropped down cross-legged opposite him. He sat neatly, disposing his outer robe over his knees so it was not crumpled. His golden fais glinted below the hollow of his throat in the open neck of his shirt.

I resisted the impulse to scrabble at my throat to make sure no fais had snaked up to strangle me. At least the impulse was faint now, more habit than compulsion. But it was still there.

Pain will do that.

I picked up another tart. I wasn't all that hungry, but long habit prompted me to make the most of any meal I came across.

"Talk to me, Elenderi," Raifas said.

"About?" I countered, trying to figure out the best way to sidle the subject toward Hlanan. The problem being, never in my life have I ever been subtle.

Raifas held up a palm. "We can begin with this dragon you apparently called upon to attack us last winter."

"I didn't call upon Rue to attack anybody. And he *didn't attack*."

"So blasting out all the windows from Ardam to Icecrest Palace was an accident?"

"No," I said, swallowed the last of the tart, and wiped my

fingers daintily on the napkin beside my plate before I said, "I suspect it was a warning."

"About?"

"Well, let's talk about that day. You were there. You saw me trying to get your emperor to stop making slaves of the people and creatures of Sveran Djur. Rue appeared right around the time I freed Kaa—the great gryph you called Firebird—who was killing himself trying to get that fais off."

Raifas recoiled slightly, his upper lip lengthening with disgust. "We do not keep slaves. That is a Shinjan custom. Quite barbaric."

I snorted so hard my sinuses burned. His lips parted as he gazed at me. "Elenderi. We do *not* keep slaves."

"What do you call it when you Chosen—and especially your emperor—can torture anyone who doesn't instantly leap to obey, or who dares to disagree?"

"Torture? I don't believe that."

"Raifas, your emperor tortured *me*. But if you think I'm lying about that, then let's talk about the gryphs and firedrakes *you* kept enslaved."

"You cannot enslave animals," Raifas said. "We train them."

I hesitated, unsure whether or not to trust him with the truth about the dual-natured. His own raptor self was an almost-discernable shadow, and I was convinced he was unaware of it.

"It's slavery to them," I stated finally.

"Then what do you call it when they are content? As is Andisla, the emperor's own great gryph?"

"Some slaves settle for slavery, not knowing anything else," I said. "I don't think that makes it less slavery."

"I," he stated, "do not think it's slavery at all. But we must agree to disagree, or we will forever argue this point, and I wish to return to the dragon you say did not attack us. Are you trying to claim that dragons were—are—not the natural enemies of humans?"

"What are 'natural' enemies?" I asked.

"Do you really desire a philosophical discussion?"

"How about a simple one?" I countered, my tail sweeping back and forth behind me, my hair swirling around me as I fought to keep my temper in check. In spite of my night of sleep, I was still tired from my training time in the mysterious dragon world.

Raifas blinked at me as though distracted, frowned, then said, "Simply put, dragons traditionally killed us on sight, and we them." His slanted brows soared steeply.

"*Why* is that?" I asked.

He opened his hands. "It's the way it's always been."

"According to whom?" I asked, and then shook my head. "Never mind. You've obviously been taught that dragons are evil, just as you've been taught that torture by fais isn't torture. The thing that surprises me, considering that you insist that dragons are *natural enemies,* is how many dragons are painted all over in the royal palace, and embroidered on people's clothes."

"Dragons were an honored foe," Raifas said with the calm of complete conviction. "A worthy foe. We admire the grace and power of a beautiful and deadly enemy. Like raptors. The great felines. We respect their physical prowess and power, even if their minds are simple."

"I suspect humans are 'simply' more treacherous," I said, and when he looked at me askance, I dropped my third pastry and crossed my arms. "Would you believe me if I told you that from the dragons' viewpoint, all beings, including humans, lived in amity in the world until another branch of humans arrived from another world armed with steel — and fought the dragons over ore, because humans wanted it all for themselves?"

"What would dragons do with ore?" Raifas retorted. "I have never heard of dragons with swords."

"They eat it."

He laughed. "They eat humans, little Hrethan."

I briefly shut my eyes. Rue, are you listening?

Some of us fought with teeth, but we would never swallow such. I caught a memory of a squished human warrior that I wished I hadn't seen — though the human had been doing his best to skewer the dragon first. With the awful image I felt a tremor of disgust from Rue.

I said to Raifas, "Their teeth were their defense, as were their claws and their fire. The metal in ore makes their fire, not flesh. Ore also contributes to their scales."

Raifas tipped his head slightly, looking uncertain, then his expression smoothed out. "I gather that dragon told you that?"

"I saw it in his memory," I said.

His brows shot upward again.

"He's been around for a very long time," I added. "Centuries."

Raifas flexed his fingers, his eyes half shut, as though he were trying to remember something. Or he was being scryed? But then he sat back, as if settling in for a long chat. "So, what does this centuries-old dragon seem to want from you? Or do you want from him? Because you are *here*." He flung his hands out wide in a mocking gesture, his hands well-made, the loose sleeves of his shirt rippling over powerfully shaped arms. "After months of avoiding return to your birthplace."

Complete lies have to be remembered. Sticking to the truth is so much easier. But you don't have to tell it all. I'd liked few Djurans during my imprisonment in Icecrest Palace, and trusted fewer. Raifas was in the first group, but not the second—and handing someone you don't trust all your truths is handing them a weapon.

So I said, "Rue woke up when the great gryphs called for help, that day on the terrace. Kaa is, oh, like one of you Chosen, and the other gryphs didn't want him to claw himself to death."

"All right, I'll accept that. Provisionally. Their behavior that day, cutting the fais from one another, seems evidential, even if it's merely instinct and not an act of will." Raifas rested his hands on his knees, and sat back on his cushion, the golden fais glinting at his throat. "So we come to now. The few great gryphs we have remaining show no disposition to leave. We've not been successful in catching any wild ones since. Our young are the ones born here, what we call the egg-civilized. So what was the purpose of your recent arrival with what appeared to be an invasion fleet of wild great gryphs?"

"They wanted me to meet Rue," I said—with a generous

stretching of the truth. But it was not quite a lie.

"And so you reappeared with a squadron of great gryphs, wild creatures none of the rest of us can come near without weapons to protect us." Raifas leaned back, smiling. His gaze traveled over my silver hair, down the midnight blue wrap, and then he said, "I strongly suspect if we were to marry I would never be bored."

"But how about me?" I countered indignantly.

His lips parted, and a breath escaped, half-laugh, as he acknowledged my insult. I liked him more than I ever had in that moment—it wasn't just that he was handsome, which I could enjoy. Attraction sparked when he laughed. "Oh, I trust I could find ways to keep you entertained," he said, stretching out a hand toward my hair, palm up.

His words might have been mere male brag. I didn't have the experience to know. When others were getting their experience in the dance of courtship, I was wearing a layer of stable droppings and old cheese to keep people at a safe distance in order to hide my secrets.

And yet, inexperienced as I was, I understood his gesture to be entreaty, not demand. So I flexed my hair, letting a lock draw across his palm.

His brows shot upwards. "It feels as soft as down," he said.

"It *is* down."

The last strands snapped away, and his gaze rose to meet mine, and once again I saw invitation. Not demand. The shivery heat of attraction fluoresced through me, but even if I was ready to act on it, which I wasn't until Hlanan and I came to some under-standing, I had to be friends first. I didn't trust him enough for friendship.

I said, "Are you now satisfied that nobody is attacking you, so you can leave the great gryphs alone?"

Raifas hesitated, and once again I suspected he was going to say one thing, then changed his mind. "That's not my decision to make."

The door opened, and Jardis Dhes-Andis, emperor of Sveran Djur, walked in.

Oh yes, Raifas had been scryed.

I let out a strangled squawk and leaped toward the window.

"Truce, Elenderi," the emperor said, raising a hand.

Naturally I didn't believe him, and naturally he knew I wouldn't; as I reached the window and drew a breath to hurl myself out and transform to my bird, he said, "Note the archers."

I froze against the windowsill, my hair and tail floofing around me as I stared wildly out. Imperial guards, in full armor, on the two towers east, along the walls, and even stationed on the slope to the north: I stared across the intervening distance at a woman with an arrow notched to her bow. She gazed with determination straight at me.

I whirled around, then watched in amazement as Raifas flashed a rueful grin, and said to me, "We had a wager going, how fast you'd fling yourself through the nearest window."

"Well, who wouldn't?" I snarled, scowling at them both.

Raifas chuckled. The emperor narrowed those slanted light brown eyes the same color and shape as my own, his face framed by a smooth, long fall of shining blue-black hair.

He walked in, dressed differently than I'd seen him. Instead of the usual complication of imperial robes, or the stark black and white of the shirt and trousers he dueled in, he wore shirt and trousers of black, and over that a long robe of a rich brown embroidered with gold geometric patterns and sprays of kings-blossom in strands of three. The robe's high collar framed the glint of the diamond-studded fais at his throat.

Raifas gracefully performed the imperial bow.

Since I wore no fais to be tortured by, I stood where I was, arms crossed and knees locked, but my heart banged frantically against my ribs. Bad manners or not, I refused to bow to him.

The emperor made a gesture, inviting Raifas to sit in his own castle. I remained by the window, my hair clouding up and around me, outer reflection of the irritation I did not try to hide, and the fear that I did.

"The great gryphs are *not* making war," I stated stonily.

"I did not think they were," Jardis Dhes-Andis retorted as he sat down gracefully at the head of the table, Raifas at his right.

A silent servant swiftly removed our breakfast things, and another soundlessly replaced those with fresh food and drink, all of which Jardis ignored with the disinterest of one who has always had plenty of the best to eat and drink whenever he wished.

"What," he said, "would be the point? Unless they enjoy target practice on humans?"

"The way some human do with birds?" I snapped back.

He lifted a dismissive hand: obviously *he'd* never wasted his time this way, but he didn't care if others indulged in this sport.

"What I wish to know is what they're doing here," he said. "We've seen them gathered in hundreds around the mountain for weeks. The Am-Jalads of both pennons were convinced that they were attempting to draw out the dragon for another attack, as Raifas I am certain explained."

So he hadn't scryed my entire conversation with Raifas. Or was that what he wanted me to think? I had learned the hard way that he was extremely adept with his scry stone.

"Rue didn't attack," I repeated. "He flew overhead as a warning. I think, if he'd wanted to attack, there'd be nothing left of your palace."

The emperor's eyes narrowed, then he said, "I told you when we first attempted your tutoring that Mount Dragon is a place of power, though imperfectly understood. It appears that you have been selected to be the recipient of information denied the rest of us. We had not even known that a dragon lay in residence."

The suspicion in both men's faces hadn't eased. But I was wrong to assume that they thought the same: Raifas was a warrior and a commander. He thought in terms of attack and defense. Jardis Dhes-Andis was also a warrior—I'd been a reluctant witness when he beat that horrible Darus to his knees using their wicked dueling sticks—but he was above all a very powerful mage. One who made long plans.

He turned that narrow-eyed assessment onto me. "Did you learn these secrets while you were in residence at Icecrest?"

"No," I said. "I was as surprised as you were when Rue burst out of the mountain."

"But you are acquainted now."

My instinct was to try to hide even that, but of course it was too late. Anyway, perhaps if he thought I had a dragon as my ally, he'd leave me be. "We are," I said.

"Does this dragon communicate with words? I wonder how that is possible with such a jaw and teeth."

"It's… more like scrying, rather than speaking. But yes. Words. He's very wise, as well as old."

Then Jardis Dhes-Andis surprised me. "Excellent." He gave me a short nod, and I sensed that this was a negotiation, that we had left behind commander and unwilling prisoner. In other words, a modicum of respect. "I want to meet that dragon," he said. "Face to face. In return, I will give you anything you wish. That I am able to provide," he added with mordant almost-humor.

I caught myself before exclaiming, "Hlanan!"

I needed to know if he was even here, first. And if the emperor had sent Darus to nab him. I also knew that Jardis Dhes-Andis was more far experienced at forcing people to his will than I. If they held Hlanan, and they knew how important he was to me, there wouldn't be any trade. There'd be more demands.

So I set Hlanan's situation aside, impatient as I was for information, and reached for another important issue, my father. Jardis did not hold *him* prisoner.

"Excellent," I said, mimicking him. "The previous emperor laid a horrible spell on my father, and the Hrethan transformed him into bird shape to save his life. That spell is still on him, all these years later. I want that spell removed. If that happens, I will ask Rue to meet you."

In the time I'd been the emperor's prisoner, I had been forced to learn every subtle change of Jardis Dhes-Andis's expression. When his mouth tightened, or his pupils dilated, excruciating pain usually struck in the next heartbeat. I stilled myself, willing away the heat of remembered pain, and the bracing of my body to endure it. I was no longer his prisoner—I was now a firebird's descendant, and not dependent on Jardis Dhes-Andis's whim.

His expression hardened, and my heartbeat thumped frantically, but I stood my ground.

Then he said, "It has been many years. Your father cannot resume human shape. No human can, when forced into transformation that long." His calm tone made it clear that he was completely satisfied to have it so.

"Nevertheless," I said, thinking of my father listening intently to music, and commenting through my mother. No real birds paid the least attention to our music. But again, I was not going to give the emperor any facts he didn't already possess, because I knew he'd use them as a weapon against me. "That's what I want."

His eyes narrowed to a considering look, as if he wondered what I hid. But then his expression smoothed. I did not dare listen to him on the mental plane. He was a master scryer, and he'd know I was there. But I sensed that he was confident that anyone forced into bird form for that many years would in effect remain a bird, even in human form. Therefore no threat to him.

"Very well," he said. "When you assure me that I shall meet this dragon, then I will remove the death-ward on Prince Danis."

Fury ripped through me like lightning at this acknowledgement that he did know the deadly magic his father had set up. That he could have removed it at any time after the death of the former emperor. But I struggled against showing it. I didn't want to reveal anything that could be used against me, including how much this meant to me.

"Meet," I repeated. "Not attack."

He looked askance. "Attack the only dragon left in the world? What a waste that would be." Just as I'd learned all the subtle changes of his expression, I knew all the shades of his voice, and sincerity rang in his words. "Meet."

"Done."

He then said, "My last question concerns the Most Noble Darus Bas Veremi. Where is he?"

"*Darus?*" I repeated, making no effort to hide my surprise — or my loathing. I bit back an exclamation *That's what I want to know from you!* And told the truth: "I haven't seen that rot-crawler since

I left Icecrest. A fact that I've rejoiced in every day since!"

I waited for the gloating threat about Hlanan, but the emperor just gave me a skeptical glance, and seemed more perplexed than angry. "And yet he left a formal letter stating that he wished to restore his honor by returning you to your birthplace. And sailed forth to Charas al Kherval to accomplish it."

All right, so that much connected with what Thianra had said. But... where was he now? And Hlanan?

"If that doesn't sound *just like* him," I exclaimed in disgust. "Trying to take me prisoner because *he's* the one who ruined himself by trying to get me killed. What a rotten thing to do!" And again I waited for mention of Hlanan.

The emperor turned to Raifas. "I believe you may be correct. We will discuss this further on your return to Icecrest."

What?

Raifas rose and bowed, as Jardis Dhes-Andis also rose. He flicked a glance my way. "I await your further communication about that dragon." Then something glinted in his fingers—a transfer token—and he vanished.

A puff of air blew about the room. He was gone; I glanced out the window, and saw the raised bows lower, and the imperial guards begin to retreat down the mountain, leaving Raifas's people on their regular patrol route.

I let out a breath of relief.

Raifas laughed. "You did not believe the words of truce?"

"No."

Raifas gave his head a shake. "My cousin may be many things, but a liar is not one of them. He seems to want to meet your dragon. Arrange that, and I expect he will let you go your own way, since you so plainly reject your Djuran rank and heritage." He held out his hands, palms out.

"I don't, really," I said. "It's still new to me. What I reject is being controlled by a fais. And being ordered around by *him*."

Raifas's white teeth flashed as he uttered a soft laugh. "That, I'm afraid, is the nature of emperors the world over."

"I know. I don't trust any of them," I said, remembering that

Hlanan's mother, Aranu Crown, had been the one to hand me off to Jardis Dhes-Andis. Oh yes, she'd explained, and I even understood the decision she'd been forced into. But I didn't have to like it. Or trust her.

To get away from the subject of emperors, I decided it was time to get some information for my secret mission from Rue. And here was one of Jardis Dhes-Andis's naval commanders. "Do you have maps?" I asked. "I think I saw one here before, didn't I?"

"I do indeed," Raifas said. "What map have you an interest in, Elenderi?"

His voice was tolerant, amused — as if expecting further entertainment. That was fine. I didn't care what he thought of me. Though my quest to find Hlanan had just set me back to the very beginning, there was still my new quest, and I meant to see to both.

To locate Rue's dragon eggs, I needed to match the land Rue had shown me with a map. If I was to protect whatever innocent humans lived below that volcano, I'd better bustle at locating it and discovering some way to get those eggs to safety.

Raifas stepped to the door and spoke to someone, and shortly after, one of his liveried servants returned with an armload of rolled paper.

One by one Raifas opened maps as I looked them over, shaking my head again and again. Until at last he unrolled an old, crackling map. There, beautifully drawn, was the same shape that I had seen in Rue's memory while flying overhead.

And when I looked at the neatly lettered label, I gulped.

That volcano lay smack in the middle of the mainland of another empire, one with an even worse reputation than that of Sveran Djur: Shinja.

Now what?

I'd been thinking I could fly somewhere, maybe with the gryphs, to find the eggs, then get back to my search for Hlanan. But... Shinja? I didn't want to go *there*. And I certainly didn't care what happened to a lot of evil Shinjans! I'd had a few close calls with them, all horrible, and I knew that Hlanan and Ilyan Rajanas had been forced into slavery as small boys. Who cared if their volcano exploded? That might give them something to do besides try to grab innocent people and make them slaves.

"Have you seen what you wanted to see?" Raifas asked, his tone odd.

I glanced up, to see him watching me closely.

"Yes." I pushed away the map.

Raifas said, in that same tone, "Then in my turn, I have a question for you."

"What?" I squawked, instantly suspicious. "I thought we were done."

But Raifas wasn't thinking of dragons or eggs. He said, "Darus departed on the eastern waters, which fall to me to defend. It's my duty to discover what happened to him and his company. Elenderi, you must understand that this question could lead to war."

"War?" Where did *that* come from? Surely they did not know who Hlanan was! "Why? With whom?"

"Possibly with the Kherval—which is where we knew Darus was seen last. Our ambassador at Erev-li-Erval is quite definite about that. Darus walked on land once, one of the ambassador's servants taking him within the palace itself."

"So Darus was in the royal palace?"

"So our ambassador insisted. He was seeking your scribe. The one who risked his life in a storm, and being taken by our island patrol, just to bring you a letter—" Raifas broke off to watch me narrowly again.

I stared at him in growing horror. "Spit it out."

"There's the troubling news of the burnt remains of a ship fashioned in our style, within the limits of our territorial waters, and one of my patrols had spotted Shinjans prowling the area—"

Sick with worry, I interrupted. I had to know for sure if Darus really had taken Hlanan. "So Darus might have left Erev-li-Erval? Say, with a prisoner, if that prisoner wouldn't say where I was?"

"Quite possibly. He might have been bringing your scribe back to the emperor, in default of better intelligence about your location."

"And he got attacked? By Shinjans?"

"Again, possibly. I need more proof before bringing this report before the emperor, as the result is almost certainly going to bring about a war. But that's my concern. My question is, is that scribe one of your pets? I remember Darus thought so, though Cousin Jardis scorned the notion."

Pets, I remembered, was the Djuran idiom for flirts and lovers below your rank, therefore not to be taken seriously. Kal, my head servant during my imprisonment, had been half-brother to Jardis Dhes-Andis—his mother a servant, one of the previous emperor's pets. So Kal's life was constrained to service. And that wasn't the very definition of slavery?

The attraction, and the friendship, that I had felt for Raifas vanished like smoke.

He went on in a gently chiding voice, "...that scrawny idiot who could scarcely put two words together in our language. Really, Elenderi, you can do better than that."

Shipwreck—captured—galley slaves—didn't they kill anyone with their slave tattoo still on them? Hlanan still had his!

"There *is* no 'better'!" I scowled at Raifas in exploding fury, tears scalding my eyes. "You're *stupid*."

And I threw myself out the window.

Fourteen

ANOTHER SUMMER STORM TUMBLED and towered over Mount Dragon, but no storm could be stronger than the one inside me. I landed as my human self and flung myself onto long summer grasses, weeping and raging.

First against Raifas, and his superior assumption, *You can do better*. Of course Hlanan had been very careful to present a lowly, harmless scribe to the world, but just the same, I excoriated that world for its value of hierarchy, power, rank—all the things I had the least respect for.

Raifas was my target until I'd exhausted the first wave of tears, and then it was the Shinjans. Evil Shinja, the empire that had forced Hlanan into slavery when he was small. At worst he was dead, and at best, if Shinjan slavers had really taken that yacht, Hlanan would have been thrown back into gallery slavery. But not if they found his tattoo from those early years! They *always* put to death escaped slaves.

The thought of that sent me wailing afresh, until my head ached as much as my heart. I managed to thoroughly exhaust myself—and I was still no closer to a solution.

But there was a dragon to ask. I shut my eyes, mentally building a thick wall between me and Jardis Dhes-Andis, but before I reached for Rue, I remembered his telling me that all humans were pretty much the same to him. I didn't know if Hlanan would regard a mental contact—assuming I could manage it—as a trespass.

Of course thou canst. Regard not distance in the realm of thought as the same as that we fly.

So Rue was still listening, a quiet presence at the back of my mind. I could wall him off, I knew, but I didn't feel the need.

I readied myself, aware of tension, even trembling. I knew why. What if I couldn't find Hlanan — what if he was dead? When I didn't know where he was, there was always the chance of finding him. The terrible news I'd heard from Raifas pretty much destroyed that hope.

But I had to know.

So I closed my eyes, readying myself the way Rue had taught me. And brought Hlanan before my mind's eye.

And there he was, but lost in a tumble of horrific emotion, his thoughts like scattered bits of something that had been ripped apart. Disturbing images — a dark cell, hunger, an old woman's blind face — and then there was my face in memory, and his mind turned toward it, his hand reaching, reaching, but I drifted away —

This was a dream.

I pulled away, my head throbbing anew. The emotions had been loud as thunder, nearly unbearable. When the echoes of his unhappiness faded, joy welled up inside me: he was alive. And in a prison somewhere. I thought back, damping the effect of his emotions as I considered the jumble of languages running through that dream: Elras and also Shinjan.

Was it possible he was there, in Shinja? But it was an empire, like the Kherval, which covered much of the continent above Meshrec, and Sveran Djur, which was an empire of hundreds of islands, and some territory on other continents. Shinja lay far over the ocean, on the other side of the world, too big to be an island, not quite a continent. It ruled all the islands around it, and the coast of another continent, though I vaguely remembered some gossip about some sort of revolt not long ago.

I transformed to my bird and took to the sky to think. As I soared upwards, I looked down through the large splats of rain toward the harbor, where a burst of activity was taking place.

Curious, I drifted down closer. Three ships were being readied.

Not the big war ships, or fat-bellied trade ships but smaller, faster ones. Scouts.

I drifted closer, flying among the seabirds wheeling through the sky as workers rolled barrels over the ramp onto a ship tied to the dock. Their voices sounded like barks from above, but I caught the word *Shinja*, and then a man spat over the side.

A gray-haired woman in warrior garb, who had to be a captain, put her fists on her hips. "Less talk, Nal! Unless you'd like to carry your opinions about Shinja to the Most Noble?"

"No, Captain, no."

This expedition had to be going after Darus. Raifas had probably given the orders as soon as I flew out of the window of his tower. But I still didn't know if Darus and Hlanan were in the same location, much less if both were in Shinja. Assuming either of them were even alive.

I circled around the foremast and flew up to the hill where no one could see me, and transformed back. In my bird form all my attention was on managing myself in the world as a bird. Maybe someday I could visit the mental realm while flying, but not yet.

I drank some water, settled myself, and reached for Hlanan again. He was still asleep and dreaming. The intensity of emotions was painful, but I did not want to wait until he wakened: if he knew I was there, he might be glad, he might feel betrayed at the invasion of his mind, he might be sorry, be angry, be confused...

I didn't know how he would react, but one thing I was certain of, he would do everything in his power to dissuade me if I said I was coming to rescue him.

From what I saw in the dreams, he had enough stress. Unfamiliar words—galk—kip—Sig. Barrow. *Shinjan* words.

Then... Darus.

I chased a memory image with Darus, and there was Hlanan, staring in horror at Darus with broken arms. That smeared into Hlanan bent over Darus as magic gleamed and glittered...

I felt as if I'd tumbled into the murk of lava, his emotions were so painful. My mind recoiled, booting me back to the here-and-now, but fragments of images remained: they were together, in some sort of prison. Somewhere in Shinja.

Hlanan was there, the eggs were there.

I was going to Shinja.

But how? I knew I wasn't strong enough to fly across a vast ocean. Then I remembered the ships Raifas was sending out. Why not go with them? I wouldn't be able to hide aboard a ship as a person, of course, but no one paid attention to birds.

I arrowed back to land, and transformed so I could gather as many seeds and nuts as I could. Summer had advanced enough for there to be plenty to find. When I'd gathered enough in one end of my wrap, I knotted it tightly. The food made a bulky weight. Would it transfer? I remembered that vast dragon, and concentrated on compassing myself, the wrap, the food — and transformed back into my bird.

By then it was late, the crimson rim of the sun sinking in the west, as overhead the last of the clouds sailed away.

The three ships had departed on the last of the outward flowing tide. I beat my wings, racing into the brisk wind until I reached them, and spiraling gratefully down in the fast-falling night to perch on the topmost yard of the largest of the three.

It had been a long, exhausting day. I needed rest. In my bird form, the gyrating yard was like a wind-tossed tree branch. I tucked my head under my wing, and slept.

During the night rain came and went, but I scarcely noticed, except to sleepily untuck my beak to drink from the falling water, then tuck up again. Exhaustion so overwhelmed me that I didn't waken until the mast vibrated under clambering figures midway through the next morning.

I took off, overhearing a sailor saying, "Look at that bird. What kind is that, all silver?"

Whatever answer anyone provided was lost as I quickly sailed away. I didn't want them taking notice of me.

———⊰◉⊱———

As the ships sailed on the wind toward Shinja, I stayed in bird form, except when I wanted to eat. I had to wait until nightfall, the late watch. While most of the crew was asleep, I'd transform to myself on the highest masthead of one or another of the ships, unwrap my bounty, and eat my fill.

The problem, I soon discovered, was that though I kept my bird form most of the time, feeling little hunger or thirst, when I transformed, the hunger hit hard. I clearly needed to eat to preserve my human form, even if it was in other-space. And so the nuts and seeds I'd so laboriously gathered, thinking they would be plenty for weeks... weren't.

So I began scanning the ships for possible meals before I ran out entirely. I'd tried to avoid the command ship because I figured that one would have the most armed guards who might decide to amuse themselves with target practice on a pesky bird seen too often. I was still angry with the Djurans for shooting at the gryphs.

But the two consorts only seemed to serve cooked foods of the sorts I don't eat. In desperation late one night I drifted along the open stern windows of the lead ship, golden light pouring out. I looked into a plain cabin with a swinging bed, and a bolted table on which square containers rested.

Since the cabin was empty, and I'd already seen that gray-haired captain walking her deck, I drifted in and looked down. In one of the containers sat ripe fruit, and in the other a bowl of mixed nuts.

This captain liked my kind of foods? I transformed and gobbled down a plum, a peach, and a tiny spray of grapes. Then I helped myself to a handful of the shelled nuts, and while I crunched those I stirred the rest with my knuckles to flatten out the spot I'd raided.

Much refreshed, I flung myself out the stern windows and transformed before I reached the water, then spiraled up, noticing upturned faces as I sped away.

Over the next stretch of days, that was the pattern: when I got hungry, I waited for a time when the captain was on deck, and flew into her cabin. Each time I was afraid I would find nothing. The fruit did diminish, but the container of nuts stayed full, often replenished.

And so the ships sailed on through storm after storm. In bird form, I weathered these storms without trouble, though sometimes I crouched in the lee of a sail when the winds whipped so high they threatened to blow my body off into the sea—or hurl me away through the air so that I would have to struggle back.

I shifted to my human self only to raid the captain's cabin for food. That was the pattern until I flew in one blustery day, the rising seas gray-green. I transformed in midair, a process I was very good at by now, but even so I stumbled as the deck slanted steeply, fell to my knees, hopped up and was reaching for the nut container when the stern windows slammed shut behind me, cutting off the watery gray light.

I whirled around to face a determined young sailor, his nose red from the raw wind that had been racing straight into the cabin. He must have been hiding beside the windows despite the terrible weather howling in.

I raised my hands, readying for battle when the cabin door opened behind me, and the captain strode in.

"Bird-person!" she bawled. "Here you are at last!"

I whirled around again, fire forming on my palms.

She stuck her fists on her hips, riding the bucking deck like the expert she was. "I just want to talk to you! But you are too quick to catch!"

I stared at her in surprise. I'd thought I'd gone completely unnoticed.

She advanced slowly, one hand out, as though offering an apple to a skittish horse. "The Most Noble Raifas said that a silver bird, which becomes a feathered person, might fly with us, and to put out fruit as long as it lasted."

Her dark eyes shifted to my hands and up again. I remembered my fires, and—feeling a weird mixture of betrayal, wariness, and stupidity at being caught flat—rubbed my palms together to quench the flames.

She and the sailor behind me both breathed easier as I said, "Raifas expected me?"

She gave a slight nod. "He ordered us to prepare for you. Said you might want to go with us on our mission, and if so, I was to try to get your help, if you can."

"My help?" I repeated.

I scowled at the bowl of nuts recently refilled. Of course no one had been eating them but me. The wariness faded, mainly leaving me feeling stupid that Raifas had so easily predicted my movements, and planned for them, all without me figuring it out.

How was I going to rescue Hlanan, if I was really that predictable and slow?

I didn't try to answer that thought, though it made me itchy inside. I said, "I don't know how I can help. Or even if I should."

The captain smoothed back her gray hair, which was frizzing up in the dampness. With the stern windows shut, the air was close and smelled of canvas and damp wood. "The Most Noble Commander said that you would probably go into Shinja directly, which we will not be doing. Our orders are to stay well out of their area of patrol, and gather intelligence of fleet movements. But if you find out anything about the Most Noble Darus, he requests that you get that news to us any way you can. Or to him."

I had no idea how I would do that. Furthermore, I didn't care what happened to Darus. But they clearly did, they weren't threatening me, and here were the nuts and seeds. "If I can, I will," I said easily.

The captain nodded, then flicked a glance at the sailor, who hastily opened the stern windows. The cold wind drove in, and he hunched, pulling his jacket about him.

Impervious to the cold, I made a good meal, for once not having to gobble it down, then took off through the window.

After that, I didn't try to hide myself as either bird or human. Some of the sailors took to hailing me when they saw me, and a couple of the youngest apprentices on their off-watch begged me to transform and back again. While they were friendly, it was with a kind of complacency, as if I were a kitten or pup. I might have the title of princess, but none of the awe or fear of their Chosen.

When I recollected how much the Djuran nobles despised the

notion of the two-natured—how definite Jardis Dhes-Andis and the rest had been about their fais keeping the human form intact, as the superior nature—I resented them. But an enemy who looks down at you is a careless enemy, I'd learned over the years.

And I was still trying to figure out my own nature, something I had no intention of discussing with any of them.

Still, the rest of my time with the fleet was more pleasant than I could ever have imagined, until the day I woke on my high perch as usual, and looked down to startlement—the clean, austere sweep of the vessels overnight had been cluttered with messy nets, barrels all over, and even the sails had been replaced with picturesquely patched canvas, ragged at the hem.

The captain hailed me as I sailed down. "Silver bird!" she called. "Princess Elenderi!"

I landed on the deck in my human form. "The ships are all changed," I said.

She smiled. "We are now fishing vessels, and we will soon break away, each to its assigned cruise. For we have reached the edge of Shinjan territorial waters, and we are now going to become Shinjan fishers." She shifted to the Shinjan language, her accent—I discovered later—that of the coastal kingdom Shinja ruled on another continent. "You will have to fly from here."

"Where?" I said. There was no land in sight.

"Come look on the chart."

She showed me their position, which was measured by some magical means. She even explained it, but the words drifted by me. I was never going to be using Shinjan magic to navigate ships. Instead, I stared at the careful drawing of the enormous island, or small continent, that was Shinja's mainland. The capital lay near the center, on a long spine of mountains, the sight of which reminded me of the dragon eggs.

I had to get to them before Rue felt the need to tear off the top of whatever mountain they were hidden in, which would be destructive to anyone who lived below.

I'd think about that later.

I scooped up all the nuts the captain had remaining. As I tied them into my wrap, she said, "Princess Elenderi, I will ask you again to contact the Most Noble commander if you discover the whereabouts of the Most Noble Darus." She added seriously, "This becomes a matter of war."

I stared back at her, remembering my earlier easy lie.

Did this mean... if I ignored their request, Sveran Djur might sail against Shinja on Darus's behalf. Oh, yes, that sounded like Jardis Dhes-Andis. He wouldn't care how many lives were spent.

But I did.

"I'll try," I said, and this time I meant it, then flew out the open stern windows and away.

Fifteen

TIME DRAGGED ON IN the Barrow, marked off by the daily dump of scrapings, and twice by tremors. Each long day passed like the others in that dank, dim atmosphere. It was impossible to tell one day from another save by the occasional rainstorm, and sometimes the sounds of voices in the distance.

The guards stayed tense, keeping their time to a minimum: no one was pulled out for fighting, or even approached Hlanan for the promised questioning. Apparently the arena was working its way through the prisoners taken after whatever rebellion had been put down before Luenro was sent to the cell.

Hlanan used time laboring through the Djuran drills, then running back and forth until he reached two hundred turns. As he ran, he let his mind range free. Sometimes he wondered what had happened to Darus out there. Strange to consider how the greater threat had brought them to a kind of truce. Strange, and sad. He would have rather never been enemies. But that choice was not given him.

He continued to keep water and food free of impurities, though shadowy figures had taken his place in tending the princess.

He returned to his usual place, and had just settled down to review his magic lessons to speed time along, when the hissing shuffle of footsteps approached.

The big woman had escorted Princess Luenro to Hlanan.

She knelt down by him, felt for his arm, then pulled him gently close. She whispered, "Did you not say that you are a mage?"

"Student only," he said.

"Then you cannot use your spells to transport us away?"

"No. There is a—" What was the Shinjan for *ward*? "A magic wall. No one can get out that way."

She turned away, then turned back, though she could not see him. "Can one get past those who guard us, without being seen, using magic?"

"Possibly," he murmured. "Though difficult. It would require a distraction. And I do not know what lies outside there, or what the cost might be if someone goes missing."

"They count," the big woman said, low and flat. "Every time."

Hlanan had suspected as much. Though illusion could help there, too. But he was not going to discuss illusion. Yet.

The princess's chin lowered. "I must think," she murmured, as she propped herself up with one hand, as if her strength failed. "I must think, and regain my strength, such as it is."

<hr>

Hlanan continued to purify the food, and to exercise, and every time the guards showed up, he watched them narrowly for the slightest hint of inattentiveness. They were arrogant, and careless, but sheer habit kept them clumped together. The only way out would be to cause a distraction.

As the days turned into a week, then two weeks, his routine was the same: rise, exercise, disinfect food. That former female guard, nearly as tall and strong as Sig, guarded and served Luenro. She came to get the scant scrapings to take to the blind princess, who ate and slept, still and frail.

In sunlight and air, with good food and medicine, the older woman might have regained her strength in a few days, but a string of chilly, rainy days made the cell a misery of cold dampness, and the inadequate food kept her not only weak, but caused her to slip into fever.

At first the big guard would not let anyone near, but

eventually fear brought her to Hlanan, begging him to "Do something."

Heartsick with dread, he moved at once to the princess, who moved restlessly on the unforgiving stone, her flesh dry and fever-hot. "She has to drink, as much as she can hold. And everything purified," he said. "I can't do anything else. I'm sorry."

"Listen to him," came a breathy whisper.

The woman jerked her chin down. She surrendered her sash, which Hlanan murmured the purification spell over, and then began long, wearying trips to the water, soaking the sash and holding it so that the princess could draw water out of it.

At first she was too weak to suck on the fabric, and the woman and Hlanan traded off wringing the sash so that water dropped in a thin dribble between Luenro's parched, cracked lips. But gradually she gained enough strength to reach for it herself, and then to eat a little. One very bad night passed, with no one in the cell sleeping until Luenro sank into exhausted slumber, the fever broken at last.

By then Hlanan had long lost count of the days of his imprisonment. His entire world had constricted to the care of this woman and maintaining his own strength. Especially as cold days alternated with the waning warmth of summer—indicating that harvest season had come. So high up on the slope of the great mountain, where the weather could be crueler than that in the lowlands, the slightest dip in anyone's health could be fatal.

Slowly Princess Luenro returned to the world, until one day, she stopped Hlanan when he'd come to check on her. Her thin fingers groped, caught his wrist, and tightened in a brief grip. "Stay," she whispered—in accented Elras. "Stay." She struggled to sit up. "I must speak in my childhood tongue. Which I was forbidden to use once the marriage treaty was made. It is good to speak it again."

Hlanan said, "Your marriage was the price of Akerik joining the Kherval, were you not?"

"Yes," she whispered. "It was a price I paid willingly, for we needed the empire desperately. And the little I hear from home, it has been good news. But I must not waste my strength on the past. You said you are a mage, yes?"

"A beginner," he said cautiously.

"Can you do illusion?" she asked. "My understanding is that such are basic to magic knowledge."

"Yes."

"Then please, you must cloak yourself in illusion. And see if my son lives. Please. Please. I beg of you." Her voice faltered. "I can endure anything if my son lives. I know Avejo means well, often. Zeltzi—she wanted my eyes gouged out, but Avejo overrode her, insisting my countenance must not change, in case I was to make public appearance. I know he desired to spare me pain, though his was the hand that did the magic to ruin my eyes. But he has been raised to consider political gain first, always through war. Avejo is..."

The princess paused, and Hlanan, not certain what to say, waited.

She drew a shaky breath, and continued. "I very much fear that to preserve power Zeltzi will kill Invey if she can, possibly Avejo if she must. I need to know if Invey lives, and if he can get away to safety. I would have him flee to my homeland if he can." Then she switched to Shinjan. "You have magic, and it seems to have escaped the notice of the imperial guard."

"Yes," Hlanan replied in the same tongue. "I've been careful to keep it that way. But I should warn you that I have been watching for an opportunity to get past our guards, and they are too tightly placed for anyone to pass them to leave this cell. An illusion is just that. It breaks if anyone touches the person or thing under illusion, or even looks right at it."

"Then we must cause such a distraction that they break formation," Princess Luenro stated. She turned her head to smile in the direction of her fierce and patient guard. "Can that be done? Would you go, mage? For you are the only one of us familiar with magic, even a little."

The guard shifted, looking uncomfortably from the princess to Hlanan, and even in the profound gloom, he made out distrust in every line of her body. "They count, every time. How could he get out?"

"I could create a false image of myself, which will remain if no one dispels it," Hlanan said, and was aware that he spoke too readily.

Luenro to turn sightless gaze his way. "And so you would escape altogether, yes? You owe nothing to us."

The guard woman hissed in her breath. "If one goes missing, we will all die at the post, a shameful death."

"Not to mention painful," Hlanan muttered.

The former guard sent him a quick look. Expressions were always somewhat difficult to make out, but Hlanan heard the seriousness in her tone as she said, "All punishments and executions for galk are painful. But we in here? We are all—were all—captains, and captain-chiefs, or rank taken, our selv-sticks broken. And yet we retain this much honor: we would rather fight in the arena, and take our chance dying by a warrior's blade, than flogged like a criminal."

Selv-sticks? Hlanan thought, then remembered that 'selv' was a medium of exchange, or credit—akin to coins in the Kherval and its continent, and other types of trade elsewhere in the world. The Shinjans had once traded the shellfish that afforded the brilliant crimson dye so valued through the entire world, a means of trade that had evolved into these sticks.

Though the former guard's voice had not risen, it was clear others listened, for the hiss of shuffling steps and the rank odor of grimy bodies closed around them. Sig said, "Nenor of the Residence Wing Guard speaks for me. I willingly risk flogging if it means bringing Prince Invey to us."

"And I."

"And I," echoed through the room.

Hlanan did not know how many prisoners he shared the cell with—unlike the guards, he had never counted—but Sig seemed to know. He raised his head. "Palcas? If it is to happen, it is with agreement from all."

The oldest of the prisoners shuffled into view. "This here is a foreigner," he stated, pointing at Hlanan. "What's to keep him from scouting off, if he gits out? I say, he uses his spells and sends one of us."

"That's right," someone else said.

"Good notion."

"Yes."

And just like that, Hlanan had the first sliver of an opportunity of escape snatched away into a foggy future: there had always been a chance that some fight, or other distraction, would break out among the prisoners, and Hlanan could have slipped away, but now he knew what would happen to those he left behind. Further, he was beginning to suspect why they were there. These were not the murderers and thieves he'd expected; as Nenor, the former guard, had said, they were all military, and though he did not know for certain what had caused their incarceration, he had a strong suspicion that much of the reason was due to politics on high.

So… either he sought to escape at any cost, or he paid the price of … No, he had to face the word square on: honor.

As soon as he thought the word, he knew what he had to say. "I won't run." It hurt to speak. The idea of escape had been his only real comfort. But circumstances had closed in on him. "However I need to know where to go, if I am to make it back before the illusory self would dissolve."

"How long would that be?" Princess Luenro asked, as the other prisoners whispered in the background.

"Illusions are flimsy at best. They have to be renewed, and if anyone walks through it, it vanishes like fog. But I can make one last until the next morning, when I'd return to be counted."

Nenor looked up at Sig. "Well? Do we trust this foreigner to reach our prince?"

The others fell silent as Sig bent his head, thinking. "He's done right by us so far," he said slowly. "But he's not one of us."

Hlanan sighed. "I'm from the Kherval. I've never tried to hide that."

"No, I meant military. Oath-maker. We all took oaths, to the good of Shinja, and all its people."

"That's right."

"Yes."

"So we did—though look what it got us."

Sig turned his head. "None of that, Vlekin. We know who'll betray us—and who won't." He turned back to Hlanan. "Prince Invey, we believe in his honor. The other…"

They still wouldn't say Avejo's name. He had to be a very powerful mage, or more likely have powerful mages at his side, for the guards to believe that mere mention would bring his retribution upon them.

Paralleling Hlanan's thoughts, Luenro said, "My son is not political in nature, but he is a prodigious mage. Perhaps he can help. The wards and protections have of late fallen to his care. It is too great a task for a single person, but my nephew has sought… other directions for his magic."

Hlanan remembered the appearance of her eyes, and could easily guess what those directions were. "As a healer, I already took an oath to do no harm. To help as I can. Betraying everyone here would break that oath."

Sig nodded slowly. "You've done right by us so far," he repeated, and Hlanan sensed the big man's own anxieties.

Luenro lifted her voice. "I, as you all, have been reduced to the level of slave in all but name. I cannot make commands. So I ask, do we have an agreement? Shall we unite in sending this healer to Invey?"

Sig said sturdily, "I agree."

That caused the others to echo him.

Hlanan sighed. All right. Honor forbade an escape. And he was aware of a strong urge to speak to this Invey. If he was so good a prince, how could he permit situations like this prison, and the area awaiting them, to exist?

How could he live with slavery?

Princess Luenro said, "To be successful, you must know the palace ways. I will teach you."

Hlanan crouched down. "That was my next question. How big

is the palace?"

The princess uttered a very soft laugh. "Huge, healer. Huge. It is going to take time to learn the ways, and the traps."

Hlanan gave a thought to Darus, whose fate was unknown — but who had obviously not told the prison commanders that Hlanan knew magic, or he doubtless would have been warded by now, if not outright killed. "No time like the present to begin," he said. "Let's start with this court, or whatever it is, outside the grill."

Not only Luenro but some of the other captains crowded around. There could be no map made. Everything must be memorized. As they began talking over one another to describe what was obviously an ancient building whose rambling wings had served various purposes over the years, Hlanan listened closely, repeating everything. He ended that day with a headache from constant contradictions, interruptions, and corrections.

The next day was little better. The third was worse, because they all expected him to have what amounted to the ground floor memorized, and he kept forgetting entire wings. During the night he suffered nightmares, but woke remembering something I had told him about my thief days — that the best way to quickly learn new territory was by landmarks.

He explained this to the many helpful teachers, and then they argued about what constituted landmarks.

It was Luenro who gently suggested that royal statues might be a beginning in that direction. Meanwhile, Hlanan began drawing with his finger on his upper leg, hoping that repetitions of word and touch would cement memory.

Luenro alone retained her patience, and by the fourth day, she had begun talking in a singsong, as if telling a story to a child. "First we walk through the hall of stone to the great gate of Emperor Nothvar with the feathered crest and the scaled robe, and go through to the Hall of Arches."

"Pass the niches with the busts of royal princes and princesses," Hlanan said. "On my left."

"Good! And at the archway off the bust of Prince Kelebit,

holding his acanthus staff over his heart..."

On she went, making a song of it. By the end of the week, Hlanan could unerringly recite the entire area from the massive prison wing to the public area of the palace, below the imperial wing.

This, they all promised, was where the going would get tough. But by then he was getting used to building a mirror palace in his mind—and he began creating illusions of his road, which Luenro of course couldn't see, but the others offered corrections.

Two and a half weeks passed, during which the troubling sounds from outside occurred again, and twice the guards appeared to pull out prisoners for the arena. Once one of those quakes silenced everyone.

They all felt the pressure of time. Luenro and Nenor had to finish teaching Hlanan the private residence wing where the imperial children had been housed. Nenor, a former kip, knew all the service routes, and the princess the routes only available to the imperial family. Both pointed out repeatedly that all might have been changed again.

But every day brought new dangers, and no one knew what new threat there might be, or who was prevailing in the struggle whose outer edges they could hear. Meanwhile the cold days got colder.

It was time to plan the distraction, and for Hlanan to make his try.

Though it had taken a couple of weeks to prepare for Hlanan's break from the cell, the distraction to get him past the guards was relatively simple—once everyone agreed to it.

He woke up with a jerk very early the day he was to try, restless and uneasy as another tremor, this one the sharpest yet, ground the stone above them as it rocked the ground.

When Hlanan stirred, Nenor was at his side, as if she had been on the watch.

"You are awake betimes," she whispered. "You have changed your mind?"

"No," he whispered back, hearing in the tightness of her voice how anxious she was. "Dreams. I woke from a dream, sure that someone ... from my home... was here." He breathed out, trying to shake the dream, which was even more intense than the jumble of dreams of a silver bird darting about and calling his name that he'd had during the first terrible weeks in prison. "But she's home. She's safe," Hlanan said firmly, as if stating the words made it true. "That's the one thought that keeps me sane."

"Sane is good." Nenor thumped him on the shoulder with her fist. "You must stay sane." She cast a quick glance back, then murmured, "It is not my place to say more than this: she will not live long if you fail her."

Hlanan sat up tiredly. There was no chance of getting back to sleep now. He was already tense enough. Nenor's words didn't help, but he said nothing. Everyone was tense. If he was discovered, they would all pay for it.

He moved slowly, quietly, warming himself up as the first blue of dawn began to outline the barred windows. Then he cast both of his spells. When the guards came at last, he stood against the inner wall before the cell doors, where it was shadowy. He had created a simulacrum of himself at the far end of the water trough, which everyone else vigilantly avoided, so that he would be counted.

Princess Luenro, as the most important prisoner in the whole of the Barrows, had only to stumble and cry out, "Oh, my heart!" just before the wheelbarrow of disgusting mush was dumped for the day. She swayed as if about to fall.

"She's fainting!" Nenor called, and another, "She's *dying!*"

That sent a shock through the guards, some of whom started forward, others hanging back. All froze, looking at their captain for orders as Hlanan bent low and dodged among the legs. He only had a couple of heartbeats before the captain motioned violently for the guards to close up again. Two heartbeats after he slipped through the cell doors, the guards had snapped into position, weapons out, as their captain hovered over the princess, barking questions at her and those around her.

Giddy with relief, Hlanan suppressed the desire to laugh,

because now the toughest part of the challenge lay before him.

He crept next to the wall, and began to chant Luenro's singsong to himself. The military area was swept clean, the air smelling so different... oh. It didn't stink.

Hlanan made it to the end of the hall, then ducked into the turn of an archway as a couple of guards marched through and away.

One of them turned to the other, exclaiming, "Augh! That reek from the Barrow gets worse every day..."

A squad of guards marched up, and turned into his archway. He pressed back, eyes down, though instinct pulled at every nerve to look up. But eyes could not meet eyes, Hlanan knew from experience playing around with other apprentices when young. Instinct was too strong for that. He needed to avoid anything that might cause deep-rooted instinct to prompt the guards to scan their environment more closely.

The footsteps tramped away, and Hlanan let his breath out, then resumed the walk, and the litany.

The first layer of that wing was military, and his only protection was how busy the guards were, rushing to and fro. As soon as he reached the public areas, he searched along the niches, and there, just where expected, was the almost invisible door to the slaves' corridor.

As soon as he got inside, he sank against a wall in the near darkness, his head swimming. They had discussed the fact that he would not be able to purify the day's dumped food, of which he would get nothing. Hunger was now an old companion, and he had learned how to portion out his strength. It was his head that protested, with a wooziness that threatened to worsen unless he rested, drawing in slow gulps of air.

When he could trust himself to move without clouds of dark fuzziness at the edge of his vision, he pushed away from the wall and forced himself onward. Here was the most obvious evidence that Shinja was in trouble. The military areas and the imperial residence were clean, lit, and polished, but the slave halls went unswept, the magical lights in the windowless halls dim and neglected.

Slaves scurried quickly to and fro, causing him to halt frequently, head down, but no one so much as looked his way, judging by the unchecked rhythm of rapid steps. Every time he halted, he used the moment to lean against a wall and breathe away the lightheaded sensation.

When he reached the second level that connected to the princes' wing, the danger increased, for this was the kips' territory.

But Luenro had insisted that he leave the slave halls. Guards were posted along them, as well as busy slaves. She had asserted he would be better off entering the royal chambers, which would be largely empty, and Nenor had told him where guards were likely to be posted.

He listened at the door to a reception hall for the count of fifty before he eased it open. Empty.

And now, at last, he saw windows for the first time in uncounted days. His eyes teared. That was caused largely by the glare of sunlight, but the tightening of his throat, and the heaviness of his chest, was entirely due to the sight of the sky.

He wrenched himself away from the windows, and bent his will to the task.

Slaves were forbidden to walk through the beautifully decorated rooms with their pale carpets worked with twined holly leaves and berries in threes. Furnishings of white and gold sat before mirrored walls, and archways with beautiful paintings of idyllic scenery, each room decorated around a specific season. Luenro's breathy voice sang in his mind, summer, fall, winter, spring, off which led two doorways. To the right, Avejo's rooms, which Luenro was certain had been abandoned for the imperial wing itself. Invey now lived alone in this wing, at the top level.

Hlanan was about to essay the left chamber when he sensed a change in the air. Instinctively he retreated behind a table inlaid with gold, crouched down, and worked on his breathing as dizziness threatened, and his hands trembled.

A pair of kips emerged from a side archway, their footsteps soft on the thick cream-colored carpet, their armor and weapons clattering.

Hlanan stilled. The light-filled room would reflect in his illusion, but any sense of movement at the corner of the eye would draw attention, especially if the guards were alert.

Their swords and red-worked armor rattled past as they marched in step straight to the door, then Hlanan heard their footfalls on the steps. Now the question was, follow or wait.

He decided to shadow them and tiptoed after, sliding on one's heels through the slowly closing door. The pair marched into a shadowy stairwell. Glad of his bare feet and ragged clothes too thin to rustle, Hlanan scurried behind the two, who talked as they marched up the steps at a vigorous pace. Hlanan matched their pace, his effort causing glittery lights to twinkle around the edge of his vision, but he held his breath until one spoke.

"You got gut trouble?"

"No worse than usual. Xienu said the betting has gone up into ruby."

"That's what I heard, too. Tchah! I don't trust rumor."

"I trust it as long as Zaffi is running the show. Nothing'll happen to his prize Djuran, not while he's grabbing selv right and left."

The other uttered a snort of laughter. "Trust Zaf for that. But soon's the Djuran falters..."

They both laughed, then fell silent for the last ten steps or so. Hlanan had eased up directly behind one, trusting to the shadows. The two reached the landing, where a couple of bored guards waited.

"You're late," one said.

"Alarm," replied the kip Hlanan stood behind.

"What else is new?" was the response, but the asker's tone was impatient, not a real query, so Hlanan was not going to find out what the alarm was about. Sure enough, the guard went on, "There you have him, at the desk, no visitors. Wouldn't go to the arena."

The off-duty guards started down the stairs, and Hlanan backed away and looked around. He stood in a narrow, undecorated hall. Doors marked the walls as far as he could see.

He eased farther away from the guards, who settled against the wall so they could see in both directions and down the stairs. He stilled each time one or the other's face turned his way, and moved only when they looked away again, clearly expecting to see nothing. The rumble of their voices continued as Hlanan retreated slowly down the hall in slow increments.

At each door he stopped, his fingers moving slowly as he tested each latch. Locked. Locked. Locked. Voices inside the fourth room—he passed on by, remembering that the prince was alone. Locked. The sixth one down was open, and he cracked it, listening to the unmistakable silence of an empty room.

He slid inside and eased the door shut behind him, then stood with his back against it as he surveyed a small antechamber filled with the scent of... food.

His mouth watered, and his stomach lurched as he stared at what had to be a way-station for the suite. Trays of various food and drinks sat on a long side buffet. Hlanan moved to it as if propelled by the strongest magic spell in the world.

He blinked down at the food, keeping his hands behind his back until he had considered everything, though he was nearly reeling from the hunger that roared inside him. It would be stupid to throw himself on the trays and dishes. What could be more obvious a hint that someone was lurking around than food missing that wasn't supposed to be?

So he looked past the unbroken bread still steaming from the oven, and the tarts and the meat pie. His gaze lit on a basket of little biscuits. He grabbed two of them, and hastily rearranged the rest to fill the empty spaces. He sank his teeth into one, and the flavor burst on him with all its freshness. He fought the instinct to gobble it down and forced himself to chew slowly, and to take small bites: he remembered that first horrible week in childhood when he'd been snatched off the streets by Shinjan slave-takers, how desperately hungry he'd been, and how he and the other children had gobbled their food when it finally came—just to lose it all again.

The two biscuits not only stayed down, but the weird lights at the edge of his vision began to recede, and he did not have to gulp for breath as much. Carefully, concentrating on staying alert, he ranged along the table, stopping at a tray with plain apple tarts next to a plate of smoked fish. This plain food was probably for the guards, and from the looks of the half-empty tray, some had grabbed their share of the meal already. There was plenty left. And plain food might be easier to stomach.

One, two fish slices, an apple tart, and he knew he ought to stop. He promised himself another visit on his way out, and moved on, constantly checking. He'd been assured that there were six kips on duty directly in the prince's suite, and of course two patrols of regular guards directly below. He seemed to be safe. Still, Hlanan was not going to be careless this close to the goal.

He reached another room, with slanting ochre rays in the bank of tall windows indicating that he had spent an entire day in moving, waiting, moving, waiting. He wondered if he'd slept on his feet without realizing it: it wasn't until he'd eaten something that he understood just how fuzzy his thinking had become.

There at last were the double doors with stylized red dragons carved into them. Odd, that the Shinjans used the same symbol that the Djurans did. Then he remembered his discovery when he first heard what the Shinjans called the Dragon Tongue. He made a mental note to look at the ancient history of both empires, as all he'd studied about them had been from the time they began interacting with the Kherval.

He reached the doors, drew in a deep breath, and laid his hand to the latch. It was unlocked. Both the princess and her ex-guard companion had insisted that Zeltzi would never permit him a locked door. The guards checked on Invey periodically.

Hlanan walked in as he banished the illusion over him. The room was huge, with a bank of windows overlooking the palace cut into the slope below, and below that, the city. Lights began to glow faintly in houses, twinkling like golden stars; the room was lit by glowglobes set on golden holders carved in the shape of stylized ivy vines.

Hlanan shifted his gaze to the ranks of book and scroll shelves, which reminded him of his father's archive deep in the royal palace at Erev-li-Erval. And nearly hidden behind a stack of papers and books on a fine carved desk, a dark red head.

Imperial Prince Invey didn't even look up. If he was aware of the door opening, he didn't seem to care, but of course he was interrupted regularly through his day.

Hlanan approached, studying the prince in the light of glowglobes set on rods shaped like laurel leaves. His hair was a darker red than his half-brother's, and he wore fewer braids. He, like Avejo, had his father's strong jaw, but on him it was narrower. Same jug-handle ears, though Avejo had done his best to hide his with the braids. Invey didn't bother. His few braids were bound back out of his way, his sleeves rolled. Ink splashed his fingers.

He's me, Hlanan thought, then gave himself a mental shake. This was a Shinjan imperial prince, who commanded hundreds of slaves. To presume a kinship of minds just because the fellow seemed to like books and got inky fingers was stupid and dangerous.

"Prince Invey," he said.

The prince looked up sharply. Then he rose, fingers reaching among his papers and coming up with a throwing dagger. Hlanan stood where he was, and the two eyed one another for a heartbeat or two. Then Invey tossed the knife back onto the desk with a thump. "You're not an assassin."

Hlanan breathed a soft laugh. "I suppose I look worse than I think."

Invey's head tipped slightly. "You look as if you'd blow away in a breeze. But my thought was, if my brother turned on me he would do it himself. And as for his mother, she'd probably want to watch, and rant at me while I died," he finished dryly.

Hlanan leaned against a table. "And I thought I had family problems," he said, then wished he hadn't. "Sorry. That was stupid."

"You've an Elras accent." Invey's brows knit warily, his pale gaze steady. "Who are you? How did you get in here?"

"Your mother sent me," Hlanan said.

Invey's breath huffed out as though he'd been punched in the gut. "What? Where did you see her?"

"In the prison. What you call the Barrow. I'm locked in with a lot of former officers, I think. Though you call us galk." Hlanan kept his voice even. He could see the effect of his words in the tightening of Invey's mouth.

"I don't..." Invey passed a hand over his face, then came out from behind the desk and moved to one of the windows, which he threw wide. Hlanan noticed a tremble in his fingers. "Every day brings another—"

"Disaster?" Hlanan asked. "We can hear the noise of fighting, and occasional screams, behind our prison bars."

Invey's mouth now thinned to a white line, then he said, "Why are you even here in Shinja? What did you do?"

"Nothing," Hlanan replied. "I was taken hostage by Djurans. Their fleet was attacked by slavers. I don't know what happened to the crew, but the chief of the Djurans and his personal guard were brought here along with me, and put in the Barrow."

Invey looked puzzled. "You were taken hostage by Djurans? For what purpose? Are you a person of importance?"

"I don't believe Darus is in the Djuran military," Hlanan said, sidestepping the other questions. The fewer details offered the better. He owed Darus that much, seeing as Darus had protected his own identity as a healer, but no more than that.

"He's not?" Invey asked, a twisted smile flaring then vanishing. "Perhaps we are talking about two different Djurans, then. Because the one twice put in the arena trounced all the competition. I am told the betting is going into unprecedented realms. Which is," he sighed, "the exact diversion the empress my step-mother wants." He thumbed his eyes, then frowned at Hlanan. "I'm too tired. Not thinking. Who exactly are you? How do I know you came from my mother?"

"She thought you might not believe me," Hlanan said, avoiding the first question. "She told me to say to you, 'Remember what I promised you on Eferrit Day when you were ten years old?'"

Invey dropped into his chair. "Then she *is* alive."

"Yes." Hlanan said, and his knees nearly buckled as his insides cramped. "I need to sit. I'm..." He groped vaguely, as dark sparkles clouded the edge of his vision. He swallowed once, and again.

Invey's voice buzzed. Hlanan looked about him, and made it the four steps to a low chair before the darkness threatened to close in. His head dropped into his lap and he gulped in air, again and again. Gradually the blackness receded, and he became aware of Invey standing two paces away, leaning down with his inky hands on his knees as he peered anxiously into Hlanan's face.

"What is it? This chamber is warded against any kind of strike," Invey said as he opened another window. "I did the magic myself—before I was warded."

Interesting that his first thought was magic attack. "It's hunger, then sudden food," Hlanan said tiredly, his head throbbing. But the nausea was slowly subsiding, along with the clamminess.

"Hunger?"

Hlanan sat back. "Am I not sufficient evidence?" As the physical reaction diminished, he was left with a heady sense of unreality.

No, not unreality. He knew what was real. Right now, he was alone with one of the leaders of the enemy, books and ink-stains notwithstanding. Invey could call his guards at any time.

But Hlanan launched into a blunt description of what life was like in the Barrows, a life Invey's mother now shared. And he saw the impact of his words in the prince, who flinched once or twice, his face more and more strained.

Finally he burst out, "Is it true that Avejo used magic to blind her? And not the burning rod that Zeltzi demanded?"

"It was magic," Hlanan said, and as Invey turned away, Hlanan added, "You can check yourself."

"I can't, actually," Invey said. Then, as if he felt he'd talked too much, his expression shuttered. "What exactly did my mother send you to say?"

"Her initial purpose was for me to see if you are alive. Your well-being."

"And she trusts you. You are from her homeland, yes?"

"I'm from the Kherval," Hlanan said.

"How did you get past the imperial guard? That cannot have been easy. I don't remember hearing about an escape in the last several years."

"I used illusion. I'm a scribe, but I learned illusion for fun."

"Illusion is easy to learn, but dangerous in that it is so easily broken."

"I know. Yet this is the way I must get back, or they will all be killed."

Invey tipped his head back, his gaze ranging over the ceiling, which was patterned in pleasing geometric shapes around stars. Then he said, "No transfers in or out, that much I know." And, "Yes, you'd better go. The guard will be in soon to check that I'm not conspiring," he added with fine irony. Then his tone changed. "Thank you for bringing that message. Please. Help yourself to the food. Take some to my mother, if you will. I can order more."

"May I take some back to the other prisoners, too? Even a scrap of fresh food will be better than the scant, maggoty leavings we get once a day."

"Maggoty," Invey repeated hoarsely, his chin jerking back slightly, as though the maggots had sprung up in front of him.

"Which is," Hlanan said with the deliberation of weeks of imprisonment for utterly no reason, "what your mother is eating. And very little of that. She has trouble standing, she's so weak." He was not about to admit what he had done for his fellow prisoners.

Invey flinched as if struck, then turned violently away. He prowled around the perimeter of the entire chamber. Hlanan stayed where he was, watching. He still had the return sneak ahead of him, plus a wait of however long before the guards returned. And then he'd have to be able to get inside.

"It will only be worse if I act," Invey muttered to the exquisite mosaic on the floor. "I absolutely believe that threat." He turned sharply, and blew out his breath. "Yes, yes. You must get back, before you are discovered. I can give you a basket," Invey said hurriedly.

"Do you have any words you want taken back to Princess Luenro?"

Invey prowled the perimeter of the chamber again, his expression changing from a scowl to perplexity and then to grim determination. Finally he shook his head. "I don't dare make promises I might not be able to keep. She must already know that she is hostage against any action I could take."

Invey spun away and opened a trunk. He brought out a basket woven from rice stalks. Hlanan reached for it, then realized he would be left with a piece of evidence that would have to be hidden by magic. He stepped back. "I can't," he said, and walked out.

He cast another illusion over himself and made his way to the food. Here, he packed as much of the plainest food into his shirt, this time paying no attention to emptying plates. Some of the bread things began to squish together inside his shirt, but after what the others had been forced to eat, he knew no one would complain.

Then he cast another illusion spell over all, just to make sure.

And he began the long, dangerous trip back.

Sixteen

HLANAN TOOK MOST OF the night to get himself back down to the Barrows. When he smelled the cells from a distance, his stomach threatened once again to revolt, and he had to pause and rest to reaccustom himself to the stench.

He was weary and shaky when at last he made it to hallway in which his fellow prisoners were incarcerated. There he crouched over the food he had folded into his shirt, glad of the deep gloom. He renewed his illusion spell and half-dozed, jerking awake at every little noise.

Finally the familiar tramp of the guards shocked him into wakefulness. He eased directly against the wall opposite the cell door. He did not know if the others would try to distract the guards again. He only knew he had one chance to get back inside.

The guards walked in a loose group, the one with the wheelbarrow pausing as the man with the keys marched up to the door. Everyone's attention was on the door.

Hlanan drew in a breath and crouched down, his grimy shirt folded over the food held tightly against him. As the key clattered in the lock he shifted around a pair of boots and scooted directly under the wheelbarrow.

Counting on the noise of heavy boots tromping on the stone floor, he crawled frantically under the wheelbarrow until he got just inside the door, then rolled away. A boot hit him as the formation closed up tight.

He froze, gazing up, but the guard cursed at the man next to him. "Watch your big feet, Taz."

"Watch yours, fish-face."

"C'mon, galk," bawled the captain, drowning out everyone else. "Come and get it! Seasoned with extra meat today — all of it crawling, ha ha ha!"

Hlanan made it to the wall, where he stilled, except for his wildly galloping heartbeat.

As the counter counted (Hlanan was relieved to see his illusion had held, though it was fading), the captain peered into the gloom in the direction of the princess. Then he grunted and wheeled about. The tightly packed formation withdrew, the door clanged shut, and the guards tromped away.

When it was quiet, Hlanan let the illusions drop.

Every person in that cell let out a sigh of relief.

"I brought extra food," Hlanan said, putting his load on the mess before them. "Let me take the rot and grime off it."

Over the shared food, Hlanan told them about the conversation with Invey. At the end, someone at the back sobbed once, choked it off, and afterward Hlanan could hear the suppressed breathing of tears confined in an aching chest.

"He's a prisoner," Sig rumbled.

"But alive," the princess whispered, her thin hands pressed against her chest. "Though for how long? I know Zeltzi will kill him if she prevails. It is only Avejo's fondness for him keeping him alive, but..." She shook her head.

Hlanan wanted to ask what the 'but' meant, then shrugged it off. Whatever family dynamic was going on here was not his problem. These imperials all countenanced slavery, and used the lives of people in their internal wars.

However, this was their homeland, their laws and customs, the sound of the winds and the daily weather familiar as breathing. His part was not to deliver his opinion, but to listen.

And somehow, his contact with Prince Invey caused all the stories to come out. Hlanan heard two threads, punishments for petty crimes, mostly issued by the empress, and association, even by rumor, with 'Xin.'

It took time to discover who Xin was, as the name was only a whisper at first, but gradually it became clear that Xin was, or had been, a slave — and had led a rebellion, which not only slaves had joined, but many city people, until it was put down brutally by Avejo's forces.

Not all the former guards agreed with Xin's revolt, it became clear from harsh breathing here, and a shuffle there. One woman muttered that one riot can turn into a hundred, and there would soon be no order at all.

"Shut your mouth, you—"

"Please." Luenro spoke gently, but such was the influence of her presence that the mutters ceased abruptly.

The princess turned toward the woman, barely a shadow among the other shadows. "You all know I am from the Kherval, where we do not keep slaves. I have never pretended to know how best Shinjans would be served. But right now, my concern is how to keep any more from losing their lives — and to save my son, if I can, from she whose actions have proved that the lives of all Shinjans mean little. For her, the acquisition of power, glory and endless worship is more important."

The silence was still fraught with tension, but less violence, Hlanan thought as the princess turned her sightless gaze in his direction. "Please, Hlanan. You must return. You did well, but there are questions that must be resolved, such as what wards lie upon him—"

"I beg pardon, but it was clear to me that it's your life he fears losing most," Hlanan said.

"Yes. But you must make it clear to him that if there is a chance of preserving others, my life can be sacrificed. This is *my* will. He must act to save the kingdom. That is the message you must take to him. It is my command."

Hlanan's heart sank at the thought of another dangerous journey through that castle. But he'd do it, partly to ease the princess's stress, partly just to get a decent meal. And he'd return because he felt bound to his fellow prisoners, who were no longer enemies, even if they were not friends. A quick thought: though he knew several languages, he could not think of word for the relationship of those bound together in adversity. Yes, 'fellow prisoners' would do, both words of equal importance.

Luenro went on, "Invey is of a scholarly turn of mind, and has been withdrawn ever since his ... oh, call him his foster-brother, though Kenji was actually a hostage. Invey was tutoring him in magic, before he vanished. My son desires peace — does not believe Shinja will regain its greatness through more war. His wish is to review and overhaul the laws, that Shinja might recover..." She paused, chin jerking up as a sharp tremor rumbled through the building. Here and there grit hissed down from the grinding stones above. Then, as the rumbling began to ease, she finished on a husky breath, "... its former greatness."

Such was the force of her will that once again, the entire group of prisoners united behind her. Hlanan wondered if they expected Invey to harbor some brilliant plan, but he kept his questions to himself: since he was the one going, he might as well ask Invey directly.

And so, the next day, the princess once again suffered a fall just as the wheelbarrow was brought in. The guards broke formation, some starting toward her until their captain barked out an order to close up. But by then Hlanan had slipped between them and out.

As he slunk along the familiar passages, darting into shadowy alcoves and twice behind statues of former emperors, he wondered how Invey was supposed to save the kingdom even if he wanted to.

How could *anyone* rescue this situation? If Hlanan's older brother Justeon were there, he'd know exactly how to organize a revolt. But he wouldn't have been stupid enough to walk onto an enemy ship without speaking to anyone, or even leaving word. Not that Justeon would ever go anywhere alone. He didn't move without his honor guard, banner carriers, and trumpeters. Even so...

As a patrol clumped by, weapons rattling in their sheaths, Hlanan crouched behind a statue of an emperor wielding a long selv stick in one hand, and spear in the other, and pinched the bridge of his nose. Justeon was *not* there. Anyway, his solution would be more bloodshed.

Hlanan made his way up to the prince's wing, after many pauses, and this time he helped himself to the food. Then he proceeded to the study, where he found Invey at the desk, but surrounded by different books and some very old scrolls.

When Hlanan eased inside, Invey looked up sharply, and his expression altered to question. "It's you again—"

They both paused as a mild tremor rolled through the castle. And here, too, grit sifted down onto the beautiful tile floor.

Invey thrust his hands through his braids in a gesture Hlanan found very familiar: frustration. "The quakes are getting stronger and more frequent. And it's overcoming the magic restraints."

"I was going to ask if you've thought to renew them," Hlanan said.

"Three times. Twice the court mages, third time I went myself—with Avejo's entire guard surrounding me. I think we are protected against a destructive quake, but I can't be sure because I do not know the cause."

"This mountain above us is a volcano," Hlanan ventured.

Invey looked up, his tired, thin face sharpening. "Yes, but it's been quiescent for centuries," he said in a we're-not-stupid voice. "*Centuries.* Some say far before the last dragon left. And it's not smoking, which the records insist came before explosions." He rubbed the palms of his hands over his eyes, then dropped them, resting his fingers on his desk. "Why did you return?"

"Your mother sent me," Hlanan said, and relayed the message.

Invey's mobile face changed, but at the command to sacrifice his mother's life, his lips thinned into a line as he moved to open the windows.

It was that sign of concern that prompted Hlanan to ask, "Assuming you can escape, what will you do?"

"What can I do?" Invey sighed. "Make my way to my uncle— my father's youngest brother, who has been Zeltzi's most dedicated enemy for years. I don't want war, either external or internal. But I'm beginning to wonder if fighting is the only way to cut the canker that is my step-mother before she destroys Shinja in her thirst for greater power."

"She's the empress. What greater power? Unless you mean expansion of the empire."

"That is Avejo's solution," Invey said. "The truth is, the treasury is all but empty. We've had several revolts, each one from different directions, the latest a slave uprising, which only succeeded in binding all the imperial factions together just long enough to put it down. A slave revolt endangers everyone. But then they were right at each other's throats again, every province with its own grievances. After my father died, the empress made some very foolish promises in order to shore up her hold on power—but, like this building, the cracks are worsening."

He looked up at a crack in the ceiling, then thumbed his eye sockets. "What she desires is abasement of all her enemies—she revels in seeing the more powerful brought low. That includes allies and even family. She turned on hers, and destroyed them one by one. Now her poison arrows are aimed at the imperial family, who I know she regards as secretly conspiring against her."

"Are they?" Hlanan asked.

"I don't know. I'm kept *here*." Avejo held out his hands. "Probably. My uncle certainly is. Anyway, her solution to the empty treasury is to take their wealth and put them to work in the most menial positions. Busy, orderly slaves being another sign of power."

Hlanan sidestepped what he wanted to say, knowing that a judgment against their entire system of government would be less than welcome. Instead, he said, "How did she gain the throne? Both you princes are of age."

"My father, in dying, handed her the imperial tally. She forced him to by magic. Avejo knows it. I know it. The mages know it. We could all see it. But the household guard all saw the proper transfer of power—though Avejo's own are still angry. He was the heir."

Invey sighed. "My uncle, I know he'd raise his entire province at the slightest sign. Half of a sign from my mother, for there are many in this palace who would do anything for her. It was their loyalty that caused my step-mother to maneuver against her in the first place—she convinced the emperor in his last years that Luenro was secretly building power to wrest the crown to me. A crown I *never* wanted." Invey's mouth twisted.

Hlanan asked, "If it comes to that. Assuming your uncle is successful. What then?"

Invey blinked. "What?"

Hlanan remembered the hope and conviction in Luenro's face, and said, "Will your uncle be a good ruler?"

Invey's shoulders came up in a sharp shrug. "Same as Father, I expect. They're all the same. Except my step-mother, if she continues rule as she has begun, her reign will be a lot bloodier than many previous rulers. Once she is sure of her hold, my mother and I will be the first to go, and my uncle and his entire household no doubt the second. The empress supports Avejo's campaign to solve our problems by taking more land. Rich land. But once he does that? She's promised him the crown then, but I don't believe she'll ever relinquish it. He thinks she will."

Hlanan took a step nearer. After weeks of misery, he felt a curious compulsion to speak, though he knew it was dangerous. "Didn't your father, and his forebears make promises to the kingdom, to protect them, and to—"

Invey looked up at the ceiling carved with complicated interleaved trees, branches, and leaves that looked curiously like dragon scales as he recited, "... 'promise that I shall govern our lands and maintain true peace, protecting and upholding the laws of my forebears, I shall enjoin mercy and equity in all judgments, and I shall protect the rights and customs of our empire.'"

He looked down. "I heard it often enough from our tutors when Avejo and I were growing up. We had to copy it out a hundred times, to improve our handwriting. My plan for recovery was to examine those old laws, remove those no longer serving, and discover ways to implement new laws for the greater good.

My brother even listened, back when he was heir."

Hlanan sighed, aware that he ought to shut up, but his endless stint of misery brought words boiling out of him. "Why," he said, "should anyone be loyal to your brother, or his mother, or even your father? Has he kept any of those fine-sounding promises?"

"He would have said he had. He certainly governed, and passed judgment, though how much mercy... well, what's your point, foreigner?"

"Don't look at me as merely a foreigner. Look at me as one of a pack of loyal Shinjans down in your prison, whose lives depend not just on my returning, but on someone in this palace making an effort to win justice."

Invey sat down abruptly. He said in a much milder voice, "Go ahead, speak if you will."

"I'm not speaking for myself. I just want to know... if everyone is aware that what the emperor says is mere ritual, that the words mean nothing more than the meow of a cat, or the squeak of a rat—why should not the ordinary person give loyalty to the ones who words do mean something?"

"Like?"

"Xin."

Invey sighed. "But he was a *slave*. Of course he ranted on about freedom for all, and equality before the law."

"You sound like you don't believe slaves are persons."

"According to the law, they aren't."

"Then shouldn't the law change?"

"*You* sound like my mother," Invey said, one side of his mouth lifting in an almost-smile.

"Weren't the slaves persons before you forced them into slavery?" Hlanan persisted. "I understand that you see them as commodities, and you can force a semblance of acceptance because you wield the sword, but in their own minds, are they not still persons? You can see the anger and resentment in the uprisings."

When Invey seemed about to protest, Hlanan whirled around, the words wrung out of him, "No wonder we humans seem to have to rediscover civilization every couple of generations. It's not just slavery. Every artisan your brother forces into his army to kill or be killed destroys civilization that much more."

"Oaths are honor, my brother says," Invey retorted. "He'd tell you that rank comes with responsibility and promises, and one risks one's own life to keep those oaths. He does lead from the front. No one is faster." Invey's smile was surprisingly tender — it was clear to Hlanan that Invey, at least, cared for his brother.

Hlanan shook his head. "From what I have heard so far while a prisoner in your kingdom, it seems to me your honor is predicated on gaining rank and wealth at the cost of others' lives. Of course they'll fight back when they can. As for you imperials, you aren't risking your lives, except against one another." Hlanan paused to draw breath. "And a whole lot of people have to die before you get at each other. Come down to the Barrow with me, and deny it if you dare."

Invey gripped his hands together, then flung them outward. "Now you're saying there is no honor?"

"I don't have a definition of honor," Hlanan said, rubbing his hands through his greasy hair in a gesture not unlike Invey's. He wandered the length of the room, his bare feet slapping the cool tiles at every step. "I don't even like using the word, because the entire concept arises out of privilege. I'm more interested in trust. That is something everyone can keep, which contributes to the building of civilization. Keeping its peace. And creating the art that benefits all."

Invey uttered a bitter laugh. "Now you sound like — like someone I used to know." His gaze shifted away, his mouth tight. "For that matter, you sound like me when I was that age."

'That age.' Hlanan wondered if Invey was referring to the young hostage Luenro had mentioned.

Then Invey's head came up, and Hlanan paused to listen. He made out the faint tramp of boots.

"Go, quick," Invey said. "They are coming to check on me. But come back, will you? I need to know that my mother is alive."

"If I can," Hlanan said.

Invey sat behind the desk again. "Why do you think I confined my studies to magic? I wanted — still want — to find a way to peace through magic. Except there isn't any spell to force peace into the hearts of those who crave blood," he finished on a sour note.

This was so very much like something Hlanan would say that he stopped, bewildered by sharply conflicting emotions. Then moved to the door. "The thirst for blood usually arises out of anger," he said — and turned to look at this man who was so like him, and so unlike. "If I make it back, we will discuss the difference between rights and power."

He slipped out, grabbed extra food to stuff into his shirt, then had to dive beneath a table carved to look like a crouching dragon with folded wings. The wings came down to the clawed feet on either side, hiding him from passers-by.

The guards' rhythmic step didn't pause, but his heart crowded his throat until he had slipped down to the servants' halls again.

As he made his way along the dim, dusty corridor, he scolded himself for what he knew was a growing sympathy for Invey — which made him argue with the prince. He knew it was risky, maybe even stupid. For what was to keep Invey from turning him over to the guards?

But the urge to reach Invey was so *strong*. Possibly, maybe, at least some of Hlanan's questions were ones Invey'd been either wrestling with, or trying to ignore, on his own.

Seventeen

BACK TO ME, TO catch up in time.

I flew for days, surrounded by nothing but sky and sea.

When I first left the ships I pointed my nose in the correct direction, but as soon as I was out of sight of them I began to worry that I'd lose my way. There was no land around me to navigate by, much less landmarks — then I remembered the sun overhead. And at night the stars.

I remembered the slantwise direction on the map, which matched the way the ships had gone in reference to the sun's daily journey. I oriented by the sun rolling slowly overhead, and when it sank behind me (for I was flying south of morning), I used the stars to guide myself by.

I drank from rain, and learned to glide above the currents carrying the clouds, or I don't know if I would have survived. There would be no carrying me — I was far beyond where the great gryphs flew. They were strong, but their large bodies needed frequent feeding.

Hunger began to tax me. I flew and slept, or rather flew in and out of the world of dreams, until even the currents seemed unable to hold up my increasingly heavy body.

Bear up, young firebird. Thou art nearing the land of my young, came Rue's inner voice. *Use thy fire.*

My fire?

How could I aim my fire unless I transformed — at which time I would plummet to the sea far below with a nasty splat.

Draw on the sun, came the vast voice, calm and shimmering with humor. *Thy strength will come if thou drawest the sun's fire into thee. Thou hast the skill. Thou must sharpen thy will.*

I struggled to find a way until I thought about dragons. Stupid me! Dragons breathed fire, which meant taking in warmth as well as expelling it. I was at least part firebird, so shouldn't I be able to do it as well?

I opened my beak the way I did to drink rain, breathed in warmth and light and air, then made a mental pinhole through which I shot fire.

Which I then almost flew into. I banked, tumbled, righted myself, dizzy and shaky.

Below thee, young firebird, came Rue's voice. *Let the air carry thee.*
Oh.

I shot flames underneath me—and reveled in the warm air boiling up. Somehow the air currents were affected, and for a short time I rode high, barely having to move my wings.

When the sense of heaviness bore me down again, I made more fire. And so on, until I learned how to shoot the fire best into the wind, so that the new current would carry me higher and farther.

I did this until my flames began to weaken. And then at last came a time when I couldn't find any fire in me at all, but as the sun rimmed the world, there jutted on the horizon a dark mass.

Slowly, slowly, I glided down, unable to beat my wings anymore. I had just enough strength to reach a shore of many colored pebbles rattling in and out on the waves. I dropped more than alighted onto a massive black rock, breathed out as I transformed... and dropped into heavy sleep.

I clawed my way out of sleep, into increasing awareness of discomfort. My arms ached. The sun burned on my eyelids. I was desperately thirsty and hungry, but I couldn't seem to move.

It took all the effort I had to open my eyes to the pearly-blue light of very early morning. I gazed up blearily into a circle of faces staring down at me. My gaze traveled down armor, to hands, most of which held a variety of weapons.

When I tried to sit up — to move — I discovered that I'd been tied up with rope.

"What *is* this creature?" A new warrior sauntered up and asked the circle around me.

It was such a relief to have my inner ear back again: no language remained a mystery as I heard the meaning and intent with the words. But I was too enervated to respond, my mouth too dry for speech. Just as well, I decided. Even thoughts came slowly, as if working their way through a gigantic vat of honey.

"I've never seen one before," another said.

"Nor I."

An older one shouldered into the group. "Good job. Secured, all according to orders. Put her in the cage."

Right then I didn't care what those orders might be. Rope meant I wasn't about to be killed. Everything else could wait.

Two bent down, one with hands under my armpits and another grabbing my feet. "It's like down," this one exclaimed, examining my ankles with wide eyes at the same time the other one said, "She's light. I can tote her." With only a slight huff of breath, the warrior hefted me over her shoulder.

Crunch, crunch, crunch went footsteps. All I could see were the swinging straps hanging down from her armor, and her boots. It seemed a long walk, but then we reached a rutted road with tufts of grass growing between missing stones. Another walk, then voices surrounded us.

"What's that?"

"Great work! Took two squads to capture a... six-year-old child?"

Through the guffaws, another commented, "Is that a tail? It's got a tail!"

"I've heard of those people," another voice, higher, butted in. "Feather people. But aren't they supposed to be blue? And... birds? And they live on mountaintops."

"In the volcano?" a deep voice rumbled, sarcastic.

High Voice responded with just as much sarcasm, "Not every

mountain is a volcano. Just the really big ones."

A nasal voice thrust its way in, "What's it doing *here?*"

"That's for the captain to find out," Deep Voice said. "Tiger Squad said a kelp-scavenger saw something fall out of the sky onto the shore. When we went to see, all we found was this here feather person."

"Looks to me like it climbed out of the ocean," High Voice said doubtfully. "Look at all the sand, and there's kelp tangled in that purple thing it's wearing."

A new voice barked, "Put that prisoner into the cart and get back on your patrol!"

"Uh, what about our rope?" High Voice asked.

"Untie it, of course," the new voice snapped impatiently. "How far do you think that scrap of... whatever it is... can run?"

So someone untied my hands, which dangled down the warrior's back, then she dropped me onto a flat surface that smelled like sour clothes and old vegetables. I opened my eyes to find myself in a cage made of wood, set on the back of a cart. Two warriors looked in the open door at me, an older woman whose hair was dyed a garish red, and a young fellow with fiery red hair and thousands of freckles. I wanted to leap past them and escape but it took all my strength to struggle to a sitting position—and I was dizzy. I opened my mouth, then decided that I might learn more if I pretended not to understand Shinjan. So I motioned to my lips and made drinking gestures.

Garish Hair merely shrugged, but Freckles unclipped a flask from his belt, and held it out.

I barely had the strength to take it, and almost dropped it. My fingers clutched the sides of the flask, which squirted warm, stale water into my mouth. It was wonderful. I gulped it down until I almost choked, water dribbling out of my mouth on the sides.

"Hey! Don't swill it all!" Freckles snatched it back.

"You can get more," Garish Hair said. "My guess is, it—she—got thrown off the masthead of some ship. That would explain looking like she fell out of the sky."

Everybody laughed at that, and someone muttered a crack

about how many bottles it took before everything looked like it was falling out of the sky.

Garish Hair snapped, "Shaddup! Unless you want to continue your clown act while doing extra stable mucking? No? We'll report that she was stuck in the sea until the tide washed her up. She's so light she must have floated on the surface."

Everybody accepted that as reasonable—the door to the cage was shut and locked—and I, thirst relieved, looked around. A swarm of Shinjan warriors organized themselves, two groups marching in opposite directions. One group stayed with the cart, guarding it as shabby villagers looked on from a wary distance, silent and cold-faced.

Behind them, equally shabby buildings leaned into each other, roofed largely with some sort of fronds. Everything looked dilapidated.

Escape would be easy enough. I could transform to my bird self and get through the cart's bars. I could also set them on fire, for they were wooden. But I wasn't strong enough to get farther than a few steps.

For now, I decided, danger was relatively minor. Let them do the traveling for me, while I learned more.

I curled up in a ball and fell back into slumber.

Eighteen

THAT SAME MORNING, HLANAN had to force himself to stay awake until dawn light grayed the long windows of the princes' wing. His journey was aided by a thunderstorm that crashed and roared overhead, blue-white light glittering in the gemstone eyes of the statues and reflecting off the gold in their ornaments and hands.

Still, the night seemed to last forever. When at last he heard the familiar tramp of the morning guard, he renewed the illusion spell on himself, and slipped up on their heels.

When they reached the cell, a scummy tide of rainwater sloshed out past the bars. Hlanan crouched, desperate to keep from splashing. There was nothing he could do about the water rilling around his feet and hands as he slid himself under the wheelbarrow. At least this duty was so rote, the light so bad, that none of them bothered to look down.

As soon as the door was unlocked, Nenor tromped toward the guards, hands on her hips as she said, "If Prince Avejo truly does not want the imperial princess to die, then she will need a blanket at least."

"Get back," the captain of the guard snarled. "Back, galk!"

"Call me what you want, but come and look at her! She can't get up—she's cold." The woman's voice trembled with stress.

Three of the guards peered into the cell as if that would improve their ability to see the murky gloom, unconsciously taking a few steps out of their formation. That's when Hlanan slid out from under the wheelbarrow, eeling between two.

At once their captain roared at them to close up in formation if they didn't want to see themselves up close and personal what the galk cell looked like from the inside.

Hlanan pressed up against the wall. He was thoroughly wet in dirty, icy water, but the illusion held and he remained unnoticed.

The captain jerked his thumb. The food got dumped, and the guards retreated. The door clanged shut, the prisoners looked around—and Hlanan dropped the illusion.

Once again an exhaled breath sighed through the cell.

"What news?" Sig asked.

"Little," Hlanan said. "The inspection guards were right behind me. Then it took a long time to get back."

Nobody questioned that—they all knew how dangerous it was.

He moved to the food, cleaning it up by magic.

While everyone was eating, Hlanan moved up to Luenro, and said in Elras, "We spoke, but he did not tell me his intentions. However, he asked me to return in order to reassure him about you." And he gave a quick summary of their conversation, to which she listened intently. He finished reluctantly, "He might not have a plan. He spoke of his idea about overhauling laws as past tense. He seems to have accepted that the empress will consolidate her rule, after Avejo goes out to conquer more land, or else his uncle will lead a bloody civil war to get rid of the empress, and everything will go on as usual."

Luenro's unwinking gaze was blank, as far as he could see in the gloom. She sat with her hands hugging her arms, and he made certain to keep his wet, clammy self from getting near her. "I have to think," she said finally. "But know this: until the emperor died, and Kenji was done away with by Zeltzi, or ran off, Invey's goals were... different. He has lost faith in himself," she whispered.

⸺⬥⸺

Now that I've caught Hlanan up in time, and we're getting

closer to each other in place, I'll have to switch back and forth between us a bit faster.

I woke up a couple times then went back to sleep again. They opened the cage and slid in a jug of water and a wooden bowl of some kind of boiled grain with some very limp greens floating about on top. I inhaled it, curled back up, and slept.

When next we stopped longer than to change the horses, I felt a great deal better. Not by any means full strength, but my mind had woken up again. I could sense Rue, very much like that quiescent lake of boiling lava, below the surface of my mind. I liked knowing he was there, though I wondered what my mind was like to him, a gnat buzzing frantically about?

No answer.

I was going to curl up again when I heard the creak of rusty hinges. I turned around, and saw that we were approaching an enormous iron-reinforced gate in what looked like a castle or outpost.

I sat up, the urge to sleep forgotten. Now maybe I'd find out where I was in Shinja, how far from the capital and Hlanan.

We rolled through the gate. People pressed away to either side, staring at the guards and at me. Most remained still and quiet, except for a few furtive whispers and a couple of pointing fingers. Once a little girl dashed up, laughing as she exclaimed, "Fish-colored galk!"

I widened my eyes and stuck out my tongue at her. She stuck out her tongue at me, until what looked like an older sister cuffed her and dragged her back—and a whip cracked right where she'd been the moment before.

"Get lost, you rabble! If you have no work, we'll find some for you!"

The people scattered, the more bold looking back and scowling.

The cart turned into a courtyard with a smaller gate that swung shut behind us. Servants ran to the horses' heads, I was glad to see, because both were thirsty, which made me thirsty again.

Then I saw a sight that sent horror thrilling through me: a line of youngsters was marched out, each with a bare arm freshly tattooed. Some clutched bloody fingers over their tattoo, others let it bleed. The youngest were crying as they were hustled toward the barber to have their heads shaved.

My cage door swung open. I had enough presence of mind to maintain my pose of weakness, though by now I had recovered most of my strength. There was no chance I would let them put a tattoo on me, and as for shaving my scalp, it would hurt as much as cutting off a limb. The thought made my hair lift and cloud about my head instinctively.

The guards to either side of me actually dropped back. I hadn't lifted hair or tail in the cage, so this startled them.

"Inside, inside," one barked at me, too loud, as if yelling would make me understand Shinjan.

I hesitated. I could fly away right then. I knew I couldn't go far, but at least I could get out of the city—but a glance at the sentries, each armed with crossbows, halted me. They could easily shoot me out of the sky.

I tried to think of other plans as they led me inside, but upstairs, not to where the other youngsters stood under bared steel.

The two guards took me to what was obviously a commander. He scowled at me, then said to the guard, "Does it speak?"

"We believe it's a she," Guard Two said.

"Does *she* speak?" the commander said, with dire irony.

"Not as we've heard," Guard one replied. "We think she's one of those mountain bird people."

"Bird! Does it look like she's sprouting wings to fly away?" And as bored guards lurking at the door barked laughter, the commander said, reasonably, "Wouldn't you?"

Guard One stated stolidly, "Whether or not she's one of them animal people, I haven't seen one like her before. Therefore she comes under imperial order."

The words 'imperial order' sobered everyone up fast.

The commander quickly divested himself of responsibility

with a quick, "Whether or not she's one of a kind is up to the empress. You did the right thing. Take her straight to the menagerie. If the empress already has one, it'll be *her* decision whether or not to brand this creature or toss her in the Barrow."

Barrow! I remembered that word from Hlanan's dreams. If the menagerie and the Barrow were close, and it sounded like they might be, it seemed I was about to get all my traveling done for me, while I rested and recovered my strength.

⸻ ⬦ ⸻

In the capital—specifically in the Barrow—the air had turned cool, and at night, cold.

The guards tossed in a blanket after the next day's wheelbarrow delivery. This blanket, old and smelling of mildew (indicating that someone had been tasked specifically to find the nastiest one available in the palace) was passed hand to hand to Luenro.

She coughed when she shook it out. Hlanan went to her, concerned. He took one sniff and did the cleaning spell over the blanket. It was so ugly and worn no one would know the difference, but at least the princess wouldn't be breathing mildew.

Though the weather was inexorably chilling toward winter, and the tremors shook the ground more often, Hlanan's heart buoyed at every evidence, however small, at how his fellow prisoners had banded together. There was no more need for Sig to use his superior strength; the food was shared out in an orderly manner each morning. The miraculous had slowly become the norm.

Many had begun sleeping back to back for the warmth. Hlanan was going to stay by himself as long as he could bear it; he dreaded saying something in the middle of the night that might reveal his background, and there was the tattoo on his shoulder that he couldn't risk exposing if his thin, grimy summer shirt ripped at last.

Over the next couple of days, as my cart rolled toward the

capital, he exercised to give his body something to do while he went back through his conversations with Invey.

He regretted how badly he'd expressed himself. He was too tired, and too hungry, to think well, but one thing for sure: it seemed arrogant to a ridiculous degree to be arguing with an enemy prince about his own homeland. And yet Hlanan's heart cinched tight at the mere thought of shrugging it off.

He knew why. He owed it to all those slaves he had known years ago, who hadn't managed to escape. Many of whom might not now even be alive. But they still deserved justice.

Maybe it was futile—even arrogant—to think that he could make any difference, but he wasn't going to stop until either he got away (without breaking faith with his fellow prisoners) or Invey sicced the guards on him.

Luenro's worry on her son's behalf spread to everyone there in that prison cell. Dangerous as it was, they all worked together to slip Hlanan out again.

At least they had it down to a kind of drill, relying on the guards' anxiety about anything happening to this precious prisoner. Any day—and time—they might come to take her away to another cell, but, as Sig muttered in Elras where Hlanan could hear, the empress relished cruelty, and she probably laughed at the notion of Luenro being imprisoned among the brutes in their pit.

Hlanan reserved judgment about the empress, having never met her, but one thing struck him: Sig had begun to trust him, or he would never have shared so dangerous an opinion. Especially with both of them knowing that Hlanan was getting outside the cell.

They let a day go by, and then a couple more when the guards stayed too close together and Hlanan couldn't get past the legs.

Then came a morning under a roaring storm. Sleety rain poured in through the grating, flooding halfway across the slimy floor. At Sig's gesture, a couple of volunteers pushed water over to the doors, and sure enough, a couple of guards slipped as they came in to dump the day's food.

Once again, Hlanan slipped out, shivering from the icy water that he had to lie in. He warmed up by running the now-familiar route to Invey's, where he found the prince looking up in a kind of strained expectation.

Invey had food waiting, this time right in his study. But he'd scarcely let Hlanan get a bite before speaking what was clearly words he'd been mulling.

"You said," Invey stated as he came around the desk and opened the windows, "you wished to discourse on the difference between a right and a power. Enlighten me. Are they not the same?"

He turned to face Hlanan, arms crossed. His tunic was black silk, embroidered in gold with falcons in flight, their eyes glinting in the light: rubies.

Hlanan was briefly distracted by Invey's impressive clothing. Previously he'd resembled the scholar he seemed to be by nature. But then he raised his gaze to Invey's furrowed brow, and his tense expression.

This talk actually seemed to matter to him. So Hlanan forced his mind back to the question. "When the Kherval first was formed into an empire," he said, "power was grounded in force. When nobles swore their oath of fealty on being confirmed in their titles, they laid their sword at the feet of the emperor or empress: their rights lay implied in their power."

"It is the same here," Invey muttered, pacing back along the wall.

"After many bloody disputes, our laws acknowledge that a right is fundamental to civilization. And civilization cannot be based on force, it has to be free agreement between all. Everyone in the Kherval is guaranteed certain rights, from the smallest street sweeper to the richest prince."

"What rights can there be outside of the right to protect your own land?" Invey said.

"The right to live your life as you wish. Of course there are limits, defined by laws. Doing no harm. Fair trade. So on. As for the ownership of land, if you were to talk to the Hrethan, for example," Hlanan said, "you would discover that they find the concept inconceivable. Even laughable, were they given to scorn."

"How can that be?"

"They would ask you how you could possibly own land that exists long after you are dead."

"But that is implied in family continuity—handed down from owner to heir, and so on. An orderly progression, the reason we *have* laws."

"Well, then we come back to defining property, which extends to the ground one lives on, and the things we make. Then there is the question of other living beings. We believe that liberty is a natural right if we are to consider ourselves civilized, therefore no sentient can own another sentient."

"If it's so natural," Invey leaned his elbows on his knees, "can one not use it, sell it, give it away as one wishes, and still remain civilized?"

"I...reserve judgment on that," Hlanan said. "But our discussion centers around that right being taken. No one agrees to slavery."

"I know *that* isn't true," Invey rejoined calmly. "The poor often sell their children, sometimes themselves, into slavery. Debtors will become bond-slaves for a given time until their debt is paid off. Children are sold so that they will always be fed and housed. There is no violence in that."

"Not physical violence. But other kinds? I'm not so sure," Hlanan retorted. "See yourself as a child of five or six. Your mother or father incurs a debt, or some other disaster of which you are unaware, and suddenly you are ripped away from your family, branded, and put to work scrubbing the floors of a stranger. You did not, at any time, surrender your liberty—it was taken away, in an act that to the emotions is every bit as violent as if that parent had suddenly taken a stick to your back for no reason that you could perceive. Worse, because after the beating, you presumably take up your life again, in the home you know. But as a slave, your life as you knew it is gone—your identity is gone. You are now a thing, with the value of a chair or a cup. Less, if that cup is golden."

"Identity isn't gone. That happens only in death. One gains a new identity." Invey waved a hand. "And slaves with skills are worth a great deal. My mother taught me to treat kindly with our slaves. They compete to be chosen for our service. Others speak of their gratitude for warmth, food, shelter."

"Perhaps some are." Hlanan lifted a shoulder. "Others might trade all that for freedom, had they the chance."

"This is what my foster-brother kept insisting, before he..." Invey turned away, then back. "How can *you* know?"

He shot the question with such skepticism that Hlanan's temper flared, and he jerked the open neck of his flimsy shirt over his shoulder, where his old tattoo was plain to see. "I was a small boy when Shinjan slavers took me off the streets of a harbor," he said. "I was not poor, or helpless. I had an apprenticeship, and a life of my own choosing. As a slave I hated every single day, every night. Every crust, every slap of the cords. I nearly killed myself, but for a chance to escape, and a friend to see it."

"But...you're..."

"The magic tracer was removed. The tattoo wasn't, for reasons irrelevant now. Trust me when I tell you that I do, in fact, understand what slaves say among themselves where those holding the whip can't hear them. And also, I refused, with my entire being, to accept that identity. The moment I escaped, I shed that identity."

"And yet," Invey said, "you bear the tattoo still."

Hlanan said, "That was in the nature of a vow, to rescue any others that I could."

Invey's head jerked up. A moment later Hlanan heard the approach of tramping feet. "It's too early for them to summon me," he murmured. "Something else must be happening. You must hide." Invey looked around wildly, as if a label might appear in his room with the helpful legend HIDE HERE.

Hlanan wasn't that much better at figuring out where to stash himself—what experience he'd had with sneaking and hiding had been with me.

At least he knew enough to avoid diving behind the curtains, which would have bulged with a person-sized lump. He dropped under the desk, behind the thin panel of wood pierced in graceful patterns.

Invey moved to the buffet. He was picking up a second bun, twin to the one Hlanan had half-eaten (now crammed into his shirt) as the door opened.

Hlanan could see the entire room through that pierced panel, and hoped he was in enough shadow under the desk that he couldn't be seen. Instinctively he flung an arm over his face, in case there was some stray reflection of light that might shine through the hundreds of piercings in the wood onto his face. At least his formerly white shirt was dark gray-green with dirt and slime.

An impatient hand thrust the door wide, and in walked Crown Prince Avejo. Still wearing armor, though he wasn't loaded with weaponry. "Stay outside," he told his honor guard.

"Brother," he said to Invey. His gaze went from Invey to the food and back. "You didn't get enough at Mother's sumptuous meal?"

Invey's fingers trembled before he pressed them to his side, crumbs falling everywhere. "Sometimes I get hungry," he said defensively, with such a guilty expression that Hlanan knew that buffet *had* been ordered specifically for him.

Avejo let out a bark of laughter, then crossed the room, and nearly caused Hlanan's heart to bang its way out of his ribs as he made straight for the desk. But he whirled, and hitched himself onto a corner of the desk, one booted foot swinging barely two hands' distance from Hlanan. "Why do you look as if someone's about to take a knife to you? There was Mother, pretending we're a happy family!"

Invey said wryly, "That was frightening enough."

Avejo laughed.

Invey went on quickly, "She refused to let me bring up the subject of *my* mother. "Where is she?"

I told you that, Hlanan thought—then realized that maybe Invey wasn't supposed to know that. Or he wanted to double-check.

Avejo's voice softened. "Safe. I promise."

"Where?"

Avejo sighed. "She's in the Barrow. You *know* Mother," he added quickly as Invey's face tightened. "At least she's safe there. Really. I agreed only so that she wouldn't do anything worse. And it's my honor guard there overseeing the mucks in charge of that end of the prison. They know they'll lose their lives if anything happens to Second Mother Luenro."

It was Invey's turn to sigh. "Since there is little I can do about that, or anything else, why are you here?"

"To see *you*. To talk, where no one can hear us."

"About?"

"First, have you seen the hostage?" Avejo asked suddenly.

Invey stilled. He didn't even seem to breathe, then, "Not since he left. I hope you aren't bringing bad news?"

"If I knew any I would. Bad or good. Not that there's anything good about that animal. No, don't start with me, Invey, you *know* he's an animal, or part animal. Your calling him foster-brother doesn't make him one. I think the proof is in how he took up with Xin's rabble, in spite of us treating him like a prince of true blood."

"Rumors." Invey set the crumbled, uneaten bun back on the buffet with the absence of one who has never gone hungry except by choice.

Hlanan loathed seeing fresh food wasted—he had to force his attention back to the brothers as Avejo said impatiently, "He's part animal, he consorted with runaway slaves and thieves, then ran off. And *you* saw fit to teach him magic," Avejo retorted.

"Rumors," Invey repeated, looking out the window. "You can find a rumor saying anything."

Avejo shifted on the desk, his armor rattling. The heel of his boot began gently kicking against the panel not far from Hlanan's nose, *bang, bang, bang*. "All right, we'll never agree about our former hostage. Except to say that, thanks to Kenji's stupid actions, if Mother's people catch him, he'll be formerly alive. And she'll blame his death on the rebels when she sends me to the islanders to renegotiate the treaty."

"You mean, to conquer them?" Invey asked, so gently Hlanan almost didn't hear it.

Avejo sighed sharply. "It's orders. You *know* I have to obey orders, too—until I can get the kips sworn to me as emperor."

From Luenro Hlanan had learned that the imperial tally had a lot of magic on it preventing it from being wrested by violence, and the Household Guard, the kips, were sworn to obey the holder of that tally.

Therefore, every Shinjan knew that the holder of the tally controlled the kips, who controlled the empire.

Avejo went on. "And we could use Iwarna's wealth. We'll govern them fairly, if it helps. In fact, *you* could do that—it would keep you well away from Mother's eye. Speaking of her. You've always been the one with your nose in dusty old archives during our magic tutoring days. What do you know about dragons?"

"Dragons," Invey repeated, incredulous.

"That's what I thought. Long dead, maybe altogether myth. Until our spies reported seeing one flying over Sveran Djur's royal palace last year."

"I still have trouble believing that."

"As do I, but what we think doesn't matter, because Mother seems to believe it. What's more, I found out she's got the entire scribe staff delving into the oldest archives, looking for dragon lore—and that possibly includes those mages she sent away years ago, who are now back. Though apparently none of us are to speak to them. I wish you would find out if that is what those mages are actually doing."

"Why?" Invey asked. "I mean, the dragon lore sort of makes sense—we've got the Dragon Festival coming up in a few days. She might want some other kind of fete besides the same old dragon dance we've been doing for generations, another way to keep the populace from thinking about the quakes and the empty stalls in the market where there should be food."

"Agreed."

"But why should I investigate her mages? She doesn't trust me as it is. You know enough magic to speak to them."

"You know more."

"Why can't you talk to them?"

"Because she ordered me to stay clear of them, saying they have work to do, and I have enough to do overseeing the army. I can't argue with that."

He sighed. *Bang, bang.* His heel struck harder against the desk. "The only information I've managed to glean, from one of the under-scribes, is that she has apparently taken it into her head that these quakes we've been having are the signs of a dragon erupting out of the mountain right above us now. Unless we do something magical to stop it. My army not being much use against dragons, is the implication."

"But there *is* no dragon in our mountain. Or anywhere else. The old archive is clear enough on that—there were hundreds of witnesses to that old dragon falling into the sea in flames centuries ago. It was the last one."

"Hah! So everyone thought until one flew out of the Djurans' volcano and attacked their imperial palace."

"I still think that might be garbled rumor. Someone mistook one of those big purple gryphs they have there."

Avejo said casually, "I know. I put the question to our pet Djuran down in the arena hold."

"He's still alive?" Invey asked, turning his face away, but Hlanan could see the tightening of a grimace.

"Alive, and he's even become a kind of pet to the populace," Avejo said. "They love to hate him. The stands have been filled every time we post one of his duels. It's great! I've been able to keep the city quiet because everyone wants the credit to get a seat to watch him fight our best. But he wouldn't talk to me. I hauled out a Djuran slave to blather to him in his tongue, so I know he understood the questions. Wouldn't peep about dragons, or anything else."

Invey sighed again.

Avejo said, "I know you hate the arena, but you should really come see him fight. It's *art*, I tell you. And our people are under strict orders not to kill him if they do manage to win. So far, they haven't. So you won't be watching a death match. Even Mother is keeping her hands off, though she says when the Dragon Festival comes, she wants me to fight him, and win or lose, she'll give him a state execution that—"

"Stop there." Invey raised a hand. "I don't need to hear any more."

Avejo's foot banged harder, once, twice, then he jumped off the desk. "Well, I wish you'd comb some of these old scrolls of yours and find out about the dragon lore, at least. I'll see what I can find out about those new mages. I really don't like it when she doesn't tell me her plans."

Avejo crossed the room as rapidly as he'd moved into it, and banged the door open. "I'd liefer know what cometh before she springeth it upon us," he added in their royal Dragon Language, and was gone with a ringing of boot heels.

Invey remained where he was, staring sightlessly at the plates of food on the buffet as Hlanan slowly climbed out from behind the desk, then joined him. Hlanan glanced down at the buffet table, wondering how many hands the soon-stale food would go through before the remains would be dumped on the floor for the galk.

And Imperial Princess Luenro.

Invey looked up, his expression tight. Hlanan understood then that the prince was determined not to discuss his family affairs with the outsider when he said, " So you pay laborers? Then every farmer no matter how small a plot must be wealthy beyond belief."

"No," Hlanan replied, making a hasty mental backtrack. "Value is a constant negotiation. Not just in gold, but in skill, knowledge, trade."

Invey shook his head slowly, his hands revealing tension in how they flexed and tightened. "You say negotiation, but is it not really a struggle? Our struggle is in part due to the need to pay our warriors on land and on sea. Our laws are based on the principle that they who risk their lives gain their reward in winning. It is only through martial success that one gains — land to the captains and above, *selv* to those below, who in turn use it in the markets."

Hlanan had learned from his cellmates that selv was essentially credit: the sailor or warrior carried his or her selv-stick, from which an exact accounting was made by merchants, who in turn, at the beginning of each season, was granted an equivalent in raw materials from crown lands.

Invey sighed. "With the famines, and the scarcity, and now with the mountain shaking so much that we fear magic cannot hold it from exploding, the empress — and my brother — believe the only way back to wealth and peace is to conquer new territories. From which the crown shall gain new materials, making the merchants content. And of course bringing fresh labor to bring about those materials. The selv sticks we grant are understood to promise this future."

Hlanan now understood those brooding looks on the streets — surrounded by the unrepaired houses in both the harbor, the outpost, and in the capital. "And so the warriors demand goods from the merchants at swordpoint? Because the crown is not honoring its debt?"

Invey twitched at the word 'debt,' as though no one of royal blood could owe debt, except perhaps to another noble. Debt seemed to imply a degree of equality between debtor and grantor. The crown could not possibly be in debt to lowly merchants. The Shinjans had another word for their portion of the selv agreement — which kept social distinctions intact.

"We cannot control famine." Invey smacked his hands down on the pile of books. "What do you think I've been doing this past year?" He shook his head. "And I've failed at that. Go ahead, tell me how you'd govern Shinja," he added bitterly.

Hlanan suppressed an equally bitter retort. "I don't know how to govern Shinja," he said, striving to keep his voice even. Calm. "But you wanted to talk about trade. And so I'm offering an answer. I'm not saying it's *the* answer, but it doesn't trade in human life. Our medium of trade is coinage. This is a form that acknowledges no social distinction. No obligation based on a future that might not come. Its worth is established right now."

Invey shook his head. "How can order — hierarchy — be maintained if a two-year warrior, barely trained, if *anyone*, can issue the equivalent of selv?"

"Because the individual is only given an amount of whatever you agree as your medium of exchange — whether it's redshells or copper, gold or pearls — equal to one day's labor. That might be a different amount in peace than in war, in a dangerous setting as opposed to a simple one, and it can be scaled for trained artisans. But I can assure you, from our own history, that to take all that imperial gold and silver decorating your palaces and vaults, and convert it in some form, even your marked sticks like your selv, and make that the new medium of exchange instead of lives, will earn you the accolade of being benevolent by future generations. But." Hlanan tapped his own shoulder. "You must free the slaves first."

Invey frowned into the distance. "So they all are given selv sticks according to a day of labor?"

"That's one measure."

Invey tipped his head, his eyes narrowed with skepticism. "And yet, the first complaint will be from, oh, the stone mason, who trains very exactly. Or the goldsmith. They will be offended to be given the same measure as a laborer in the field."

"Expertise gains one more measure," Hlanan said. "But think about the effect in the rest of the world, which knows the trade of coinage for goods: the power of the sword replaced by the power of the coin. There is no destruction, no loss of life. Each party walks away with what they want."

Invey frowned.

Hlanan said, "If the crown owns all the labor of an individual, what causes that individual to work hardest, other than the constant vigilance of the hated labor-master? Who is usually a bully, and must be constantly watched lest he, in his vile entertainment, damage the workers and so lessen the product, while stealing in secret from his master?"

Invey spread his hands, then stiffened as another tremor rolled through, rattling the glass in the windows.

"Reward. Gain," Hlanan said. "If the laborer works harder, and sees a material gain in the extra labor, then there is incentive. And no bully necessary."

A distant bell clanged, and Invey started. He pressed his hands to his temples, making Hlanan wonder how bad a headache the prince had.

Not surprisingly, Invey said, "You'd better go. Take some food to my mother?"

Hlanan was already stuffing bread into his shirt.

Nineteen

THE MORNING HLANAN WAS able to sneak out under cover of the storm, my carters and I reached the palace, and proceeded around a warren of side buildings to a huge garden complex, in the middle of which was the empress's menagerie.

Once we passed beneath a graceful gate, the guards walked almost on tiptoe, their posture stiff, as if under the scrutiny of a captain, but no one was in sight. I looked around in amazement. It was the first time in my life I saw such beauty and sensed such an atmosphere of silent wretchedness.

The menagerie's garden was made up of flowers, shrubs, and trees chosen for their rich colors and aromatic blossoms, leaves, and bark. Cages had been set amidst decorative groupings of shrubs and trees and flowers, each under a platform with a tiled roof. These roof tiles were in complicated patterns, and the cages' bars were covered in gold leaf.

It was beautifully designed and maintained, and guarded sedulously, as this, I discovered by listening to whispers, was the empress's personal retreat.

Everything, in short, to please the eye of a single human, with absolutely no thought to the proper environment of the prisoners. Oh, the cages were scrupulously clean—I'm certain not for the sake of the prisoners, but to spare the nose of the empress. They were set amid artistically landscaped plants and trees, which effectively isolated the cages from each other's view.

I had to shut my inner eye tight against the desolation around me, especially when I sensed words in the searing misery. Some of those imprisoned in this glittering, artistic torture chamber were dual-natured, but forced to stay in their animal form by magic ward.

Apparently my being human in size and dimension earned me a larger cage. My guards peered warily through the sheeting rain as if their lives depended on their vigilance—a quick peek at their blaring thoughts, and oh yes, their lives did depend on my being safely transferred from the barred cart to the golden bars of a menagerie cage. Else a very, very nasty and prolonged fate awaited their captain, and the rest would go straight to the Barrow.

Barrow, there it was again.

I tamped down my impatience, and moped into the cage, giving no sign of the relief I felt that the cage bars were wide enough for me to squeeze my bird body through.

The cage had been set with a sort of reclining bed with cushions, and some decorative plants in pots around the edges. It afforded comfort, but no privacy other than the shrubbery at the sides and back, keeping those in the neighboring cages from seeing me. But nothing would impede the empress's gaze when she came around the front side to view her collection of living oddities.

The golden door swung shut, the lock snicked, and the squad breathed collectively in relief as they splashed away with their empty cart, leaving me safely locked up.

Or so they thought.

I went straight to the bars, which I tested. Solid iron beneath the gold. But! In my bird shape, I'd fit through just fine. I considered leaving right then, but that inner instinct that had been honed all my life, and sharpened even more after my time as Jardis Dhes-Andis's prisoner, warned me that someone unseen was watching me.

My instinctive suspicion was the empress. I don't trust emperors and empresses, who in my experience are much like thieves, only worse, because they have law on their side. A regular thief might go to prison for grabbing you, but an emperor can nab you, and nobody makes a peep.

Except this was her private play area, so why would she hide? Unless that amused her, of course. Anyway, I decided I didn't want to reveal anything about myself. After all, a hidden empress could have hidden crossbow archers planted all through those decorative shrubs, and while the rain was very heavy, making visibility difficult, it would also slow my flight.

So. I was in no pain. The cage was shelter. Maybe I'd get food! I decided to wait, and learn what I could before making my next move.

The rain increased steadily. No one came. So I finally curled up on the cushion, which looked pretty but smelled of mildew, a familiar smell. I won't call it comforting, because so much of my childhood was spent hiding. In any case, I fell asleep.

When I woke, the storm had passed, leaving a world of plinking, splashing drips. Servants in soggy livery came around with a cart full of different baskets and barrels of food. They went from cage to cage. In some, they chucked contents, and in others, they waited for the prisoner to point at something.

When they came to me, they stopped. I put my elbow over my nose at the smell of meat, and pointed at the baskets of fruit and one of grain. Interesting that nothing was cooked. I wondered if this was a sign that they didn't consider any of us sentient, if not human.

Small portions were laid right on the floor of my cage. All right, clearly I was regarded as a lower being in their scale.

I'd just bit into a slightly squashy peach when a horn blatted some distance away.

I would have ignored it, except the soft whispers just barely audible from the direction of the far cages, and the mutter, coo, and cry of creatures, all stilled. Warning tightened the back of my neck.

Up the main walkway, which the carters and the food people had avoided, processed six banner carriers, each bearing an enormous oval banner of crimson with a huge crown centered, and around it an embroidered red dragon, winking with precious gems. Behind them walked a woman clothed in sober gray.

The gray woman walked in front of a huge palanquin born on poles by twenty husky men. This palanquin had an elaborate tiled roof, and fantastic carvings, mostly painted—red the chief color—around the doors and the side windows, which were curtained.

Behind the palanquin armed guards marched in step.

At a signal, everyone stopped. All those servants—more than fifty people, all to accompany one woman—stood as still as statues, except for the palanquin bearers, who set their burden down gently.

From the palanquin stepped a woman. She was as different from Hlanan's mother, also an empress, as could be: her hair was such a flaming red that I knew it had to be colored by a mage, probably a fresh spell every day, to make it so bright. Empress Zeltzi was very thin, her face painted to emphasize her eyes and mouth, the skin stretched in a way that suggested magic alteration. At a distance she looked no more than twenty, but as she approached, her neck and her hands revealed that she was far older, maybe even older than Aranu Crown.

She wore an elaborate gown glittering with jewels, and rings on every finger. Her red hair was half done up in a complication of braids on which rested a diamond-studded crown. The rest hung down, flame-red against the deep black panel of the back of her gown, which two servants picked up and carried over the soggy ground.

She walked right up to my cage, and her painted lips thinned in a kind of smile. "This *is* one of a kind. The rest of these creatures are blue. I have never seen one this color," she said to a gray-robed woman at her side, standing with bowed head.

I was considering what to say—my days of blurting out whatever I was thinking had ended with my stay as prisoner of the Emperor of Sveran Djur—when the empress said to the woman in gray, "Make it speak."

It? You have to realize that there are several ways of saying 'it' in Shinjan. There is the word for non-living things, then the one for things that crawl, without identity or gender, such as worms and slime and flies. A being whose gender was unknown would get a different pronoun. For me, the empress used the pronoun for worms and slime, the ones the ocean patrol guards who'd found me had used.

Stung, I stared—and that was when the women in the gray robe at the empress's side made a gesture, spoke a word, and green light lanced out and struck me with the same horrible pain as the fais 'correction' used so generously by Jardis Dhes-Andis.

No surprise these Shinjans knew similar magic for causing pain, I thought hazily as I let out a yelp. I almost began cursing, but managed to clap my teeth shut.

Suddenly I didn't want that empress knowing anything about me, including that I could speak, much less that I understood her.

So I faked a faint, letting my hair settle over my face, which was turned toward the front of the cage so I could see what was coming.

The empress tutted softly. "I didn't say to kill it, mage."

The mage bowed low. "I used the mildest degree of the fire-strike. The creature must be ill, or weak."

The empress turned away, saying, "Weak it may be, but it does seem one of a kind. If it's still alive, see that it stays that way. Genru! Send the reward to those who caught it. And make certain that imperial generosity is proclaimed. I want the world to know that I am very generous when my wishes are served."

The servants carrying the train scurried in a half circle to keep up with the empress, who trod back to the palanquin. She climbed in—leaving her wet shoes behind. No doubt someone would have fresh ones waiting for her wherever she was going next.

The procession started up again. It circled around the garden so that the empress could finish gloating over her one-of-a-kind prizes.

As soon as the last soldier was out of sight, I rolled to my feet, went to the front of my cage, and spat in her direction.

There was nothing to do but finish eating, then sleep again. I was fine with that—I still wasn't quite at full strength yet. At least this place provided shelter of a sort, and food. A few more meals and naps, and I'd leave. But there was nothing preventing me from exploring once it turned dark, right?

When I'd eaten everything they left me, I curled up and slept, waking at the distant brassy sound of a gong. The shadows had lengthened to the blue shade of just-past-sunset.

I looked around very carefully, for I still had that neck-tightening sense of being watched. But the decorative shrubs around my cage were still, and no one was in sight. So I transformed to my bird, and took wing, aiming for the space between the gilt bars.

The same moment a nasty sensation, like hot metal, repelled me, someone said urgently, "Don't!"

In a blink I was a Hrethan again. I staggered against the bars, looking out as a teenaged boy emerged from behind a trellis of trumpet lilies across the way.

Tall and thin, he wore ragged clothes. His feet were bare. A shiny blue-black braid swung out and knocked against his elbow as he sent a fast look around, then he sauntered up and grinned through the bars at me. "I knew you were one of us," he chortled.

"Us?" I asked, wondering what group he could possibly mean, as he wasn't Hrethan. Until very recently I hadn't belonged to any group, outside of beggars and thieves.

"Dual-natures." He tapped his chest, blurred into a wolf with blue-white fur, then back again.

"Oh!" I grinned back. "Yep. There's magic on the bars?"

"Right. I know how to break the spell," he said, "but *she'll* know. Or her mages. Same thing. The grays are all snitches."

"Who are you?" I asked. He didn't seem like some sort of spy for the empress—why would she bother? But you never knew, with these royal types.

"Kenji Jach Mirel. From Iwarna Islands."

"I don't know those," I said.

"We're on the other side of Shinja, you might say, from the continent of Charas al Kherval." He pronounced it carefully, the "r" sound a trill. "Ten years ago we fought Shinja to a standstill despite all our islands together being less than a tenth its size."

"But you're not a hostage now?" I asked.

The last of my doubt vanished as his mouth pressed into a line. "The empress is sending Avejo against us as soon as the fleet is ready. She wants me dead first. A tragic accident." He grinned again. "I ran, to...friends. But I'm not going home again until I figure out how to free *them*." He waved an arm, encompassing the entire menagerie. "I was learning magic. I don't know enough. Yet."

"The empress let a hostage learn magic?" I asked, wondering if he'd had a life akin to mine when I was the prisoner of the Emperor of Sveran Djur.

"Hah!" Kenji gave a gust of laughter. "My...Invey was teaching me. The second prince," he added, seeing my confusion, then his gaze shifted. "Invey is...was...different. I think. I can't get near him to find out if he knows about the invasion."

"Sounds like politics to me," I said. "Like a midden heap, it stinks, and sticks to you if you get thrown into it."

He snorted another laugh. "It is when you have Empress Zeltzi handing out white streamers right and left."

"White streamers?"

"They hang down from the imperial seal on death sentences. White for bone," Kenzi said. "Everyone here grows up knowing that. Since she became empress, it's not just those who speak or act against her, it's their entire family. Three streamers, three generations."

"That's horrible!" I exclaimed.

"Yes. Which is why I joined... Well, what I meant to say was, even if she's offering a gold piece to volunteers for a special ritual for the Dragon Festival, and a month's rent forgiven for their families. People take it and pretend a smile, because they all celebrate Dragon Festival anyway, but they know her special ritual gold is just buying them off."

As if a single gold piece would fix all the problems underlying those dilapidated houses and ruined roads.

Before I could voice that, a quake rumbled through, rustling the leaves and making the cell roofs creak.

Kenzi looked around quickly. "Almost time for the evening feeding. I'll be back. I just wanted to warn you about the seal ward, and to let you know you're not alone. I'm still working on finding the magic to destroy this place."

He began to turn away, but I said, "Wait! Do you know what the Barrow is? Or where?"

"The imperial prison." He made a sour face. "Other side of the palace. Why?"

"I've got a friend who's a prisoner there. I mean to break him out."

Kenji's brows shot upward. "How?"

"Well, I'm still figuring that part out, now that I'm here."

He whistled, then looked around again. "It's impossible to get into the Barrow unless they toss you in."

"Impossible?" I asked. "Why? What's so special about it?"

"People who go into the Barrow don't come out," he said. "Except through the arena."

"The arena? What's that?"

"It's where they stage battles, sometimes to the death, to entertain the city. And collect wagers," he added with a derisive sneer. "Even I can't get into the Barrow, wolf or human. Got to go. I'll be back when it's clear."

With a flick of his long braid, he was gone, leaving me clutching those bars in an agony of worry.

Hlanan in an arena?

No!

While I would stake him against evil mages and scoundrel politicians, poor Hlanan would never be able to defend himself against a mad chicken, must lest a bunch of bloodthirsty fighters. I had to get to him NOW!

I began to reach mentally—then slammed the inner door when I remembered how appalled he was—how appalled everyone was—when they discovered that I could in effect scry minds without having to use a scry stone. Even Jardis Dhes-Andis, that master at invading minds, had to use a scry stone.

What were the rules here? The time to learn them, of course, had been while I was among the Hrethan—but that was the period I was too frightened to breach that inner wall.

If only I could reach the mountain where my parents lived, and—

Then I stopped. Blinked at my hands. My hair lifted and swirled around me as I struggled with impatience. Dullwit! I didn't need to be on the mountain. I could scry them from right where I was!

Deep in the lowest layer of my conscious mind, I felt more than 'heard' a low chuckle, like a bubble of laughter from beneath the deepest sea. Rue was still with me.

I shut my eyes and settled myself, then reached for Rue. "These quakes. Do they have anything to do with the eggs?"

I didn't really think the two were related—so I was surprised when he didn't say 'What quakes?' *Yes. The quakes are the result of the eggs forcing their way into what thou callest the physical world. Their mother is not there to aid them.*

"Is this bad?" I asked.

It is not good, but the emergence of the eggs into their nest in the caldera is slowed. I cannot come—I am too large—but I can hear the eggs, and send what comfort I can. Their birth is slowed, but time is still short.

"So I have a few days?" Worry serried through me—so much going on. I couldn't abandon Hlanan now, not when we were so close, and he a prisoner somewhere in this benighted place. Yet I could not abandon the eggs.

I sensed from Rue that he was waiting—that there was yet time. All right, then. I needed to get busy.

I resettled myself and reached for my mother, expecting to make a great effort. But then her voice spoke in my head as if she sat beside me, and I jumped. This was as easy to speaking to Rue.

Elenderi, came her warm voice. *We worried. You are safe?*

How to answer that? Don't worry her, I told myself. *Safe enough. I found Hlanan. He's here, but I can't get to him by foot, and I'm afraid to open my inner door in case it's one of those rules I never knew about that I'm always breaking. Is there some kind of etiquette about scrying this way?*

Her inner voice brightened with humor. *The custom is the same for all ways. You think of the person. You will know when they sense you, and if they do not want the communication but are unable to... shut the inner door, as you say, then you shut your own door.*

Oh. I was expecting a lot of safeguards, with maybe some arcane magical spells thrown in for good measure.

My mother caught the sense of what I was thinking. *Such things are for those who breach trust, and fear to be breached. But training oneself to maintain the inner wall suffices.*

Good, I returned. *Then I'll try him now.*

Unless it is an emergency, there is someone here who has waited so very long to know you.

And then I was aware of my father's presence, benign and endlessly patient. My mother's inner voice vanished, and I caught an image of her sitting with some people who were busy turning their harps.

Father?

Beloved daughter, precious beyond worlds. For the first time, I heard his inner voice. His love reached across the distance between us and bathed my spirit. Just as I'd felt when I rediscovered Mother, it was like one's first awareness of safety, after having had none for so long that one forgot there was such a concept. It was the glow of sunfire without glare or burn.

It was...healing.

I wanted to shut my eyes and float forever in that bliss, but my original purpose hovered at the top of my awareness. I think he became aware of it, as I sensed his question, *What happened?*

He was very powerful with mental scrying. My inner wall had come down, and he could have ventured to my memories, the way I could enter others' dreams, but he waited for me to welcome him—and I understood that I was getting a lesson in how to scry properly.

I was still anxious about Hlanan, but my father, so long shut off from me, was important, too. So I turned my inner eye to memory and let him see it all. His benevolent, compassionate consciousness flickered, quick as thought, through my isolated childhood, meeting Hlanan, my adventures with Thianra and Rajanas, my first encounter with Jardis Dhes-Andis, the half-brother he had only known as a very small boy.

I felt a change in his perception, a focus, attended with regret. That feeling intensified as he took in what happened to me in Sveran Djur.

Then I was with my parents on their mountain, and he saw how terrified I was at the prospect of using my inner voice again— it was isolation once more, self-chosen.

After that, my flight with Tir, my meeting with Rue. I did not know him well enough to descry his thoughts or reactions, and I was far too intimidated to blunder my way there, but I did sense a meeting and a blending of awareness with Rue. And a sharpened interest on the part of the dragon.

But—as yet—no words.

From there, my longer flight over the ocean, charged with my important mission. Father stayed wordlessly with me, sustaining me with his love, appreciation, understanding, until he reached my brief encounter with Empress Zeltzi—and my meeting Kenji, the prince from Iwarna.

Then my father offered words. *You have done well, my child. Heed me now. I am aware of certain patterns of movement in the realm of magic. It may aid you to know that the Empress of Shinja has recently welcomed the return of mages she sent in secret to master blood magic.*

Blood magic! I'd had a horrible brush with that not long ago. Both Hlanan and I. *That can't be good,* I thought.

It was once a method of healing, but has long since been distorted from that. The Kherval Magic Council cannot interfere. There is no treaty with Shinja. There is no more that I can tell you.

Then I'd better get going. How was I to end this first, very important conversation? But again he gave me a hint with another wordless embrace of that love, and then I felt his inner door close.

I opened my eyes.

Scrying like that had in the past been tiring, but not this time. It felt as if I'd had a day of rest. I wasn't certain if that was a gift of my father's, or if my time with Rue had somehow strengthened innate talents I'd always had. These same talents that, I'd learned after my acquaintance with Hlanan, were considered immoral unless people were willing to open their inner door. I'd always known how to do what I thought of as voice cast (which was bad) and mind cast (which I discovered was far worse, though Jardis Dhes-Andis wanted me to practice it—on others, not on him), and so I had stopped, even before I found myself unable to do any of them.

But to do these things at all, I needed what I called the person's range. That meant becoming used to their voice, and sensing their patterns of reaction and intent, without using any doors. Hlanan's range I knew very well. My parents had given me theirs.

I considered from all angles, and decided it was time to reach for Hlanan and knock on his door. I would know if he thought it wrong.

I resettled myself, shut my eyes again, and this time thought of Hlanan, imagining myself standing outside a cottage door with him inside. I gave a mental shout, *Hlanan?*

Lhind! A maelstrom of worry, elation, exhaustion, and plain physical hunger battered me. *How are you? Where are you? Are you scrying from Erev-li-Erval? No, you can scry without...*

A confusion of images and memories as well as emotions assaulted me, and I took a mental step back, struggling to focus only on his inner voice, and shut out the rest. *I'm here. In Shinja. In fact, I'm in the empress's menagerie, which I'm told is on the other side of the palace —*

No! You can't be —

If I'd thought his feelings and words an assault before, that was nothing to the storm that hit me.

Hlanan! I am here with two purposes. One, to get you out, but there's another VERY IMPORTANT one, and I don't have much time. A lot has happened.

I felt him bring himself up short. He was excruciatingly tired and hungry and also filthy—I could feel his awareness of that. I tried again to narrow my focus, as regret suffused me on his behalf. Every bit as strong as the regret I felt from him that I was caught in the Shinjan web.

It was time to reassure him. *I'm here but I'm not helpless. And I can scry again — I couldn't, which was why you didn't hear from me. I didn't know about your letters until… oh, it can wait till we meet. But I can scry, and find out things. Like, I just learned from my father that the Empress of Shinja got back some mages sent to learn blood magic. You and I both know how bad that is.*

Now his astonishment hit me like a storm wind. But that was an improvement over his regret and worry. *Truth? How does he know? I thought he was a bird.*

He is. But he can scry mind to mind, like the Hrethan. He is in contact with your guild mages. He says they can't do anything because Shinja won't do a treaty with the guild, or some such. The thing is, see, I can find things out.

This is vitally important, he returned. *If true. And I am inclined to believe it, because I believe this empress would use blood magic, or any kind of magic, to solidify her hold on the empire.*

Didn't being an empress mean you've already *got* a hold? I mentally shrugged it off — I didn't have any interest in Shinja or its political messes. I just wanted to find Hlanan, get him out of there, and rescue those eggs.

But I sensed that somehow the current situation here had become important to him. His thought came: *I don't know where to begin.* With it another whelm of exhaustion, hunger, worry, and the like.

All right. For whatever reason, Shinja mattered. So I'd help in any way I could. I sent back: *I met someone here, named Kenji, who promised to visit again in the morning. I'll know more then. Why don't you sleep?*

Kenji? Invey's foster-brother?

He said he was a hostage, but he mentioned Invey, who taught him some magic.

Hlanan's inner thought came, *I must risk another journey.* I didn't know if I was supposed to hear that or not. Then he mentally formed words for me: *I must sleep — I'm too tired to think. I need to conserve my strength. Can you scry me tomorrow so we can plan?*

Sure. And smiled inside and out. Once again, I had become his partner in adventure. My inward smile reflected back from him before I felt his mind turn inward — he didn't even think about closing his inner door. So I closed mine, and curled up to sleep.

Twenty

HLANAN WANTED TO SLEEP, but couldn't.

After that long silence of months, during which he had no idea where I was or why I hadn't answered his letters, I was suddenly back in his life—but as a fellow prisoner, there in Shinja, the last place in the world he wanted me to be. Except maybe Sveran Djur.

But it seemed I had been busy during that period of silence— and I'd brought grim news. He lay there as a sharp quake rumbled through the massive stone walls. He had to consider whom to tell what, for though he had come to like many of these Shinjans on a personal level, there remained the fact that he was a slave against his will, under death sentence, and for no reason whatsoever. That made them enemies.

He considered telling Sig what he'd discovered, and as quickly vetoed the idea. Sig would ask questions he couldn't answer, and anyway, he wasn't really the cell's authority anymore. Luenro was.

So when light began to lift, he worked through the exercises that had become habit as he figure out what to say, and then made his way around to those who were ailing or wounded. When he stopped by her, he whispered, "I was scryed last night, by a mage from the Kherval. There is news I need to tell Invey."

And Luenro beckoned the group to decoy action once again. This time one of the people slipped and fell in the slime, before the food could be dumped. Before the guards could kick and punch the woman out of their way, Luenro felt her way to the fallen woman's side, forcing the guards to back up rapidly, which broke their tight formation.

Hlanan tucked, rolled, and slithered—then he was out. As he loped noiselessly away, he wondered if getting easier to escape was due to that Djuran drill, or just because he was getting used to having to dive between all those legs.

Another benefit (so he thought as he made his arduous way up to the residence wing) was Invey's being kept a prisoner in his own suite made access so much easier. Ordinarily a prince could be anywhere.

The way was clearer than it had ever been. He was too tired to question that; it seemed a part of his finding it easier to run up flights of stairs, which of course was completely unrelated.

Instead, his tired mind was full of questions for me, beginning with how I'd managed to end up in Shinja. He couldn't believe he hadn't asked that first thing. He was still thinking about me, wondering if it was a good thing or an impending disaster to have me so very close by when he reached Invey's study.

The door was open. Hlanan paused, listened, heard no voices, so he walked in—

And was immediately flanked by armed and armored warriors, swords drawn.

Invey sat behind his desk, face tight with tension. Avejo perched on the edge of the desk, head tilted to one side. Diamonds glittered among the many long braids in his hair, otherwise he was dressed for war.

He raked his gaze down Hlanan, then laughed. "I think you can sheathe the swords, boys," he said with a casual wave of his hand.

The hiss of steel sliding home preceded Avejo saying, "I thought I recognized the reek last time I was here. But I could not believe Invey was entertaining a prisoner from the Barrow. And... not by anyone's orders. How *did* you get out? More importantly— right now—who *are* you? Not Shinjan, I can see that much. Why aren't you running for the gates as fast as your feet can carry you?"

There's nothing like shock to wake up a tired mind. Hlanan realized he should have seen the empty halls in the residence as sinister, but now was not the time to be mad at himself for carelessness.

His gaze shifted to Invey, in whose face he saw only tension. Then the sense of Avejo's words hit him, specifically what was missing: Invey had not told Avejo that Hlanan was an escaped slave, or the conversation would have begun very differently.

"I'm a scribe," Hlanan said in his Elras-accented Shinjan. "I was taken prisoner aboard a Djuran yacht before your navy captured it."

Avejo's eyes narrowed. "A scribe? Why would a Djuran noble bother with a Kherval scribe? Especially *that* noble? He's so damn stiff-necked when I tried talking to him, you'd think *he* was the imperial heir."

Hlanan's mind had begun running fast, ahead — he hoped — of the questions. He could feel death hovering in the air, and he had to save as many lives as he could. "I'm one of many imperial scribes. I was taken while answering a summons. From what I understood, the Djuran emperor wanted to know the whereabouts of one of his kin who is outside Sveran Djur. People seem to think scribes know everything." None of it was a lie.

Avejo waved a hand. "Right now I'm not interested in Sveran Djur or its emperor. Unless they're coming at us, in which case I'll be very interested."

He paused, and when Hlanan just stood there, he waved a hand, the other still resting on his sword hilt. "All right, so you were very much in the wrong place at the wrong time. Now, how did you get out of the Barrow, and why are you here?" He waved a hand toward his brother behind the desk.

Those were the questions Hlanan had expected next. "I'm sent most often between the mage guild and the imperial palace. I have friends among the mages. One of them taught me illusion magic, which is fairly easy for anyone to learn. I used that to get out."

Avejo nodded. "It's easy, but equally flimsy. So flimsy I don't think we've ever bothered warding it down there. I'll have to fix that. So you used illusion to get past my guards. Then they aren't asleep on their feet. Very well. Why Invey? What kind of conspiracy do you think you can work up with my poor brother here? He says you've been talking about history, but I believe that about as much as I believe Little Moon is Big Moon's bouncing ball."

"I promised Princess Luenro I would see with my own eyes if her son was truly alive and well. Her origin, like mine, is the Kherval, and her health right now is very fragile. I'm trained to serve." Hlanan held his hands away. "As for our conversation, Prince Invey did ask me about Kherval history."

As he spoke, he was watching Avejo carefully. He had heard plenty from the prisoners about the two princes, specifically how well they got along, in spite of Empress Zeltzi always trying to set them against each other.

And so, to forestall any more questions about his motives, Hlanan brought the subject back to Shinja's problems. "But this time I came with a specific purpose, again at the princess's behest. I was scryed last night by a mage from the Kherval."

"Scryed," Avejo repeated under his breath, frowning.

Hlanan had learned that the Shinjans regarded scrying with deep suspicion. Everyone in power had wards against being scryed — Princess Luenro's scry stone had been taken away from her not long after she'd arrived to marry the emperor, they said for her own safety.

Hlanan went on, "They searched for me, and no one could find me, so I was scryed to discover my whereabouts. But this is the important thing. The mage guild in the Kherval discovered that your empress sent mages to learn blood magic. They recently returned after training for some years."

Hlanan watched that impact both brothers. Avejo straightened up, then turned to Invey, who was already looking Avejo's way.

The brothers exchanged tense glances, then Avejo turned back to Hlanan. "Blood magic is illegal in the Kherval as well as here, is it not? But they let these mages learn it?"

"Nobody *let* anyone do anything," Hlanan said. "First, your mages could not have learned it in the Kherval, or they—and whoever taught it—would indeed be imprisoned, and an envoy sent to your government about the mages. It had to be taught somewhere else, but mages all around the world apparently talk to one another, and share information like that. Because as you say, it's forbidden by every government that I know of."

"Of course Mother would..." Avejo said under his breath, one hand pinching the skin between his brows.

Then his hand slapped against the desk, sending a pile of papers fluttering. "If that's true, it would explain a lot." He kicked his boot heel against the desk again, *rap, rap, rap,* then jumped down. "Invey, go ahead and talk history with your scribe if it amuses you." He sent a narrow look at Hlanan. "I'm going to find out the truth if I can. I'm inclined to leave things as they are—if you're right, you've done us a very great service. But see that you return to that cell after your history session."

"Of course," Hlanan said. "I promised the princess. And I know what would happen to everyone down there if one of us got away."

Avejo grunted, then cast a rueful look at Invey. "I can't believe you managed to find someone as bookish as you are among the galk."

Shaking his head, he crossed the room in three strides, whirling a casual hand in the air. His guards clattered silently after him, leaving Invey and Hlanan alone.

Invey got to his feet and moved to the windows. His fingers trembled as he pushed them open.

Hlanan sighed as he understood an action that had he'd managed not to notice until then. "Sorry about the prison reek. Though there is nothing I can do about it." He still was not going to mention how much magic he knew, until he trusted the Shinjans far more than he did at present.

But Invey's mind had already moved on. He stood with his hand on the window latch. "Blood magic," he repeated in a strained voice. "If he confronts the empress, she'll no doubt claim that she's just looking for stronger magic than anything we know, in order to bind the mountain."

Hlanan said, "Except she sent those mages years before the quakes began, right?"

"Yes. Oh, I know what she wants—what everyone who tries to get blood magic wants: a way to prolong life. She would love being empress forever. The other rumor I've heard is that it can be used to force others' will to one's own."

Hlanan wanted to say that it didn't work very well, according to what he'd discovered after his own brush with blood magic, but he squashed the impulse. A scribe wouldn't know that.

Invey went on, "This is bad. Terrible. I..." He looked toward his desk, then over at Hlanan. "Why don't you take what you want of the food, and return? I'm afraid that my thoughts are too disordered for converse. Give my respects to my mother."

Hlanan considered mentioning Kenji, then decided against it. What he'd learned from me about blood mages could be palmed off on 'a mage' (strictly speaking, I was one in that I could do magic) but it was too much of a stretch to believe that any Kherval mage would know a thing about Kenji. Or, for that matter, if it was a good idea to bring up his name, since Kenji was apparently living in hiding.

So he gobbled down some food, loaded more into his shirt, and departed.

———◈◈◈———

I woke feeling restless and confined, which meant I had pretty much recovered from that long flight over the sea. So I did some handsprings back and forth across the cage, and then—after looking around carefully—transformed to my bird-self and flew fast around the cage, practicing darting and diving. I needed the exercise, but mainly I wanted to be able to dodge arrows if I had to.

Kenji came back, as he'd said he would. "I'm a little late. It's the coming Dragon Festival—everything is turned about. Except for our friends among the volunteers, who don't even have costumes yet!"

"Costumes?" I repeated.

"They make up the dragon's body. For the Dragon Festival parade. There's talk of this one being the longest dragon yet, a hundred pairs of legs. But the costumes—the legs have streamers of gold and red—need to be fitted to each wearer, and the volunteers keep being told the materials are still coming. Hundred or not, it'll still look shoddy, which is all I expect of the empress. Anyway. What did you want to know?" he asked. "In turn, will you tell me about where you come from?"

"Nothing easier," I replied. "But first, I have two worries. One is the friend I told you about, but the second one I found out yesterday when someone scryed me—"

"You escaped having the scry ward forced on you?" he asked, looking astonished.

"What scry ward? No, tell me later. I don't have a scry ward on me. This is what I wanted to tell you. I learned that Empress Zeltzi has blood mages. Is that common here?"

Kenji's eyes widened. "No!" Then he frowned. "Really? Who told you that—how do they know? Blood magic is illegal *every-where*, I know that much. Except of course, the empress only pays attention to laws that benefit her," he added bitterly.

I gave him a quick summary of what my father had told me, adding that the senior mages in the world all seemed to know magic business, without much regard to political boundaries.

At the end, he muttered, "I have to go—I have to tell Sanvi."

He was gone before I could ask who Sanvi was.

The feeders came around a short time later. I made eating last as long as I could. When the empress showed up to gloat over her captives, I curled up into a ball with my back to her, and fell asleep.

I woke after dark, sat up, and reached for Hlanan.

I could sense that he was no more rested than the last time. But stronger was his joy. I asked him where he was—if we could find out each other's stories.

His emotions rippled again, reminding me of the strength and variety of wind currents high in the sky. I knew that scrying with a stone was different than my scrying—there was a frame to it, so to speak. When I scryed, there was no wall or ground or air, there was intent and emotion, unless I closed out one or another.

But I was learning to do that. To help him to adjust—and to save the effort and time of mentally forming words as one speaks—I gave him my memories.

At first I thought it might be a mistake. He was so upset at himself for not understanding how much damage my time as Jardis Dhes-Andis's prisoner had done me, until I reminded him that I hadn't told him. But his response, quicker than thought, was that his mother had sent me away so fast that we hadn't had time to understand each other.

It's over, I said. *And Rue helped me. I want to get to those eggs, but first I mean to help you get out of here.*

Whoosh! Another whirlwind of emotions from him, then he shut it all down. I could feel his effort—he had learned from me, just as I'd learned from my father, as I'd hoped. But he was learning fast, for someone who didn't have mind-scrying inborn.

He then gave me his memories, as you have seen. I can't say how long it took, only that we were in the middle of discussing whether or not he should tell Invey that Kenji was alive and well when the sound of guards coming to the cell silenced the prisoners.

It was never good when they came off-schedule. Especially when they recognized the uniforms of the kips, instead of the regular guards. Everyone backed away as the doors were unlocked.

The leader peered in as two of her subordinates held torches high, then she rapped out, "Which one is the Kherval scribe?"

Hlanan stood up.

"Out."

"Where?" he asked.

She gave a short laugh. "Jaw Box."

A hissing of whispers cut short when she glared into the cell.

In silence, Hlanan walked out as the kips closed in around

him.

They walked a short way, then the kip commander stood aside, and pointed into a small cell that—unlike the one held just left—was more or less clean. In the cell was nothing but a wooden bucket full of water.

"In," she said. And as one of the subordinates tossed fabric onto the floor, she added, "Make yourself clean. If you are still offensive when I come back for you, we'll do it for you, with a wire brush."

A shove, clang! The door slammed, leaving him alone. I was still with him—he hadn't shut me out, though I'd shared my father's instructions about that.

I wondered if I ought to shut myself away when he said out loud, "What do you think, Lhind? Ice water straight from the river?" He bent, swished a finger in it, and said, "I thought so. Frigid."

He was talking to me—he wanted my company. *Splash it around the room before you use your magic?*

He shucked the filthy clothes. "I didn't think of splashing the water. Excellent idea," he said.

A short time later, he stood barefoot in a pool of water next to the empty bucket. He was clean for the first time in what felt like forever, wearing a badly woven long shirt-like thing over loose trousers. Neither item fit him, but at least they had ties.

He was just cinching up the trousers, which were far too long, when the door opened again,

The kip commander gestured him out, sniffed at him, uttered a grunt that he guessed was approval since no wire brush was in the offing, then led the way down the hall, the subordinates falling in behind.

Do you want me to stay with you? I asked.

As long as you can, was his silent reply.

His heart drummed. But he was resolute: if whoever had summoned him was the empress, he might have a chance at transferring away, as long as he had a moment free, in a space not warded. Though he didn't want to—to him that would be a defeat.

He had shared his memories, but that didn't mean I understood his ardent desire to reason with Invey, or to help him. Who cares about a bunch of slavers? But I kept my own reactions behind a mental door.

Then the kip commander halted, and waved him through.

He stepped into a stone room with a table, a heavy wooden chair with clamps, and racks of very sinister implements. The room had been swept but it stank of old blood.

Hlanan took another step in, to find Prince Avejo sitting behind the table, Invey standing behind him. Hlanan stilled, bewildered—aware that these were supposed to be enemies, though what constituted an enemy seemed to be a fuzzy distinction of late.

Unless he was about to be executed, or tortured...

The moment the thought winged from him to me, I closed him out and though I didn't have the princes' range, tried to open a door to Avejo—and the chaos of a strange mind, with all its unknown experiences and ways of thought smacked me right back into myself. At the same moment, through Hlanan's eyes I saw Avejo stiffen, wince, then rub his temple.

It took me a few heartbeats to recover, and to cautiously reopen the door between Hlanan's mind and mine.

Avejo was saying, "The extra mages were hired to help with designing a new ritual for the Dragon Festival in a few days. Which makes me wonder who your informant was, and what their motivation."

Hlanan said, "I can't prove anything from your prison. All I can do is pass on what I was told."

"To drive a wedge between us? To cause alarm at the worst possible time—"

A sharp jolt, followed by the low rumble of a quake caused Avejo to stop and look around. They all did, as deep inside my mind, Rue stirred, and reminded me wordlessly that the eggs were waiting.

But not for much longer.

Avejo cleared his throat. Then said, "My brother insists your intentions are benign, but then he has always been easily taken advantage of."

Invey flushed, but didn't move.

Avejo said, "You will have to furnish better proof." He stopped there, but tipped his head to one side—Hlanan suspected that was the direction of the arena.

Hlanan's thought reached out to me, awash with stress: *Lhind! Are you certain that was your father?*

I answered in the affirmative, alarmed and frightened on his behalf. And angry. He'd risked his life repeatedly, and what was the result from these Shinjans?

But getting angry wouldn't help. How could a prisoner offer proof when he couldn't even get out of his cell except to visit a prince who was also a kind of prisoner?

Well, he had me. And Kenji's words to me. But I wasn't going to tell him to give Kenji away. What could those mages really be doing? I thought over what little I'd been told—and then sent a thought to Hlanan, *Ask them if the mages are making illusion for the hundred legs of the dragon.*

Hlanan repeated my words—and then halted when Avejo and Invey stared back at him in surprise.

"There's no hundred legs," Invey said at the same moment that Avejo said, "What hundred legs? The parade will use the same dragon we've used ever since we were boys. Its body can hold no more than twenty, if that."

Hlanan said—at my prompting, "According to what I was told, the empress herself has called for volunteers from the people. They are being housed in a special place, their families given a gold piece each. They are wondering why they don't have their costumes with the streamers down the legs, as usual." He added, "Obviously I can't prove anything here. I am only passing on what I was told."

The detail seemed to surprise the brothers more with each word. On 'streamers' they looked at each other.

Hlanan added, "I have no idea what streamers are, but these are the words I was given."

Avejo's gaze narrowed with question as Invey said, "They are colorful strands of fabric hanging down. To look like fire, as the people who form the legs of the dragon dance and weave down the street."

Avejo said to Invey in Dragon Tongue, "How might this prisoner know that? Unless everything he hath said be a lie, the scryer who giveth him these things could be anywhere. For certain there be a spy in our midst."

Invey said softly, "Ought we to put the ward against scrying on Hlanan?"

"Not yet. At the first sign of threat, or misinformation, yes—for the short time he liveth beyond that. Find out, if thou canst, with whom he speaketh."

Avejo got up and walked out, followed by his guards, except for two at the door, obviously there for Invey.

Leaving Invey alone with Hlanan, prince and prisoner.

Two princes.

The two princes eyed one another, both prisoners in some wise, one Shinjan and the other Kherval. Then Invey said softly, "What would you do if you were me?"

Hlanan shook his head once. "I was born a prince, and spent time in your galleys as a slave, yet I am the same man. Whether I have a prince's power or the slave's lack, as long as I still possess will, I shall choose mercy. I will always choose mercy. If I live beyond this choice, I will then look back at the merciful act, and so it shall be until I can no longer choose."

Invey drew in a long breath. Took a step away, then back. "Tell me this. Is it Kenji who is revealing these facts that you could not possibly see yourself?"

Hlanan saw the hope in Invey's face. I saw it, shared by Hlanan, whether he was aware of it or not. Then Hlanan said, "I can't answer that."

To his surprise, Invey bowed his head. "I understand. To know he's alive would be enough right now." And to the waiting—listening—guards, "Take him back, please."

Hlanan turned, then stumbled. I caught a wash of nausea in

him—then realized what he was trying to hide: my presence, alongside his, gave him a kind of double vision or awareness that gave him vertigo. It was easier for him to sustain this scrying while sitting with his eyes closed.

Chagrined—and far more tired than I'd realized—I closed the inner door, while he was returned to the cell. And so materially had his status changed among the prisoners that no one jumped him and took his nice new outfit, much as they might envy him.

Twenty-one

A SHARP QUAKE WOKE me abruptly. The eggs — making their way inexorably to the surface. Nobody in Shinja knew that but me, though they were about to celebrate their Dragon Festival.

Another thought was how Shinja and Sveran Djur both used dragons in their art, language, and custom, as symbols. It made me wonder for the first time how their histories were connected. Not that there was time to ponder history.

Before I could reach for Hlanan, the rustle of shrubbery and Kenji's quick, familiar step caught my attention.

"Who is scrying you?" he whispered urgently. "Sanvi saw Avejo's personal man sniffing around the volunteers for the Dragon Festival. Avejo's never cared about the festival before. What did you tell them?"

"What you told me," I said in surprise, and alarm. "Without your name attached."

Kenji made an impatient gesture. "I don't care if they search for me. I have been on the run for a year, now. They'll never find me. But if your scryer is here, Sanvi says to warn them. She thinks Avejo is going to be calling out the torturers sooner than later."

"What? Why?"

Kenji bent over, hands on his knees. "They're all desperate. And they're all lying to each other — the empress, her son. And the people will pay the price. As usual."

His head jerked up. He stood poised, listening, then flitted back into the shrubbery and was gone.

A short time later the empress's entourage came around. It was time to get out of there, I decided. Torturers—the endangered eggs—even the festival was beginning to sound sinister for reasons I couldn't fathom, but my instinct was all I'd had to trust for so much of my life I wasn't going to ignore it now. It was time to act.

I knew that I risked being tossed in the arena, if not executed outright, if I left the menagerie, but I figured there would be more chances of escape than there were now. If it was to be the arena, I might even be put where Hlanan was, however briefly.

First, to get out of that cage.

I'd learned that the menagerie imprisoned those the empress considered one of a kind. I had to let the empress know that I wasn't unique, but in a way that wouldn't get me killed outright. Emperors and empresses, in my experience, were used to everyone around them bowing and backing up. Respect, obedience. If they didn't get it, they had a tendency to hurl nasty things at you. Or hurl you somewhere nasty.

The entourage made its lumbering way, complete to banners, and when it drew near I moved to the front of my cage and bowed repeatedly. I gave furtive peeks each time I came up. When I saw the empress looking my way, I *fwooshed* my hair and tail up around my head as I bowed.

One… two… three…

I didn't see the signal, but the entourage stopped. The empress looked out. She said something to the woman who walked next to her palanquin.

The woman came over to me. "Her imperial highness wishes to know if you comprehend our language."

"A little," I said chirpily.

"You crave a boon?"

"Oh yes," I said, even more chirpily. "May I send a letter to my family to tell them where I am? My cousins will be looking for me, I know."

"Your…you have a family?" the woman asked.

"Oh, yes. In our mountains. Actually, on several islands. We all look alike," I said.

The woman's face didn't change. She turned abruptly, walked to the palanquin, and murmured.

The empress waved a hand, and the palanquin moved on.

I wasn't left wondering very long. Before the sounds of that parade had died away in the distance, a bunch of those warriors turned up and used some kind of token to break the spell over the bars of my cage. When I saw the greenish flash of light I was glad I'd listened to Kenji.

Before I could get out, one of the warriors grabbed my arm in a hard grip. He pulled me out, and a second warrior took my other arm. Her grip was just as hard, if not harder. I tried—tentatively—scrying them, but again the chaos of unfamiliar experience and perceptions acted like a hammer on my mind. I shut the inner door tight, swaying on my feet. Both the guards reacted with flinches, the one on my right shaking her head as if something had gotten into her ear.

But one emotion lingered, amplified by two: they were afraid of my getting away, because it meant they'd be in the arena instead of me.

They put me in a box with a tiny air hole—far smaller than my bird—and the wooden-wheeled box bumped unmercifully over endless stones until a dank, damp smell filtered in the airhole. The box opened before a tiny cell, I was shoved in, the door slammed before I could recover from the shove.

And that was that.

I sat on the grimy floor, put my elbows on my knees, and shut my eyes. I needed to think over what I'd learned, beginning with Hlanan's determination to convince Invey of... what?

I didn't think he was even certain. He only knew he had to try. But he'd always been that way. When we first met, he did his best to talk me out of being a thief. I hadn't liked that attention, seeing *me* instead of a noisome thief. It was the first time that had happened in memory.

That same determination he brought to his efforts to talk to Invey. There was no use in trying to talk him out of those risky sessions with an enemy who was also a hostage. He was always going to do what he thought was right.

I had to get him away — I had to get us both away.

When they came for me, I said, "What happens now?"

"Arena," one guard said, laughing.

Another one said, "If you give 'em a good show, you might live."

That was all the warning I had before we started up a long tunnel toward the surface. A continuous roar resolved into a crowd. Vendors passed out food as entire families sat, awaiting blood sport.

I halted when a spear fell across my front, and I looked up at a big guard with a nose like a potato, her dye job looking like iron rust. "Wait there," she said. "You're next." She shoved me next to a gaunt woman with a child.

"What are we supposed to do?" I asked.

The guard snorted a laugh without her face showing any humor. Just boredom. "If you entertain 'em, you live." Her chin jerked outward, and then she turned to the gaunt woman. "You got one last chance to say where we can find Sanvi Xin."

The woman stared blankly.

"That's it, then," the guard said, and moved down the tunnel.

The three of us stood there some paces from the gate to the arena. I said, "Who is Sanvi Xin? Any relation to the Xin who raised a slave revolt?"

The woman looked dully at me, and away.

The child wrinkled a snub nose and said, "What *are* you?"

"Hrethan — partly."

"You got *fur*," the child said, round-eyed.

The woman's thin hands pulled the child away from me, and against her body.

I turned away, sighing. It was this kind of response that had kept me alone for so long. I would have left them to their fate without a second thought. But life with Hlanan had pushed me in another direction. There I was, imagining the horrors the woman had experienced—and the ignorance—to bring her to this place. I'd have to save her if I could.

So what was I up against? I ran the few steps to the gate, and peered out, against a roar of laughter and heckling. I had always avoided battles, duels, and the like, as much as I could. When I couldn't escape, as Rajanas had pointed out that morning before I took off with Tir to meet Rue, I'd used whatever I could in order to get away. So assessing fighting strategies is not my strong point. But from what I'd learned—mostly from Rajanas—many fights didn't last long. It was easy to get out of breath, especially if weighed down by armor and heavy weapons.

The fight I glimpsed out in the arena was no short slug fest. The victim (not a guard, dressed mostly in rags) was clearly not very good. He kept backing up and backing up as the spectators jeered. An ineffectual block or two was followed by a hard strike to an arm. Blood ran, spattering the ground, and the victim fell to his knees.

The spectators whooped. I turned away, my stomach roiling. But then I forced myself to turn back to see what I was facing. Guards dragged the victim away, his legs twitching futilely. He was alive.

From Hlanan's shared memories I recollected his shock when his cell mates were taken out, then tossed back in some time later, badly wounded. This, here, was what happened in between.

The guard tromped back up the tunnel. "Your turn, galk," she said breezily. "Weapons along the walls. If you can get to them. Give 'em something to laugh at, or bet on, you'll live—even get something to eat."

The gate creaked, and the three of us got booted out, the child sprawling in the hard-packed dust. As the mother bent down to pick up her child, I walked away from them, making a fast scan.

Potato Nose had not lied when she said there were weapons in racks, but from what I saw, they were rusty and dull. There were other things, like sand, probably for soaking up blood? Stacked in racks, more equipment like buckets and rakes.

I glanced back to see what the mother and child were doing:

standing there completely frozen, the woman's work-worn hands pressing her child's scrawny chest against her.

No help there. I turned away, just in time. A hulk of a guard lumbered toward me, sword held loosely in his fingers, a bored look on his face. I began trotting in a diagonal, drawing him away from the mother and child. He took longer steps to close the distance, still bored even when he swung the sword at me in a lazy arc.

I leaped up and somersaulted over his head. The crowd whooped in surprise. The moment I landed I began pelting toward the weapons. A quick look. Remembering what Rajanas had said, I rejected anything that looked heavy. I was terrible with a sword, so I wouldn't even try.

I reached the buckets, and skimmed along the rack, throwing them behind me to bounce and spin, slowing up the big fellow thumping after me. As I ran, I tried to spot the archers who would shoot at me if I transformed.

One thing I'd learned from Hlanan's memories was that being a mage would get you killed. He had let Invey, the one he 'liked' the most (if like is a useful word for an enemy), think he was a scribe only able to do illusion. I had an arsenal of magic skills I could use, such as turning into a bird, but these must be saved as a last resort.

The guard had much longer legs than I, and came at me from the outside, trying to pin me against the wall. So it was time for another leap. He was ready, swinging his sword upward—but that was clearly not a move he'd practiced (who expects to fight someone right overhead?) and his step faltered.

I flipped in the air as the sword whizzed below me, vaguely aware of the crowd WHOOOing like a pack of ghosts. Once again I set out running. The crowd roared as a second guard issued from one of the tunnels, coming at me from another direction.

The buckets lay where they'd stopped, scattered useless all over the arena. I jinked to one side and hustled for the wall where helms had been stacked. When I got close I could see that these were wrecks—two of the top ones had giant holes in the top.

Maybe it was funny to see victims try to wear them?

But I wanted them as weapons. I paused long enough to send them rolling and bouncing at the two guards, who had to break rhythm to hop out of the way.

While they were busy dodging the helms, I ran for the sand pile, scooped a helping into my wrap, and twisted the fabric to capture the sand.

I wondered where Hlanan was, reaching instinctively. His thought blasted into my mind: *Lhind, is that you? Hlanan.* As clear as if he stood next to me.

I hadn't meant to contact him. That wall between us was mighty thin. *I can't talk now.*

I felt him rein his demands, his worry. The emotions still curled through me, like ink dropped into water, and I nearly stumbled. But then he focused. *Lhind, the guards are talking about a silver creature escaping the arena fighters. Is that you?*

A third guard issued forth from one of the tunnels. The three began running at me from three directions, jinking when I jinked. I ran this way and that, fwooshing my hair and tail every now and then, which distracted them and raised more yells from the spectators.

Yes, I responded mentally. *Busy trying to stay alive.*

Sig says, put on a show.

A *show?* Like this was a theater? But of course it was—for the audience, who came every day hoping for excitement and blood, and to win bets.

All right. If a show would keep the archers at bay, a show they would get. So when the three slowed, closing in, I flourished my tail around front, hiding my hand as it plunged into the sand.

Then I brought it out and in a gesture I'd perfected as a child escaping alleyway bullies, slung it around in a circle at eye level.

Not surprisingly the third guard turned her face away, but the first one howled curses and clawed at his eyes. And so it was over his head I leaped, somersaulting three times before I landed.

Once again the audience howled, and I imagined side bets going up about how many somersaults I'd put in as I ran for my life. Entertainment! I wanted to give them 'entertainment' — for *me*, and see how they liked fear and terror. But I remembered what Hlanan had said about mages — and the fact that he was still stuck somewhere out of my reach — and fought the instinct to hurl fireballs.

I ran. I leaped to walls, using those to bounce myself over the heads of pursuers. I veered to pass the rusty swords and broken spears to grab a rake, and used that to vault over the heads of a pair who came at me, arms out.

Then, as the audience howled and yelled, I turned and chucked the rake between their legs. One fell with a slam, the other hopped, lost her balance, and windmilled her arms as she righted herself, losing her momentum.

When I paused for a few desperate heartbeats to catch my breath, I discovered that an entire squad had come out. It looked at first glance like an army. The mother and child stood pressed against a wall, completely ignored. Well, I'd wanted to draw attention from them.

It was getting harder to dodge. I had learned I was no good at mind cast without knowing range, but one thing I could do: if I met someone's eyes, I could push an image, for no longer than a heartbeat. But that was all I needed. One, then another, a third, and so on, thought they saw buckets or helms underfoot and stumbled, or hopped, or leaped sideways away from nothing. The audience loved it at first, then got bored.

And I couldn't keep it up forever. I was getting slower, and there were more of them, so the inevitable happened — I jinked in the wrong direction, someone made a diving tackle, and in leaping over them I got caught squarely in a net two others threw.

Wham! I hit the dirt, whereupon half a dozen bodies dropped on me like a landslide of boulders. My face pressed into the dirt, I heard whoops and panting and someone muttered, "It's not hair, it's … like feathers!"

"Who cares," someone else snarled, panting. "This one is a mark. Let's put it safely away and hope we're not slung out here for incompetence."

"Eh," said a third voice. "The crowd likes him. Her. Whatever it is."

Various hard hands grabbed portions of me and toted me along. I could only see a sliver of ground as my hair and shoulder were mashed against the net. At one point someone said, "Orders are, that one is a mark. Goes up against King Gabby, before the Festival. Put it in the next cell over."

"Hoo, that should raise some betting!"

"Already quadrupled."

Mark—I knew what that meant. My hopes soared—surely I'd be tossed into Hlanan's cell.

But the tiny cell that I was shoved into had no one in it.

The door slammed. The lock engaged with a raspy clunk.

Free of the net, I sprang up. The door had a small opening just above the level of my head, with a single rusted bar cemented in. No human could get their elbow past that, but as a bird, I was fairly sure I could squeeze through. I reached up… no magic. They didn't even think to ward the cells.

I was free. Or could be very quickly.

I heard men's voices nearby. Next cell over: could that be 'King Gabby'?

The rise and fall of those voices was familiar. And not in a good way. Not Shinjan… *Djuran?*

I strained to hear…and then came a familiar voice, saying shortly, "Quiet."

Abruptly the other voices ceased.

I knew that commanding voice.

It was Am-Jalad Darus Bas Veremi. Otherwise known as the Most Noble Darus of Pennon Veremi of Sveran Djur.

Twenty-two

I FLUNG MYSELF DOWN onto the bare floor, ignoring the strong scent of mold. It was time to let Hlanan know where I was. I reached—and there was his inner voice, sharp with stress: *Lhind! You're back!*

So I learned that though his voice was as clear to me as those of my parents, he couldn't reach me on his own.

Sensory impressions overwhelmed me with vertigo: I was there in the Jaw Box again, facing Invey and Avejo, and not there. I was tall, I was…

Hlanan staggered, clutching his head. Giddiness echoed back and forth between us until I snapped that inner door to a pinhole, shutting out his physical impressions except for sight.

He drew a shuddering breath as Avejo barked, "What happened?"

Invey's eyes widened. "You were scryed. Weren't you?"

"Yes," Hlanan said. And to me, *Where are you? You're all right? Cell. I'm fine.*

"It's Kenji. Isn't it?" Invey asked urgently. "He's the only one who'd be able to communicate with those volunteers. He has to be connected to Xin's daughter…"

Avejo raised a hand. "If Kenji is scrying us right now—"

"No." Hlanan exhaled the word. "I don't even know who Kenji is. But my scryer can contact him."

Avejo scowled. Invey's face cleared in relief. "Brother," he said in Dragon Language—probably an attempt to keep the 'scryer' as well as Hlanan from comprehending. "Thou must trust once. We cannot reach the volunteers else. Thou knowest…"

While Invey went on to coax his brother, Hlanan's urgent inner voice aimed at me: *Lhind, Invey is certain that those volunteers are going to be sacrificed in a blood magic ritual on the Dragon Festival day. There is nothing but circumstantial proof, but far too much of that.*

Kenji knows all those people, I answered, sick with horror.

Can you get to him from wherever you are now?

I can try. After dark. But even if I find him, I don't know if he'll trust them. He thinks Invey turned against him.

Hlanan said to Invey and Avejo, who had fallen silent, eyeing each other, "My scryer can contact Kenji. But there needs to be a gesture of good faith."

I wouldn't have put it that way — it wasn't what I meant — but to my surprise, both brothers reacted with instant comprehension.

Avejo said, "I need those people out of there the night before Dragon Festival, unless they want to be part of the ritual. And I can't get anyone near Sanvi Xin or any other rebels to get the warning to them, without raising the suspicions of my mother's guards. Even supposing they believe me."

Invey leaned toward Hlanan. "Tell Kenji — have your scryer tell Kenji — that I myself will remove the ward locks on the menagerie cages."

Avejo scowled at him.

Invey said softly, again in Dragon Language, "I have heard thee, thou also revilest against that place."

Avejo made a warding gesture. "Thou knowest I find Kenji's arguments about souls, dual souls, and animal wills the prattle of boys. Merely that place offendeth the hunter in me."

Invey smiled sadly. "For thou, always the chase, and not the kill."

"The kill is fine against a worthy foe. Which is not some brute beast," Avejo said. "But the chase, yes." He grinned — and it was clear that this was the greatest divide between the brothers. It was then that I understood one of the underlying tensions in those conversations Hlanan had held with Invey: Avejo looked forward to tackling Kenji's islands, as a worthy chase. In that he reminded me of Raifas of Sveran Djur.

But Invey saw only the cost.

Avejo's smile faded. "However, it be not that. It be Mother."

Invey looked down at his empty hands.

It was Avejo's turn to say softly, coaxingly, "She was handed the imperial tally before all witnesses. To go against her be to rebel in the eyes of the royal clan."

Invey looked up at that. "She coerced the emperor our father, on his deathbed, by dire means."

Avejo's answer was so quick and so tense that it was clear this was old ground for the both of them. "But that hath not been proven before the army."

Avejo lifted his head, turning Hlanan's way. "We need a diversion here at the palace, so that I can bottle up Mother's kips before the ritual."

Remembering what I'd overheard, I said to Hlanan, *I can do a diversion, in the arena. They're putting me in there anyway.*

He suppressed his reaction to that, and said to the brothers, "I believe I can give you that diversion."

Invey looked up full of hope, and Avejo with distrust. He opened his mouth to speak as a jolt caused the building to sway. Grit sifted down from above.

Invey said to his brother in an urgent undertone, "The empress might be able to bind the mountain, but if she is successful, there will be no stopping her requiring rivers of blood in order to command more power. And if she believes she can extend her life forever—you *know* that will be her next project, however many lives it takes—you and I will be among the first sacrifices."

Avejo fixed Hlanan with a narrow stare. "You can really arrange a diversion?"

"I believe it will be effective," Hlanan said, and I responded, *It will be very effective. But can you get out?*

Avejo said at the same time, "What's the cost to us?"

"Cost?" Hlanan repeated, rubbing his temples. I reduced my scrying to a pinhole, so that I was not reacting to his reactions, causing him to react to my reactions to... well, if that sounds confusing, imagine the echoes inside one's head.

"Your mystery scryer is a Shinjan?" Avejo demanded.

"No. Another prisoner. But who can provide a diversion in your arena."

"A prisoner?" Avejo's expression cleared. After all, what could prisoners really do, other than putting on a good show? They had plenty of guards around Darus of Sveran Djur, who had proved to be a formidable warrior, and popular with the crowd. "Even so, no one does anything for free. What is the cost?"

"The freedom of everyone in that cell with me," Hlanan stated. "Including Princess Luenro."

Avejo smiled. "Done," he said easily. It didn't take any effort to hear the same tone I'd given Raifas's captain the first time she asked me to find Darus: he had no intention of bothering with it.

Invey stared down at the floor. Then looked up at Hlanan. "We'll talk later." He gestured for the guards to take Hlanan back to his cell.

I stayed with Hlanan, who on his return reported the gist of his conversation to the anxiously waiting Sig and Luenro and whoever else wanted to hear. Except he left off the question about the cost.

When he was done, he began another session of the exercises the Djurans had taught him (he was now doing them several times a day out of restlessness). I asked why he'd not reported his demand. *Won't they be pleased?*

His response was, *They'll be pleased when they're actually free. Until then it seems cruel to offer hope when I can't guarantee the princes will agree, or heed me if they win. What happened to you in the arena?*

I showed him, relishing his delight when I managed to escape being grabbed, but I had to shut out his sharp spike of worry at how close I'd come to those waving weapons.

You didn't tell me before they put you in the arena, he thought when I finished.

No. I needed to concentrate, and what could you have done? I discovered I much preferred finding out your adventures after I knew you were alive. Though I hated the long silence, if I'd known at the time you'd been captured, and about the storms, and about the Shinjans getting you, I would have been sick with worry. And I wouldn't have known what to do to help. I hate being helpless. So do you.

You're right. You're completely right. Did you see what happened to the fear-frozen mother and her child? Of course Hlanan would ask that.

I can't say for certain. I couldn't see much once the guards got that net around me, except I saw no bodies as I was carried out. All the guards had been chasing after me, so I suspect they just stashed them back in the prison.

And there, unspoken, was his gnawing worry about whether it was right to help princes who could abide such situations as helpless prisoners being forced out there to possible slaughter, just to please the spectators. Yes, they were raised to it. Their slaves and their arena were everyday to them. I don't know if he was even aware of his sharing when he determined that questioning everything one was raised with was not just right, but a necessity.

Another quake broke my focus. I hadn't noticed until then that I was tired after all that effort, both physical and mental, but hadn't eaten all day.

I'd tangentially noticed that guards tromped by my new cell every so often. Judging by the steady rhythm of their tread, they didn't stop to peer into the peepholes of these cells. Even so, I waited for the next round, then jumbled my wrap into a corner in hopes that if someone did peek into the gloom they'd think I was curled up there, and shifted into my bird.

I hopped to the grating. It was a squeeze, but I got through, and flew off, staying a finger's length below the ceiling. It was a relief to discover that night had fallen, for I was so tired it had begun to seem that day would never end.

I searched along the corridors, learning my way. Once I perched on a moldy beam as guards walked by below me.

When at last I sailed through a barred window into the free night air, excitement lent me strength. I knew it was temporary. I had to find food.

I also had to learn my way about. So I flew in ever-widening circles, keeping low to roofs and diving into alleys as I watched for places between sentries. A thin, sleety rain began to fall, blurring vision. The sentries all looked down, to keep the cold wetness off their faces, so I soared upward.

That made learning my way about much easier. The imperial complex lay below me like a map. I found the menagerie, and flitted among the ornamental trees and shrubs until I smelled fruit left to fall and rot. Same with the nut trees — the empress obviously didn't need any of that bounty, and wouldn't let anyone else have it.

I got a good meal into me, and then flew wider, hoping that I would find Kenji. I crossed the menagerie twice. He was not there.

So I transformed back to my Hrethan self, and walked among the cages, saying over and over, "Who is friends with Kenji?" for I did not know who among the prisoners was dual-natured, and who not.

Finally someone called softly into the rain, "Who asks?"

"I was here until this morning," I said. "I have a message for him. Can you get it to him? It's important..." And I sensed interest all around me heightening when I mentioned blood mages.

As I made my way back, I became aware of a deep, discordant hum, so deep I felt it in my bones more than heard it in my ears.

It was Rue.

I returned to my cell and shifted to my Hrethan self, comprehending that I'd been sensing that hum rising gently for days. It was a reminder that the eggs, one of two goals for me, represented the last living family for this dragon who had believed himself alone for centuries.

Yes, it was time to get out. If I could take Hlanan with me, excellent, but if he chose to stay and get involved in Shinjan imperial politics, well, I'd been alone before. Though it hurt to think about it —

I was wrestling with that realization when the tramp of guards approached. But this time the rhythm broke into separate footsteps, then stopped. Lamplight swung wildly, lancing golden beams through the grating in my door.

Glad I was safely back, I sat up as the door creaked open. Lamplight filled the cell, limned by a man's silhouette. He lifted a hand, and most of the light retreated to the outside of the cell, leaving me alone with the figure, who set the lamp between us. He was no longer a silhouette — he was ... *Invey?*

I remembered then that I wasn't supposed to know who he was.

But he was faster. "You recognized me," he said quietly, then added, "I've never seen one like you before. I heard the report of your episode in the arena."

I considered pretending I didn't understand, then remembered how I'd gotten out of the menagerie. They knew I understood Shinjan.

"Are you the scribe's diversion?" His eyes narrowed, the light from below emphasizing the sharp bones in his face. He was very thin — and in that moment he looked a lot like Avejo.

While I was considering possible answers, he again was faster in putting together clues — but after watching him in Hlanan's memories, and now listening to him in person, I was getting his range.

"Are you — you must be his scryer." His gaze shifted around, as if looking for a crystal or a mirror.

"Yes," I said, sensing the real question. "But I only scry him."

Sure enough, his expression eased in relief. He knew so little about scrying he was imagining a spell that permitted two people to scry. "Why are you here?"

It was time for me to push the conversation the way I wanted it to go. "I came," I said, "to... quiet your mountain." I decided not to mention that actual dragons were about to be born. This was not the time — not until I knew those eggs would be safe. I went on quickly, "Then I found out a friend is here as a prisoner, though he did not trespass or transgress your laws."

"Quiet... the mountain," he repeated. "They said you are from mountain people. Do you have magic to quiet mountains — is it blood magic?"

"Ghack, no!" My hair and tail fwooshed out as I recoiled.

He took a step back, blinking.

I said, "We Hrethan firmly believe that blood ought to remain inside the vessel of origin. We do not even eat meat." I whipped my hair and tail behind me, and he blinked again as I said, "I will give you a diversion. I guarantee it will draw the attention of your palace guards. Then I want my friend free. After that I will ascend your mountain before it's too late."

"What's too late—an eruption?" he asked. "The mages have bound the mountain. Why isn't it working?"

I knew, of course that the binding magic was straining against the emergence of Rue's eggs from the weird world-between, but I spread my hands.

He pinched the skin between his brows. "One day. We have one day, and if we're not successful..." He made a warding gesture, walked out, and the door slammed. Locked.

Not that that would keep me in!

I flopped down cross-legged, and reached for Rue. "What *is* the Dragon Festival?"

When I was young, our kind and thine celebrated the season of birth for dragonets. They are generally born at this time, as the sun turns farther away, for winter's cold and the distant sun keeps them in the nest until they have the strength to fly. But after the death of our kind, the humans used this festival to commemorate our extinction, thereafter assuming dragonish trappings to celebrate human strength and power.

Well, that must be really dispiriting to the last live dragon, I thought behind my inner wall.

The eggs ought to be hatching now, Rue added. *We have at most two turns of the sun before I cease to hear them in this world. I will rip open the mountain before I let that happen.*

Twenty-three

THE SUN BARELY CRESTED the eastern horizon, creating a silvery blue world—the same shade as my feathers. I flew out to the menagerie again.

This time I found Kenji lurking around. As soon as he saw me, he gave a great sigh of relief. "The magic is gone from the cages," he said abruptly, as if continuing a conversation. "But I don't know if it's a trap."

I said, "I think Invey kept his promise. As for freeing them, and the people the empress wants to sacrifice, wait until you hear the uproar."

"What uproar?"

"From the arena. I'm going to cause it. You won't mistake it. And it should draw all the guards within hearing, so you should be able to get away."

Kenji grinned. "Done." He took a step closer. "The volunteers are now throwing away the special food and drink the kips bring, but pretending to eat and drink it. And come midnight, we'll get them away—it's *my* illusion magic that'll protect them." He tapped his chest proudly.

Illusion magic? I'd completely forgotten that! Illusion might help with another problem I knew Hlanan would expect me to solve, which was the Djurans.

A noise—the approach of the morning feeding—and he vanished into the shrubbery. I gathered a handful of tiny berries from a nearby tree, wrapped them in a broad leaf, then transformed to my bird. I clamped the rolled leaf into my beak and took wing back to my cell.

At that same time, as two strong quakes shook the palace, Hlanan was once again summoned to the Jaw Box, escorted by a squad of guards. He passed into the grim room, aware that this third visit might be his last—he could feel tension in the air.

Inside, only Invey awaited him. He got up, and while Hlanan stood there as usual, barefoot, cold and shivering in the biting autumnal air, Invey walked back and forth, then around him in circles, asking random questions: "Do you know Prince Kenji?"

"No."

"Have you ever been to the Iwarna Islands?"

"No."

After several more questions like that, Invey passed by Hlanan, and pressed something into his hand. Hlanan gripped it, and stilled, thoroughly bewildered.

But Invey walked on, asking random questions without a break—"Have you had military training? Does the Kherval use scry stones in the military? What is the magic concerning them, does it differ from state to state?"

Hlanan kept up his litany of *no, I don't know*, and *none*, until he was waved out. He let the worn sleeve of the now-grimy "new" shirt fall over his hand, hiding whatever it was he'd been given, until he was once again locked into his cell.

Then he moved to the grating, and using the weak light that filtered in, opened the tiny strip of paper Invey had given him.

> *When your scryer causes the diversion, I will send my personal servant to open your cell. Stage an escape, but my mother is to go with my servant.*

Hlanan looked up, then held out the note for Sig to read out loud to Luenro.

They began discussing it while I was talking to Kenji. On my return, I reached for Hlanan, rejoicing in his genuine relief and gladness that I was there.

He told me the above.

I said, *Having his mother taken away makes me wonder if you're being set up.*

Half of the inmates here agree. Princess Luenro has promised them that she will refuse to go with the servant — whatever is to happen to us will happen to her.

On that grim note, we had to part, as someone wanted his attention, and I could feel that sickening flutter of vertigo he got when we were connected and someone else spoke to him.

Besides, I had work to do.

I unwrapped the berries, and, using the basic magic I'd been forced to study when in Sveran Djur, laid illusion spells on each one, tied to Darus's name.

Time crawled by; I checked with Hlanan one more time, to find him and his cellmates intending to rest against what might be a very long night. But they weren't resting. After all this time, wondering what would happen to them while those in command waged a silent battle over how they were to be used, pardoned, destroyed, the end had finally come. None of them could sleep.

Hlanan let me listen as they talked in low voices, mostly reminiscence. He said little, to them or to me, but I sensed that he found my presence comforting. It was strange, this connection, not quite courtship — especially as we had yet to lay eyes on one another — and yet more intense than friendship.

When some of his companions dozed off, he and I reminisced over our first meeting, when he saw me escaping a local bully and using one of my small magics to deflect my pursuit. It really wasn't all that long ago, but it felt somehow like another life, so much had changed.

Finally we both dozed, leaving the pinhole open; I caught him dreaming a jumbled array of memories from Erev-li-Erval's splendid palace overlooking the waterfall, and Thianra, and galley slaves.

That roused me. I was thoroughly awake when the guards came for me. "You get to start off the Dragon Festival," one said. "First blood is one of you — maybe all of you. It's to the death!" And the braying laughter of one whose heart had turned to callus.

I said nothing as I walked out, my arm pressed against the seeds tucked into a fold of my wrap. The soft murmur of voices I'd heard intermittently from the next cell over had ceased. The Djurans were already at the arena.

When I emerged from the long tunnel, the first impression was a wall of sound. The stands were packed. Hundreds of paper lanterns hung, brightening the arena to gold as the eastern sky began to lighten.

I walked into the arena.

Someone started a shout, "Kill it!"

The crowd took it up, stamping and shouting, "Kill it! KILL IT! *KILL IT!*"

Darus and his four liegemen stood erect, in a defensive square facing out, at the center of the arena. Darus stood outside the square. I was shocked at how much he'd changed. Hardened. And he hadn't exactly been a pastry puff to begin with.

As I approached, I took a closer look around the arena. All the garden stuff, the old helms, and the old weapons were gone. Instead, what looked like an army of Shinjans in full battle gear stood along the wall, steel in one hand, spear in the other.

Darus and his men had new swords. Shinjan swords. Darus's had a red tassel hanging down. I realized what I was seeing as I closed the last distance: I (or rather my death) was to be the show opener. Once the Djurans killed me, the Shinjans would charge and finished the Djurans in a bloody fight. I could feel their anticipation, and the focus on Darus in particular.

When I was maybe twenty paces away, I saw Darus's eyes widen in recognition. Then those blade-sharp cheekbones flushed dark in the weak light of predawn. "You!"

"Yes, me," I cut in, as his men encircled me. "And no, it was *not* my fault you're here. That was *your* stupid mistake—"

He moved so fast I barely escaped losing my head. A corner of my wrap dropped, along with wisps of my feathered hair as the tip of his blade passed a fingernail's width from my head as I vaulted in a somersault over his head.

The crowd roared. I shouted against it, "I'm here to get you out!"

He whirled and came at me again, the sword cutting the air with a hiss I felt as I flipped away.

"Listen," I yelled against the bloodlust of the spectators. "I'm about to take this place apart—"

"What?" He stepped back, and whatever fog of fury he'd been in broke. Leaving him still very angry, but puzzled.

"I'm going to *destroy* this place," I said. "Go ahead, swing, but don't cut me—I need to give you something."

His eyes narrowed. I braced, but he took another swing, this time the tip of the blade deliberately clearing me as I flung up my hands and backed up a step. He closed the distance.

I dropped the seeds. "Get someone to pick these up," I said quickly. "Hand one to each. There's an illusion spell on them—tied to your name. You'll look like Shinjan guards. Go out the tunnel that way over there." I waved my hand as I whirled over his head once again. "Right, right, right, left, and stay off the roads, all the way to the sea. Don't let anyone touch you. The illusion will—"

"I understand illusions," he snapped. "I don't believe you."

"Believe what you want. I don't care what happens to you," I sang out as he made another strike, and I somersaulted overhead. "You, and your emperor, can both jump in a volcano and I'll celebrate. But Hlanan cares. I'm doing this for him, before I take this arena apart."

"How?"

"Watch!"

And as he raised his sword overhead to bring it down, I shot a small fireball at his feet.

Just a little one, testing myself. Oh yes, I was ready.

His mouth dropped open. He flung himself back and barked something at one of his men, who bent and swiped up the seeds.

I opened my hands and shot fireballs at the feet of each man in quick succession. They began to run.

Some of the Shinjan guards bolted toward them to intercept.

I began zapping arrows of flame toward these Shinjans

thirsting to start the fun of slaughter, and as they scattered, I turned my attention to their fellows gathered along the wall.

Zap! Hiss! Splat! I shot fireballs in all directions. Their fine formation shattered—no one paid the least attention to Darus and his Djurans.

All attention was on me as I shot fire in all directions.

The guards jumped, ran, and some dove over the wall, all shouting, but no one could hear above the tumult of the crowd going crazy.

That was when the sun rimmed the jutting towers of the east.

Rue had taught me to draw sunfire from beyond clouds, from the stars, even from the sun on the other side of the world, but there was no doubt about it: when the sun appeared, it was much, much easier.

I turned to those hundreds of lanterns, now dim as fading fireflies, and blasted them with flame that gouted upward in showers of sparks that rained down on the crowd—it was time for those spectators to get something to think about besides bloodlust.

Sparks spattered outward, singing faces, hands, clothes. The crowd panicked. Stampeded as I shot flames at the detritus they left behind—wood, cloaks, cushions, baskets of food, and so forth.

The Djurans were gone, or mixed into the crowd of Shinjan guards running about. Somewhere a bell began clanging frantically, soon followed by another.

"Over to you, Kenji," I muttered.

Then I planted my feet, drew in a deep breath, and beamed spears of fire into quake-made cracks in the stone supports.

A sinister hiss on my left. Instinctively I leaped: an arrow sped past my shoulder. I whirled around and raised a sheet of flame around myself, which burned arrows to ash.

I bent all my strength at focusing fire into the stone supports of the stands until the hairline cracks spidered outward, became gaps... and as another quake rolled through, huge chunks of stone teetered, toppled, then in an unstoppable tumble smashed down, crushing the stone benches below.

Through it all, Rue hummed.

Dust billowed upward, spreading outward in a brown haze laced with smoke. I transformed to my bird and soared upward, hiding in the haze from the Shinjan archers as I circled the ruined arena. I knew that destroying the arena was wasted effort—nobody was stopping them from building another one—but at least it wouldn't be today.

I flew above corridors and alleyways crammed with guards and kips. No one thought to look up as people ran about in a frenzy. Hlanan and his cell mates were now out, but that didn't make them safe.

I couldn't see any one person in that sea of heads below. So I first reached for Invey, as an experiment. I was fairly certain I'd gained his range.

His emotions were so intense I was glad of the physical distance between us. I confined my inner door to the tiniest pin-hole as I listened to Luenro saying, "What's amiss? Oh, don't tell me the peace between you brothers, which is the joy of my life, is threatened?"

Invey hated seeing his mother groping blindly, her gaze blank—he had sent the servant to her side to guide her as well as to protect her. But he knew the more difficult questions were about to come.

He hesitated, words ready on his tongue, but he did not speak. All the disparate pieces fit together: Avejo, who if he hadn't been born an imperial prince, might have been the most successful horse breeder in his village or town because of his expert eye, and his expertise in training for speed. But because he had been raised to the sword, and believed in its use, Avejo would probably end up using that sword against Invey unless Invey gave in, whatever he believed.

The decision might come after many tossing nights, even after weepings of bitter tears, but it would happen, because violence gave Avejo purpose. If the entire system of slavery were brought down, Avejo saw chaos, an even greater danger than his lying, grasping mother.

"It's nothing," Invey said—puzzled. Was he sensing my

presence?

I shut the pinhole and began to glide, reaching for Hlanan. *I am in the sky. Help me find you.*

Vertigo nearly struck me out of the air as his exhausted, strained emotions smote me: *They did set us free, but Princess Luenro refused to be separated from us. And so we all just arrived at what is supposed to be the sacrifice site.*

Alarm burned through me. With his thought came what he saw; I soared high, then higher, until I spied what seemed to be an ancestral monument at the extreme end of the palace boundaries, separated by the city by a river crossed by a fine, arched bridge.

People lined the bridge, filled the street along both banks, and surrounded the area, as Avejo's kips strained to keep the crowd from overwhelming those gathered on the steps of the monument. As a Hrethan I would never have gotten through.

As a bird, I fluttered down once I spied Hlanan's familiar silhouette—for a short time I only had eyes for him. As I approached, shock rang through me at how tired he looked. How thin. He was all bone and muscle, his brown hair unkempt as it straggled down his back. But at least he'd been able to do the cleaning spell for them all—I recognized the Princess, standing with vacant gaze next to Invey, whose drawn face was even more exhausted-looking than Hlanan's.

So intent was I on Hlanan (who was not yet aware of me) that at first I didn't notice the drama on the steps not two paces from Invey.

Because of the susurrus of crowd noise, I could not hear anything as Avejo, in full armor, emerged from a group of captains and approached the steps, sheathed sword in hand, golden tassels dancing. His ruddy braids swung against his gleaming armor as he leaped up the steps three at a time, then took a stance beside his mother.

The empress stood at the top of the steps, in front of an elaborately carved stone table. She was dressed in red and black and gold, wearing an enormous crown that came halfway down her forehead, just above the slanting eyebrows so much like Avejo's.

And like mine.

"The palace is now ours," Avejo said in a clear voice accustomed to field command. "The harbor was ours last night. The city as well. We must—"

He stopped, as a strong quake rumbled through. Glass broke with a tinkling shatter in one of the shops lining the river road, and somewhere someone screamed.

Rue spoke in my head, *They are very nearly here.*

The empress shouted, "This is *exactly* what I shall control! Avejo, choose any number from this mob, and—"

"Your blood mages are dead," Avejo interrupted. "Saw to it myself."

The empress turned on him, frowning in disbelief.

Avejo said, "They seem to have eaten whatever that was your victims at the Thistle Retreat were supposed to ingest. They were sound asleep when I cut their throats." He tossed down something at his mother's feet.

I couldn't see what it was, but she seemed to recognize it, because she blanched.

Avejo said, "Brother?"

Invey took his mother's hand, and guided her up the steps.

"What is *she* doing here? Or are you trading her life for..." The empress's words faltered as Invey spoke two words. I could not hear those words, but that neck-prickling sense of strong magic made me shiver.

He had released a very powerful spell. The empress blanched. Then she bared her gritted teeth, her face flooding with color. Her hands shook as she fought against a coercion.

Invey said, so softly that few beyond the immediate circle could hear her, "Dost thou recognize this spell, Step-Mother? It is the selfsame spell thou once laiest upon our dying father. Relinquish the imperial tally to my mother."

The empress fought mightily—probably much harder than the emperor had—but the magic was stronger, laid (I found out later) on that crown she cherished so much. There were apparently so many wards on it that she never knew what spells had been removed and replaced.

The empress trembled as she fought, but her hands inexorably removed something golden from inside the front of her elaborate gown, and laid it into Luenro's outstretched hands.

As soon as the tally reached Luenro's palms, a sort of soughing noise, more voice than a sigh, rose from the crowd, followed by a hissing of whispers, and then a great shout.

The empress gazed, eyes distended, at all those open mouths now able to express their hatred of her, as Invey whispered a spell over his mother. The greenish snap of magic made her stagger, and tremble as she leaned against him. But then she blinked rapidly, and looked around her as Invey whispered yet again, his face blanched of color, his gaze locked a continent away as he concentrated.

Avejo took a step toward him, then stepped back as Luenro cleared her throat. "My first act as empress of Shinja will be to declare the fate of my predecessor. She will remain here at the door to the family tomb, a symbol of what happens to those who abuse the people's trust."

Invey gestured once, sharply, and before everyone's amazed eyes, Zeltzi's colors leached to gray, and all the soft curves of flesh beneath her chin, the rich folds of her silk, hardened to stone.

It was not a mere stone spell, which is easily lifted—it was an enchantment, bound to some object that only Invey could identity. Unless you had that object, you couldn't break the enchantment, and I was willing to bet he transferred it to the bottom of the ocean on the other side of the world.

Avejo watched, looking extremely ambivalent, then turned away—this much had obviously been worked out between the brothers.

Luenro raised her voice. "People of Shinja."

She had to speak twice before those crowding the front—including Hlanan and his former prison mates—fell silent, and those behind strained forward to hear.

"I do believe that Shinja ought to be governed by Shinjans. And I also believe it is time for change."

"Wait, what change?" Avejo stepped forward.

"Brother," Invey said, taking both Avejo's hands—and for the third time, he murmured a spell before letting go and stepping back.

Before the astonished eyes of everyone there, Avejo's face blurred, changing shape. He stooped, arms reaching down—then reshaped into hooves. Between one heartbeat and the next, the warlike imperial prince was gone, replaced by a splendid springbok gazelle.

Everyone stilled.

Avejo stilled. He sent a look of betrayal at Invey's distraught face. Then the long-legged, graceful animal looked about wildly, liquid brown eyes wide, and with two breathtaking leaps, he was gone.

With a rustle of foliage he vanished off into the trees behind the monument. "He has always loved the chase," Invey said softly, but his downward gaze made it clear how much this betrayal hurt.

But the invisible weight of responsibility didn't leave him time to grieve. Luenro raised her voice; this time it rang clear. "My second act, therefore, is to cede this empire to my son Invey, who will dedicate himself to making the changes that will restore Shinja to greatness."

She laid the imperial tally in Invey's hands.

Some whooped, cut off when another quake rumbled through.

The guards keeping the crowd back looked angrily at one another, as if waiting for a signal to... do what? Bring Avejo back? Fight?

Invey moved to the middle of the top step, looked about—and the tension in his face eased when he saw me.

"As my first act," he said, his strained voice lifting, "I command the Hrethan to calm the mountain."

Me?

I opened my mouth to point out that he was no emperor of mine—nobody ruled me—I was just there to protect Hlanan until he could use his magic transfer. But I had never closed the pinhole between Hlanan and me, so his thought came urgently, *Go.*

I AM going – but not at HIS command, I returned indignantly.

Don't you see? He is beginning a new rule without bloodshed. He knows he is not your emperor. He knows, better than anyone, that he is nobody's emperor. Power happens two ways. One is force. The other, it's chosen. Give these Shinjans something they can choose.

Between one heartbeat and the next I remembered a conversation we'd had before we parted, about why people follow other people. Out of love, out of habit, out of a conviction that they will be safe. They follow because others follow, because they wish to be left to live their lives while someone else deals with the matters too overwhelming for the individual.

I glanced around. Yes – these people were poised. Anything could tip them into violence. Avejo's loyal guard already looked halfway there, except for the captains who gazed rigidly at that tally resting on Invey's palms.

So in other words, Invey needed a gesture.

Well, if Hlanan liked him, why not give him his gesture.

I could feel the sun at my back. I ran halfway up the steps, turning so I could feel the sun on my face, my hair and tail lifting. And after all these weeks of working on the inner voice, and inner command, I knew what to do.

I lifted my hands, pulling Sunflame deep within me…

Then I transformed into a firebird and shot like a comet straight toward the sky.

Twenty-four

I NEARLY LOST MYSELF in the fierce joy of that flight.

Poor Avejo, I thought: now I understand your love of the chase. But I don't want to catch anyone, certainly not to kill anyone. It's the exhilaration of speed, the pure sunlight, the scouring wind.

Up and up I flew—it would have taken me days to flap that high in my bird shape, I was so fast.

But at last I caught myself, and looked down onto the snowy peak of the volcano. Then I turned my mind in question to Rue, and he guided me back down, and through a tremendous crevasse full of smoke and the stench of burning rock. Heat rose through cracks in the floor. In places steam billowing up.

I winged through, dropping lower and lower until a vast cavern opened. And there, in the center, glistening in a pulsing light whose source I could not name, lay a clutch of eggs. Several of them rocked. Little bumps knocked against the smooth gray shells.

In spite of the fact that I had seen Rue, I had still imagined the eggs to be something that could be carried out in a basket. Maybe a large basket.

These eggs were my size, I discovered when I shifted to my Hrethan self. *I'm here*, I sent to Hlanan. *The eggs are here!*

Do you need my help?

I didn't know what he could do, only that it would be good to have him there, as reaction had set in. I swayed on my feet, staring

at the enormous eggs as Rue hummed inside me with an urgency
that buzzed in my bones. Through Rue I understood that the eggs
had finished pushing their way through into real space. But they
had to be helped out of their shells immediately.

I looked away, memorizing a spot nearby, and sent the image
to Hlanan to use as a magic transfer destination. He appeared,
falling to his hands and knees, his face ashen. Invey had obviously
removed whatever wards had prevented Hlanan from doing
transfer magic, but even when one is feeling fit and strong, that
kind of magic *hurts*.

He got one foot under him. "What do we do first?" he shouted
hoarsely over the hiss of steam.

Rue sent a heartbreakingly vivid image, perhaps a memory: a
silvery blue dragon curled around a clutch. She clawed open the
shells, breathing fire over them.

I understood then. "They can't get out on their own," I
bellowed to Hlanan.

He looked back at me in bewilderment. We had no weapons,
and our human nails would be useless — it was clear that those
eggshells were thicker than storm sail on a ship.

Fire, Rue said.

Fire would not hurt them — they were dragons. And I was a
firebird.

I drew on the ferocious heat beneath the cavern, then aimed at
the nearest shell.

At first nothing happened, save more rocking, and some
bumps from the inside. But then, quite suddenly, the shell
stretched, a hole appeared, then the edges caught fire and
withered, revealing a knot of dragonet folded together, its tiny
arms and legs working weakly as it tried to disentangle its long
body and tail. It raised his head, peered around at us, then opened
its mouth. A squeaky hiss issued forth, as its mind keened: *hunger!*

Rue sent an urgent image of glittering rock.

I looked around helplessly, then waved at Hlanan. "Ore! The
dragon mother picked this cave because it's veined with ore! Fetch
it..."

I leaped to the next shell, as Hlanan began picking up tumbled rock in his arms. He carried it to the little cloud-colored dragon, whose head bobbed weakly, until its snout nosed the ore. The dragonet opened its mouth and its tongue flicked out to take a rock. Crunch! Then another.

The more it ate, the more the creature wakened to alertness. Hlanan gave up carrying rocks, hauled off his tunic-shirt, and filled it with ore, then dragged that to the dragonet, who trembled as it fought to raise itself to those little clawed feet, tail twitching.

By then I'd opened a second shell. Rue's hum had changed again, a sound like the deepest wind instrument ever played, losing that terrible harshness, as the second shell cracked and a new dragonet appeared, this one silvery green.

By the time I'd freed the third dragonet, the first one had toddled its way drunkenly toward the ore on its own. So Hlanan began dragging the ore toward the newborns.

One by one we got them out of their shells, until the cavern floor crawled with small dragons chomping and crunching with their tiny teeth. Tiny! Those teeth were the size of my little finger.

It was then that the first one, who I was already thinking of as Cloud, unfolded its wings and gave them an experimental flap or two. When nothing happened, it went back to nose out another vein.

At last Hlanan and I collapsed on a flat boulder, side by side. "We did it," I said stupidly, over and over. "We did it."

Presently a dragonet, then two, bumbled our way, pushing snouts against us, their breath warm. I felt their questing minds: we did not smell like food. Then the first one wavered sluggishly, and fell over, eyes torpid.

Rue? I called in alarm.

Fire. Bathe them in fire.

I cupped my palms, drew on the distant sun, and laved each dragonet in fire from nose to tail. That perked them right up. They wobbled toward one another, then one by one, they lay down in a heap and slumbered.

When all were still I counted seven: three cloud-colored, two a sandy brown with reddish highlights, and two greenish with bronze highlights. Hlanan and I sank down onto a rock side by side. I snuggled up against him, sublimely happy to be with him at last. When his arm came around me and pulled me to his side, every part of me scintillated with starfire.

But his breathing gradually shortened, then hoarsened. I am not exactly experienced in intimacy—for most of my life survival depended on keeping people at a distance—but this one man had succeeded in dissolving my lifelong barriers. So I had learned what he sounded like when he was caught up in ardency as much as I.

And this breathing was not ardency. It was pain.

"Hlanan?"

He didn't remove his arm, but he stiffened slightly, then slowly—I could feel his reluctance—admitted, "Lhind, it is so very good to be with you again. But you are... really, really ... *warm*."

I looked down at my wrap. Was it *smoking?*

Hastily I let go, and he took in a shuddering breath. Not that the air in that cavern was much cooler. "Sorry! I guess I'm still learning how to be my various shapes." I peered anxiously at him, my insides squeezing at how weary he looked, his face glistening with sweat. The way his lips moved made it clear that he was desperately thirsty.

"Hlanan," I said. "You do not have to stay. In fact, I think you should go *home*. Not back to those Shinjans. You did more than enough for them."

He leaned back on his elbows, eyes closed. "I promised I would help you. You certainly helped me."

"There is nothing for you to eat here. No water. They don't seem to need it. Yet. If I get thirsty I will shift to my firebird, now that I know how to. But this place is too hot for humans. The little dragons are fine. They are fully in the world, and safely hatched— the quakes are done. Rue will tell me what needs doing." I grinned and tapped my head. "I can find you this way."

He let his head drop back, strands of damp hair sticking to his forehead and straggling over his shoulder. "Even if I wanted to return to Shinja, I don't think I ought to."

"Why not? Ah, though I *completely* agree with your staying away, it seems to me Invey liked you. The princess certainly did."

"Because I suspect the sight of me would be a living reproach." He sat up and turned my way, his tired brown eyes earnest. "I said a lot of things to him while we were both more or less prisoners that might not sit so well with a new emperor. He has to begin to think like one," Hlanan added wryly. "Which will make him less..."

"Human?"

"Sometimes being human isn't all that laudable. Less approachable? I suspect he's less likely to hear free speech from an outsider—and it almost has to be that way, doesn't it? He has to learn to keep enough distance to prioritize what would be best for the majority. Even if he wanted to he cannot listen to the wishes of each of thousands and thousands of individuals." He shut his eyes and whispered, more to himself, I suspect, than to me, "It's a terrible form of government. But people... follow. They turn to each other, then to a leader, good or bad, when they don't know what to do. What else is there?"

"I don't know, and I don't really care, since no emperor yet—and I've met two, no three, no *four*, if you count that terrible Zeltzi—has asked for my opinion. But this much I know. You said it yourself once. The best ruler is one who stays in their palace and lets people get on with their lives."

"I've blathered a lot, haven't I?" Hlanan sighed. "In any case, Invey has his mother now. She's Kherval-raised, but she has Shinja's wellbeing in mind, so she will be the best source of advice. Kenji is also there. When I left, Invey and Kenji were talking as fast as they could. If Invey needs a voice of conscience, I trust those two to provide it. Invey will endure it because they mean something to him."

I had been thinking over what we'd seen at that monument. "Did he tell you he was going to do all those things, like turn Zeltzi into stone, and Avejo into a gazelle?"

"No. All that preparation, when he had only himself... He

must not have slept for days." Hlanan wiped his sleeve across his brow. "Yes, I had better go. This heat is nearly unendurable. But I am not ready to deal with my mother yet. I think I'll go to Ilyan Rajanas, and send a note to Mother through the scribe desk. At least she'll know I'm safe."

I leaned over to kiss him. "You taste of salt," I said.

"Because I'm sweating like a horse. You taste of smoke and sweetness."

I laughed, and he got slowly to his feet.

He had just enough strength left to endure the transfer, and I was alone with the sleeping dragons, Rue's deep joy humming like a thousand harps through my mind.

I slept.

⟨●⟩

I woke to the hissing chirp of hungry dragonets. Once one was awake, all were awake.

And so time slipped by.

I had no idea how long it was. The measure of days lost all meaning as I began living more and more in firebird form. My Hrethan self does best in cold weather, with plenty of water and fruit. My firebird self required only the heat.

I remained Hrethan long enough to drag ore to the dragonets via my wrap, until they got strong enough to nose out the veins themselves. Then I stayed in firebird shape, losing any sense of how humans measure time.

The dragonets' mother had chosen well. There was plenty of ore. Though the cavern was not nearly large enough for Rue, it was perfect for inquisitive little dragons to nose about, climb, and eventually to test their wings.

They ate ravenously each day, and pooped a sort of dusty grit that they began leaving in a place where the wind swept it out, which was my first evidence that they were in silent communication with Rue. Between him at a distance, and me with them, we tried to mother them as best we could. They flapped, flopped, tumbled, they tussled and played, and when they hurt themselves, or just wanted warmth, they came to me and I bathed them in fire.

Rue was a continuous presence in my mind as well, benign, content. Longing to meet the little ones face to face, as soon as they were strong enough to fly outside the cave.

Every so often I listened for Hlanan, as there was no telling if it was night or day, and anyway I wasn't certain how far apart we were sunwise anyway.

No surprise that the first three times I checked, he was deeply asleep. Each of those was farther apart as the dragonets grew in strength and size. Before long it was all I could do to keep them from hurting themselves with their attempts to fly out of the cavern into the frigid air. It was a relief when they tired themselves out at last, and fell into a heap to slumber. Then I got to rest.

I was asleep when my mother's voice whispered in my inner ear, *Elenderi. Your Prince Hlanan seems to be trying to scry you.*

Mother! Quick as instinct I shared everything that had happened, and caught the fact that she, and my father, had been following my adventures from their distance as much as they could. My spirit lifted, buoyed by their approval and support, something I hadn't known I needed until I got it.

I was shaking off sleep and readying to contact Hlanan when Rue's thought reached me: the dragonets had reached the stage of their growth at which they could endure the shift between spaces without getting lost in the mystery of that between, though they would need Rue's physical presence to guide them there.

That meant it was time for him to fetch them. *As soon as they waken,* came his thought.

I looked at that slumbering pile, and settled back and reached for Hlanan.

Lhind! There you are! Tir is here.

I'll bet Tir went back there after leading me to Rue, to wait on your return.

I think so as well. It's good to have Tir here again. Sometimes I lie in bed and watch the aidlar go in and out the windows. My sister is here as well, just arrived.

I felt his question. *I'm fine, though I'm having to live as a firebird — all I have as sustenance is the heat from molten rock and sunlight drawn from outside the mountain. But not for long. Rue is coming to get the dragonets. You are well?*

Rajanas and Ovlan seem to be competing against each other to stuff me with my favorite foods every time I poke my head outside my door, and then scolding me back to rest.

I pictured the silent Ovlan, and grinned. *How does one scold in hand language?*

Very, very emphatically. Rajanas wants you to know that he finds it disturbing that we can scry without a scry stone, and of course it would be you who would break centuries of custom.

I snorted. *The Hrethan talk mind to mind all the time. Ignore him and tell me how Thianra is.*

She keeps offering to play music at me day and night. I must look a lot worse than I thought I did. Hlanan's thought changed tenor, and I sensed he had walked out of the room where the others gathered. *Lhind, Invey scryed me. I don't even know how he did it. The Shinjans have distrusted scrying for untold generations, and had in place many wards.*

You're safe from them. You did what they asked. What does Invey want?

Nothing I can point to. We talk, going over ground we already discussed when I used to sneak up to his suite. He released all the Barrow prisoners, and as a first step, removed their slave status. His mother is delighted, but the lazy uncle, who has lived for decades a single man tended by a hundred well-trained slaves, is threatening to raise a rebellion. And of course those who own slaves, who make their living in the trade, are angry — and many of Avejo's army captains he suspects are conspiring against him. Now Sanvi Xin is Invey's steadiest ally, though also his harshest critic. He seems to want to talk to someone who isn't Shinjan.

With Hlanan's words, everything came rushing back — Invey's revolution, my long flight.

My promise to Raifas, which seemed so long ago.

And my promise to Jardis Dhes-Andis to introduce Rue to him, in order to get that cruel spell lifted from my father.

Guilt smacked me straight in the heart. I had totally forgotten! I'd been living as a firebird too long. I was forgetting my Hrethan self, and her ties to the world.

How to fix that? To begin with, I didn't even know where Darus was—if he and his men had survived. Bleakly I contemplated the long, exhausting flight back to Sveran Djur, just to tell Raifas news that was old before I even left.

Rue's amused inner voice reached me. *Thou foolish little firebird!* With the gentle admonishment came a wordless reminder that I knew how to shift between spaces. It was the same concept as taking my wrap with me when I transformed, just involving distance and not things. I had only to see where I wished to be, and I would be there. It was what the complicated spell for magic transfer, with its tokens and Destinations, tried to emulate, though in a clumsy, painful form.

I experimented, shifting from one side of the sleeping pile of dragonets to the other. I did not like the way a deep chill gripped my bones, though usually I never minded cold. But this was visceral, made me gasp, and it left me giddy after I'd done it several times. Whereas in Rue's image, dragons did the shift in midair, while flying, as well as while still. Also, I recollected that there were degrees of shift, instinctive to dragons—that was how I'd first met Rue, partly present in the center of that volcano, and partly not.

I dropped onto a boulder to shake the chill and the last of the light-headedness. Remembering Hlanan's words, I reached for Invey—

And nearly fell off my boulder as I recoiled from the fury and anxiety roiling in the new emperor of Shinja.

"...sent the eldest of the slaves to beg you not to force them into starvation and homelessness."

Invey faced a much-freckled woman with thick reddish blond hair. Awareness seeped through the roiling emotions: through him

I realized that this was Sanvi Xin, daughter of the executed leader of the slave revolt.

"They don't seem to understand that their owners will either have to pay them for their services, or pay the apprentice fee for them to train in something else," Invey said. "How can I make it clearer? I sent out an imperial order for everything to be read thrice daily in the market square. I can make a proclamation myself at noon before the monument, I suppose."

"What I can tell you is this: most slaves cannot *get* to village or town squares to hear the morning, midday, or sunset proclamations because they are *working*."

"Then I had better make an appearance and command the entire city to gather so that all can hear me declare it."

"Do that," she said. "I think the owners are either confused, or are deliberately frightening them, especially the older ones," Sanvi stated, muscular forearms crossing beneath an enormous bosom. "And you have to make it clear that there is plenty of work! My cousins in the guild set out signs saying we would train anyone in stonework, but we've had maybe a fourth of the expected numbers come..." She was clearly settling in for a long rant.

My head panged violently and I shut the inner door. Was I losing my human self? I reached for Hlanan, reassured when he was there again, as clear as before. *I am in the courtyard at the back of the Gray Wolves learning warmups,* came his voice, rueful with laughter. *I will never be any good with a weapon, but I am getting very good at handstands. It was quite gratifying to see Rajanas's jaw drop when I walked on my hands across the training court here.*

Should I go away and leave you to it? I asked, a little wistfully. Still a bit light-headed, Invey's anger, anxiety, and yes, beneath that a sense of betrayal, all lingering like the tang of poison.

No—for this is inescapably boring. Now I remember why I was always skipping out on the physical training master and going to hide in my father's archive when I was small. His laughter cleared out the last of the poison.

I made the mistake of listening to Invey. Those Shinjans are so greedy! I shared what I'd heard from Invey.

Hlanan's anger vanished. *It's fear. Not mere greed, but fear of so much change. Now I understand what he tried to hide from me, why he needs to scry. He must be hearing conflicting wishes on all sides... I should go—*

No!

Hlanan hesitated, then his conflict tumbled through my mind like rainclouds. *I can't be an authority, foreigner that I am, with no easily pointed at status, but I can at least listen.*

Emperors ARE authority, I pointed out. *That's what the crowns and thrones and thousands of guards mean, right?* Crabbily, I thought to myself that if Invey didn't want to be emperor, he shouldn't have enchanted his brother into a gazelle.

But that was even short-sighted for me: if Invey had done nothing, then Avejo would at this very moment be leading the navy to conquer Kenji's islands and take their wealth in order to shore up slavery, instead of racing across the plains beyond the mountains, eating the last sweetgrass before the snows reached the river-carved valleys.

Hlanan's thought paralleled mine. *At times like this the weight of accepted authority is so useful, even reassuring, as much as anything in human endeavor can be. That in essence is why people follow. No one likes chaos.*

If he wants an authority above emperors, there are always dragons, I cracked—and then I thought to myself, Why not? Better than Invey asking Hlanan to come back to Shinja, and like as not blame him if everything went wrong.

The worst of it was, I knew Hlanan would go, even if everyone else considered the risk greater than the reward.

Yes, this problem I was going to take care of myself.

I opened my memory to Rue: the day I first saw him, when he shocked Jardis Dhes-Andis and the Djuran empire by flying out of the mountain around Icecrest palace. He had roused at the plea of the gryphs, and in so doing had awoken out of his death sleep enough to hear the eggs.

I sent tangled images and words, not at all certain how to express it—or even what to say—in hopes he might make a similar flight around the mountain before taking the dragonets away. Maybe his appearance would scare those Shinjans into ... into what?

Rue understood better than I did. *Little firebird, for me to frighten these humans is to foster bloodshed between our kinds once again. I will fly because I must, but it is for thou to carry what message thou wilt to thy kind.*

"Not my kind," I muttered—but I knew that I was closer in kind to the Shinjans than Rue was.

I thought about everything Hlanan and I had been talking about, and was still debating just how foolish I was going to be when the dragonets began to waken.

Rue was coming.

For the first time, I did not block the dragonets from attempting to escape the cavern. Excited, they began fluttering from rock to boulder on their way out, until we reached the crevasse that looked out over the slope toward the land below. To my surprise, the world had turned white while I was busy with infant dragons. Snow sparkled in a clean, frosty blanket down the mountain, topping the roofs of the imperial city on the lowest slopes.

Rue appeared as a dark spot far on the horizon, then swiftly grew. From high in the sky he began to drift lower, his long body eeling gracefully, until he was nearly motionless, sliding beneath the ledge of our crevasse. I remained in firebird form in case one of the dragonets fell, for none were strong enough to recover from the thousand-stride drop below our ledge, especially in that cold, which was already making them sluggish.

But nothing dire happened. One by one they fluttered to Rue's back, one batch of four, and then he circled around again for the last three. Once they were settled down on his broad back, sheltered between his wings, Rue gave an inner nod to me, sailed out over the city, then banked and headed toward the sea, wings beating the air with a thunderous *clap!*

Once he was over the water, he shifted out of sight, taking the dragonets to their new nest in Rue's volcano on Sveran Djur's main island.

By then I was already drifting down toward Shinja's capital there on the slope below. I stayed in firebird form, though already I was having to work hard to draw enough fire from the low sun of wintry midday. I could sense that the moment I let myself go back to either bird or Hrethan I was going to be desperately parched, and probably hungry as well.

Below lay the imperial complex. A quick glance showed the menagerie empty, the cages gone, and only the garden remaining; the arena lay under a forgiving white blanket, the contours of the ruin softened by snow.

Much of the city had gathered on the streets, moving toward the monument where Invey had taken the crown. At Rue's appearance they had frozen in place, faces upturned toward the sky.

Now the crowd began to move again, until they saw me. Unlike previously, there was no panic or pushing, just a steady, inexorable flow with intent. I didn't understand the mood of the Shinjans. Nor was I going to stay long enough to find out.

I needed to make a gesture on the imperial scale, foreign as such an idea was to my nature—I was still uncertain what to say. My mind raced with snatches of words, all discarded. I am not the stuff heroes are made of. Those awe-inspiring figures of legend and song who make euphonious speeches that stir thousands to action? I'm not one, I know that much.

But for a few heartbeats I could pretend to be one.

I glided silently, my silvery feathers glowing a bright enough gold that I cast no shadow, then I soared low between rooftops, over the heads of the crowd.

I could see word spread in a rush of hissing wind until all faces turned upward, eyes and mouths round. My fire reflected off those faces as I drifted toward the monument.

An instant before my feet touched the stone I shifted to my Hrethan form. Static lightning crackled through me, lifting my hair and tail, throwing off sparks. The world's worst thirst dried me from eyebrows to toes.

But I held to my plan as I looked into Invey's startled face. He'd begun to speak, but took a step back. Remembering what Hlanan had said about authority, I first performed a low bow.

Yes, that was right—I could hear it in the soft murmurs of the crowd. That established hierarchy: I was a figure from legend, bowing to their emperor.

I lifted my hands, letting my hair fwoosh up around me as I intoned, "The age of dragons has begun anew!"

A low roar of question swelled, then subsided as those in back pressed forward trying to witness. I glanced at the patched wall of a house, the missing tiles on a roof, and bawled my loudest, "Commencing a new era of peace, to once again bring Shinja back to its ancient greatness!"

That was the stuff! I could see it in smiles and nods. Everyone liked greatness. And they were ready for peace.

But my throat was already scratchy, and it would be bullfrog raw soon.

"The era in which *all* Shinjans are born free to achieve that greatness! There shall be no more slavery!"

The last word was more squawk than voice, but it got across. As the front began to cheer, I turned to Invey, who gave me a wry look. I bowed again, and transformed into my firebird.

The thirst died away. My flames caused the front of the crowd to take a step back as I took wing directly over their heads. I kept flying until I knew I was out of sight, and then I fixed my mind firmly on that pretty little stream on the side of Rue's mountain, and...

I tumbled to the snowy ground. The stream had rime along the edges, but the water was still running. I threw myself in, embracing the delicious cold, and drank and drank until I could drink no more.

Then I crawled to the bank, and slept.

Twenty-five

I WOKE RAVENOUSLY HUNGRY, but at least the thirst had abated. For now. Grumpily I made myself shift to my bird to fly to Raifas's castle. Time to keep that annoying promise about Darus.

I flew in an open upper window. The room was empty. I opened the door and ran down the spiral staircase, toward voices. I recognized Raifas's among them, so I followed the sound to a large room off the entry with the gigantic indoor tree. Raifas stood surrounded by Djurans, all in dragon-scale armor, with battle tunics worn over it in their pennon colors.

Behind Raifas was a table set with a plate of hothouse grapes, and some kind of pastry. I arrowed straight for them, paying no attention to the Djuran military captains, who stopped talking and stared at me.

Raifas's lip curled. "I wondered if you'd ever turn up again." He tipped his chin toward the door. "I'll be with you presently."

The warriors waited for me to leave, and at an impatient glance from Raifas, realized it was they who were being dismissed. They shot various sorts of stares my way before exiting, the last closing the door.

In the short time it took for them to leave, I'd nearly cleaned the plate. As I crammed the last of the pastry into my mouth, Raifas said, "You're too late. Or almost. While you've been lolling around..." He glanced at my plate, containing a few crumbs and the grape twig, and amended, "or whatever you were doing, the emperor has decided to move against Shinja. The attack was to commence today—in fact it might already have, if the weather cleared. But he sent me back by transfer because a message arrived saying that the dragon was sighted attacking the mountain." He gestured behind us. "I was sent to assess the situation."

"Rue is not attacking anybody," I said impatiently. "I wish you'd get that through your skull. Of course, your idiot emperor probably wants him to attack so he can play war. Beg pardon. He's *already* playing war."

Raifas's mouth tightened into a line. "I did warn you."

I'd eaten, but I was still light-headed. I rubbed my temples as I said, "Darus is *fine*. Was. The last time I saw him. Um. I don't know when, exactly. I don't even know the date right now. But!" I said as Raifas stirred impatiently. "I can find him. Right now. But how is he going to communicate? I can, um, transfer myself, but not anybody else."

Raifas's eyes widened, then narrowed. "Here." he reached behind his neck, and unclasped his fais.

Easy as that. I couldn't help a gasp—the fais Jardis had forced on me had zapped me with excruciating pain if I so much as touched the clasp. I shook off the remembered cruelty, and gingerly took Raifas's fais, still warm from his neck. I would rather have handled a poisonous, angry snake—though I knew the thing couldn't possibly attack me. But memory is memory. Remembered pain makes its own scars.

"Be right back," I said. "This time I mean it."

I didn't want to do the slide-shift again, but I forced myself to concentrate on Darus's well-remembered face. Handsome, you could say, but about as inviting as an ice pick.

The memory became a reality—a sweaty, grimy reality—before the ground lurched beneath my feet. My balance was usually excellent, but the moving ground and my light-headedness combined and I fell with a splat.

That was not ground under me, but a wooden deck. The smell of brine hit me next. Then sound—shouts, the groan of wood, the racket of wind in sail, creaking rope. I sat up as Darus, ragged and filthy, stared down at me incredulously. "You!" His expression lengthened from disbelief to amazement to betrayal as he blinked at the glittering fais clutched in my hand.

Betrayal? I looked at him in astonishment, inadvertently reaching mentally. Then shut the inner door, but not before I caught a blast of his emotions. Anger, of course foremost, but beneath that total betrayal because I was there and not his emperor. Who was a very powerful mage: if I could find him even though Darus's fais was missing, then Jardis Dhes-Andis could.

Behind him his crew stood, staring at me in amazement. I counted them up. Not only had he and his four made it to safety, but somehow he'd managed to locate and extract the rest of his staff and crew, or most of them.

"Here," I said, hopping to my feet. "Raifas sent this—we have to be fast, or there is going to be a war. I—yow!"

An arrow zipped by, yanking a few strands of my hair with it. I whipped my hair behind me, turning.

Darus's ship was being chased by another ship, which had just reached arrowshot. I recognized the flag fluttering from the foremast, and the long, lean style of that oncoming ship.

"Pirates?" I yelped. "You're being chased by *pirates?* How did you end up..."

Darus's lip curled as he wiped back stringy, grimy hair, then gestured with a long curved sword. "Do you really want to hear it?"

"No." I breathed the word out. Leaped up onto a mast, and peered across the choppy gray seas at the chase.

I held onto a rope as I drew in as much sunlight as I could, then I sent flames shooting across the intervening sea. When the pirate's sails were all on fire, I took care of the next two pirates flanking that ship, then hopped down to face Darus. "That'll keep 'em busy. You can handle it from here."

He'd already clasped Raifas's elegant fais around his neck, over his grimy shirt, and stood with eyes closed—in communication with someone. But the tight mouth of betrayal remained. There was no joyous reunion here.

Then it hit me that Darus missing was probably more useful to

Jardis Dhes-Andis than Darus restored to his place in the Djuran hierarchy, as an excuse for war. Whatever the emperor was saying at that moment to Darus over the fais. But then, his emperor was not in the habit of explaining himself to anyone.

I was done there. Before he, or any of his followers, could react, I slid back to Raifas's room, then caught myself against the table and shivered.

Raifas stood where I'd left him, arms crossed. "I was beginning to wonder if you were trying to pawn my fais," he commented.

"Pirates." I spat the word, spied a jug of water, and drank from the thing, holding the jug in both hands. Half of it slopped down my front, because jugs are not made for drinking from, but that felt good.

I crashed the jug to the table, flexed my scalp and my hair shook off the water. Raifas backed up, letting out a bark of surprised laughter. "You did say *pirates?*"

"Darus was being chased by three. I gave them something else to think about. He should be doing whatever it is you do with those fais things when you're not being tortured. There! Done. Promise kept."

His expression went through a series of changes that another time might have made me laugh. Then he flung out his hand, one palm toward me. "No. If I start asking questions, I suspect I will never stop. I have to get back to the flagship."

He took a token from a pouch on his belt, grimaced as he braced himself—and transferred, leaving me alone. I drank off the rest of the water in the jug, and took a deep breath. Already felt better.

And I was free—

And then came the mental equivalent of a polite tap at my inner door. *Mother! So that's how you do it!* I winced, regretting how I'd been barging through Hlanan's inner door without that equivalent of knocking. Oh, and Invey's, though I didn't feel any guilt over that—at least he'd been too tired, and too busy, to know I'd listened so briefly to his thoughts.

My darling Elenderi, I really think you ought to be here with us.

Us?

She obliged with an image: standing aboard a great navy ship under the long banner of Charas al Kherval snapping in a fierce wind.

I drank the last of the water, braced myself, and shifted. At least this time I didn't fall down, though I swayed as my body leaned into the plunging ship. Spray shot high on either side of the prow, under a sky wild with thunderclouds. I smelled ... dragon fire on the wind.

Confused, I looked around for my mother. She stood on the foredeck, with my father resting on her forearm, his head turning sharply, one eye then the other. The moment I saw him, I felt his reassuring thought flow into my mind.

Steadied by their appearance, even if I didn't understand it, I whipped tail and hair behind me, flattening the feathers against my back the way my mother did, to keep the storm winds from tearing at them.

The aidlar Tir hovered in the air not far from my parents, flapping hard to stay in one place—and there was Hlanan, a long black cloak too large for him flatting in the wind. I recognized that cloak. It was Rajanas's.

"Lhind?" Hlanan exclaimed.

I ran to him, and we fell into mental exchange—by now we were so much faster than spoken words. A lot had happened while I was asleep, beginning with Invey scrying Hlanan to ask if he had sent me. I caught a brief, heart-lifting burst of pride from Hlanan as Invey told Hlanan about my appearance as Emissary from the Great Dragon of Peace.

But Invey never got the chance to finish relating my speech when he was interrupted by a note from the commander of the Shinjan western fleet that they had sighted Sveran Djur's war fleet hull up on the horizon.

After that, scribes at various imperial desks were busy sending notes back and forth. The Kherval scouting party that had been shadowing the Djurans ever since Hlanan had been traced to Darus's yacht was included in the note sending.

The ships converged before nightfall, just as an enormous storm blew in quite suddenly—right around the time I tumbled into sleep on the side of Rue's mountain. The sky had begun to clear this morning, and the ships were now ranging for battle.

As the mixture of image and voice enlightened me, I peered past the plunging bow toward the Djuran ships. I make no claim to naval expertise, but even I could see that Sveran Djur had pretty much all its navy there, while Shinja had only a part of its—Avejo had had the main Shinjan fleet in harbor, poised to sail against Kenji's islands when Avejo became a gazelle.

Lightning still crackled between high, tumbling clouds. Winter thunderstorms are rare; I wondered if anyone else could smell the dragonfire.

Rue, I thought. Sometime during the night, while I was snoring on the bank of that stream above Raifas's castle, for whatever reason, Rue had shifted to the sky somewhere above the two fleets and the shadowing Kherval scouts, and shot enough fire through the sky to change the character of what otherwise would have been a regular winter storm.

I recollected Hlanan's last words as my gaze returned to the ship I stood on. Over at the side stood a middle-aged man in Kherval livery. I didn't have to ask: he had to be the empress's eyes on the scene.

Then I recollected what Raifas had said: Jardis Dhes-Andis was about to launch his fleet against Shinja. Only the storm winds had delayed him.

"Oh, no, he's not," I muttered to Hlanan.

"What?" He gave me a startled glance. "Who?"

The ships were slow, but moving. Very soon they would be in arrow shot. Or worse, if Raifas had any of the trick weapons Jardis had been encouraging him to develop.

I reached inside for my firebird, but I was too depleted. It felt kind of like hitting a deep bruise. So I leaped up and transformed to my bird, second nature now. I rose higher on the wind, barely having to flap—though Tir kept pace with me.

I sent a mental greeting to the aidlar, whose calm bolstered my spirit. Tir, I thought as I rose higher, was a lot like Hlanan, as much as bird and human could be similar. Was the aidlar a witness for the dual-natured as well as there as Tir's companion?

From Tir came an outflow of support. Yes, there were more witnesses to this crisis than those two-leggers standing on the various decks.

Now I could see everyone on board the Kherval scout, including a young person wedged between two barrels, bent over... a sketchpad? I opened the inner door for a heartbeat, catching the artist's ardent desire that there might be gold in the offing for a painting of a historic moment.

Well, and why not, I thought as I let the wind carry me across the foaming seas toward the lead Djuran ship, to where Jardis Dhes-Andis stood on the quarterdeck of the Djuran flagship.

Raifas looked splendid enough in his burnished bronze dragon-scale armor, with the battle tunic over it in Ardam's colors of crimson, black and gold, but he faded to insignificance next to his emperor.

I'll say this for Jardis Dhes-Andis, he knew how an emperor should dress. His armor was worked in pure gold, with black as the background, intertwined stylized symbols in triplicate, the gold matched by the coronet he wore on his brow, that single huge diamond in the center flickering unnerving reflections of the lightning crackling overhead.

I flew down. At first he didn't see me. He gazed through a spyglass at the Shinjan ships, then impatience tightened his face, and though I would never venture near the steel and stone door I had erected between him and me mentally, I knew he had sent a mental command over the fais—then recollected that Raifas did not have his.

He turned to say something, and stilled as I fluttered down and lit on the deck of the Djuran ship, and transformed to my Hrethan self.

The creak of bows made my shoulders come up, but Raifas raised a gauntleted fist, and the archers in the yards held their weapons ready.

"Elenderi," Jardis Dhes-Andis said, amused.

I snarled. I had just gotten used to my name, after a season of hearing it lovingly said by my mother, but hearing it from him threw me right back to the misery of my captivity in invisible chains of pain while surrounded by deceptive luxury.

When in doubt, be as rude as possible. He hated rudeness.

And he could no longer touch me.

Though I was aware that Darus had used Raifas's fais, presumably to contact his emperor, I said loudly, "Did Raifas forget to tell you that Darus is fine? He's busy outrunning pirates."

Jardis Dhes-Andis said, "Not quite," and glanced to one side.

I saw Darus coming down the deck, his expression like marble in winter. He must have been summoned by transfer magic. He didn't even look my way as he dropped to his knees before Jardis, and at a gesture rose and took his place beside Raifas, looking even more ragged by contrast. He handed over the fais, as Jardis went on, "We are redressing the wrongs of the Battle of Athaniaz Island, if you should like to witness."

"You mean that's your new excuse?" I squawked, horror chilling me worse than a thousand of those transfer-shifts. How *could* I have forgotten just how sinister Jardis Dhes-Andis was in his complacent superiority?

He wanted a battle, and he was going to have one. Furthermore, he knew he was going to win this battle, and here he was, looking forward to the pleasure of watching it happen.

And there was nothing — *nothing* — I could do. Even after all my efforts.

He smiled at me, and I knew he was very aware of my thoughts, and was even postponing his pleasure to make sure I knew it. His gloved hand began to rise.

Then Rue was back in my mind. *Remember thy promise, little firebird.*

One again, I had forgotten! But apparently, so had the emperor of Sveran Djur.

Wildly I grasped at this last possible deflection. "It's too bad," I said even more loudly, to suppress the tremor that threatened my voice, "that you'd rather slop around out here than meet the dragon I'd promised you could meet."

Jardis Dhes-Andis stilled, and his hand dropped. His eyes narrowed under his slanted black brows as he eyed me skeptically.

"I am sure you know that the dragon flew out yesterday—but I guess you weren't there to be met," I babbled, inventing as I went. Rue was silent in my mind, which I took as tacit agreement, so I kept on. "Too bad you didn't want to meet him. Dragons," I added, "live for hundreds of years. He might not come out again for a century. Maybe even two."

Jardis Dhes-Andis's lips parted. "I want him at Icecrest."

I shrugged. "That can be arranged. Now," I added—though that would only postpone the inevitable. But any postponement at least allowed for coming up with a brilliant plan to circumvent the battle. "First," I snapped, "*your* promise."

The Djuran emperor flicked a look at Raifas, who bowed, and I knew a silent command had gone from mind to mind. Jardis Dhes-Andis vanished, transferring back to his palace, leaving his entire fleet waiting, just so he would have the pleasure of witnessing the attack on his return.

I groaned inwardly, braced, and slid back to that hated place, to the highest of Icecrest Palace terraces, from which Dragon Mountain could easily be seen. Above me, glistening towers of white stone threw back the bleak wintry light, as dark clouds roiled high overhead.

I'd won a little time... what next? How to stop a war?

Jardis Dhes-Andis stepped out of a door, a fine piece of jade resting on one palm. With an air of mock courtesy, he held it out. "It's now bound to your name."

I took it, turning it over on my palm. It was beautiful, carved in the shape of a dragon's claw. I felt magic on it, but that could be any kind of spell. I was about to express my doubt when *tha-DUD!*

Distant lightning framed a magnificent sight: a mighty crimson dragon, wingtip to wingtip the size of the island, rising from the mountain and gliding directly toward the Icecrest.

Courtiers ran out through the doors, staring upward, their fine paneled robes blowing in the rising wind. Then most of them cowered back as if those walls would keep them safe.

Jardis Dhes-Andis stood alone on the terrace. He lifted his head, lips parted as the wind rose, blowing his long black hair in ribbons down his back. He held a ruby in his hand, which he raised, and as the dragon passed overhead, spoke a word.

Horror gripped me as shimmering greenish netting spidered out from the gemstone, creating in an eyeblink an enormous net that settled over the dragon.

I knew what that was. Jardis Dhes-Andis had spent all these weeks creating the biggest fais ever made, in order to force Rue to his command.

The emperor's right hand extended toward that greenish light just as lightning branched from the clouds overhead.

"The lightning's struck the dragon!" someone shouted.

Light flared around Rue, causing the glittering net to flash ruddy gold.

Then quicker than a heartbeat, that fire lanced down from the fais-net and Jardis Dhes-Andis stood limned in a glory of sunfire, face upturned toward the sky, eyes wide, the ruby blazing on his palm like a sunset.

"No! The lightning hit the—"

Emperor and gem both vanished, the scouring wind sending their ash whirling over terrace wall to the sea.

Twenty-six

FOR A SHORT TIME I stood there staring stupidly down at the jade dragon's claw in my hand.

A courtier screamed. Another shouted, "Lightning struck the emperor!"

"It hit the emperor *and* the dragon!"

"Is he *dead?*"

"The lightning —"

More lightning crackled. I smelled dragonfire.

"Get inside! Get inside! Lightning..."

Another mighty thud rattled the windows in the palace at my back. Rue's wings flapped as he passed overhead, sliding to the beyond in a wink of light before he reached the mountain.

I stood there witlessly for a few breaths, the jade forgotten in my hand, as I comprehended that Rue must have known all along what Jardis Dhes-Andis intended. The dragon had drawn down lightning in order to negate the magic of that fais — while it was still connected to Jardis Dhes-Andis. Calling down lightning was a measure way beyond me, but Rue seemed unharmed.

Hail pelted down from the wild clouds, stinging me. Awareness returned to my physical self, and I remembered the stone in my hand.

Father, I thought.

One more slide, and I was back on the Kherval ship. Numb with reaction, I held up the jade, and as my mother looked at it first in puzzlement, then astonishment, Father lifted from her forearm, wings flapping.

I whispered my name. Green light snapped over Father, destroying the death binding. A heartbeat later Hrethan magic shimmered over my father, resolving into a tall man who looked at first glance unsettlingly like Jardis Dhes-Andis. He wore a very old-fashioned three-panel stole over the pleated trousers and long shirt typical of the Djurans. He was barefoot, evidence of his having been getting ready to sleep before he was attacked with evil magic by his own brother.

His face so much like Jardis Dhes-Andis's wore an expression of tenderness and joy that was completely unlike his half-brother's. My father threw his arms around me for a fast, convulsive hug. Then one arm lifted, and he brought Mother into the three-way hug before they kissed over my head.

For an endless time the three of us stood like that, rocking on the plunging ship, but then I became aware of voices. I let go, stepped back, and reached through the inner door to both parents, sharing what had happened. *But what now? There is no heir. Jardis Dhes-Andis didn't let any of his lovers have a child, and he killed everyone else in the family —*

"Everyone," my father said gently, "but you, and me."

I gawked at him. I knew that Mother, and the Hrethan, had spoken with him mind to mind over the years, keeping him from succumbing to the fate of those forced into another form.

What I was beginning to realize was that though he had been a bird living out of Jardis Dhes-Andis's reach deep in Hrethan mountaintops, he had, through various sources, kept up with developments in Sveran Djur.

My instinctive protest died on my lips. He looked around with a faint smile, then tapped me on the shoulder. "Time for duty," he said — understanding my residual fears.

I gazed back, questions whirling through my brain. Duty. He had been born a prince, raised to rule before he was cheated by his brother. But he had watched the Djuran empire from afar ever since. I was beginning to intuit just how much he had longed to set things to rights.

He had always been a mage. He transferred to the deck of the Djuran flagship. I used my shift to join him, catching my balance as he walked barefoot to Raifas, his long black hair flagging in the wind.

There was no mistaking who he was. He even looked Jardis Dhes-Andis's age, as magic had frozen him in time physically. "My brother," he said to Raifas, "lost himself to a lightning strike. He is no longer with us. That leaves me the sole representative of the Andis-Sveranji blood. I believe the time has come to sail home."

Everyone stilled. Poised for... What?

The ship rose and fell on the surging waves, packets of foam splashing over us all. Intensely worried, and sensitive to every sound, I thought I heard the creak of a bow. Perhaps Father did too. At any rate he raised his hand, and greenish magic flared.

Then every arrow on the ship sprouted leaves, steel arrow-heads falling to clatter on the deck, or to vanish into the sea.

I know enough about magic to understand that such spells have to be prepared ahead of time. Perhaps he and Mother, speaking mind to mind, had readied it during the brief period I was gone—as the moments streamed by, I began to suspect that the unseen but listening Hrethans had been the first to know what had happened, by whatever means. Maybe even through Tir.

The effect of that sudden magic on the Djurans, raised to respect power, was stunning. Darus was the first to kneel. Then those on deck dropped to their knees. Thuds sounded around as Djurans descended from the yards and ropes to join their fellows.

Raifas sighed softly and dropped to one knee, his head bent. It was clear he really regretted having what was for him the chance of winning a nice little battle taken away—he wasn't the kind to relish bloodshed the way his former emperor, with whom he'd grown up, had been, but he did see the coming battle as an exhilarating game.

Father said, "Commander Raifas of Ardam Pennon. Set sail for home. You will find me waiting in Icecrest." He turned my way.

I sent the thought, *Those courtiers in Icecrest are running around in a panic.*

Let them. The imperial military is all here. Courtiers will do little harm before I get there. We will clean up this mess first. Back to the Kherval flagship.

I was gone on the word 'flagship.'

As soon as I regained my spot near Mother, Hlanan took a step toward me. "What happened? What happened?"

It was faster to show him through the inner door. When I reached the end, his expression hardened to the one I was beginning to recognize. It was his duty face. "Invey is over there on the Shinjan flagship," he said. "He needs to know."

"I don't suppose we can't just send a message," I muttered, giddy, tired, a sense of unreality fluttering behind my ribs. I was half a breath from giggling inanely, out of relief, out of escape... out of joy at seeing my father, even if I was about to lose him.

I was about to lose him—I turned, in time to see him appear a few paces from Mother's other side. He made the grimace that everyone who does magic transfer can't avoid. At least I wasn't losing him yet.

Hlanan looked my way in silent question.

Yes, I would go with him to Invey's flagship.

The humans did magic transfers, and I did my slide. We staggered on the deck of yet another ship. Invey stood with red-haired Shinjan captains, all with high command chevrons on their jackets.

"Jardis Dhes-Andis is dead," Hlanan said without preamble. "He has been replaced by Danis Dhes-Andis, Lhind's father." He opened his hand toward me. "The new emperor of Sveran Djur is on the Kherval flagship for now, if you wish to negotiate a treaty. I know he wants peace," Hlanan added.

"Well done," Invey breathed, his gaze resting on Hlanan. A gaze of admiration... and tenderness.

Hlanan didn't see that look of longing Invey gave him, because he was smiling my way. "Thank Lhind. It was her doing."

"Actually," I said, "it was the storm. Lightning struck the former emperor while he tried to put evil magic on the dragon

Rue. Who also wants peace."

Invey glanced from one of us to the other. Then he drew in a deep breath as he straightened his spine, his expression inscrutable as he turned to one of his commanders. "Give the signal to prepare for return to Shinja."

The commander laid hand to chest and walked away, followed by the rest of the captains. "How do we do this?" he asked, when it was just the three of us.

"Come aboard the Kherval flagship," Hlanan said quietly. "It being a neutral party. It was shadowing the Shinjans for reasons no longer worth going into."

Invey gave a short nod, then said with a speculative glance. "One of these days, I trust you will tell me who you really are."

"Hlanan," said he, his fingers sliding into mine and tightening their hold. "Merely Hlanan. Anything else is like clothing, can be put on and taken off at need. Beneath it all is just me."

"Ah."

If you want all the details of the diplomatic negotiations, you can find different versions in Elras, Shinjan, and Djuran archives. All sufficiently full of pompous posturings, I'm sure. You can tell by the name they agreed on, The Three Oceans Thousand-Year Peace.

They all will insist that the treaty was written at the place where the territorial waters meet between the three empires. That is a particularly human idea, the ocean being vast and ever-changing in spite of boundaries humans try to impose.

But if pompous posturings (including my own) is what it takes to win a generation or two of peace, I'm all for it.

My father lives in Icecrest now. Mother went with him for a time, mostly to be there when Father outlawed the enforced fais of dual-natured. Though I was disgusted that he didn't banish fais altogether, at least he made the correction spell conditional for parents, and forbade the level of pain that had been used on the great gryphs to "tame" them—and, incidentally, on me. Some of the dual natured stayed where they were, content with their lives. Others took off in human or gryph form. It was now their decision.

Mother said that for a time she will spend winters there, and summers in the Hrethan mountains among the snows; I wonder if I'm going to have Dhes-Andis brothers and sisters presently. I'd like to have more family. Especially if one of them gets roped into being the imperial heir.

The Djuran court, Mother says, will take time to change, but she is beginning with music.

Sometimes I even turn up, usually when least expected, and get in some harp lessons with her. But I never stay long. Icecrest has too many bad memories, and anyway I prefer Dragon Mountain, where the dragonets are growing steadily. Rue says they will be flying out on their own in ten to twenty years—short for dragon time. Already I hear them in the mental world. Cloud, Sand, Spring and the rest all kept the names I gave them—though dragons don't use names among themselves, as they don't need them in the mental plane, they recognize them as useful for their interactions with beings who speak or sign words to communicate.

Hlanan and I returned to Rajanas's place, but we weren't there long. As soon as the treaty was carried back to Aranu Crown, Hlanan's mother, she sent a summons to Hlanan, adding that if it took an army to get him home, so be it.

He transferred to Erev-li-Erval, and said with an injured look that she didn't have to make threats. Thianra hastily intervened, before the two could start sparking as steel meeting steel tends to do when clashing.

The empress cleared her schedule with a summary wave of her hand, and then it was Hlanan's turn to talk.

Talk he did. I was there for some of it, listening by mind, until the empress figured out that we were indeed scrying without benefit of stone.

"Hlanan," she said. "Please invite Lhind. Tell her, *invite*. Doors all open if she wants to, ah, fly off."

I shifted right then—and she jumped. Then eyed me. "So," she said gruffly. "I was completely wrong about you. I beg forgiveness."

Hlanan blinked at his mother. I stared, my first impulse to laugh. But I managed to quash it; I had an idea what that must have cost her to say. She might accept the laughter as her due, but she would never forgive me. And relations between son and mother were uneasy enough.

So I gave her the bow I gave Invey, and sure enough, saw the tension around her eyes relax, even as she said even more gruffly, "Now, none of that. The fact is, I don't know what to do with the two of you."

"Why should you do anything?" I asked suspiciously.

Her mouth twisted. "One of you vanishes into the clutches of a Shinjan noble, the other flits off, and before anyone hears from you again, between the pair of you, you manage to bring down two imperial governments. There is a lot of speculation about you both in this part of the world, let us say."

"None of it would have been possible without a lot of help." I waved a hand.

"We were merely catalysts," Hlanan said more austerely, hands clasped behind his back.

To which the empress retorted, "Anyone who recognized themselves as a catalyst is even more dangerous. I want harnesses on you. Hlanan, I am making you my heir. Don't even try to argue. Thianra has been dropping hints like boulders for years. Even your rock-headed older brothers agreed, after hearing of your recent exploits. And you, Hrethan, I want you by his side."

Hlanan turned his sweet smile on me, and I gripped his hand with my right at the same time my left was waving her off. "No, no. No thrones. No robes and crowns. No *courts*. I'd die of boredom, and you *know* I'd get into trouble."

"I think it would be good for some of 'em to find themselves in trouble now and then," she muttered, then turned to Hlanan. "Well?"

"Lhind will be my consort while she is in Erev-li-Erval, but she is to have her freedom," he stated firmly. "She has family on this continent, and in Sveran Djur, and right now she is the only one who speaks to dragons."

The empress opened her hands. "Could I really hold you?" she asked, brows raised.

I didn't answer—wisely or cravenly, you be the judge of that—but turned to Hlanan. He met my gaze, his thoughts open. *So... can we at last begin our courtship? Except I'm not sure where to start.*

I rubbed my hands, reflecting that though I had even less of an idea, at least we've got the rest of our lives to practice.

ABOUT BOOK VIEW CAFÉ

Book View Café Publishing Cooperative is an author-owned cooperative of over twenty-five professional writers, publishing in a variety of genres including fantasy, romance, mystery, and science fiction.

BVC authors include *New York Times* and *USA Today* best-sellers; Nebula, Hugo, and Philip K. Dick Award winners; World Fantasy Award, Campbell Award, and RITA Award nominees; and winners and nominees of many other publishing awards.

Since its debut in 2008, BVC has gained a reputation for producing high-quality e-books, and is now bringing that same quality to its print editions. Find out more and sign up for our newsletter at https://bookviewcafe.com/bookstore/newsletter/

CPSIA information can be obtained
at www.ICGtesting.com
Printed in the USA
FSHW020720240520
70551FS